Pray For Him

Tyler Battaglia

Content Warnings

Pray For Him is a horror story and may contain upsetting content. Please be advised that the story includes the following:

religious trauma

adoption-based trauma

homophobia (external and internalized)

ableism (off-page but alluded to)

transphobia (off-page but alluded to)

child abuse (past and present, off-page but alluded to)

domestic violence (past, alluded to on page but not described in detail)

alcoholism (past, alluded to on page but not described in detail)

loss of autonomy (including through possession)

accidental animal death (wild bird – note: there is a cat, but nothing bad happens to her)

emetophobia

sexual harassment

body horror

dangerous driving

gaslighting

I

"God is love."

Standing at the pulpit in front of the attentive parish that filled the church's main room, Isaias regarded the churchgoers. He was glad to have the grace to be in front of them and preaching God's word. He was pleased with this place that he had built up from little, from next to nothing, in fact, to this church that he was lucky to call his own; it was a beautiful place, and the morning sunlight shining through the stained glass made him love this place. Isaias felt dizzy with it all, with the elation of preaching God's good works to his parish in the centre of this community that he had fought so hard to build. It felt to him like he was a part of something bigger than himself, *representing* something bigger. And it was true, he supposed—to be present here, speaking from the heart of the Bible, he was not simply Isaias, a lone man in the face of God. He was in his home away from home, right where he was standing, and his parishioners would follow him blindly in almost any cause because he was more than just a man. He was a man of God.

They would take his word for the word of God.

There was a strange comfort in his insignificance in the face of God. He did not matter. Only God mattered.

Isaias continued.

"And not only is God love, but *love* is *God*. Or, more accurately, love is Godly. Take the Ten Commandments for example—and, yes, I know that they don't explicitly mention love by name, but don't doubt that they are *about* love. Love God, love your parents, love your fellow man, love your wife... none of these are worded as such, but God's law, above all else, is to commit to God's love, to commit to Godly love, and to commit to loving God. Just as God loves you—each and every one of you. Jesus told us, 'Love one another as I have loved you'. He commanded our love for each other. It is a divine order that we should love each other."

Isaias trailed off into a pause. He let it linger. He didn't look down at his notes, but in fact looked at the devoted parish in front of him. He held back a shiver. It was chilly in the church, he noticed; why was it chilly in the church? A side effect of the old building, Isaias supposed. He wasn't sensing anything—he wasn't detecting anything unusual at all, at least not on the surface. It was just a draft. His hands felt tense where they were gripping the pulpit on the dais where he stood, the one at the head of the chamber on the raised platform that put him at a higher level than the devoted masses before him. Just a slight distance from everyone else.

Scanning the crowd of churchgoers, the ones that came from all walks of life in their little suburb, Isaias noted that it was a sizable crowd for a parish as small as his. It was a far cry from the few stragglers he had started with. The congregation in the Sacred Heart had come out in a respectable number that early February day.

The Sacred Heart. It was a fitting name for the locale where Isaias was delivering a sermon on this topic, but truthfully, he had wondered on more than one occasion what might go into the renaming of a church. It was the only thing he didn't like about his church. It suited his humble house of God, but the name felt like it should belong to someone else's. He did not want to be ungrateful by denying the history of this place assigned to him by his bishop, it had been an honourable cross for him to bear, but he felt unworthy. What did Isaias truly know of love? Even knowing the workings of the heart of all the people before him—and, truly, if he dared, he could tell what every person in the pews was feeling, what their hearts truly wanted—did not make him worthy to preach of love.

Knowing what was in the hearts of others meant little when it came to *understanding* what it meant to feel those things. To love. And Isaias was not one who knew love. It wasn't his place.

"Now," Isaias continued, voice surer than he had felt all morning, putting years of practice behind the words, "I know that with Saint Valentine's Day next Sunday, it's tempting to give in to commercial love—but that is not what God intends when he tells us to love one another. Venerating a saint by buying gifts, consuming chocolate, indulging in—well, indulging at all—that's not what love is really about, is it? Not Godly love. Not the love that God intends for us. No, what He intends for us is to love with our whole beings: heart and soul and mind. Because love is an act of devotion. It is a choice that we make. And remember, that's going to be as true of today as of next Sunday as of the next. Valentine's Day may remind us to love but it's not the only day on which we should hold love as paramount in our hearts."

Isaias closed his eyes for a moment, taking his time to centre himself on the feeling of being in the room. The quiet psychic energies pulsing in the room were—well, they were a reminder to himself of what he could, and did, love. He was a Catholic priest and had been raised in the church by a God-fearing family of religious practitioners where love was doled out under only the strictest, and most proper, circumstances. When one was truly deserving of the gift of love. But above all else, Isaias loved God Himself, and that love certainly mattered more than anything at all. He didn't need anything else in life—so long as he was worthy of God's true love.

But was even God's love unconditional, as he had been told? Isaias doubted. And to doubt was to walk the path toward sin.

Isaias kept those thoughts to himself, never to be confessed to another living soul.

If he needed to preach about God's love, then he needed to believe in love. It was that simple.

Carefully, his eyes still closed, Isaias reached out to the room and took a moment to centre himself on the feeling of being in that place. To remind himself of what he *did* love that was Godly. His parish. His duties. God Himself. He reached out to the thoughts and feelings of the congregation, trying to ground himself in *their* faith, *their* belief, *their* love. He felt the positive emotions that they felt, wanting to let himself feel what they felt. Even an echo of someone else's emotions was a start—better than feeling like his own heart was empty. The room was full of love, mostly, and attentive expectation. Compassion and, he noted this last one with a small smile to himself, a bit of boredom. From the children, he would hope. The ones whose presence at Sunday Mass was reluctant in the first place, let alone on the topic of *love*, a baffling mystery to most young children.

Isaias related.

But there was something else, under the psychic remnants of love. A darker feeling. Something pulsating. Something hungry that wanted to overtake and consume all the love in the room. Isaias thought that if the others could feel it like he could, it would be let into their souls. That it would poison them, devour the love in their hearts, leave them empty. Isaias gripped the pulpit tighter. The feeling was cloying; it stuck to the skin of his soul. For a moment, it was so powerful that Isaias had to wonder if it was his own feeling.

Was Isaias's own heart where this feeling that railed against love came from?

But what did Isaias have to be afraid of?

What did anyone have to be afraid of, under warm stained-glass sun and listening to a man preach a sermon of *love* of all things?

But someone was. Someone was scared. And it wasn't Isaias—slowly, he unpacked it. Picked it apart. It clung to his soul, his heart, it was frighteningly familiar, but it wasn't his own feeling.

Hurry, an imaginary voice seemed to beg him, giving words to the feeling. *Please hurry.*

And just like that, the emotion scattered, slipping from Isaias's grip as the other emotions in the room crowded it, winning out. There was too much going on in the church, too many people all at once. The emotion, which had been at once recognizable and strange, disappeared into the cloud of emotions around him.

Isaias searched again, just for a moment, to try to find the feeling. He was afraid to find it again, he thought it might try to overtake him, but he worried for whoever was so scared. Several times he imagined that he almost had it, but it darted out of his grasp, like an insect that he was trying, and failing, to capture in glass.

Isaias tried to press a little more, to track it. There was something familiar about the texture and feeling of the emotion, like something once loved that was now wilting, but—

Isaias opened his eyes and paused when he realized that everyone in the room was staring at him expectantly.

Oh, no.

Funny, he thought, *to be a priest experiencing performance anxiety.*

Isaias smiled to the crowd, or tried to, his lips straining to mimic the expected emotion, another façade he had practiced, before he looked to his notes to pick up where he had left off. He let go of the pulpit, his knuckles white and his hands shaking, as he shuffled uselessly through the pages. The lingering residue of the emotion, dripping sluggishly down the stone walls of the church, was distracting.

"Sorry, my apologies. I was simply—overwhelmed by God's love for a moment." Isaias laughed softly, and the congregation laughed with him, but it was the kind of laugh that happened mostly because you thought it should. An echo of something someone else felt. Another thing that Isaias related to.

Isaias kept thinking of the impatient, anxious feeling he had feared for just a moment was his own.

"The point," Isaias tried to continue gingerly even as he tried to lock his emotions down into something silent, a regular struggle to curtail anything he might have felt, "is that we should love daily. We should love each other, and we should love God. With every fibre of our being. For what's the point if we don't love open and honestly? Is that not what the Lord intends? Our lives should always be centered on love. We should live our lives *with love* and *in love*. Even if the only one you are in love with is God Himself. So long as the love you hold is Godly. For love—Godly love, anyway—can heal all ills. Love is kind, yes, but love is more than that. Love is restorative. Now, as we discussed earlier..."

Isaias droned on, trying to follow his gut and not just his notes, but his heart was no longer in it, if it ever had been. He had to keep referring back to what he had taken down, to words other people had offered, quotes gleaned from other preachers at other pulpits, to the things he knew he was supposed to say during a sermon about love. He'd recited all of these words a dozen times, a dozen ways, at weddings, at funerals, at any event where someone wanted to be reminded of *the healing, redemptive power of love.* Love upon which to build a marriage, love to build a bridge through grief, love to baptize a life into Christ's path. But Isaias had only ever known the kind of love that kept intimate company with fear.

The notes didn't feel like enough when Isaias was confident that everyone in the parish could see him for a liar.

The sermon ended quicker than he had hoped.

Clearing his throat gently, Isaias, drew the sermon to a close with an invitation. "Please, let us conclude with the Lord's Prayer." This was familiar. This was a prayer Isaias could recite in his sleep, under duress, without pause or question. And there was an impatient insect of a feeling crawling under his skin telling him he should conclude. "Our

Father, who art in Heaven, hallowed be Thy name; Thy kingdom come, Thy will be done, on Earth as it is in Heaven...

"... For the kingdom, the power, and glory are Yours, now and forever. Amen," Isaias finished, with an echo throughout the church as the parish murmured the collective conclusion to the sermon, joining all of their voices to praise the Lord. "I know many of you will be tempted to miss church next Sunday, given the date, but God won't accept such an excuse—you can bask in God's love that day, too." Isaias made sure to punctuate this with a wink—he would let the parishioners make their own choices about how much their faith would outweigh other things that day. But he knew where he would be. "And with that, I wish you all a happy week-before-Valentine's-Day."

Isaias tucked his notes into the Bible and closed it with a too-loud thump, amplified by the church's acoustics, giving a certain finality to his sermon. It was a good enough signal for the parish, and people rose and gathered their things and their families. Isaias didn't watch them, instead stepping down from the pulpit and into the aisle of the nave.

Isaias tried again to capture the feeling from earlier, to reach out to the heart and soul that the fear was coming from. He peered into the slowly dispersing crowd, coloured still by the stained-glass sunlight. With the amount of people thinning out, it took only a few moments more before Isaias found the anxiety again. The feeling was somehow both loud and muffled, like an emotion screamed into a pillow like that could suffocate it, and for a moment that fear again threatened to overtake Isaias in a way that he had avoided for years. It could be dangerous, feeling other people's emotions—sometimes the tidal force of them was more than his own heart could endure, subsuming his entire sense of self into someone else's being.

Carefully trying to parse the emotions away from his own, Isaias was overwhelmed briefly with the uncomfortably stark mental image of wilting flowers, something beautiful but dead too soon, starved of light. He stumbled slightly as he tried to pull back from the mind, dizzy with the whiplash. A parishioner, an older gentleman, caught Isaias to stop him from slipping and falling.

"Are you alright, Father?" the man asked. He squeezed Isaias's arm gently.

"I'm just fine," Isaias murmured. He gave an embarrassed smile, bashful for having slipped for no discernable cause. "Thank you." The man helped steady Isaias, not letting go of him until it was clear that he was ready to stand on his own again. "Thank you," Isaias repeated once he was steadied, patting the man's arm before he veered off, back toward the pews.

The mental image he had received, the pressing force of it, was helpful. Isaias scanned the church, milling about the aisle and paying no real attention to the typical 'thank you, Father's and the 'lovely sermon, Father's, the whole time deliberately weaving his way through the crowd to try to track the emotions. It was easier now that he had such a strong sense of them.

He wasn't surprised when he saw Violet Montero sitting in the pews. Once he had felt the sense of flowers, felt a flash of emotions that reminded him of a warm purple, he had been certain that it was her. The teenager was the only one still sitting, dressed in a soft purple blouse and black pants, her forearm crutches leaned on the bench on one side of her, always within reach. Her dark, slightly curly hair was tied back in a messy ponytail, several large strands coiling out the sides and framing her face. To her side was her friend Poppy, clad all in black save for the red beads that dangled from her hearing aids. Violet was watching Isaias with a steady gaze. Despite the dread of emotion that coated her presence, her eyes betrayed no hint of feeling. For a moment, Isaias watched her back in wonder. In the five years he had lived in this community, preached at this church, he had never once seen Violet or her father in the Sacred Heart. They were alien to the church, to the religion of his heart.

It did make sense, though. The smell of flowers.

Isaias said goodbye to one more parishioner before he made his way over to Violet and Poppy.

While he didn't have children of his own, Violet's father, Hector, was the best friend that Isaias could have ever asked for, and he cared for Violet with his whole heart. If Hector's daughter was troubled enough to come to church despite her father's general lack of enthusiasm for organized religion, Isaias was worried about her the way he imagined that he would worry about a child of his own. And if it really was Violet who was so anxious, so fearful—and Isaias was certain now that it was, and none of the same emotions were reflected in Violet's friend—then it was all the more reason to check on her.

Approaching the pew in front of the one where the girls sat, Isaias kneeled on the bench so that he was facing backwards. He crossed his arms over the back of the pew to face them. He breathed in, reached out to Violet emotionally, took in the smell of flowers, even if it opened himself up to some of her fear and anxiety. He could *feel* the way that she felt out of place, like she didn't belong.

Poppy exchanged a glance with Violet, who nodded. Poppy smiled and reached over to squeeze her friend's shoulder. "I'll be outside, Vi."

"Yeah, I'll be out in a minute, Pop." Violet's voice was quiet. Poppy paused for a moment before giving Violet a side-hug. Violet leaned into the hug for the space of a heartbeat before Poppy released her and stood up.

"I'll see you next Sunday, Father," Poppy said before side-stepping into the aisle and making for the exit. She hadn't waited for his reply. It was odd for her to leave so quickly, leaving Violet behind, Isaias thought—Poppy and her family were the churchgoers, not Violet.

Isaias waited a moment more for the last of his regular parishioners to exit, leaving the room empty save for Isaias and Violet. Despite the hollow echo as the last footsteps departed, it felt better that way. Isaias smiled to Violet. She didn't smile back, an oddity for a normally warm girl. "Hi, Violet."

"Hi, Isaias—Father."

"You don't have to call me 'Father' just because you're in the church," Isaias admonished softly and fondly, hoping to lighten the mood. "Your flesh-and-blood father might not like it very much."

"Okay, Father Isaias," Violet said plainly, and Isaias couldn't tell if she was joking back or if the joke had fallen entirely flat. Her tone revealed nothing. But it didn't matter, probably. Not when something was obviously wrong.

"How are you doing, honey?" Isaias asked instead, replacing the 'child' he was tempted to say with a more basic address. He didn't think that Hector would mind that as much as he'd mind a priestlier-sounding term of endearment. Better to be fatherly in the familial sense than in the religious one. "Do you want to tell me what's wrong?"

Violet looked at Isaias with her dark eyes. He could feel her anxiety now more than ever. It made her otherwise pleasantly familiar essence shrink down and shy away from him. She fidgeted and looked at her hands, and Isaias noticed that her often-painted nails were now bare, but for a few flecks in various shades of purple and blue, and a little ragged, bitten down to her soft brown skin. When she looked up, though, she was suddenly smiling. The look on her face didn't match what Isaias was still feeling from her. It was, unlike her nails, painted on. "Nothing's wrong," she said, a little too brightly. Even if Isaias couldn't sense her emotions, he thought he would have seen through the thin veneer of pleasantries. "I actually came to invite you over to dinner tonight."

Isaias paused. He wanted to press about what he was feeling about her, find a way to fish for why she was feeling so anxious without admitting to her that he could sense it, but the invitation caught him off guard. Why come to the church just to ask him to visit for dinner? Isaias was struck by the oddness of it. She had his number; she had texted him on behalf of her father before. "Tonight?"

"Yeah." Violet licked her lips and nodded. Then she smiled again, bright as ever. It felt familiar and distant all at once. "This isn't an invitation from Dad, but I think he'd be happy to see you."

Isaias couldn't help but smile back, more honest this time. The sentiment seemed obvious—Hector was Isaias's best friend—but it pleased him, nonetheless. "You don't think he'd want forewarning that I'm coming?"

Violet shrugged. Even that felt exaggerated. Like she was acting. "I'm cooking tonight, so he doesn't really get a say. And you know he doesn't mind even if you show up totally unannounced." Her smile faltered but came back full force in the blink of an eye, as if it had never struggled. "I think the only reason he doesn't show up at your door without warning is because the rectory kind of creeps him out. Sorry if that's, like, offensive."

"No, it's okay." Isaias shook his head. "I know your father doesn't care for the church. That's why I was surprised to see you here. I thought you would have just texted if you wanted to invite me over."

"I was in the neighbourhood and, I dunno, I thought it would be nice to sit in on one of your sermons. I know they're important to you. I thought maybe I could—I don't know, see what all the fuss is about."

"Thank you, Violet. That's very sweet. I hope 'all the fuss' was worth it. If you're sure your father won't mind, I can come over for dinner. If you're cooking something good of course." Isaias winked.

Violet laughed. Isaias was grateful to feel the spike of good humour in her emotions. This time it was real and, for at least a moment, it overtook the strange apprehension that Isaias still couldn't figure out. But he felt some of her worry persist, and he had to carefully filter out her misgivings, whatever they were, from his own, his concern for her mingling with her own anxieties. "I hadn't decided yet, actually. I was going to go grocery shopping after this and see what inspired me."

"Then I hope you feel very inspired. When would you like me to come over?"

"I don't know. Five-ish?"

"Then five-ish it is," Isaias said. He smiled to her, hoping to reassure her about whatever was causing her unease. He wanted to ask but thought maybe that was why she had invited him to dinner. He could figure it out there, when Violet was in a place where she felt more comfortable. For all she had said she thought it would be nice to see Isaias preach, he doubted it had been a pleasant experience for her. Among her anxious feelings, Isaias could feel the way that she was impatient to get through this. It was clearly not a place that she wanted to be, instead a place that she reluctantly felt she *had* to be, and it was probably making her nervousness worse. No need to let her doubt feed her nervousness more. "I'll see you then."

Violet nodded. She smoothly swept up her crutches and used them to leverage herself to her feet, a fluid movement that had her up in an instant. Isaias rose to follow. "I'll see you then. And—Father Isaias?"

"Yes, Violet?"

"You don't have to bring anything, or whatever. I know you probably want to. But just—make sure you come. I could really use you there."

The earnestness of the statement shocked Isaias almost as much as the content of it. For a moment, Isaias didn't know what to say. He started to ask, but instead just resolved to trust Violet. She was the daughter of his best friend. He trusted her father with his whole heart, so it was only natural that he trusted her, too. He hoped it meant that she trusted him, too. "Okay, Violet. I'll be there. I promise."

Violet nodded, and Isaias felt the oppressive emotions ease off her somewhat. She smiled again, then turned to leave, her footsteps and the falls of her crutches echoing in the hollowed-out body of the church.

With her departure, the church was empty, except for Isaias and the strange feelings that Violet had left with him that Isaias didn't know how to understand. He felt his heart worming its way into his throat. Was there something wrong with Violet? With Hector?

Isaias could only pray for them both that they were okay.

II

Isaias spent some time working in his church office, answering calls from parishioners and preparing himself for other sermons that week. He was distracted, though, his heart not in his work. He checked his phone periodically, which had been stored in his office desk drawer, halfway expecting a text message from Violet or Hector at any moment, even though he had no reason to. He never heard anything.

Watching the clock, Isaias returned to the rectory with some time to spare before his apparent dinner date with the Monteros. It was a short walk from the church to his living quarters, which were themselves on the consecrated grounds shared with the church and a small graveyard. The winter air was clear and crisp, a light breeze cutting through the graves on the other side of the grounds to the path where Isaias walked.

"Hello, Father Flores," Mrs. Lisette Marsh greeted Isaias cheerily as he entered the rectory where he lived, and he gave the petite, grandmotherly white woman a tired smile. She was a little round, and always warm with her plump, ruddy cheeks, and she tended to remind Isaias of home cooked meals and dryer sheets, as if she'd spent her whole life doing someone else's housework. *Poor woman*, Isaias thought. He wondered if she would have to be forced to retire at this rate.

"You know that the title isn't really necessary," Isaias reminded her for maybe the tenth time that month. It was more or less a game to them, at this point, for him to make a token protest here and there, though he knew she would always respectfully refer to him by proper address, and definitely never simply by 'Isaias', no matter how much he insisted she might as well have been his family, at this point. Or at least as close as anyone was. Anyone other than the bishop. Hector and Violet were another matter—a family Isaias had never been invited into.

"Of course, Father." She was in the middle of dusting the glass cabinet display in the hall, and she didn't look up from it, even as she spoke. She delicately held a figurine of Mother Mary and baby Jesus in her hand, brushing a thin layer of dust off of Jesus's head with a gentle swipe of her duster. "How was morning Mass? Sorry that I couldn't make it, but my niece needed a ride. Though really, she should have been in church herself, shouldn't she have been? Something to think about."

"Mass was fine," Isaias said. He paused in the front hall, debating unburdening himself, his anxieties, on Mrs. Marsh. It wouldn't be right, though, he thought, to complain about not understanding love, or not knowing how to preach about love. She was a widow. She had no children, though she had other relatives, like her niece. Isaias surely did not count. It would be cruel, wouldn't it be? To complain to an old woman about things that Isaias had no business speaking of in the first place? She had not asked for it. Why give her those worries that remained otherwise with him? Instead, Isaias reached out to her emotions, trying to feel how she felt, trying to understand what might have burdened *her*, what might have pained her. It was a process he had done often. Today, it was simple: she was content, if tired. Happy enough. Pleased that she had the time to take to clean this little display, baby Jesus and all. The whole process took only a moment, and Isaias found himself saying only the expected. "Mass was lovely, thank you."

Mrs. Marsh looked up at him, turning the figurine in her hand. She smiled kindly, and Isaias was overcome with the inexplicable desire to cry. He didn't, though, and he carefully clamped down on his emotions to prevent them from being felt by her, containing the psychic leakage as he had practiced so hard to do. "Glad to hear it, Father. When would you like your dinner?"

Isaias smiled, though it felt rocky as he suppressed the lingering urge for tears. "Actually, Violet had invited me to dinner with her and her father this evening. I hope you didn't have anything special planned for us."

"No, not at all. That's good to hear, Father. I'm glad you'll be spending some time with your friends."

"Me too, Mrs. Marsh. You can head home now, if you'd like. Enjoy the rest of your Sunday."

Mrs. Marsh smiled to him again. Isaias's heart warmed at the sight of it. "Thank you, Father. I'll take a little more time to clean up, if you don't mind, but I'll be quiet as a church mouse."

Laughing, Isaias said, "I have no doubt. Peace be with you, Mrs. Marsh, as always."

"And with your spirit, Father."

Isaias resisted the urge to say more, do more, and made for the study instead. He didn't expect any calls, and he didn't have any to make, but he thought that the quiet was a good place to be. It was his sanctuary, and he could settle himself in for a while until it was time to go to the Montero household. He closed the door behind him but did not lock it, as he had a habit not to unless he had a guest who needed privacy. His own privacy was comparatively immaterial, irrespective of if Mrs. Marsh would ever have reason to invade it. If she came in, it would be for good reason, and that comforted Isaias—everything that the old woman did was, ultimately, for good reason. Isaias trusted

Mrs. Marsh wholeheartedly. Mrs. Marsh, Hector, and Violet were his dearest friends and confidantes for a reason.

The study itself was small but comfortable, all cherrywood reds and browns, quite a few books on the shelves and just as many ecclesiastical decorations on the walls and on the desk. This desk was more cluttered than the one in his church office, as he didn't make much of a habit of staying in here when he could simply work out of the church's office. It was lived-in, Isaias would probably have to say, less than strictly professional.

One decoration stood pride of place above his desk, where it would watch him work and live: a painting of the Virgin Mary, whose eyes were full of love and pride, but never enough to be sinful. Her smile was small; bashful. It contained the beauty and secrecy of if the Mona Lisa were herself a mother.

Isaias walked over to the desk to sit but found himself momentarily distracted by a photo of himself and his bishop that stood next to the phone. It was nearly a decade old, by then, from the day that Isaias had been ordained as a priest by none other than the bishop himself. The photo was of Isaias smiling, standing next to Bishop Reid, who had his arm around Isaias's shoulders, though he visibly had to stretch to reach Isaias's taller shoulders. There was little that might have told an observer that these men were technically father and son, not at all clear from the bishop's pale skin, soft features, light eyes, or rapidly greying hair when next to Isaias's strong jawline, tanner features, and dark hair and eyes. But the bishop's eyes and smile were certainly possessing of a father's pride. It reminded Isaias that no matter how much or little that Isaias remembered of his biological parents, the bishop had been the one to raise him.

Isaias had never seen the bishop so proud in any other moment of his life, and he had since teased the man about his hubris in that moment. Pride was a sin, after all. Even pride in one's own family—flesh and blood or otherwise.

The picture brought distant feelings with it, the way that some objects could, as if they had been thought about so often that the thing itself had developed a soul of its own. It was just a photograph, so it wasn't nearly as powerful as a more significant personal item might be, but it still held traces of his mentor in it. For Bishop Reid, Isaias sensed the faint smell of rubber, like a child's toy. The colour was a soft, cloudy grey, though he knew the actual man to be wrought iron. The sensations weren't unpleasant, at least not when he associated them with the bishop.

Isaias looked to the phone in its cradle and considered calling his mentor unprompted. Isaias sat instead—he had no desire to bother the man without warning if he didn't need to. He opened one of the drawers of the desk to rifle through instead. He saw the worn old rosary that lay nestled in the dark of the drawer, surrounded by personal papers. The rosary, he was told, had belonged to his mother, and to her mother before her. He had no idea how old it was, but it always felt like a hefty, ancient thing. It held the weight of generational love and wisdom.

It wasn't what he was looking for, though, but what it rested upon: personal correspondence, dozens of letters, at times from friends long-since parted ways with, but mostly from Hector—never mind that they had lived in the same city for the entire duration of their friendship, never mind that it was easy to pick up the phone or see each other. It had begun as something of an in-joke, to exchange letters despite the proximity. Hector had started it as a way of teasing Isaias, telling him that he was such a timeless and romantic soul that writing letters to him seemed truer to form than just giving him a phone call or sending him a text. There was little substantial content to most of the early letters, truth be told, but they were fond nonetheless; pleasantries about the weather, as if they weren't in the same city, mere city blocks apart, or updates on life that they could have just as easily shared over coffee. Sometimes postcards found in giftshops for places they had both been anyway, but also a few from the rare time that Hector had travelled with Violet, declaring that they wished that Isaias had been there with them. Isaias wondered, sometimes, if it were true: had they truly wished that Isaias had been there, with them, a part of their family?

But as time went on, the letters had begun to change shape. They became deeper: fears and regrets, rarely explicit, mostly hinted at, dodging around ever admitting something too real. Isaias knew that Hector was a troubled man, and it was through letters that he had first confided in Isaias, in an abstract sense, about his struggles with alcohol; his regrets surrounding his lack of contact with his family; his terror that he had driven away his wife, Violet's mother, through his inattentiveness; how he was trying to do better, be a better man and father. It was through these letters that Isaias had first told Hector that he was afraid of losing his own family more than he already had, what little memory he held of them fading slowly away into nothing. They often felt so far away, in spirit even more than in kilometers and years. He had told Hector, in this way, confessed not through sacrament but through pen to paper, that he was lonely.

He'd even admitted, once, to being Godfearing in the wrong ways, wrote it down, sealed the envelope, then burned the paper in the old stone fireplace before he could gain the courage to post it to Hector, all of a few blocks away from him. He'd never shared those fears again.

Isaias gazed at the letters, wondering what he would find at the Montero home that evening. Violet had been fearful—but for what? Hector was a kind, earnest, gentle man. Despite his pain, he had never hurt another. He would sooner harm himself than let anything come to pass to his daughter. It wasn't anything like that.

Skimming through the letters, Isaias asked himself, how could a man who wrote, *I saw this strange little figurine of a creature at the thrift store, and it made me think of you, maybe you'd like to give him a name when no one else would*, be someone so in pain?

How could Isaias hold anything but love in his heart for a man who sent a postcard from their favourite bookstore-turned-coffee shop, that they had been to together a thousand times, that said, *Thinking of you!*

What secrets were hidden by a man who wrote, in the surest of pencil strokes, *I still dream of all the people that I've lost?*

Hector *was* in pain, that much was certain. Maybe his daughter had seen that. Maybe there was something in his soul that needed mending, that a man of God could tend to. Maybe there was something that Isaias could do to heal him. Had he not just preached that morning about the healing, redemptive power of love? God's love, at least.

But Hector was firmly against the thought of God. Isaias had tried to ask him why, and at first Hector had not wanted to commit to an answer. Eventually, he'd recited an argument that Isaias had heard a thousand times before, but he hadn't believed that that was truly what Hector had meant. *If God is all powerful, then why do people suffer?*

Isaias hadn't answered, because he hadn't thought that it was the question that Hector really wanted to ask. And because sometimes Isaias wondered that same question, despite having all the expected answers in his arsenal already.

Skimming through the letters, Isaias closed his eyes and let his heart guide his hand. Like the photo, the letters held a special significance—enough that there was a lingering emotional residue across the pages. Isaias had thought of them often, thought of them fondly, and he wondered if it was his own emotional energies that had imparted traces of Hector on the pages. The only other explanation for why Isaias sensed the faint taste of vanilla on his tongue, sweet and aromatic, when he touched the pages, was that Hector himself had poured his own heart into them. And how much time or energy could Hector have possibly spent on a postcard that said, *Thinking of you?*

The shape of vanilla shifted, turned bitter and astringent. It was still recognizable as that sweet aromatic, but it overwhelmed Isaias quickly. He resisted removing his hand from the letters to avoid the potency of it, instead opening his eyes to see what letter it was that had evoked this residual bite. He carefully removed the faded sheet and held it, the taste becoming sticky in his mouth. Had he not noticed that feeling before, when Hector had first sent it? Had the essence of Hector that clung to it deteriorated, broken down over time? Isaias unfolded the letter, not sure what to expect, and carefully read.

How long are we going to keep this up? The letter-writing. Not that I'm opposed, exactly, but Violet sometimes looks at me funny when I drop them off in the mailbox. Last time, she asked me if it was a waste of a stamp to be sending you something in the mail when we don't live that far apart. You can walk to me. I can walk to you. Why am I writing letters when I could just go straight to you and talk to you face-to-face?

When I was a kid, and my mother and I first left home, I had a few recurring thoughts. I know I haven't told you much about that, but I can tell you this: I felt like shit, and I watched the mail. At first, I watched every day, hoping that I would hear from the family that we had left behind. Eventually, I just watched around birthdays and holidays. I asked my mother if we could send something ourselves, but she just smiled sadly at me. I don't think she thought we could. Or maybe her heart couldn't take it.

Eventually I realized nothing was coming.

I stopped watching the mail.

It's nice having something to look forward to again, with you. I guess what I'm trying to say is, thank you.

Isaias remembered the letter. He remembered reading it and his heart aching for Hector, even without knowing all the details. Hector had felt forgotten, abandoned—Isaias knew that particular pain well. He knew what it was like to wonder if you were missed before, finally, realizing that you simply weren't. Isaias's heart hurt all over again. The taste of acrid, spoiled vanilla lingered on his tongue—a phantom taste that he couldn't shake despite its improbability. The shape of Hector's pain, he thought.

Perhaps Isaias could help him—through prayer or comfort or the kind words of a friend. Or perhaps not, perhaps he would find himself too weak in the face of real pain to do anything but take it upon himself, a band-aid to long-term healing, only a temporary measure. He could make the pain his for a time, but it would do nothing for Hector's soul in the end.

All Isaias knew was that he had to try. As Hector's friend—and because Hector had always been a friend to him in return—Isaias owed him everything.

III

Despite an apparent vow of poverty—he was rich in *life*, he would say, if not in goods—Isaias had picked up a certain shame associated with the idea that he should ever show up somewhere, even as an invited guest, empty-handed. Alcohol was strictly off-limits in the Montero household, so a bottle of wine was out of the question. Chocolate was a given—Violet loved it, even though she was very careful not to have too much at once—but it wasn't *personal*. Isaias wanted to show Hector that he was—well, he was thinking of him. He always was.

There was a small shop that Isaias liked to visit sometimes, at least when he was not in uniform. It was eclectic—something of a thrift store in parts, something of a plant nursery in others, and something like a new age mysticism shop in others still—but it was charming. Hector had shown it to him, after a quiet warning that Violet had told him it might have some 'witch-y vibes', in her own words. Hector had liked the plant selection, and Isaias had adored looking through old and lost things that might have otherwise been forgotten. Violet had lingered looking at crystals, though when Isaias had asked her about it, she had shrugged it off as mere curiosity.

It was there that Isaias went now. What else could he ask for than a one-stop-shop that had things both Hector and Violet were interested in?

The Second Voyage was a small little shop, tucked away on a little street called Montagne and down the road from an equally small church—not Isaias's own, but one he had visited before, nonetheless. The sign outside was deceptively colourful, the text a bright white against a splash of eclectic rainbow. It was misleading as a sign not because the shop wasn't a cheerful enough place, but because the interior was not the same colourful shades, but instead the deep mahoganies of comfort and home. When Isaias entered, he was greeted by the smell of some kind of burning incense, a pleasant floral and herbal smell he couldn't quite place, and a whole lot of clutter. And, with the clutter, the trace emotions of one hundred different memories from one hundred different people, impossible to fully place or understand. Was the lingering longing he sensed from the rose-scented candles, wicks unsinged, or the clothing rack full of lightly worn dresses in a rainbow of colours? Was the love emanating from the pile of old fine dinnerware, piled precariously high and decorated in swirling floral borders, or the stuffed toy octopus, its plush fur a dull pink and with extra stitches holding it together? Did the feeling of grief come from the old photo albums, still filled to the brim with someone else's old family photos, or from the smiling baby doll, still in its box?

And the anger, the fear? What objects here held such pain?

Every person Isaias would ever meet had a lifetime of emotions tattooed on their souls, and it saddened him that it would be impossible to know all of them to their truest extent. That a simple thrift store was able to contain such a variance of human stories told him so much about the people who surrounded him in Sainte-Thérèse, the town he'd called home for this latest stage of his adult life.

"Can I help you, Father?"

Isaias turned around to face the shopkeeper—Lena—who was behind the counter, leaning forward and resting her elbows on the Formica countertop. One arm was bent up to rest her chin in her palm, watching Isaias curiously, while the other tapped painted nails—a spectrum of pinks and oranges—on the laminate. She was smiling at him, and he could sense tinges of her amusement from there. She had caught him standing in the doorway, staring at the shelves as if he had never been there before when she had seen him there often enough to recognize him.

"Sorry, I was just—I wanted to get a small gift or two," Isaias said. He smiled back.

"For Hector?"

Taken aback, Isaias laughed. "What makes you think so?"

Lena grinned at him, all teeth. It might have been unnerving, except that she had never been anything but sweet and her emotions belied only fond bemusement, however distant they felt. Bemusement, and something fainter under the surface that Isaias could barely detect. She pushed a brunette French braid over the shoulder of her off-the-shoulder white blouse, which was embroidered with scattered blue and pink flowers. The way her blouse hung off her shoulders revealed freckles in her lightly olive skin, even in the dead of winter. "Just a guess. You tag along here with him and Violet sometimes, but this is the first time I've actually seen you all by your lonesome."

"Well, you got me." Isaias shrugged helplessly. "Yes, it's something for Hector—and for Violet, I hope."

"Do you want help? Or are you good?"

"I'm—good, I think. For now, anyway."

Lena laughed at him again, her voice ringing with fondness. "Okay, Father. Let me know, okay?"

Isaias turned his back on the counter and walked with slow steps to the nearest high shelf of trinkets and discarded goods. He was sure Lena had secured everything properly—he certainly hoped that Lena had secured everything properly—but the too-tall shelves were themselves as eclectic as the collections of goods upon them. Tall, metal shelves seemed to sway faintly in Isaias's imagination, like they might topple, taking everyone's once-precious memories with them. The mismatched wooden cabinets looked sturdier but were filled to the brim with haphazardly stacked plates and cups and even appliances, and it looked like any single object on them might lose balance at any moment. Isaias studied the collection at a slight distance, hovering his hand centimeters above each one. He wasn't sure what he expected to find—would something call to him? Cry out the memory of feeling to him in a way that made him think, yes, Hector needs this—this item properly represents the dearness of him in his heart?

But there was something that prevented him from touching anything. He couldn't tell where it came from, but there was something dark lurking beneath the love, the desire, the sorrow, the grief. Was it the anger he had detected earlier? Isaias couldn't quite identify the emotion, despite his intimacy with the emotional workings of the human soul. It felt—layered. Complex. Like a normal emotion but with a rotting, spoiled core. Something was wrong with it, and he didn't know where it was coming from. If he touched it, even by accident, what was the chance that it would poison his heart? Could a mere object hold the power to corrupt?

Isaias dropped his hand back to his side and stepped back from the shelves. He turned away, away from that poisoned emotion, and was surprised to find Lena watching him. "Can I help you, Lena?"

Lena wrinkled her nose playfully at Isaias but shook her head. "It's quiet in here," she said.

Isaias glanced back at the shelf. It was inside the armoire with its doors ajar, Isaias was sure. Watching him from the crack, buried there amongst the innocuous, waiting for its prey to come too close.

Or was it on the rickety metal shelf, painted white to disguise its identity? Was the painful object coiled there like a serpent, camouflaged among the innocent?

Isaias stepped away, closer to the counter. "Yes. It's quiet."

Lena nodded. Her smile was gone, as if it had never been there at all. Isaias wondered if he had imagined it. "Maybe try the flowers."

Isaias forced himself to breathe. In, out. *Please, God, stay my spirit.* He nodded. "Yes. Flowers. Of course."

Making his way to the portion of the store that held mostly plants and flowers, Isaias immediately felt tension leaving his shoulders and neck. Flowers were a much better idea. Flowers could do no wrong. Flowers held no expectations. Flowers were better suited for a gift for Hector, not something hidden among the shelves with that profane thing—whatever it might be.

Isaias drew his fingers across the velvet petals of a rose, applying a gentle pressure to the scarlet surface. Flowers didn't carry emotion precisely the way that people did, even objects, only distant remnants of feeling that were largely inaccessible to him—but there was something peaceful about them. Saintly. After the strangely powerful feelings of the thrift store shelves, the flowers were a comfort.

Lena appeared a moment later. She flapped her hands toward the flowers, chattering as she did so. "I know my herbs and spices better than my flowers, I won't lie, but maybe I can help you pick some out."

Isaias smiled. He wasn't sure why Lena seemed jittery, too, but he appreciated the solidarity. "I would appreciate that, yes."

Lena perused her own flowers, talking to Isaias as she did. "You know—Hector was in here, this morning, and—his daughter is named Violet, so those are probably obvious, right?—and he was acting strangely."

"Oh, he came in earlier?" Isaias hovered his hands over the violets for a moment. Lena raised a pair of garden pruners up and raised an eyebrow at him. Isaias nodded.

"Yes, he was—" Lena carefully snipped a few violets from the plant, gently holding the flowers between her fingertips before handing them to Isaias, who took them delicately— "he seemed agitated."

Isaias frowned as he examined the flowers in his hands. "Was something wrong?" Was Hector's agitation something to do with why Violet had invited him over for dinner that evening?

Lena continued to speak as she went through the flowers. Periodically, she would pause to ask Isaias if he liked certain flowers or not and, if agreed to, would select a few blooms to give to Isaias for Hector. "There was a darkness around him. Something clinging to him. I don't know, it's... You'll probably be able to tell when you see him, you're—well, you know."

Something in Isaias went cold, for just a moment. Did she know? It wasn't a deeply held secret that he knew things—sensed things—but he had always been told to keep it close to his chest. It was not befitting of him to flaunt a gift from God. It was not *right* for him to show that he was different, that he was—God's gift was a precious thing, surely, but never to be abused. Never to be put on display. Humility before pride. Charity before recognition. Service before love.

Before he could say a word, something passed through Lena's eyes, and she shrugged meekly and carried on as if she had not implicated Isaias's divine perceptions at all. "Anyway, you're his friend, so you'll see it, I'm sure. But he came here to pawn something off. I said I wouldn't pay for it—let's just say that the bad vibes were off the charts—but he left it anyway. He just wanted to get rid of it. I shoved it in a corner somewhere until I can figure out how to, I don't know, cleanse it or something."

The poisoned object. That must have been what Isaias had been sensing—something that Hector had left behind. Had those toxic emotions come from Hector himself, then? Or was he passing something along? Even if those awful feelings had not originated in him, it pained Isaias to think that Hector had come in contact with them. Perhaps others—others who felt things normally—would not be corrupted by the hurtful emotions of others, but Isaias wasn't convinced of that. It must have been true that carrying evil close to one's heart, even the evil of others, could only hurt someone. Perhaps it would not make their soul irredeemable—Isaias was not sure if he believed in such a possibility—but it surely could damage one's good graces.

Against his better judgement—and fighting the fear of an unknown object—Isaias said, "May I see what Hector left behind?"

He had to know what had hurt Hector so badly.

Lena looked at him in silence for a moment, her feelings strangely unreadable. They were there, just—muffled. Like she had wrapped them up in a protective veil. After a moment, she nodded, eyes dark and lips pursed into a thin line. She handed Isaias the rest of the flowers before walking to the more thrift-oriented portion of the shop. She dug through that old armoire that Isaias had suspected, pushing open its walnut-coloured door. Isaias held the bouquet of flowers close to his chest and waited for her, not daring approach.

When Lena returned, she cradled something in her hands that was wrapped in a soft velvet cloth the colour of communion wine. She paused just out of Isaias's reach.

"Before I give it to you—will you pray with me, Father?"

The obvious answer to such an inquiry was *of course*, but Isaias didn't manage that. Instead, he said, meekly, "I didn't think you were Christian."

Lena didn't budge. She cupped the velvet cloth gingerly between her hands. "I am, in my own way. Maybe not in your church way, but we find our own ways to believe. And I do believe—no, I *know* there is something out there. Something more. Something good, something dark, something that isn't either one. So maybe not Christian in your way, Father. But far be it for me to shun the gifts of the divine. I believe in the heart of it all."

Isaias furrowed his brow. He wasn't sure he understood the difference she was trying to express, but it wasn't his place to question it further. Her beliefs were just that—hers. If she wanted him to pray with her, he would do so gladly.

Flowers held in one hand, Isaias approached and rested his hand on top of the bundle of cloth that Lena still carried, careful not to touch her skin. He could feel the darkness in the bundle seeping out, saturating the cloth and threatening to absorb into him.

Isaias searched his mind for an appropriate prayer before he began, running through an internal catalogue of templated prayer for every need, every purpose. He closed his eyes and followed his heart.

"I take refuge in You, our Lord, and ask You humbly as Your servant to cleanse this object, and cleanse those who have ever beheld it, of all sin, all histories, and all defilement. As You cast out the enemy, so too may You cast out all evil that attaches itself to the souls of Your humble servants. I shall ever sing Your praises. Amen."

Isaias opened his eyes an instant before Lena did with her whispered, "amen." Once the words had faded into utter silence, Lena passed the velvet cloth from her hands to Isaias's properly, and he gently closed his hand around it. It still felt heavy in its wrongness, but he felt more confident to handle it with his God on his side.

I consecrate myself into a vessel for Your power, O Lord. Give me even a fraction of Your might to hold this thing bravely.

Isaias turned the cloth over in his hand and stared at it, trying to guess from the familiar shape wrapped in velvet what it might be. A string of beads. Two perpendicular bars. He felt a martyred figure carved in relief against the shape.

Isaias's heart ached at the thought of this being what had hurt Hector, but he could not know for certain what it was about it that made Hector reject it. Without unwrapping it, Isaias cleared his throat and slipped the velvet-wrapped rosary and crucifix into his jacket pocket. "How much do I owe you?"

Lena had already walked back to the counter while Isaias was distracted. She didn't look at him but waved a hand vaguely. "Nothing, Father. Consider it a tithe. Send my best to Violet and Hector, okay?"

Isaias pulled the small bouquet of flowers closer to his chest. He felt the weight of the rosary in his pocket, radiating something strange and pulling him toward the earth. He feared perhaps it would cause him to sink into the dirt, then keep sinking. But none of that was Lena's problem anymore.

"Thank you, Lena. I'll see you later, alright?"

"You take care of yourself, Father, and those dear to you."

There was nothing else to say to that, Isaias thought, so he said a soft, "you too," before heading for the exit. As he neared, his eye caught a spinning rack of postcards. Had he not noticed those before? A collection of art and photographs in readily mailable format. He gently spun the rack to better peruse the options. There were quite a few of the Basilica of Saint Thérèse of Lisieux. The Montero family wasn't a religious one, but the basilica named for the same saint as their town was a tempting image. Isaias hovered his hand over one of them for a moment, questioning the selection, before he saw a postcard that instead was decorated with a painting of a small, rustic cottage on a lake, surrounded by vast gardens of flowers. The sun was setting over the lake, and there was a single lit candle in the window of the cottage. It looked peaceful.

"One more thing, if you don't mind, Lena—and may I borrow a pen?"

Hector,

Sometimes I can't believe that a soul as radiant as yours houses so much pain. But don't they say that the best among us are those who have been hurt but choose to be kind anyway? Even God is said to be kind, but not soft. There is a difference, and I see that in you. Kind, but not soft. Like God Himself.

You don't owe me anything. You don't owe me your secrets. But I do hope that you know I will always be there for you. That you, and Violet, too, will always be dear to my heart. No matter where we go next, my life is better for having had you in it for whatever time I am blessed with. So, I hope you know I will be here for you.

I hope you know that you can always trust me.

Yours,

Isaias

IV

It was a chilly Sunday evening, in that time in early February where the weather was still undecided if it wanted to be winter for much longer, clinging to the frost on the ground, or spring, the start of snowmelt making the walkways slippery with black ice, nearly invisible but no less dangerous for it, but if he looked closely he could see grass just starting to peek through at the edge of the sidewalk, desperate to live again. Isaias told himself that he was walking so carefully and slowly to the Montero house not because he was afraid of what he would find there, but because he was afraid that, if he fell, he would ruin the gifts that he had so carefully selected for Hector and Violet. Or so he would tell himself. He balanced the small bouquet of assorted flowers from The Second Voyage and the assorted chocolates from the pharmacy—marked up in price, just in time for Valentine's Day around the corner—in his arms. The rosary and the postcard were tucked into his coat pocket, a familiar but uneasy weight.

The sun would be fully setting soon, and the remaining light did nothing to warm him. Each moment that it sunk lower, Isaias's uncertainty grew. Regardless of what had caused Violet's urgent invitation, Isaias did not know what he would find in their home. And

Lena had said—well, she hadn't said much of anything. But there had been something wrong.

There was a darkness around him. Something clinging to him.

It felt cruel to doubt what was going on with Hector when Isaias knew so little, but the fear kept growing, building, gathering under his skin as he approached the street where Hector and Violet lived. The darkness was becoming too strong, leaving a pressure under Isaias's skin that made it feel like his flesh was being pulled taut, something trying to escape him, to *break free—*

Pausing on the corner of the cul-de-sac where he would find the Montero home, Isaias shifted his gifts into one hand to free his left—then swapped everything over again to free his right. He crossed his fingertips from forehead, to sternum, to left shoulder where the flowers lay, to right shoulder. Softly, under his breath, he prayed:

"Lord, guide my hand to help me know how best to help Hector and Violet with their troubles, whatever they might be. Lead me to the truth, so that my friends may be delivered from any evil. Amen."

Isaias wasn't sure if the darkness receding was real or imagined, but he steeled himself to walk along the gentle curve of the street where neighbours had neglected shovelling the sidewalk, stepping in slush and puddles near the gutters where the road had been imperfectly plowed, down to the house a few doors southwest of the intersection, nestled between two larger homes that were complete with two-car garages, immaculate white stucco walls, and perfectly angled roofs. Under the snow, Isaias knew there would be manicured lawns with minimal decoration; dead now from the winter, but soon to be tailored to perfection for the spring and summer months. Unlike the houses that dwarfed it, the Montero home was—quaint sounded nearly condescending, but it was the best word for it. The house was a much smaller building, a bungalow, and had never been rebuilt or had additions. It had a driveway but no garage. The masonry was old, but the shutters were brightly painted in a friendly yellow. Under the snow, Isaias remembered, there was a neatly trimmed lawn that would stand out not at all among the large garden beds, which boasted not just flowers but also vegetables and berry bushes. With the snow beginning to recede, Isaias could see the hard edges of the pine board garden beds that lay underneath. The dead canes of blackberry bushes, which wouldn't come fully back to life for a few more months, emerged like grave markers. The slow melt of snow also revealed a lawn ornament of little red bird—a cardinal, maybe?—fixed in the ground, its head breaking free from the ice. In better weather, Isaias had seen its wings spin in the wind.

Maybe quaint wasn't the right word. Maybe it was 'homey'. That wasn't a feeling Isaias was very familiar with.

But as soon as he stepped from the curb to the front walk that cut through the snow to walk up to the main door, Isaias's vague suspicions and unease became a feeling that there was something more definitely wrong going on.

The sensation he normally associated with Hector, the smell of smores—something like vanilla, chocolate, and the warmth of a campfire—rose to meet him, faint, distant, but not right at all. Isaias felt a hot flash, his head swimming from the heat that could not possibly be coming from that February afternoon sun. He smelled something that had been cooking too long over a fire; the sickly-sweet smell of burnt sugar, charred beyond caramelization.

But the unpleasant sensation was gone almost as quickly as it had overcome him.

He must have imagined it. His bishop had always told him that he had a propensity to exaggerate what his Godly gift could show him. A bad habit carried over from an overactive childhood imagination. Nothing more.

At the doorstep, Isaias didn't immediately announce his presence. Instead, he took the postcard out of his pocket that he had written for Hector earlier, after the trip to The Second Voyage, and deposited it in the black letter box that hung next to their door, just below their house number. He had considered giving it directly to Hector at dinner, but it was part of their dance together—delivered confidences, mailed secrets, and posted confessions. It wouldn't be right to hand it directly to Hector. It wasn't the way their friendship worked.

Postcard delivered where it needed to be, Isaias hovered his hand over the door for a moment, wondering if it was safe to let himself in or if he should knock to request entrance. But the thought was ridiculous—in what world would Hector and Violet's home be anything but safe? Steeling himself, he turned the handle to let himself into the Montero house, as he normally did, opening the door with one hand, his gifts carefully held in the other. As he used his toes to kick off one boot, then the other, as he called out, "Hello to the house!"

Violet appeared within seconds, her white cat following on her heels. Violet's eyes were lit up with her smile, and Isaias felt her genuine relief echo through him, magnifying his own slow return to ease. She wore a red apron over her purple shirt now, clearly in the midst of cooking, leaning on just one of her crutches now. She went in for a hug—before seeing the flowers and chocolate box and stopping herself short. "You made it, Father Isaias."

"Of course I made it," Isaias said. "And now you really don't need the title, we're in your own home."

"Sure." Violet wrinkled her nose laughingly. "Oh, dad will *love* these," she said as she took the bouquet from him, careful in how she held them, gentle with the delicate petals and cradling them against her body while she leaned her weight on her crutch, "and *I* will love *those*," she added as she nodded at the box of assorted chocolates that Isaias held.

"I thought you might." Isaias smiled as placed the box of chocolates on the console table and watched Violet search for a vase for the flowers. "Where *is* your father?" It was odd, perhaps, that Hector hadn't come to greet Isaias along with Violet and the cat. Isaias had sensed him—or something *like* him—so the absence was noticeable.

"He stepped out for an errand or something." Violet shrugged. She placed the flowers into a glass vase on a side table, then filled it with water from one of the many bottles and watering cans in their living space that were sitting on almost every surface. There was almost always a watering can or some other receptacle for water on hand for the many, many indoor plants that kept Hector occupied during these winter months. "I'm sure he'll be back soon."

Hands no longer occupied with chocolate, Isaias pulled off his winter jacket and hung it in the closet, as Violet didn't need to invite him to do—this was familiar, after all—before crouching down to pet the cat behind her ears. She had waited patiently for him.

"Hello, Prue," he greeted her as she meowed. She was officially Violet's cat—clearly indicated by the way she would follow Violet around the house, keeping just out of the way of her crutches—but she was *un*officially Isaias's. Isaias had found her as a stray, named her, and only given her up to the Monteros when it had become painfully obvious that Mrs. Marsh was badly allergic. She fit in here better, anyway—the rectory was not exactly a family home, no place for a cat that needed the amount of love and care that Prue clearly would. "Did you miss me?"

Prue meowed again, and Isaias stroked her back before standing. Violet had disappeared into the kitchen while Isaias was distracted by the cat. He took another brief look around the room, halfway expecting Hector to appear from nowhere, before he followed Violet into the kitchen, while the cat followed him.

The kitchen, too, was cozy, but bordering on cramped, with spice racks, small appliances, utensils, and tools crowding much of the counter. Hector was a comfortable cook, having learned more so after his divorce, but Violet had taken to it where her father was less natural. Isaias had witnessed many homecooked meals tag-teamed by the two of them, Hector often supplying herbs while Violet did much of the cooking. His heart always warmed to see them work in unison, father and daughter making their home such a loving place.

Violet was back at the stove, now, stirring a large pot on the burner. The kitchen was warm with not just the heat of the element, but with the aromatics cooked into the stew. Violet's phone on the counter also added to the ambiance, bubbly pop songs that danced on the edge of Isaias's recognition were playing from the speaker.

"Would you like me to help with anything?"

"Nah, I'm good," Violet said. "At least until I need a taste-tester."

"Well, *that* I can do." Isaias laughed and looked around the kitchen, unsure what else to do with himself. He got a better look at Violet's crutches when he noticed the second in the pair leaning against the wall near the fridge. She had added new stickers to the purple aluminum body of the crutch, replacing some of the more worn and peeling ones, showing off lyrics from her favourite bands, a cartoon cat declaring its desire for violence, and a bee hugging a purple, pink, and blue heart. From there, Isaias's eyes were drawn to the plant wall just beside the small kitchen table, where Hector and Violet had hung pots for a variety of herbs. The plants were struggling, though, an oddity in their house—many of the herbs had been pruned nearly beyond recognition, and much of the remaining foliage was wilting.

"What happened to the plant wall?"

Violet looked over her shoulder, leaning momentarily more on the crutch she was still using, to get a better look at Isaias and what he was looking at. For a moment, she seemed surprised by the question, but then her face fell. "Oh. A bunch of them started dying recently. Just wilting for no reason, even though I think we've been taking care of them just as well as ever. I started pruning the shit—sorry, I started pruning them to save what I could. I'm drying out some of the bits I pruned off, but I'm hoping if I get rid of the rougher parts, maybe they'll recover?" Violet sounded uncertain. She turned her back on Isaias, turning around to face the stove again. "Dad always says if you cut off the parts that are struggling, the rest of the plant is more likely to bounce back."

Isaias approached the wall of plants with undue caution, not sure why he had the sense that a mere touch to the leaves would transfer some kind of poison to him. Hector—with Violet's help—grew edible plants only in the kitchen, and in fact *most* of his plants were safe for consumption, save for some of the more decorative plants. But something in Isaias warned him against getting too close—still, he touched the leaf of one herb, not sure what he would find.

He found nothing. He felt nothing. Certainly nothing of Hector's love.

Isaias didn't exactly expect plants to have their own personalities or feelings, though sometimes he was certain he felt *something*, but he had always imagined that the plants in the Montero house carried some echo of their caretakers' hearts, with all the love they gave. But this plant had nothing at all.

Violet was watching Isaias over her shoulder. Isaias finally responded to say, "I'm sorry to hear that."

As Isaias drew his fingers away from the leaves, he saw something stirring in the dirt in the pot. On instinct, he looked closer and spotted something long and thin, but with fine, barbed hairs on it, start to push out from the roots of the herb, meticulously pushing soil away from it as it emerged from under the plant. Isaias expected a spider, but the spindly wire-like appendage kept going, kept emerging, kept *growing*, too long for a spider-limb, too long for anything, then a second and third pushed through the dirt—

"You okay, Isaias?"

Isaias looked back quickly at Violet as he took a step back away from the plant. He drew his hand up towards his face, uncertain, taking in the soft scent of the plant, reminiscent of pepper and citrus, but also maybe of mildew just under the surface. Looking back to the plant, Isaias no longer saw the spider-limbs. The dirt around the plant was still. Nothing had disturbed it at all. "Sorry, I think—some kind of bug startled me."

Violet laughed. "Yeah, we get bugs in the plants sometimes, even indoors. We've had some weird ones lately. I try to catch them and put them outside if I can, but it's kind of hard to when my hands are usually occupied."

Isaias nodded, tearing his eyes away from the plant to look at Violet again. "What kind of bugs?" He wasn't sure why he wanted to know, except that something about the insect legs had unsettled him. Multiple had begun to break through the dirt, and he had known it must have been a spider, but something told him it would have been more than eight legs, or otherwise wrong, not a house spider but something that had dug out from somewhere far deeper than soil.

"Weird ones." Violet shrugged, then turned back to her cooking, unconcerned with the strange insects—Isaias could feel the indifference to the bugs rolling off her. "I tried to identify them with an app on my phone, but I can't figure them out. I'm worried they might be invasive, but I'm not sure, so they can just go be invasive or whatever somewhere not in our house."

"Fair enough." Isaias couldn't argue with that. He stared for a moment more at where the bug-thing had tried to emerge, wondering where it had gone before deciding that maybe it wasn't worth knowing—he wasn't afraid of bugs, and he loved all living things, so being so put off by a harmless insect was unreasonable.

Another moment passed before Isaias tore his eyes off the rim of the suspended pot.

The top of the board was made of cork, a DIY improvisation from Violet to turn the unused portions of the plant wall into a message board, and Isaias looked there. There were several photographs of Violet, and some of her and Hector together. Family portraits, capturing their bond as father and daughter, the two of them against the world. Then there was one photo with Isaias in it—a charity picnic that he had organized through the Sacred Heart but that didn't take place at the church itself, so Hector and Violet had come to support and had donated some items for the charity auction, as well. The photo had been taken by Mrs. Marsh, who had been volunteering as well as collecting photos for the church bulletin, and captured Isaias hovering while Hector manned the barbecue, Violet lounging nearby in a reclining lawn chair, her crutches leaned against the arm of the chair, with purple sunglasses obscuring her eyes but with her hand shading her eyes to see what her father and Isaias were fussing about. Isaias couldn't *remember* what they had been fussing about, but the photo was such a simple moment in time. His heart was full to have it included among their family portraits, albeit not pride of place. It was almost like he was a part of the family.

A sticky white webbing covered the corner of the photograph, creeping into the frame just below Hector in his KISS THE COOK apron, eating away up and into him, covering part of his likeness but consuming nothing of anyone else who was captured in the photograph. It glistened, moist and shiny under the bright white light of the kitchen. Isaias traced it with his gaze, searching for the source—

The front door slammed open.

V

The sound of the front door was harsh, magnified by the sheer unexpectedness of it. Of course, Hector had been coming back. Of course, the wind was picking up outside in the last dredges of evening. But Isaias had sensed nothing and no one approach the house, the stillness of Isaias and Violet in the kitchen having gone undisturbed, a stillness he hadn't realized had been so fragile.

No emotional sense of Hector—or anyone or anything else—had approached the house, like his soul was on a cat's silent paws.

There was a long, ponderous silence. Something like dread filled Isaias as he thought of a nature documentary, a wildcat stalking its prey, looking for signs of which way the smaller creature had gone. Scenting the air. Biding its time.

"Violet?" Hector's voice called, even and measured.

As if unknowing that she might be walking into a trap, Violet picked up her second crutch and walked to the doorway of the kitchen. "We're in here, dad!"

And just like that, the spell was broken.

There was a rush of warm air—or maybe the cold air rushed out—as the front door closed, the chill immediately dissipating. The reassuring weight of Hector's heart reached out to Isaias's. The pop music seemed to increase in volume, entering Isaias's awareness again.

It had been a ridiculous mental image, after all.

It was just Hector.

"We?" Hector called back. Isaias could *feel* the confused frown he must have worn, the innocent puzzlement that emanated from him. But he appeared a moment later in the kitchen doorway to meet his daughter and, upon seeing Isaias, his confusion melted into relief—what a strange emotion, in one's own home—and he smiled. "Isaias, fancy seeing you here."

Isaias smiled back. His heart warmed at the sight of Hector. There was something comforting about his very presence. He was a tall and broad man, solid in mass in every part of him. It was obvious there was strength in him, irrespective of him being round in his belly and in his limbs. His dark beard and short, tightly curled hair were spotting with the salt to his pepper, despite not quite reaching his forties yet. His skin was darker than Isaias's, or even Violet's, even in winter months, the richness deepened by the sun as he spent as much time as possible in the sun year-round. He was the picture of a handsome outdoorsman, unlike Violet with her art and Isaias with his books, with the collar of his worn flannel shirt askew underneath his parka.

And Isaias saw that Hector's eyes were kind, lined with laughter. He was glad to see, whatever else might or might not be wrong, whatever might or might not be worrying Violet, that Hector's eyes were still kind. Isaias admired those eyes, especially knowing something of Hector's previous life from his confessions to Isaias made under the façade of coffee conversation.

Despite the world, Hector was brave, he was strong, he was good. He was loving.

Softly, Isaias said, "It's good to see you, Hector."

"Isaias? I wasn't expecting you."

"Surprise visit," Isaias said, unwavering in his pleasantness. "Well, Violet invited me for dinner, actually."

"Oh, she did?" Hector asked. His eyes were gentle, yes, but the hesitation—the implicit reluctance—was at odds with it.

Violet, standing besides them while leaning on both crutches, now, shrugged one shoulder. "I did, yeah. I don't know, it's nice to have company for dinner, sometimes. And," she added, "I'm cooking, so you don't really get to decide who's coming for dinner, right?"

Something eased, and Hector laughed suddenly. His laugh was, like the rest of him, soft around the edges. It filled a room with joy. "Fair enough. But I would have expected Poppy, not Isaias."

"Well, I decided I only wanted to cook for three, not four, so Poppy can come next time." Violet beamed, but there was a thin veneer over it that Isaias could detect but not quite place. Something false about it. "Quit complaining, dad, I got your friend's nose out of his books and his Bible so you could have some company."

Hector's smile wavered. Just for a moment. "I didn't—" He stopped, then paused and collected himself for a moment, the deliberations playing across his face in real time. "Glad to have you here for dinner, Isaias."

"Thank you for welcoming me into your home," Isaias said—it felt stiff even in his own mouth, too formal, too unpracticed when he had been to the Montero home a thousand times or more. It was supposed to be safe and familiar. Hector always was. But for a moment he worried that maybe he wasn't welcome in their home, after all.

Violet, coming to Isaias's rescue again, suddenly declared, "Oh, dad, Isaias brought you flowers!"

And just like that, Hector melted back into comfort. Isaias became aware again of his emotional weight, the soul of a man you wanted in your corner, though he hadn't been sure exactly when his sense of Hector had wavered again. "He did?"

"Isaias, you should show him. I have to finish making dinner, anyway—won't be long, though. Promise. Maybe."

"I can do that," Isaias said. He gestured at Hector. "Your dad has to put his jacket away, anyway."

Hector blinked, slowly—like an off-guard cat—as if only just realizing he was, indeed, still bundled in a thick, down-filled parka. "Fair enough."

Hector left the kitchen back to the hall, and Isaias followed him out to the entryway. Hector's boots were placed to the side, snow already beginning to melt off of them into the boot tray, but he opened the closet with one hand as he shrugged off his parka with a twist of his other arm. He froze as the door slid open and his eyes landed on Isaias's long, black winter trench coat. He stared at it for several seconds, until Isaias stepped forward. "Hector, are you alright?"

Hector started moving again, as if God had simply paused him for a moment and then hit 'play' again when Isaias interrupted. "Yeah, I'm good." He finished removing the parka, hung it on a hanger, and put it in the closet at some distance from where Isaias had hung his own coat.

Isaias thought of the rosary in his pocket but tried to dismiss the thought. Nothing had ever indicated that Hector had any gifts that might divine something's presence, even if he had been the one from whom the rosary had originated.

Isaias wondered if he should ask Hector about it, but Hector closed the closet with something like finality and turned back to Isaias. He rolled up his red and black flannel sleeves as he did so, revealing coarse arm hair on his thick forearms, along with a thin spidering of old scars around his hands and wrists, raised welts from old wounds around his knuckles that stood out all the more as he moved. "So: flowers, Isaias?"

Isaias tore his eyes from Hector's arms and looked back at his face. His cheeks burned, and it magnified when Hector chuckled. "Uh, yes," he said. "I went to The Second Voyage. Lena helped me pick out some flowers."

"The Second Voyage." Hector seemed to turn the shop name in his mouth, as if trying to remember why it sounded familiar. As if they hadn't been there together many times. "That was nice of you—Lena may not be a florist, but somehow she manages to have the best-kept flowers in Sainte-Thérèse even when it's the middle of winter."

Isaias smiled, despite feeling like something was wrong. "Yes, she has something special."

Hector nodded, then gestured broadly with one arm to suggest Isaias show him the flowers, which Isaias was happy to do. In the living room, the vase Violet had selected stood tall with the flowers on a side table next to the couch. There were violets, of course, but also an assortment of red and white flowers along with different purple flowers to make the small bouquet. Hector approached in reverence, looking to the flowers in something like awe. As he reached out to trace the petals of a peace lily, a flower Isaias could recognize, he thought that maybe this was where Hector found worship. He may not believe in a Christian God, but Hector found divinity in other places, Isaias could tell. And how could Isaias begrudge a man his prayer, even if it was at an altar of flowers? Did 'you shall have no other gods before Me' apply when it was a religion of God's own creations? Could God truly disapprove if man worshipped, instead, the beautiful world He made?

Isaias had known since their first meeting that Hector loved flowers. He was a contractor, self-employed running a small business for renovations and construction. It was how they had met, shortly after Isaias had moved to their community. The church that he'd been charged with had been a bit run down, in a somewhat neglected neighbourhood, and Isaias had been asked to help restore the Sacred Heart to any fraction at all of its former glory. The old pastor had left suddenly, and the community hadn't had their old church in a number of months. Isaias had set about restoring it first and foremost, to make the more spiritual changes visible to the naked eye, tangible to the casual observer. Isaias had hired Hector on the recommendation of a parishioner to lead the repairs within a few weeks of arriving and, in short order, Hector and his colleagues had transformed the little church into something that people could love again, risen like Lazarus from the ashes of its former self.

Hector had done the gardens himself, as something of an enthusiast. They had been good friends ever since, and though Hector had never set foot into Isaias's church again, he did take a periodic and friendly interest in the flowers at the Sacred Heart. Asking how the gardens were doing was about as close to asking how Mass went as Hector ever got. In the dead of winter, with the gardens buried deep under the snow, he rarely if ever inquired about the church, but Isaias didn't need him to. There were other ways, now, to show each other that they cared.

But of course, Isaias would continue to gift Hector flowers if he thought that they might make his friend smile.

Solemnly, Hector withdrew his hand from the petal. He picked up the vase instead. "I'm going to put this up somewhere higher," he said. "Prue mostly stays out of my plants, but lilies are toxic to cats, so better safe than sorry."

"Oh, I'm sorry," Isaias said. Where was Prue, anyway? What if she got into something she shouldn't? "I didn't know that."

"No, it's alright." Hector placed the vase on the mantel, a splash of colour among crawling green ferns. "You wouldn't expect something beautiful to be so dangerous. And it's a peace lily, which isn't as bad as a true lily, at least."

"That's good, at least."

Turning back to him, Hector said, "Thank you, anyway. You didn't have to bring anything. I didn't even know you were coming over."

"Maybe I just like to spoil you."

Hector laughed—another hearty, warming sound—and Isaias felt more at ease again. This was normal. This was friendship, in fact, with Hector laughing again and the smell of Violet's stew wafting from the kitchen, through to the dining and living space. It was *home*, even if it wasn't Isaias's.

It was more than he'd ever had—to him, home had meant cathedral ceilings, drafty attic bedrooms, thrice daily prayer under the stern and watchful eyes of church officials. There had been few children who had been raised in the church like Isaias was, even fewer his own age, and the Bishop had always been the closest to true family that he had ever had after Isaias's parents had given up on him.

Isaias dismissed the thought. He was grateful for his gifts from God, which had singled him out as a child in order to put him on His righteous path. There was no regret in that. There was nothing *to* regret.

What more could Isaias want than God? His life was God's life.

Hector glanced back at Isaias, tearing his eyes away from the flowers, as if he could tell Isaias was deep in thought. He smiled and, for a moment, all of Isaias's doubts washed away.

"Dinner smells wonderful, Violet."

Violet beamed proudly at Isaias for his praise. "It better," she said with a laugh. She was sitting already, while her father took care of serving the stew. "I put, like, ten pounds of garlic and ginger in it to make up for the fact that you don't eat meat."

"You spoil me."

"Only because you're so nice to us. I'm going to eat so many chocolates after dinner."

Isaias laughed again before saying "thank you" under his breath as Hector ladled the stew into Isaias's bowl. Once all three bowls were served, with water in their glasses and bread on the table, Hector sat. He immediately reached for his spoon, and so did Isaias, but Violet interrupted.

"Did you want to say grace, Father?"

Hector froze. Across from him, Isaias saw his hand hovering over his utensils, paused a centimetre above. His eyes were locked on a piece of potato poking out of the broth.

"You want me to?" Isaias asked, tearing his eyes from Hector to look at Violet between them. He frowned at her—neither she nor her father were religious, and never once had they wanted him to say grace. It was unheard of. And, frankly, something he worried that Hector might not be comfortable with, and not just because he was holding deathly still.

"I don't know," Violet shrugged. "After seeing your service this morning, I thought it might be nice. I know it's important to you."

"I—"

Hector interrupted. "You went to church?"

Suddenly, Violet looked uncertain. When she answered, her voice was meek. "Uh, just to meet Isaias. I mean, it's the easiest place in the world to find him, right? I could text, sure, but I can also just kind of show up at the church and he's probably going to be there."

There was a heartbeat of silence, then another. Isaias knew Hector wasn't terribly fond of organized religion, but this level of discomfort seemed unusual. They were friends, weren't they? It was a part of Isaias's life. If Hector wanted nothing at all to do with it, then why would he ever be friends with Isaias? Unless, of course, he was only tolerating Isaias's presence for another reason.

Isaias thought of the reams of letters and postcards he had safely tucked away in the rectory and tried to dismiss the concern. Hector did more than tolerate him. They cherished each other's friendship. He felt the earnestness, the honesty, in every gesture that Hector made, even now. He could not hide his true feelings from Isaias, but he never made any attempt to, either.

But then the silence ended, and Hector shrugged. The nonchalant gesture mirrored his daughter, and Isaias was reminded of their matching familiar casualness, always self-possessed but never dismissive. Hector picked up his spoon. "It's fine, Violet," he said.

"You know I'd never tell you what you can or can't believe. That's between you and you. Nobody else."

Violet still looked and felt uneasy—yet at the same time, Isaias detected something else under the surface, something like vindication. "Sure, dad."

Isaias cleared his throat. He did not know what had caused this strange tension, but he felt caught in the middle. He was beginning to piece together that Violet really had invited him for an unknown purpose—a cunning girl, she worked in mysterious ways.

Isaias held back a smile at his private joke and instead looked to Violet and said, "If you want to pray with me, we can do it silently. Or I can teach you later, if it's something you're interested in learning about."

Violet studied Isaias. He had the sense she wanted to test his honesty, his integrity. Her round face and wide-set eyes were open, friendly, and gave her the impression of being easy to read, but he knew that she would share only what she wanted, when she wanted. Despite her father's general openness, she had developed on her own a keen sense of strategy from all the times she had been underestimated. "Maybe later," she said. "I'd be interested to talk to you about belief sometime. I've had some questions, lately."

It was enough of an answer, Isaias felt. "Well, it's my job to try to answer those questions for you." He finally picked up his own spoon, satisfied that the tension would now pass, and ready to dig in. "It's delicious, Violet, thank you."

"Thank you, Isaias." Violet didn't look at him, keeping her eyes locked studiously on her father, who himself looked calculatingly at Isaias.

Isaias was struck with the sense that perhaps he was in the middle of something he did not understand. It was not a new feeling—the strain of trying to fit into a family where he did not belong. Where he would never belong.

VI

Aﬆer dinner, Isaias was reluctant to linger, but Violet insisted that he stay a little longer. Hector said nothing. Violet engaged Isaias in conversation, sharing from her box of chocolates, which she had requested Isaias retrieve for dessert, even when he tried to insist that they had been a gift for her. Hector partook of the chocolates but continued to say nothing. Violet talked at length about lighter topics, at first, about Poppy and her friends, about the coming spring, about the art piece she was working on, about graduating from high school in a few months' time.

It wasn't until she asked Isaias, unprompted, "How do you know if God is real?" that Hector reacted.

Isaias watched Hector—tense, alert, ready to bolt—while he tried to formulate his answer for Violet. "I think I've always known," he said. "I've always felt His presence, but it's not that way for everyone. Sometimes it's not about feeling Him, knowing for certain, but believing anyway."

Violet nodded. "So, you don't have any doubt at all? But it wasn't some big revelation for you, that there was something more, that made you believe in Him."

Isaias wondered if it was true, that he felt no doubt. It wasn't something he could ever let himself think about too long. "No, I suppose it wasn't."

Suddenly, Hector spoke: "You know how they say, when someone shows you who they are, believe them the first time?" He kept his eyes locked on Isaias. His voice was level, his gaze inscrutable.

Unsure where Hector was going with the question, Isaias momentarily reached out to detect Hector's emotional resonance. With Hector, it was normally an easy jump—they were already bonded enough that it was a simple ask of his gifts to look deeper into Hector's soul. Half the time, it wasn't fully conscious—just being near Hector connected their hearts. But all evening, it had felt like Hector was at a distance from him. Isaias couldn't quite make anything out. So, this time, Isaias reached out deliberately.

Someone started screaming. The sound tore through Isaias's mind, cut a sharp wound into his mind, his soul. Isaias flinched, his heart seizing in his chest from terror reflected down to the core of his very being. He'd never felt so much fear—and he wasn't sure if it was his own, or someone else's.

Then the sound was gone, as quickly as it had begun. His heart began to pound.

"Isaias, are you okay?" Violet asked. Her brow was furrowed, and she was frowning. The feeling of her worry replaced the sharp fear he had felt mere seconds before.

"Sorry, yes," Isaias said. The noise was gone, but his ears still rang. Was that *Hector's* soul screaming? Was he in pain? Was he afraid? "It was nothing. Sorry, Hector—yes, I am familiar with the quote."

"Well, God showed me who He was when I was still a boy," Hector continued, as if Isaias had never recoiled away from an invisible force. He stared steadily at him, his gaze boring into Isaias. "He was never there, even when my mother prayed to Him or when I did. But He *was* there in the words of those who meant us harm. God never showed me any of what you see in Him, and I believed Him."

It wasn't news, exactly. Isaias knew Hector held pain in his heart, but it was the first time he had so explicitly blamed it on God. But of course, there was a reason his dislike for organized religion seemed to go beyond belief.

It was a miracle, maybe, that Hector was so willing to let Isaias into his life.

Except, it wasn't that Hector didn't believe in God's existence. He just didn't believe in what He was said to be. And Isaias couldn't begrudge him his hurt. Isaias knew all about hurt. But for him, God had been what he'd had in the face of pain.

"I'm sorry you felt that way, Hector. And I won't tell you you're wrong to think that." Isaias felt something sinister simmering just under the screaming in Hector's soul, and he pushed out with his own heart—tried to share some of his love, his care, his *empathy* with Hector. Not for God. For Hector himself. "Just like you said to Violet, that's up to you. I would never stand in the way of what your heart tells you."

Hector's features softened, his face slackened, his eyes gentled. He was the Hector that Isaias knew again. Something reached him—be it Isaias's words or the emotional resonance they had shared. "Right, of course."

It was like a switch was flipped. Again. Hector had been hot and cold, and his aura matched. The mood swings were uncomfortably rapid, difficult to track.

Hector was normally steady; strong. He was Isaias's rock.

Isaias ears still rung softly, echoes of terror that weren't quite fading, leaving Isaias shaken and unable to ignore the disquiet from Hector's unsteadiness.

He would hear those screams in his dreams and had to wonder if that was what Hector's fear sounded like.

The rest of their after-dinner conversation was much more uneventful, falling into something that felt more like the rhythm of their normal companionship. Conversation covered everything from sports—of which Hector was fond, of which Violet and Isaias were mostly clueless—to upcoming art installations at the museum—for which Violet was very excited, for which Isaias and Hector were eager to lend their support—to the weather—all of them hoping for the sun to come out more often, for the cold to prove itself to have an end. When conversation lulled, Isaias helped Hector clean up the dishes and leftovers while Violet went searching for the cat, who had been hiding somewhere since Hector had come home.

But Isaias found himself spending the whole evening waiting for the next time that Hector's mood would suddenly swing, if he would prove himself so unsteady. He could tell Violet was watching for the same thing, though with something more like calculation than wariness radiating off of her.

As Isaias dried dishes and put them away, Hector suddenly spoke. "I am glad you came over tonight." His gaze stayed fixed on the sink, his forearms submerged in the steel basin, suds catching the light where they clung to his thick arm hair.

"Of course," Isaias said. He put the last of the utensils away and turned back to Hector, but Hector didn't look up. "You know I have a very hard time saying no to Violet." Hector didn't react to that either, but he didn't feel aggressive this time—only sad. "And it's always good to see you."

Hector nodded. He resumed scrubbing at the bowl he was holding under the water. The water came away faintly brown from the remnants of broth. "It's good to see you, too, Isaias. It's—things have been strange, lately."

Isaias resisted the urge to say *I've noticed*. That was not active listening. Making assumptions or inserting his own preconceptions and observations were not useful when it came to urging someone to bare their soul. Instead, he gently prompted by asking, "Have they?"

The water ran steady. Hector scrubbed absently at the bowl, his eyes unfocused. He felt distant from Isaias, even then. "My head's all muddled in a way it hasn't been since—well, a long time."

Carefully, Isaias tamed his emotions, repressed them. Letting himself react too strongly would risk subjecting Hector to his feelings, like unwanted radio waves. Maybe plant something in his head. Hector's emotions were strangely closed off to Isaias, but that didn't mean he wouldn't receive something that *Isaias* felt too strongly. Hector was clearly already struggling—he didn't need to be burdened with Isaias's unasked for emotional interference, too. It caused a hurt in Isaias's chest that he couldn't quite place to shut his feelings away from Hector, but he bore the pain on his shoulders readily.

So, he repressed his fear.

While Isaias hadn't known Hector as anything but a single man, he knew what his friend had been like when he had been married to Violet's mother, when Violet was still just a little girl. Hector had never once been to confession with Isaias, but he had confided much in him anyway. Isaias seemed to have that effect on people. Hector trusted him just as much as Isaias trusted Hector.

But Isaias wondered what Violet remembered of the days when she had lived under the care of two married parents and when Hector had found more solace in alcohol than in his wife. Isaias did not know what that had been like—but had something now stirred those painful memories in Violet?

Carefully, Isaias said, "I'm sorry to hear that you haven't been feeling well."

Hector grunted softly. He scrubbed the bowl a little harder. Isaias was certain it was clean enough. "Yeah, well, it's an understatement."

Isaias kept his attention on Hector, trying to assess him when he lacked the emotional read—he wasn't used to it, even when he had been told not to pry into the emotions of others, it had always been *there*, he had never been in the dark for long. Without any dishes to dry, Hector obsessively washing one, he focused entirely on his friend.

Sometimes he wondered what if he *did* use his gifts to connect to Hector? Would it be so wrong, to be more open about what it meant? What if he told Hector his whole truth, instead of leaving it piecemeal? Would it be so bad to admit to not being—normal? Being touched by God wasn't something to be hidden, surely, yet Hector had only an inkling of the truth. He had the barest idea that Isaias was prone to a certain sensitivity to the feelings of others, beyond mere empathy in the common sense. He could read people, know things, more than others. When Isaias had explained, or tried to, that he was able to understand the plights of others, Hector had merely remarked, "Must be a useful skill for a preacher."

Isaias still thought about that, sometimes.

Instead of confessing all of the things that Isaias wanted to say to Hector, he whispered, "You can tell me anything."

Something in Hector softened, opened up, like a flower beginning to bloom. Isaias caught the scent of Hector's emotions as they reappeared, a comforting and familiar sweetness. "I know," he said. His voice was soft, difficult to hear over the running tap. His arms stilled in the water. "It's—family stuff, you know? It's complicated. I—"

Hector's words cut off as the kitchen was plunged into darkness.

For a moment, Isaias could only see Hector's silhouette, his body backlit by the light that still poured in through the kitchen doorway from the dining room. His face was cast in shadows, completely imperceptible in the deep darkness.

Isaias heard a *crunch* from nearby before the lights came back an instant later. That hint of Hector's emotions went missing just as quickly.

He was lost to Isaias again already.

It took a moment for Isaias to see the blood in the water, blinking his eyes to adjust to the rapid changes in light, and at first thought perhaps his mind was playing tricks on him. But no, it was blood. The soap bubbled a foamy red.

Isaias reached out to take Hector's wrist but stopped short of seizing his arm. "Hector, are you alright?"

Slowly, Hector withdrew his arms from the sink, the red-tinged suds clinging to the thick hair of his forearms. He blinked down at his hands, as if he were surprised to find both of his palms sliced open, deep gashes in the centre of both hands that looked deeper than they had any right to be. Water-thinned blood welled from the wounds. "Must have broken the bowl."

The too-calm tone of voice unsettled Isaias as much as the appearance of the deep punctures. "You must have," he said. His fingertip hovered over the mound of flesh that made up the base of Hector's thumb on his right hand, mere centimeters from the gash. "Leave the sink, let's go clean these and bandage them. I can finish the dishes once we know you're taken care of." Hector nodded, but did not reply. Isaias brushed his fingers down to Hector's wrist for a moment before gently gripping him over his pulse—slow and steady, which was strange given Hector had just cut himself so badly, but fortunate, all things considered, to prevent bleeding too quickly—and applied the gentlest pressure he could manage to ease Hector away from the sink when it became clear he wasn't going to move of his own accord. Gently, Isaias led Hector to the bathroom, helping him sit on the edge of the tub once he slid the frosted glass door for the shower out of the way. He walked and moved as Isaias directed him to and nothing more. *Shock*, Isaias thought, wondering if perhaps the sight of the blood had triggered something for Hector. He'd seen it before, Hector's hesitation and shock—albeit rarely—so it wasn't an unheard-of possibility.

Hector's pulse was still steady, but his breathing was slightly too rapid for comfort. Once he felt Hector was seated, not even seeming to notice the track of the shower door, Isaias let go of his wrist to carefully smooth Hector's curls away from his forehead—carefully broadcasting his every movement so that Hector wouldn't be surprised by the touch—to check his temperature as well as offer comfort.

Isaias didn't see Hector move, really, not registering the flash of movement for what it was, until Hector's hand seized upon Isaias's wrist, smearing blood from his palm across Isaias's own pulse point. Hector finally looked up, his eyes locking onto Isaias's. *My soul is exposed*, Isaias thought, convinced Hector was seeing into his heart, though *he* was supposed to be the empath, not Hector. Unlike Hector, though, he could feel his own heartrate spike, his pulse quickening under the bloody grip on his wrist, his heart pounding in his ears. Hector's fingers were firm against him, not tight enough to be painful, but sure enough that Isaias felt he must want to convey something.

For what felt like one too many moments, Isaias stood over Hector, his fingertips still halfway tangled in Hector's curly hair and grazing his forehead, Hector with his fingers wrapped firmly around Isaias's wrist, his blood soaking into the cuff of Isaias's shirt and one finger extended into Isaias's hand, crooked to touch the pad of his fingertip into the very centre of Isaias's own palm. Hector's hand on him, his hand on Hector, seemed to create a perfect circuit, through which Isaias's emotions flowed into Hector and from which Isaias finally started to feel what Hector felt again, some shadow of his hopes, his dreams, his fears, his secrets. More than any time before, Isaias felt that, standing there and holding him, he might have understood Hector with the utmost potential, have truly known his heart and soul, if only they had more time.

Why did it feel somehow more intimate than anything their friendship had ever held before?

And why did that scare him so much?

"Hector." Isaias breathed his name. His heart swelled. He wanted to pray—for himself, or for Hector?

Their emotions swelled together, magnifying each other and creating an echo chamber of fear and—and what? Isaias was distracted; he couldn't quite make out the nuances of the feelings that flowed through the conduit that their contact had made.

Before Isaias could say anything else, he heard the tapping of Violet's crutches hitting the tile floor as she appeared in the doorway to the bathroom. "Dad? Isaias? You okay?"

Isaias jerked his hand back and was surprised to find that it came away easily, Hector's grip suddenly slack.

He felt guilty. Why did he feel guilty? He had done nothing, just felt their emotions joining as one. For a moment, he wasn't sure if it was even his own emotion, or if instead he was still feeling the lingering presence of someone else—Hector. But what more did Hector have to feel guilty about than Isaias?

He looked back at Violet as he struggled to find his words through the misplaced guilt sticking to him. His left hand still hovered, unused, in the air, from where he had pulled away from Hector. Uncertain, he touched his right hand to his left wrist, feeling the tacky texture of Hector's blood.

Evidently, the gesture drew Violet's eyes. "Somebody's bleeding? Are you two okay?"

Hector broke through the silence, his voice sounding like his own again. "Just cut myself when I broke a dish, Vi. We're fine. Did you find the cat?"

Violet's gaze shifted from the blood at Isaias's wrist to her father's hands where the blood had originated. She frowned. "Oh. Uh, yeah, I found Prue in my room. She was under my bed. She came out when I called her but then hid again when you two went into the bathroom, I guess some noise scared her. She's fine, I think. Do you need help bandaging my dad up?" she asked, tacking the question on with a glance at Isaias. "He doesn't need, like, stitches, does he?"

"I hope not," Isaias said, but he truthfully wasn't sure. "I think we're okay, Violet. Bandages are in the cupboard, right?"

Violet nodded. "Yeah, the one with all my shit—all my medical stuff, sorry."

Isaias laughed, causing Violet to wrinkle her nose at him. Her attempts at censoring herself made him feel less on edge—maybe things could be normal, after all. "Thank you, Violet," he said, though he noticed that neither Violet nor Hector laughed. He went to the cupboard where he knew they stored all their medical supplies and fished out some large bandages as well as antiseptic.

"Help me wash the rest of the blood off your hands before we clean you up, would you, Hector?"

Hector nodded and stood, this time willing to do so of his own accord, it seemed. He walked to the sink and Isaias turned on the tap for him to wash the blood off. Hector's eyes found Isaias's in the mirror above the sink, but Isaias looked away and fixed his own stare on the faded floral tiling that made up the backsplash behind the faucet.

Once Hector turned off the water he turned his palms up to Isaias, who inspected them. The gashes were deep—maybe not as deep as he had originally thought, but still significant—but there was no blood or sign of damage, and Hector didn't seem to be in any pain, even when Isaias gently traced the skin around the edge of Hector's hand to test the sensitivity. Hector didn't react with any discomfort, so Isaias continued to marvel at the complete lack of blood, the way the injury looked clean.

He was struck by the image of Doubting Thomas, the thought that he could test, somehow, if Hector was real, pry his fingers into the wound, touch the tender inside of Hector as if that were any substitute for touching his heart. As if there had ever been any doubt that Hector was right there in front of him.

"It's really not bad, is it?" Violet asked, interrupting Isaias's thoughts.

Isaias shook his head. "No, it's—I think he's fine. Are you worried, Hector?" he asked, looking up at Hector, who was studying him.

"No. I don't feel any pain."

Isaias frowned but nodded. The rest was easy—swiping antiseptic over both open wounds, wrapping them in gauze—firm and secure but not painful, like Hector's grip before, when they had been connected—and making sure the wrap held fast. Once he was done with both hands, he let Hector go, at once feeling his absence. He also felt an ache in his temple and in his ribs.

"All better," he said, not really knowing what else to say.

Hector smiled, but said nothing, never taking his eyes off of Isaias.

VII

WHILE VIOLET HAD TRIED to suggest that Isaias stay for tea—neither of the Monteros even *drank* tea, just kept it around for Isaias's benefit—he had felt that it was well past time for him to dismiss himself and go home. His presence did not feel particularly welcome, and he needed time to think.

Violet had invited him for a reason, but he couldn't quite place what she had wanted him to gather. It must have involved her father—but Isaias couldn't figure out what was going on with Hector. He needed to reflect on everything he had felt that night—the feelings in the house, in Hector, and in himself.

"I should get back to the rectory before the blood sets," he had said as an excuse, gesturing to his sleeve, sticky with Hector's blood, "or else Mrs. Marsh will never be able to save it."

"I think it might be a lost cause," Violet had said cheerfully, but she hadn't protested.

Isaias hugged Hector goodbye first, and he felt a momentary return to their usual warmth when Hector's strong arms wrapped around him. He felt safe, there, even though something still distanced them from each other in way he wasn't used to. But for a second, it felt like they were dear friends again, and Isaias was loathe to leave Hector's arms. Hector, for his part, seemed to let the hug linger and didn't try to push Isaias away.

But at some point, a lingering hug was improper, and Isaias reluctantly broke it off. When they separated, he saw Violet watching them—both of them—carefully. Isaias looked away and cleared his throat. "Thank you again for having me for dinner," he said. "It was lovely to see you both."

"You, too," Hector said. Isaias couldn't tell if he meant it. "I'll see you later, alright?"

Isaias turned to leave—his thick jacket back on, the rosary weighted heavily in his pocket—but Violet asked, "Wait, can we talk a moment before you go, Isaias? In private?"

Isaias didn't hesitate. "Of course, Violet. Anything."

Violet glanced at her father, then said, "We can step outside for a second."

Hector frowned. "It's freezing, Vi."

"No big, I can throw a jacket on. It'll be just for a sec."

Isaias echoed Hector's frown. It was cold, and why not talk inside? But he sensed the gravity of Violet's request, the dead seriousness of her desire to have proper privacy. "I won't let your daughter freeze to death," Isaias promised Hector.

Hector's frown deepened and for a moment Isaias swore he felt another flash of heat, like fire, like something burning. But it passed in another instant and Hector nodded. "Sure. Take care, Isaias. Violet, come back in soon, alright?"

"'Course, dad."

Violet expertly put on a purple puffer jacket, juggling her crutches long enough to do so, and tugged a grey woolen toque down over her ears. She gestured vaguely with the base of one crutch for Isaias to step outside, so he did, holding the door for Violet until she had exited as well.

The sun had long since set, and the night sky was pitch dark. The only light around them was from the house behind them, and a few of the other porch lights on the cul-de-sac. None of the lights did anything to cut through the bitter cold. The weather would be painfully cold for a while longer, having barely escaped the coldest month and the winter season not ready to die. Isaias stayed close to the house, not wanting to lead Violet too far from safety and warmth. Their breath came out in puffs of steam. Above them, the stars were clear, the moon a sharp crescent.

Isaias hesitated to break the silence of the night. That time of year, in those cold temperatures, and deep in something resembling suburbia, there were few living things around. The only noise was the distant rumbling of traffic off the main road. Isaias was just hugging himself tighter against the chill when Violet finally spoke.

"You see it, don't you?"

Frowning, Isaias once again considered the delicate balance of leading Violet in the conversation without biasing her. He was meant to listen, not insert himself, not unless explicitly asked for his opinion or advice. But Violet was, wasn't she? Asking him to share what was in *his* heart, for once. "Your father?" he asked.

Violet nodded. She didn't look or feel relieved that it hadn't gone unnoticed. She must have thought it obvious—and, to her credit, it was. "He's acting super weird, right? Not like himself at all. Sad, and weary, and angry, and just—it's not like him, okay? You know that's not like him at all. That isn't him."

"No, it isn't like him," Isaias admitted carefully. He couldn't tell Violet the extent of what he had felt—that Hector felt *wrong*, somehow, like another person altogether. But did Violet even believe in the soul?

"It isn't him," Violet repeated. Her voice was low, almost swallowed by the dark. "Thank you for coming tonight. I didn't know how to explain it, Father. You needed to see him for yourself—you're his best friend, so I knew you'd know that he's not himself. You'd know. You know *him*. You can save him."

Violet's conviction was clear. He felt it, her positive certainty that Isaias could save her father. But save him from what? There was a certain amount of assuredness in her feelings. She was scared, but she was putting her wholehearted faith in Isaias to help her father. A faith she may have never had in anyone else *but* her father.

"Save him from what?" Isaias asked, wanting Violet to tell him what exactly it was that she believed that Isaias could do. Her faith was clear, but the wording troubling. Hector's soul didn't need saving—and if it did, it wasn't Isaias's business to proselytize to him without his consent. But no—she must not be asking him as a priest, but as her father's friend. He thought that her problem, whatever it was, was not Godly.

Instead of answering his question, Violet returned with one of her own. "Could you teach me how to pray?"

It was not an unfamiliar query, exactly, but Isaias would never have imagined it to come from Violet. Uncertain, he didn't answer at first. "I didn't think you believed."

Isaias couldn't see Violet's cheeks flush in the dark of the night with the way she was lit from above by the porch light, awash in an LED glow, but he felt her embarrassment radiating off her. She shrugged weakly, the movement muffled by her heavy coat. "I don't know if I do," she admitted. "But I don't need to pray to God the way you think of Him, do I? Or maybe I can, and that'll help me figure out what I think."

Isaias nodded. He didn't want to discourage her, of course, but he hoped she didn't feel she *needed* to do it, either. "Well, there's no one way to pray. For me, it is an opportunity not just to speak to God, but to reflect. To be honest with not just Him, but myself. And like you said, you don't have to pray to God. If it helps you, you can pray to come to focus. Putting your thoughts and beliefs to words can provide clarity. An honest prayer will require you to be honest with yourself."

Violet nodded, the movement so slight that Isaias might have missed it if it weren't for the bob of the pompom on her hat. "So, I just start by being honest with myself?"

"It's a place to start," Isaias said. "And pray to whoever or whatever you like to help you make sense of what you're feeling. It's a way for you to feel closer to what you believe in. It's personal, how you want to pray."

"Thanks," Violet said. She was quiet, but Isaias could tell in the weight of the pause that she wanted to say more. Ask more.

Isaias shifted, waiting to see if more would come, and the movement made him aware again of the rosary in his jacket pocket, the slight weight against his side. Would Hector be upset it made it back to his home, after he had disposed of it at The Second Voyage? Would Violet benefit from it more than if it remained lost, without a spiritual home?

Hesitantly, Isaias removed the velvet cloth from his pocket. He struggled to unwrap the cloth from the rosary to show Violet, fumbling in his leather gloves to be as delicate as he needed to be. It was his own first look at the rosary, and it was obvious it was old, worn as it was in places from prayer. The crucifix portion was perhaps the most worn down, partially broken from carelessness. The face of Christ was chipped and most of His features—the details already difficult to read in their small size—had been scrapped off. It was unsettling, but Isaias attributed it to the amount of time such a rosary had been carried in a family, loved and prayed over. It was at least as old as the one in his office at the rectory, maybe older.

"I think this was your father's," he said softly. "It seems he dropped it off at The Second Voyage. I thought maybe you'd like to have it."

Violet looked to the rosary with something like fear and awe—the two feelings intermingled on her soul in a way that made them nearly indistinguishable. She reached for it, and Isaias was suddenly struck with his own fear: what if the rosary, which had filled both him and Lena with unease, did something to poison Violet by its presence?

But when Violet closed her hand around the crucifix, curling the relief of Christ into her fingers, Isaias's panic dissipated. Whatever darkness the rosary had picked up, he suddenly felt sure that Violet would be unaffected. That she was stronger than that. That her heart was steadfast—and that, perhaps, she could return some of the righteousness back to the symbol.

"Thanks," she said softly as she tucked the rosary and the cloth into her jacket, then returned her hand to her crutch to regain her balance. "I appreciate it. Why do you think dad got rid of it?"

Isaias hesitated to answer, though a part of him was certain he knew. "Maybe it held too many bad memories."

Violet frowned but again she nodded. "Well, I won't tell him, then."

"I appreciate it. If he's not been feeling well..."

Her nose wrinkled, barely visible in the bare light. She laughed, but it sounded—and felt—bitter. "Yeah, I don't really plan on poking the bear right now."

"Fair enough." Isaias shook his head. "Well, it's cold, so we should—"

"Yeah. I should get back inside before dad thinks I'm going to freeze to death." This time, the laugh sounded more genuine, even if frayed at the edges. "Thanks again for coming to dinner, Isaias. It was good to see you, and—I don't know. I just know that you can help him, more than I can on my own. He trusts you more than anyone else in the world."

"I don't know about that," Isaias said. Hector was his dearest friend, and he had confided in Isaias in the past, but he was a stubborn man, and one who solved his own problems. Even if they held each other's trust in high regard, it wasn't inherently true that Hector would let Isaias solve whatever problem it was that he was having. And he likely trusted Violet more than he trusted Isaias—it was just that Isaias couldn't imagine a parent who would want to be vulnerable to his own child, to expose that he was struggling. It wasn't that Hector trusted Isaias more, it was that Hector was not a man who would show weakness to the one he was meant to protect. Still, Isaias had to try. For Violet and for Hector both. "No matter what, I'll do my best to help your father."

"Promise?" Violet asked. Her voice sounded smaller like that, younger than her sixteen years. It was a painful reminder that she was still a child, no matter how proud.

"I promise."

Violet shuffled closer and gave Isaias a one-armed hug, briefly leaning her weight on only one crutch. Isaias hugged her back, willing his care into her—just this once, he could share something to ease her pain. Just this once, he could let his gifts do something to help someone directly. Should he really feel like he had to ask God for forgiveness just for trying to make someone hurt a little less? If he tried to give someone scared just a little bit of hope?

Violet let out a soft sigh before she straightened up and let go of him. She sniffled and Isaias suspected she was fighting tears, not willing to let them fall even if they would be near invisible in the dark. "Have a good night, Isaias."

"Try to take care of yourself, too, alright, Violet? You can't worry yourself to death over other people."

"I'll promise to take care of myself if you promise to take care of my dad."

Isaias hesitated. It would be a heavy promise, one he wouldn't take lightly, when he didn't even know what was wrong. "I promise I'll try."

Violet nodded. That answer was, apparently, good enough. "See you later," she said, turning her back on Isaias and going inside.

When the door closed again, Isaias was left in the cold with only the dim porch light to illuminate him. He stood in the pale circle of light for a long moment before the light flickered, then shut off, leaving Isaias in near total darkness, but for the faint light of the stars above.

VIII

THE WALK BACK TO the rectory felt somehow colder than it was, like the chill of the winter night had crawled deep into the marrow of his bones. The breeze that had felt nearly pleasant cutting across the churchyard earlier that day had become brutal; biting. Some irrational part of Isaias felt convinced that he would never be warm again, the cold never leaving him. Of course, it would be spring again in a matter of weeks, and soon enough the snow would melt, and the flowers would bloom. But in that moment, the wind cutting into his cheeks no matter how tightly he pulled the scarf around his face, it felt like the sun would never rise again, and Sainte-Thérèse would be left in a perpetual winter darkness.

When Isaias returned to the rectory, he hoped for warmth but found none. Mrs. Marsh had left for home already, it seemed, as the rectory was dark and silent. Empty. It was cold, too—there was no sign of the heat stirring in the old building, and it was quickly falling victim to dated insulation. They said churches were hard to heat, but so were rectories—and, unlike the church, Isaias had to *live* in the rectory.

Fumbling for the light, Isaias flicked the switch. There was an electrical hum of protest and the light flickered once, twice, before turning on. Isaias frowned—were the bulbs failing, or the wiring? One would be significantly more inconvenient to fix, but he wasn't sure if he had extra bulbs to test with.

A problem for tomorrow, he decided. He was cold and he was tired. He took off his boots, not wanting to track snow past the mat in the front hall, and removed his scarf, but left his jacket and hat on—too cold to go without them, at least not without a thick sweater to replace the coat with.

On the console table by the door was a note left by Mrs. Marsh. Isaias picked it up as he set down his keys. His breath puffed out in white clouds in front of him as he read.

Heat's out, it said. *I called someone to fix it first thing tomorrow. If it's too cold for you tonight, give me a call and you can come stay with me and my niece.*

Well, Mrs. Marsh's note explained why it felt only marginally less cold in the rectory than outside.

A small addendum to the note read, *P.S. Bishop called this evening about 6:30.*

Isaias tugged his jacket sleeve out of the way to read his watch, seeing that it was not yet eight o'clock. Not too late to call the bishop back.

Maybe once Isaias had some tea in him.

He was beginning to regret leaving the Montero home. Normally he would be sure that if he called, Hector would be glad to let Isaias stay somewhere more comfortable. But tonight, he wasn't so sure he would be more than a burdensome presence to whatever was troubling Hector.

Besides, he told himself, he would have to hold Mass in the morning. Few of his parishioners attended daily, let alone on a Monday morning, but *somebody* had to be there, and it should probably be Isaias if he was the one holding services.

Isaias went to the kitchen to turn on the kettle. The lights there flickered, too, which was concerning—perhaps it really was a wiring issue, and maybe that was the same reason the heat was out. He imagined something living in the walls, chewing through the wires. Whatever it was surely wouldn't survive that, would decompose behind the drywall. It unsettled Isaias to think of, but he didn't sense anything like death in the rectory, either.

He turned on the kettle and hugged himself against the chill as he surveyed his mug and tea options. When the water was ready, he made an herbal tea and carried it carefully to his study. The kitchen lights flickered again as he turned them off, and the study's lights brightened slowly, as if on a dimmer—but he had never installed such a set up.

Eventually, the lights were at their full strength and Isaias resolved that yes, he should ask Mrs. Marsh to call an electrician as well as someone to look at the HVAC system. Something was wrong with the building.

Isaias settled into the chair at his desk in the office, setting his tea next to the photo of him and the bishop. The tea steamed in the cold air, obscuring the faces in the photograph. Isaias ignored the anxious feeling it gave him and picked up the phone as he sat. Mrs. Marsh had insisted Isaias continue to have a dedicated landline—something about keeping his personal number separate to preserve his mental health. He wasn't sure it was necessary, but there was something more comfortable about sitting at the desk and using the office phone to make his calls. The bishop was family, but it felt right, anyway. Once he dialed the number from memory, he picked up his tea to sip it while the phone rang until he was connected with the bishop who oversaw Sainte-Thérèse and other nearby towns within the diocese.

"Isaias," Bishop Reid greeted fondly when he realized who it was. Isaias felt some level of comfort from the voice of the man who had raised him. He was not the bishop's son by birth, nor had he been adopted, per se, but the man had taken him in when his parents hadn't known what to do with him. He had proven too difficult for them, so he became a ward of the church by the bishop's good grace. "Glad to hear back from you so soon, my child. Are you well? I called only to check in with you."

"Your Excellency," Isaias greeted, then paused. Was he well? By all accounts, yes, but he still felt disturbed by the strangeness of the evening. "I'm well enough," he decided after a short thought. "Nothing to complain about."

"You're not stretching yourself too thin, are you, Isaias? I know how you can get with your—gifts, when you're careless."

This was a typical line of questioning from the bishop, it came up in nearly every conversation they had that Isaias was gifted, had gifts, should be careful of his gifts. Isaias already knew what answer was expected of him. There was only one acceptable answer to be given when asked if he was stretching himself thin. "I have been keeping them to myself as much as possible," he promised. He kept his voice grave, even if he didn't feel it with the whole conviction of his soul. "Only using the powers vested in me by God where it is appropriate, lest I abuse them."

"That's right, Isaias." The bishop sounded satisfied. Isaias wished that he could sense something from across the distance, know how the bishop *really* felt about Isaias's answer, about whether he was using his gifts from God or not. Was there doubt in his heart, the way there often was in Isaias's? Did he really feel so certain that this was the right thing? When Isaias had been a boy, the bishop *had* encouraged him to use his gifts—but only under the strictest circumstances. Without that guidance, Isaias was supposed to keep them to himself. "Now, how are you, really?"

Isaias used his free hand to sip his tea as he used one foot to roll the desk chair closer. He sighed, the steam from his breath in the too-cold rectory mingling with the steam from the tea. "I'm alright," he said, more earnestly this time. He wanted to impress it upon the bishop. "Cold—the heat is broken. And I've been busy with the church, of course. Taking care of the parish. There was a good turnout at Mass this morning, which was nice. I was preaching on the topic of love."

"Love, eh?" the bishop asked. He sounded like he was smiling. Isaias was glad he had said all the right words. The church was well. "That's a challenging one, but certainly rewarding. God's love is pure and great. How did it go?"

"Well, I think," Isaias said. But he still remembered the anxiety from the morning that carried over into the evening, the tension, the stress. "The parish seemed pleased, anyway. It's just that—"

"What is it?" Bishop Reid asked. "Was there a problem?"

Isaias thought of Violet, and he thought of the sensation of wilting flowers. He thought of Hector, erratic instead of his usual steady self. The disturbing feelings clinging to him. Like something was wrong, off-balance. Something had thrown everything into a slightly different tilt and Isaias was trying to right it again without success. Was the parish pleased, if any individual in his community was so troubled, let alone two? Neither were truly a member of the congregation, but their worries, their *pain*, weighed on Isaias, especially after the evening had been filled with so much discomfort. They were members of his community. They mattered to him. Maybe the bishop would know what to do.

"The daughter of a close friend came to me about her father," Isaias said after his deliberation. The bishop had raised him, guided his path, and always set him straight. He had years of experience that Isaias simply didn't. He could tell Isaias what to do. "He is not a member of the parish—neither are Catholic at all, in fact, though I think the daughter might be interested in exploring it—but he's a very dear friend to me. His daughter is worried that he is not himself and I'm afraid that I have no choice but to agree after seeing them both this evening. The problem is, I doubt he would tell me what the matter was, even if he is clearly not himself, so I just don't know why, let alone what I should do for him. I don't know if I should use my gifts, or help in a more conventional sense somehow, or if there is something else that can be done."

"First, Isaias, you know you should only use your gifts when it is absolutely crucial to do so. And if he's not a member of your parish, that *certainly* isn't cause to use them. If he is someone outside of your parish, perhaps he needs help from someone outside of it, too," the Bishop advised with his slow, familiar drawl. Isaias knew it well. "You needn't worry too much about those not part of your flock when you have so many others to tend to. Your first responsibility is to your family in Christ."

Isaias lowered his head and bit back a sigh. The cold puffs of his breath were still visible. He had been afraid of this answer. He had hoped for another one anyway. He knew what was expected of him. His family in Christ meant the bishop and those who had raised Isaias in the church, and now his parish, too. But was it wrong to want Hector and Violet to be a part of that family, too? Perhaps not in Christ, but as people who meant the world to Isaias. "Yes, Your Excellency."

"I don't want to discourage you from having friends, Isaias, but your whole life is this church, isn't it? The Sacred Heart. If this friend of yours doesn't come to you for help himself, let alone does he ask for the help and support of God above, it may be best to redirect the family. Perhaps he needs counselling, or to speak to a professional of another sort."

Isaias didn't bother to say that Hector might just be his *only* friend. He wasn't entirely sure he could count those who came to him for spiritual guidance to be true friends, though he tried to be friendly with them when they came to him. There was Mrs. Marsh, of course, but even that felt complicated. Isaias didn't have many people in his life that he knew for sure were there for uncomplicated reasons—for reasons of pure care and affection, not connection through the church or otherwise.

That was wrong, though, wasn't it, to worry about? The church was his life. His life was the church's—and God's. That bond was great. That community meant something to him. It was so much bigger than him; only a man. There was a reason that the church had taken him in when his family no longer felt able to care for him.

In the pause where Isaias did not answer him, the bishop was saying, "I'm quite serious, my son. Take care of your parish and your church. Follow your duties and follow God. I don't want you hurting yourself or anyone else by misusing God's gift to you. He trusted you with your gifts. You should be careful about using them, unless it is to genuinely promote the Lord's work."

"I'm not using it," Isaias said and immediately the words felt wrong, like he was lying. When he had touched Hector, his hand on Hector's forehead and Hector's hand on his wrist, had he not used his gifts then? What else could explain the depth of everything he had felt, in that moment, for and with Hector? Isaias wasn't sure that anything else could explain the way he had felt standing in the bathroom over Hector, his emotions magnified beyond recognition, nearly too intense to manage. It had been a long time since he had become overwhelmed by the force of a single feeling, but he came close in that moment earlier that evening. So maybe he *had* meant to use his divinely inspired gifts to read into Hector's heart and soul. Maybe he had meant to know him on a level deeper than human intuition. And was he not always too aware of the emotions flowing through all those around him? Perhaps that, too, was a betrayal. "Not really," Isaias corrected himself. He couldn't bear the thought that he might be lying to the man who had raised him. It would feel like too great a sin.

"It's the 'not really' that concerns me, Isaias. As your bishop, as your mentor, and as your de facto father, you know that I love you like my own son. I have no other children, you see—"

Isaias did not sigh. He did not say 'I know'. He said nothing at all. He sat staring at the last dredges of steam off his mug of tea in the room that somehow felt colder by the moment and, as always, he listened.

"—and at any rate, you were always a troubled young man. When I took you under my wing, it was to foster your gift from God, but also to guide your path. Now, be careful, son. Please? For this old man's heart? I couldn't bear the thought of you being led astray, after all we've done together. You would be risking such a *bright* future."

Isaias nodded to himself. Said, "Yes, Father." The irony of the statement meant that it didn't quite feel like reality, but nor did it feel like it was in jest. It was a statement in some kind of purgatory, awaiting judgement from those who might deem it truth or a lie.

"Alright, there we go, Isaias," Bishop Reid said. Isaias could hear the bright energy in his voice. The man was lively enough for someone nearing his seventies. "Now, for the last time: how are *you*? Are you well? Are you taking care of yourself? Is Mrs. Mash feeding you right?"

Isaias laughed softly, but it felt dry in his throat. He wasn't sure if he should blame the cold—the air still felt damp, despite the frigid temperatures. He latched onto the opportunity to pivot the conversation. "She is," he promised. "She also left me a note promising she called someone to fix the heat."

"Excellent! Be sure to nip that in the bud—you know how those old buildings can get, after all. Say hello to Mrs. Marsh for me. She and I were friends once, you know."

"I know," Isaias said, knowing the story, or at least knowing it well enough, though he did not know if Bishop Reid had ever had any friends that he did not preach to at some point or another. He had heard many stories about many friends, but they all came back to the church in the end. "And I'm doing well. Busy with my work, and happy for it. Praying regularly, of course. How are you, Your Excellency?"

"Good, good. I'm well. Nothing to complain about that you haven't heard before; an old man's joints, et cetera, et cetera. But my heart is in the care of God, and so all is quite fine in the end. Never any need to worry about much else, is there? Anyway, Isaias, I shouldn't keep you, it's late and I imagine you want to bundle someplace warm. I had only been calling to check in, it'd been a few days since we'd spoken last. Never a bad time for a check in, is there? We'll catch up proper next time you're able to come by my little neck of the woods, won't we?"

"Of course, Your Excellency," Isaias promised, though he never quite knew when he would make it to the bishop. There always seemed to be some excuse or another to delay a visit. "I promise."

"Good. Take care of yourself, will you, son?"

"Yes, Your Excellency. You, too."

"Peace be with you, Isaias."

"And with your spirit, Your Excellency."

Isaias paused in his seat, still holding the phone cradled against his ear, and only hung it up when he heard the bishop's receiver click and the dial tone begin, telling him that man who had raised him was gone again. Their conversations always felt brief—but Isaias supposed it was only natural when they spoke often. There was not always much to update one another on if they hadn't gone long since speaking last. Tonight, all that had really been new was his concerns about Hector—and those had been summarily dismissed.

Isaias sighed as he replaced the handset of the phone in its cradle. He picked up his mug of tea and took a sip, only to find that it had gone completely frigid and starkly bitter. It figured—the air was beyond cold, and it had been steeping quite some time. Still, the tea seemed too thick in his throat as he swallowed, coating his vocal cords with the acrid taste of over-steeped leaves.

Isaias wondered again if he should sleep elsewhere for the night, but instead resolved to find as many blankets as possible to live under for a few hours. Maybe it would be a comfort, to have the weight of extra blankets on him. It might finally settle his nerves.

Putting his tea aside, he leaned forward and opened one of the drawers of his desk. He felt momentarily drawn to his favourite old rosary, the ancient, weighty thing. It was similar to the one that he had found at The Second Voyage, previously Hector's and now safely in Violet's care. But while he felt that thing carried anger and pain that

Violet was going to wash away with new love, the rosary in Isaias's desk carried something different: grief.

He couldn't explain how he could feel emotions from objects, he could barely understand how it was that he could feel them from people except that it was a gift from God Himself. But the hands that had held this rosary had felt deep grief and had left pieces of their soul behind, infused into the beads of the rosary. What had they lost, that they grieved so much? Surely not Isaias himself—the rosary would have left with him, and he had been given up willingly. What was there to grieve?

The grief-soaked rosary nestled amongst the letters and cards from Hector—he had never thrown out so much as a Christmas card—was striking, but the lights flickered again, for a longer period that time, leaving Isaias in the dark for long enough for him to count to six under his breath. In the brief darkness, he thought he could see the shape of his frosted breath in front of his face, but everything else was obscured. For that moment, he heard and felt nothing except his own breathing. He imagined, for a moment, what it might be like to be buried alive.

The lights came on and Isaias shook away the feeling. He took his cellphone from his pocket as he stood, taking his cold and bitter tea from the desk with his other hand. He wanted to check for any final messages or calls before he would go upstairs, change into the absolute thickest clothes that he had, crawl under every thick blanket he could find, and sleep until it was time to get ready for Mass in the morning. His head felt heavy with fatigue, even though it was barely past eight in the evening. He just wanted to sleep for as long as he physically could. Realistically, it would be when Mrs. Marsh returned in the morning and started tending to the rectory.

Isaias poured the remaining tea into the sink, trying to pay no mind to the way it dripped out of his mug like a thick sludge, while he checked his messages and e-mails. To his surprise, he saw a text from Hector that had just arrived—he hadn't heard it announce its arrival with a notification ping, as it had appeared on his screen the exact moment he had turned on the screen.

Sorry if I seemed like I was acting weird earlier, Hector's text said, simple enough. *I've been stressed.*

Isaias hesitated before he texted back: *Nothing for me to forgive*, he wrote, despite the way something shivered down his spine at the memory of Hector erratic and hostile, of the wounds in Hector's palms bleeding into the water, and of the way Isaias felt both thrilled and terrified to be close to him. *We'll chat soon about whatever it is that you're stressed about? I would love to help if I can.* He ended the text with an emoji of a pair of hands praying, just for good measure.

Isaias wanted to ask right then, invite Hector to join him in confessional, to bare his soul to him. But he didn't really think that pushing it would be wise, and Isaias could barely think straight—truthfully, he didn't know if he had enough spirit in him to pursue the matter again so soon.

Instead, he went upstairs to get ready for bed. He finally took off his coat, hanging it in his bedroom instead of in its place downstairs, and changed into thick pajama pants, a long-sleeved shirt, and a pullover sweater. He dug out every blanket he could find for his bed. After brushing his teeth and trying—and failing—to wash the blood out of the sleeve of his shirt, he knelt by his bed to say his evening prayer. He tried to concentrate on the spiritual wellness he needed to feel, but instead he kept thinking of the strength of Hector's hand and blood on his wrist.

He fell asleep to the smell of the radiator, somehow producing the pungent stench of something burning despite its failure to heat anything, Isaias shivering even under layers of blankets. He never did hear back from Hector that night.

IX

What woke Isaias wasn't Mrs. Marsh, but instead the sound of traffic on the nearby road, followed by the stark realization that there was a breeze blowing through the room. Isaias was positive he would have noticed if the window had been open when he went to bed, given it had already been frigid in the rectory, so the latch must have popped in the night. Old buildings had quirks—something strange would happen, sooner or later.

On the bright side, the heat was back, and Isaias could tell from the way sweat clung to his skin, sticky and humid under his clothes, and that the only chill remaining in the room was from the open window. Isaias kicked off his layers of blankets and got up to close the window before he checked his phone. Still no reply from Hector, though he supposed there had been no obligation to respond. He would talk to Hector again, soon, as he always would. It was always only a matter of time before they found each other again.

Isaias went to the bathroom, peeled off sticky clothes to have them join the bloody shirt in the laundry hamper, and showered off the musk of sweat. Something about the hot water—and the water heater was certainly working, despite the faulty heat, thank the Lord for that—rinsed off so much tension from his body. He was reluctant to leave the shower, but he knew he would have to prepare for Mass shortly. He shook off strange, sickly-sweet memories, and got out of the water into the cooler air of the bathroom, dressed, and went downstairs.

"Good morning, Father," Mrs. Marsh greeted when she saw him in the kitchen. She was making breakfast, and Isaias was soothed by the multiplying sensations of hot grease along with the constant comfort of Mrs. Marsh's presence. "The heat's back!"

"I can tell," Isaias laughed. "Thank you for getting that fixed so quickly. Was someone really able to come over so early?"

She shook her head. "It was working when I got here, already. I called the company to let them know we may have a false alarm. They said they would come over anyway to double check there are no issues with the furnace. They should arrive during Mass, so hopefully minimal disruption for you."

"I noticed the power flickered a few times last night, as well. Do you think it might be related?"

Mrs. Marsh looked up from her frying pan and raised her eyebrows. "I hadn't noticed anything. Well, I'll see if we can look into that, too."

"Thank you," Isaias said as he turned on the kettle near the stove and prepared a mug of herbal tea. Remembering how quickly the tea the night before had turned bitter, Isaias selected a different one—ginger and dandelion to soothe his nerves. When the tea was ready, he sat at the table and breathed it in, letting the herbal steam fill his lungs.

Mrs. Marsh, possessing of a sixth sense for when breakfast needed to be done, served him pancakes within moments. Still unsettled from the night before, Isaias felt he didn't have much of an appetite, so ate his pancakes and maple syrup mechanically. He sipped his tea for the ritual of it, a necessary rite and his own private sacrament before he would deliver Mass. He had few comforts that were his alone, and he had to allow himself this, as he allowed himself his friendship with those few people outside of his church that he held dear to his heart.

He thought of the bishop's words, about how Isaias's parish came first, his duties to the parishioners held above his debts to his friends. Isaias kept his eyes low when he stood from the table. "Thank you for breakfast, Mrs. Marsh," he said softly. "I'll have to go get ready to deliver Mass, now."

Mrs. Marsh looked at him with concern in her eyes that he could feel radiating off of her. He left the room before she could say anything, and before he could examine her emotions too closely.

Like his breakfast, Mass and the other duties of the church mostly involved going through the motions for Isaias that morning. He delivered his sermon and served communion and he spoke to parishioners about whatever they might require to have their community needs met: he worked with a member of the parish on her spring bake sale plans to raise funds for the church's community library; with an administrative assistant for the nearby elementary school on bringing some kids in on afterschool programs; with volunteers seeking to set up a small farmer's market at the church on the weekends once the snow was good and gone; with a recent widow on working through her grief following the death of her husband the past fall.

This must have been what Bishop Reid had meant the evening before, about not getting involved in the affairs of those outside of his church when his *community* needed him, but he couldn't bring himself to turn away from his friends. Surely, his service to his parish didn't mean that he had to turn his back to his own loved ones, who equally needed him? Violet was a member of the community who had asked for his help, it shouldn't matter if she or her father were active members of his parish or not. And Hector was his only friend. Isaias loved the Montero family as his own. They should be just as much a part of his life of service.

But he was distracted, wasn't he? Or perhaps more accurate was to say he felt drained—each person he spoke to wore their hearts so strongly, and Isaias had trouble not taking on their emotions as his own. He was filled with all of the weariness and pain and ambition of his parish. He *was* the parish, in many ways, or at least his heart was.

When Violet appeared in his church in the early afternoon, Isaias was tired enough to be taken off guard. He wasn't sure how to talk to her about whatever weighed on her and her father—not when he still wasn't sure what to make of the night before. His emotions were already stretched thin, he hadn't had the time to unpack everything he had felt the night before.

He knew that he had to, though, for the sake of her and of her father both.

Instead of jumping straight in, Isaias tried to break through his uncertainty by asking, "Isn't today a school day?"

Violet, with her curly hair tied back and wearing her purple backpack slung low over her shoulders, shrugged and cheerfully said, "Nope."

Isaias raised an eyebrow at her backpack as Violet beamed at him like she wasn't even trying to fool him about school, but instead trying to convince him that her skipping was acceptable. The cheer was a thin façade over the real emotions she felt—the same anxiety he had felt from her the day before.

"Well, did you want to talk, then?" Isaias asked. "Since you don't have class."

"Yeah. Please."

Isaias led Violet back to his church office to make sure they would have privacy if anyone came to the church unexpectedly. He let the receptionist know he would be offering counsel in his office before leading Violet there.

Isaias's office was one of the places he spent the most time besides the rectory, where he managed the necessities of life like sleep. The office wasn't a totally private place—plenty of parishioners had been inside—but it still felt personal, somehow.

In front of Isaias's desk were two comfortable enough chairs, where he now indicated Violet to sit. He watched her select the one that was farthest from where Isaias himself would be sitting at his desk, though it was by only a marginal difference. Instead of worrying about it—actually, it suited him better to keep a touch more physical distance, given his lack of emotional distance in all things and how he was already feeling worn out from an emotional day and a half—Isaias looked at the mahogany bookshelf behind his desk for a moment, walking over to it to re-shelve the copy of the Bible that he had used in the sermon that morning but not yet put away. Most of the contents of the shelves were books on theology, but there were a few children's books, also of a religious bent. He kept them in a few different languages, just in case, though mostly he had them in English and French. One book wasn't shelved properly, leaning against some of the other children's books. It was illustrated with a cartoon of Noah's Ark complete with the animals, two by two. A book of Biblical stories, written for a younger audience than could understand much of the Bible.

Isaias poured two glasses of water from a pitcher on a side table, placing one in front of Violet before he took his seat behind his desk, shuffled a few of his papers to busy his hands for a moment, and then looked up at Violet, who was carefully settling into the cushions of the chair and leaning her crutches against the arm, where they would be within easy reach if she needed them. Isaias leaned partially onto his desk, hands clasped together and his body weight on his forearms. Attentive and listening. It was a well-practised pose. He needed it, on some level, the role to play—he was tired, but he needed to give Violet his full attention. If he went through the motions of it all, it would be easier to be who she needed him to be.

Isaias weighed whether he should ask her outright what she needed, or if he should let her start the conversation. It was difficult to judge, because Violet had refused to actually tell him anything, and Hector had been even harder to read. What gave him a clearer answer was the way her emotions felt: her feelings were conflicted, uncertain, confused. A little bit angry, in places. Hard to pin down. Not a single emotion stayed in place for long enough for Isaias to really grasp onto them or understand them. The only thing he could say with much authority was that she was just as anxious and afraid as she had been the day before. Though now, against all odds, it was tinged with the slightest bit of hope.

None of which told Isaias much of anything, except that he should take whatever she said next very seriously.

For a long moment, neither said anything. Then, Violet nodded to the bookshelf behind Isaias and asked, "Do you really believe in this stuff?"

Isaias started, caught off guard. "The stories of the Bible?"

Violet frowned. Her eyes were fixed on the cartoon ark, the man leading a pair of lions to salvation from the impending flood, followed improbably by a pair of gazelles. "Yeah, those," she said. "I guess some of them sound kind of silly, to me."

"I do believe in them," Isaias said without further hesitation. Then he paused before adding, "It's complicated, though. Some stories might be just that, stories with moral teachings. Maybe even pure metaphor in some sense. But I think at least most of them are truthful at their core, that what the story is telling us is *God's* truth. I believe in God with my whole heart," he added for clarity's sake. It felt like a necessary addition, that he should pre-emptively defend himself. "It doesn't matter if the events happened exactly as described in the Bible. The truth of them is there."

"I kind of figured." Violet didn't seem wholly convinced—Isaias couldn't tell if she was happy with the answer or not, and something in him was scared to try to read her emotions to find out. It would be a violation of her trust in him, anyway. He *couldn't*. He watched her pick up her glass of water instead and take a sip. "Thanks," she murmured.

"Of course. Now, should we talk about—your situation? How are you doing? How is your father?"

Violet held the glass in both hands, staring into the water. "I'm tired. And, you know, I'm really worried about my dad. He's not himself lately and it's kind of freaking me out. Like a lot. You saw him."

"Do you want to tell me more about that?"

Isaias could feel Violet close off from him in real time. "I was kind of hoping you could to your own conclusions. *You saw him.*"

"I know," Isaias said quickly. He had to do damage control. "And you're right, he wasn't himself. But he's your father—whatever is going on, you know him better, and you've seen more of what's happening."

Violet sighed and stared at Isaias's desk. He got the impression she wanted to lay her head down on the laminate surface and just sleep. She stayed brave, though, and kept talking. "Yeah. Well, that's kinda the thing. He's being really goddamn—sorry, he's being really, you know, moody, and he won't talk to me at all. And there's been weird stuff…"

Isaias rose his eyebrows. "'Weird stuff?' What do you mean?"

"Like—" She stopped. "Okay, no. What did you see when you were with my dad, cleaning up from dinner last night? What do you think?"

Isaias paused. He did have his hypothesis, but he had no proof at all. Nothing had indicated that Hector was drinking again, after all these years. It would be unfair to accuse him of such a thing, wouldn't it be? Hector had worked so hard on his path to recovery—and while there was no shame in relapse, it wouldn't be right for Isaias to doubt him, either.

He wondered instead at Violet's theory. She seemed to have one, but she wanted Isaias to come to his own conclusions. She was a scientist in this situation, not wanting to bias him with her own assumptions. "I think he likely just has a lot on his mind. He mentioned something about being stressed. Maybe some kind of—family problem?" A shot in the dark, and one Isaias knew must have been false the moment he said it.

"What kind of family problem could there possibly be?" Violet asked. There was a scoff in her voice. She felt frustrated, her private emotions bristling like an irritated cat. She put her glass of water back down on the desk with a definitive thud and leaned forward, her cheeks flushed. "He doesn't talk to his family. It's just me and my dad. There's nobody else but us. That's why this matters so much, Isaias. We've only got each other."

Something in the words cut Isaias's heart, but he didn't want to examine it any closer. This wasn't about him. It would never be about him. "Maybe someone reached out," Isaias pointed out carefully. He didn't want to deny Violet, but he also didn't want to doubt Hector that it was anything but stress. Hector wouldn't lie to him. He never had before. "There are rational explanations that tell us there's little to worry about. Stress is normal, and so is behaving differently when under stress."

"Bull—sorry, Father. That's not it," Violet insisted. She leaned back in her seat, but did not deflate, was not defeated. She reached for one of her crutches and grasped the handle, seemingly just for something to do with her hand. "I don't want to hear anything about how, like, it's all perfectly normal stuff. Okay?"

Isaias frowned. "I know he wasn't himself, but I'm sure there's a reason why he's not talking to us about it. Maybe he needs to seek counselling?"

Violet gave him a hard stare, and Isaias immediately felt her anger and his own guilt. Well, there he was. Deflecting the problem, just like the bishop had suggested that he should.

What happened to helping your friends, Isaias? he asked himself. *Or are you just going to listen to Bishop Reid and make them no longer your problem?*

But that thought felt unfair, too. As if Bishop Reid had not had the best intentions, after all. Isaias was sure that that wasn't true. His bishop was his father and only ever had the best of intentions. He had never steered Isaias wrong—at least not deliberately.

Isaias tried to save the statement before Violet lost her faith in him. "Violet, I—"

"No, I get it. You haven't seen enough. One dinner wasn't enough. This isn't something that, like, therapy will fix, Father. This is—different. You have to believe me that it's *so* different from that."

Isaias paused. He didn't want to accuse, and yet—well, he didn't know where else to begin to help her, if he was going to at all. If it was alcohol, counselling *was* the answer. Alcoholics Anonymous, or something like it. A support group who could help him. Experts. People in the community who cared and knew what they were doing. Isaias could direct him to the resources, but was he the right person to help? He could support Hector, be there for him as a friend and an ally, but he was one man. A man of God, certainly, but Hector didn't believe in God. God's word couldn't save him if he didn't want it to.

"I didn't see any signs of it, myself," Isaias said carefully, not sure where else to go, "but have you considered that he maybe started drinking again?"

"No," Violet said immediately. Her eyes narrowed. Isaias was making mistake after mistake. "No way, Isaias. Sorry, Father. He wouldn't do that. Not to me. He hasn't drank at all since mom left, he never would again."

"Alright," Isaias said, and he felt the intensity with which she believed this. She was impatient and frustrated, but she held fast. The shrinking Violet who had come to his church yesterday was strong and confident and sure again, more than just an echo of her former, headstrong self. It was hard to deny her when she held this belief with such conviction. It struck Isaias again that she really *did* have a hypothesis, and it wasn't a return to substance abuse. But Isaias couldn't figure out what she was trying to get him to propose; to vindicate. Whatever her theory was, the 'family problems' story didn't fit into it, and neither did recurrent alcoholism. He didn't know what was left, and he didn't think that he was going to validate her beliefs without understanding them, whatever they were. "What do you think is going on then?"

Violet looked at Isaias with gravity. She hesitated, and he could feel the fear mingled with utter conviction in her heart, the kind of steadfastness that Isaias normally saw in only his most devout parishioners, and rarely even then. For a moment, he felt doubt in her. She believed in herself and her conclusions, but maybe she didn't believe in Isaias. That hurt, too—that doubt in him.

Violet said, "I think my dad's possessed."

Isaias stared in shock. That was Violet's theory? He didn't know where to begin, so stupidly repeated, "Possessed?"

"Yeah. It's the only answer, Father. It's why I came to you. You're his best friend, but you're also a priest. You'd know how to handle this."

"As in, by a demon?" Isaias asked, as if she had not already confirmed by insisting that it was Isaias's role as *priest* as much as his role as *best friend* that made her think he was well-suited for saving her father. Isaias tried to rein in his surprise, his disbelief, his doubt. None of them were fair to Violet. Not when she was so deadly serious—he had never felt anyone more committed than she was in her belief now.

"Yeah," Violet said, and she looked away. She was certain, he could feel that in the intensity of her thoughts; she believed in her words without a doubt, but he did feel that she felt shame. As if she was being scolded for saying something that she shouldn't have. Reprimanded. "That's what I meant."

"Violet, I—" Isaias couldn't help the disbelief in his voice, despite his efforts.

"You said you believe the stories," Violet insisted, cutting Isaias off before he could try to find an argument against her. She looked back at him again. She nudged her glass of water away from the edge of the desk and leaned forward with the force of her conviction. "In the Bible. You said you believe in these things. So why not possession?"

"You've been rehearsing your arguments, haven't you?" he asked, softening his incredulity for her. She had been ready for his doubt. Somehow, that brought him a strange sense of comfort. Violet was not speaking rashly, at least not in her own mind. She was coming from a place of rationality. But just as quickly as it comforted Isaias, it chilled him to the bone: Violet, coming from a house of atheists, was deadly serious about this being a matter of the Devil. Isaias swallowed hard, and leaned back in his seat, putting distance between him and Violet, but kept his eyes on her. "Honey, I said that much of it wasn't literal."

He wondered, did that make him a bad Catholic, to not be willing to jump to the explanation that came from Heaven and Hell? Violet believed it, her fierce emotions told him so, radiating off of her with the surest conviction. Why didn't he?

"You believe in God," Violet pointed out. "Wholeheartedly, you said."

"Yes. Absolutely, I do."

"You believe in angels?"

"Yes."

"So why not the Devil and demons?"

"I didn't say I didn't *believe* in them—"

"So why couldn't dad be possessed by one of them?" Violet retorted, smacking one hand against Isaias's desk, causing the water to jostle in its glass, almost spilling, and nearly making Isaias wince while she was at it. "If they're real. And not a metaphor, like you said some of the stories are."

"It just seems—unlikely," Isaias said carefully, pulling his hands into his lap, his arms tight to his body. He had to tread carefully, to be careful not to hurt Violet, or himself, in this process. He had to be careful to not acknowledge the fear that was clinging to him. Was it Violet's, or his own? Did it matter, if the fear was real, leaving a stench like rot in his nose and a taste like something spoiled in the back of his throat, where he couldn't reach? "Not impossible, but unlikely. While I do believe in Hell, and the Devil—the possession of ordinary men and women is not exactly a commonplace occurrence, even in the Bible. Not in the sense that you mean."

"Well, if it's not drinking, and it's not some non-existent family problem, and it's not a ghost or a demon or something, then what is it?" Violet demanded. Her eyes shone with something undiscernible. He felt her fear, but also her righteousness. She might have made for a good priest herself, in some alternate world: passionate and fierce and devoted. Perhaps she was a better soul than Isaias could ever hope to be. "How do *you* explain the way he's been acting? The strange things happening? The cat won't even be in the same room as dad anymore."

"I'm sure there's a reasonable—" Isaias stopped himself, knowing he wasn't going to convince her with logic if he didn't at least hear her arguments first. Her anger, her worry, her fear, her belief—they needed to be heard out, all in equal measure. She could not be swayed if she didn't have her chance to sway him first. Isaias loosened up his arms, uncoiled himself from his defensive stance, and instead forced himself to open up by picking up his glass of water on the desk, taking a sip to steady himself. The water felt painfully cold against his tongue, but it washed away some of the taste of doubt in his throat. "Okay, Violet. Tell me about the strange things that are happening. This isn't the first time you've mentioned them, but you haven't explained to me what it is that you mean. Let's start there. What is the proof you have been gathering?"

Violet pulled back from Isaias's desk. She crossed her arms over her chest, for a moment, then promptly unfolded them and pressed her palms to either side of her neck, elbows pointed out and at Isaias. "Okay, so: last week, dad took a phone call in the middle of the night. Like... past midnight middle of the night. I shouldn't have been up, but I was because sometimes I hurt too much to sleep, and I heard it. And he was talking all quiet and intense and then abruptly he stopped. Not even like he got cut off, he was just suddenly dead silent. All this intensity, then nothing. I was worried, so even though it hurt to get up, I went to ask him if everything was okay and he, like, snapped at me to go to bed. That was the first time I noticed him acting particularly weird. You know my dad: he's quiet when he's mad. He doesn't yell at you or anybody. Even if he was mad that I was up or whatever, he wouldn't have *yelled* at me."

That was commensurate with the fact that Hector had been behaving strangely—even somewhat aggressively—but Isaias didn't think it was terribly convincing as arguments went. It was the same pattern they had already observed and could have been caused by any number of things. Whatever the call was had upset him, which could even explain why he had been so stressed as to be behaving strangely. But Violet wasn't done—Isaias could sense the energy bubbling to the surface of her emotions, ready to explode. Isaias had told her that he would hear her out: that was as good as any promise. So, though he shifted uncomfortably in his seat, he said, "Go on."

"Okay, so, Prue, the next morning, she hisses at him, right? I'm out of the room, but I swear to *God* I heard a second hiss and then she bolts out of the room and past me. So, I go in, and I ask dad what's up, and he says Prue saw something in the window that scared her, no big. But that's the last time I know of that the cat was even in the same room as him without hiding from him, like she's scared he's going to kick her or something, even though she used to love him so much.

"And then, I start hearing these weird noises around the house. No more creepy calls, but like we have rats in the walls or something. Or upstairs. You know, the second floor that we don't have? Like scratching above our heads. Something creeping around between the roof and house, ready to drop on us. Dad keeps talking to himself, and there's this *smell* in the house that I can't figure out. Like something is burning, but I can't figure out what. And I keep finding things moved and just... I don't know. Things aren't normal." Her eyes were beginning to well up with tears and she dropped her hands back into her lap. Isaias felt guilty to see her so defeated, even though he had caused nothing. But she was desperate—and coming to him to fix things.

Softly, Violet continued: "I was watching some horror movie about demons, and about exorcisms and stuff, and dad kept *laughing* at it, like it was funny even when it was super freaky. Like I was watching a comedy, not a scary movie. It was weird, but it got me thinking that maybe... I can barely sleep right now, Father. Worse than normal. Everything is so fucking *creepy* all the time. So please. Please, you have to help my dad."

Isaias hesitated. The smell of flowers had grown almost sickeningly sweet with the force of Violet's insistence. He didn't doubt *her* belief in a demon inside of her father any more than Isaias doubted the existence of God Himself. But it wasn't much to go on. Odd occurrences were one thing. Demonic possession was quite another. Just because she believed in it, didn't mean it was true. But still, it bore asking, "Was it the movie that made you believe your father is possessed?"

Violet shook her head emphatically. "No. I mean, it got me thinking and all, but I wasn't *sure* what was going on until last night."

Isaias frowned. He had been there for dinner the night before. Had something happened after he left? Had he missed something that Violet felt was proof? "Last night?"

Violet took a deep breath. Isaias knew, suddenly, that this was the nail in the coffin of her arguments—the final piece. "After we talked, I—I prayed, last night. I don't know if it was to God or to someone—something—else. Maybe it doesn't even matter, as long as *someone* heard me. And I think someone did." Fishing her phone out of her jacket pocket, Violet started swiping her finger across the screen. "I slept easier than normal, better than I have since dad started acting weird, but then I woke up really suddenly in the middle of the night, at like three? And I heard something outside. It was too quiet to hear. And dad had installed those cameras at the front and the back of the house because he's paranoid something will happen to me, so he wants to have that extra security. So, I checked the app for the cameras. There was nothing in the backyard. But in the front..."

Violet turned her phone toward Isaias. The image was grainy, and Isaias couldn't immediately recognize what he was seeing, but once Violet deftly pressed the play button on the video from behind and the video came into focus, Isaias understood.

In front of the house, standing in the middle of the quiet suburban street, was Hector. Isaias instinctively recognized him—he would recognize Hector anywhere. Hector stood in the middle of the street, underdressed for the weather, his arms outstretched on either side of him, making a crucified figure. Hector was still, but the video had audio, proving it was playing. The noise that must have woken Violet was clearly heard.

Something was *screaming*.

It was the same voice that Isaias had heard over dinner, when something had broken into his mind. And while the voice on the video was distorted, Isaias was surer than he had been the night before that it was Hector's voice.

Suddenly, there was movement on the video—while Hector remained perfectly still, the texture of the light around him changed. In an instant, the shift in light became headlights, became a car barreling too fast down the quiet residential road—coming quickly for Hector.

Isaias's heart dropped, suddenly sure he was about to see the car collide with Hector, crushing him. He was filled with dread that he was about to witness the death of the man he cared about more than anyone else in the world.

The video went dark. Then silent.

Violet pulled the phone away from Isaias. Despite his heart pounding in his chest, he fought hard to keep his emotions from leeching out, reaching Violet. Because as terrified as Isaias had been that he was about to witness someone he loved die, Violet was calm. She had to be calm for a reason.

"I screamed," Violet said. "I was sure I was about to see my dad *die*, and I couldn't do anything. I chucked my phone and started grabbing my crutches because he would need my *help*—and then there he was, in my bedroom door. He turned the lights on and for a second, I couldn't really see him because my eyes weren't adjusted, so he was just this huge shadow in the doorway, but it was my dad. And he was fine."

Isaias's heartrate didn't slow. He was amazed at how calm Violet was being in the face of saying that, maybe twelve hours earlier, she had been convinced she was about to see her father die. For his own part, Isaias was sure that he was going to play that video in his dreams—only this time, the car would connect, and he'd witness Hector's death. Isaias swallowed, trying to get his throat to work with him. It felt painfully dry, and the acrid taste of his own fear was overpowering, so he picked up his glass of water and took a large drink. His hand shook. "Hector's okay?"

"*Completely* okay. I told him I'd had a nightmare and he tucked me back into bed like I was a little kid again. This morning, he drove me to school, so we could catch up he said, and he talked to me like normal. For the entire drive it was just... normal." Violet shrugged weakly. For a moment, her expression wavered, and Isaias felt some of her carefully crafted emotions shift with it, revealing the anxiety beneath. The doubt. She looked down and away from Isaias, hiding her face from view. "I started to doubt everything. Like maybe it was all in my head, and dad is fine, and *I'm* the one with something wrong with me."

"I'm sorry, Violet." Isaias felt for her. Doubt was familiar to him. Doubt was one of the most painful feelings in the world. And to doubt oneself, one's own mind, was worst of all—Isaias understood deeply the fear of uncertainty in your own beliefs.

Violet nodded. She was quiet for a moment, then took a deep, shuddering breath. She looked up at Isaias with tears in her eyes, but renewed conviction. "When I got to school, I hid in the bathroom and watched the video on my phone again. And again. I had to convince myself again that I saw what I saw. I downloaded the video to make sure I don't lose it—which is good, because the video is just *gone* off the app, now—and watched it again. Sometimes I think that when the screaming stops, I hear a *crunch*, like the car really did hit my dad. Sometimes, the screaming seems to continue in my headphones even after the video is over. Sometimes, I think I hear tires screeching and then the video keeps playing even though there's no more sound or video. But one thing stays the same every time that kind of weirds me about above everything else, I guess just because it's such a consistent weird thing."

Isaias couldn't imagine what one thing stood out to her, in a video like that. He kept replaying it in his own mind's eye. "What's that?"

"The fact that the light went off *right that moment*," Violet said. "It's on a motion sensor, so it's supposed to turn on when it senses people or animals. And then there's a time delay before it turns off again. It's supposed to stay on for like 10 minutes after it detects no more movement of anything alive. How long was he standing there, so still like that, before that car came? And how come the car didn't see him?"

Isaias wasn't sure if he would agree that it was the strangest thing about the video, feeling deeply uncomfortable about it from start to finish, but it did raise even more questions than the video originally already had. Taking a deep breath, Isaias considered his next words carefully. He knew what Violet wanted from him—and he couldn't doubt her, not when he knew how much that alone would hurt. "I'll do my best to help your father," he promised her before he could second guess himself or her again but held up a hand to caution her from getting too excited. "No matter whether Hector behaving strangely is mundane or hellish, I'll help, okay? I can't make any promises right now, when we don't know what the exact cause is. If it is possession—and I am not saying that it is, Violet, we have to be careful—then that's a very serious matter and I will do my best to get Hector whatever help he might need. But it's a hefty accusation, and you're describing strange things happening, not anything that can't be explained." Even the video had to be explainable. It had to be. "Experts believe that 'possession' was often misattributed. Illness or 'otherness'. I'm not saying it doesn't exist, it's not impossible, we know of it through scripture, yes, but I'm just saying that the accusation has been abused in the past."

It was the necessary disclaimer. As much as Violet had convinced herself that it was true, as much as everything she was saying was leaving *Isaias* doubting in his previous assertion that it had to be ordinary, he just couldn't take her word for it without investigating. Violet believed it, but it was something dangerous to put your heart into.

It was a warning to himself as much as to Violet. Isaias knew his heart could be weak—he had been told his entire life that he was too liable to let his heart be swayed, to put his whole self into something, and to become hurt because of it. He believed too easily, when all he really needed to believe in was God.

Violet nodded firmly. "I know that, Father. I did my research, I promise. I wouldn't have said it if I weren't sure of it. My dad isn't himself. And I was doing research on the signs and symptoms and... so many people still believe in it. Your church does, doesn't it? The Vatican and all that? It still happens. I can't accept any other explanation."

It was funny, in a dark way, for Violet to be so convinced of demonic possession, of the influence of Hell, when her father was such an irreligious man. Isaias would have assumed Violet just as deeply atheistic as Hector himself, but she had *prayed* for her father. Maybe her father being taken over by something was an easier explanation than something that she would have seen as a betrayal, her father making a choice that hurt his only family.

For his own part, Isaias would have preferred something mortal. He could handle that. It wasn't beyond him, or Violet, or a little bit of outside help. If it was demonic, that was another beast altogether.

Even if he felt like he was lying to Violet—because here he was, sitting across from her and not telling her about his own gifts that proved *divine* intervention was possible, refusing to accept at face value that the influence of the Devil could be at play.

But he couldn't dismiss Violet out of hand, either. Her experiences were odd, at the very least. And had Isaias not smelled the burning scent, like she had described? He'd thought it was a sensory vision, the kind he got from his abilities to tap into the emotional signatures of others. Had he not felt those strange emotions swirling beneath the surface with Hector's bloody hands on him? But maybe it wasn't Hector he'd felt.

Isaias took a deep breath. "Okay, well, first step, Violet," he said, trying to be the logical one still, "will be to find evidence. We need to be very sure of what our diagnosis of the problem is before we act in *any* way. How about you ask your father to come see me in the rectory this evening? I'm sure I'll be able to suss out what the problem is so close to the House of God." Isaias hoped it was as good a plan as any.

Violet nodded eagerly. "Okay, Father. I'll tell him to come."

"Good. I hope for the best, Violet." He fell silent for a moment before he continued. "And I hope, for all of our sake's, that you're not right about the reason for your father changing. Because I'm not—it would be something else altogether if that was the problem."

Isaias simply hoped that he could prove her wrong. He'd rather Hector be overtaken by the figurative spirits of alcohol than by those of the Devil itself. Recurrent alcoholism, as troubling and heartbreaking as that would be, was a tangible, solvable problem. Something that Isaias could figure out how to handle. Not abstract. Concrete.

What was one man, even a priest, to do against the torments of Hell?

X

Isaias anxiously awaited any word at all from Hector while he tidied up his study in the rectory. He had sent Mrs. Marsh home for the evening already, irrationally afraid of what she might witness, and he'd prayed for a time; for himself, for Violet, and, of course, for Hector.

Isaias didn't want to risk missing Hector, so he stayed downstairs, looking through old documents. He was able to do so comfortably, now that the heat was miraculously working again. While his office in the church itself received far more use from Isaias on the day-to-day, the study happened to be what he actually preferred to work in. Messiness aside, it contained more personal items, though he had few in the first place, and the room felt a little more like a space he didn't have to curate to the expectations of his parishioners. While the Sacred Heart was God's sanctuary, the office in the rectory was Isaias's. It was why it was home to the photo of himself with the bishop, the rosary in the desk drawer, and his letters from Hector. Unlike the bookshelves in the church office, which all served specific purposes, his shelf in this office had classics of romantic literature mixed in among the theological texts, as well as a handful of romance novels he'd scavenged from church book sales at the Sacred Heart. Whenever no one else had seemed to want them, Isaias took them himself, surreptitiously leaving a donation for the church fundraiser. That was his justification, anyway: it felt better to Isaias that they had a home on his shelf than if they might have been discarded. Even if most were left unread to that day, Isaias sometimes feeling too embarrassed to be seen reading books he'd heard described by women at the church as 'bodice rippers'. At least Mrs. Marsh had never judged him, though she had certainly seen the books tucked shamefully between textbooks and study Bibles.

The shelves showed more of his personality, with little ceramic figurines of odd-ball creatures he had been gifted by Hector, a parish of small little monsters and cryptids that Isaias had never identified but had named anyway, lined up in rows. There were some small pieces of framed artwork, paintings Violet had created for school and had wanted to throw away before Isaias rescued them. The books, of course. Here, his individual touch was safer to display, even if he had tried not to make it too obvious.

It was the rosary he was focused on that night, tracing his fingers over the beads and counting them off in his head as he prayed. The rosary reminded him of roses and of sandalwood. It left him with the comforting presence of who his parents could have been. He could almost remember being a toddler held in his mother's arms, smelling her perfume as he clutched the rosary and she sang him sweet lullabies. Had that been home, all those years ago? He had been too young when his parents gave him up to remember anything more than impressions, but he wondered now—were they happy in this life without him? He held no bitterness to this last gifted remnant of his birth family. His parents had given him up for blameless reasons. For who could ever force someone to raise a child, if that child was better off directly in the hands of God?

Still, he wondered how different life might have been if his parents hadn't felt alone. Would he have still been such a difficult child that they felt their love was not enough, if someone else had been there for them?

Isaias finished counting off the beads as he lost himself in reverie, before tucking the rosary away into his pocket. He could only stave off thoughts of demons, metaphorical and metaphysical, for so long, and Hector would be there soon. He hoped that being able to pray with his foremothers would help keep him steady in the face of whatever came next. He could use all the strength that he could get.

He was pacing the floor of his study, not looking forward to a visit he normally would have longed for, when his phone rang. Not his cellphone, but the landline on the desk that no one but the bishop used. Isaias frowned—he had just spoken to the Bishop the evening before, was something wrong?—and answered the phone regardless of his trepidation.

"Hello?"

"Isaias."

It was Hector's voice—Isaias was sure of it—but something about the quality of it sounded strange, slightly *off*. And while he knew Hector had the number for his landline, he had never once called it. Isaias suspected that it was another way of distancing himself from the church. "Hector, is everything okay? Are you on your way?"

Hector did not reply. For a moment, Isaias stood there on the phone listening to Hector breathing. The sound might have been comforting any other time, but instead it sounded pained. It was ragged; too sharp, too fast.

"Are you okay?" Isaias asked again. For a moment, Hector only continued to breathe into the phone.

Isaias heard tires screeching, a sharp intake of breath from Hector—then silence.

The phone line went dead. Isaias could smell melted, burnt rubber.

Taking a shaky breath, he hung up the phone. He went to find his cellphone—to do what? Call Hector back? Call Violet?—and saw that he had a text from only a moment before from Hector. It had just come in, so Hector was—he was fine. He was fine.

Isaias swallowed to soothe his dry throat and opened the text.

Why exactly am I coming to your rectory?

Isaias paused, unsure what Violet had told him. He didn't want Hector to put his guard up anymore than he likely already would have. He texted back, *I wanted to see you.*

A mere moment later: *Violet said it was important. You swear it is?*

Yes.

OK. Be there soon.

Isaias forced his shoulders down, away from his elbows, shook his arms out, and took a long, deep breath in. He held the breath for several seconds before releasing it. The tension didn't quite disappear, but it did fade away into nothing but background noise, which was the goal. Isaias did not, and could not, live a life without anxiety, it seemed; he was always picking up emotions whether he liked it or not, and so he was always feeling *something*. Prayer brought him as close to peace, and thus as close to *God*, as was possible for him.

But through his brief effort to dispel the worst of his stress, he felt more secure in meeting Hector. If he thought about it for too long, he would be afraid again, so he tried to avoid letting himself linger in his own feelings. It wouldn't help to risk accidentally spreading his fears to Hector. He needed to be objective; clear-headed. He needed to tend to *Hector's* emotions, not his own, and so his own had to be ignored.

Putting the phone away, he went back to tidying his desk. He normally didn't concern himself with keeping it *that* tidy, actually, but if Hector was coming, he did want it to be a little neater, a little *less* lived-in. At least enough so that it didn't look like he regularly carried on like this, when truthfully the only problem was that Mrs. Marsh declined to touch Isaias's personal possessions, and he rarely had the time and space to clean it properly. He spent just enough time in the study for it to collect clutter, but not enough for him to dedicate the time to keeping it as neat as the office in the church. Nowhere else in the rectory itself would ever be allowed to look anything less than pristine, not under Mrs. Marsh's watchful eye.

There was something vulnerable about Hector coming and seeing into the mess that Isaias had allowed his study to become. It was a vulnerability he couldn't spare. Just like his anxiety, it would be better to put everything back into its proper place.

It didn't take long enough to put the desk into something resembling order and get it looking presentable enough to entertain Hector. Which was ludicrous—it wasn't enough time for Isaias to forget Violet's words—*I think my dad's possessed*—or the feeling of Hector's blood or the sound of his screams.

Maybe it was petty for Isaias to worry what Hector might think of him, what he might see in him, when Hector's soul might be on the line.

Nothing Isaias did was of any significance in the face of the Devil, was it? Forces of that magnitude—the Devil, let alone God Himself—would surely be indifferent to Isaias.

Isaias had only seen Hector the night before, but he suddenly missed his friend terribly. He longed to see him again, to satiate his loneliness—and knowing that he would be there soon did nothing to comfort him.

Because would it truly be Hector who walked through that door?

Isaias found ways to pass the time while waiting, anything to distract himself from what might come to pass next once Hector arrived. He was standing at his shelf, flipping through a theology textbook from seminary—which unhelpfully reminded him that possession was a serious matter and that steps to amend should be taken only by someone absolutely certain of its cause and that that someone should be a fully ordained priest, authorized by their bishop, and that such a priest should be, above all else, pious, prudent, knowledgeable, and possessing of integrity—when he felt something strange invade his senses. Low, in the pit of his stomach, was a sinister feeling that made him nauseous. After the illness gripped his stomach lining came the other senses, including the smell of burning that was quickly becoming familiar. This time it was not just the sickeningly sweet smell of burnt sugar, but the sulphurous odour of charred hair and something else stomach-turning, putrid but not quite identifiable.

Was that what a demon smelled like, felt like? Like sickness and death?

With ringing in his ears, Isaias went to the front door to see if Hector was there. It was wrong to assume that the feeling of that dark soul—or lack of a soul—was somehow attached to Hector, but he didn't know what else to believe.

He was scared, above all, that maybe Violet was right.

Out on the street, nearer the church than the rectory, was Hector. He was difficult to see in the dark, and with the snow picking up and blowing vigorously, but Isaias knew it had to be him. He was underdressed for the weather, in a flannel shirt that read almost black in the night, jeans, and only boots for winter wear. Isaias wasn't dressed for the weather, either, but was suddenly more worried that Hector would get frostbite than he was about any demon. He pulled his boots and coat on unceremoniously and rushed outside, ignoring the bite of cold against his face and neck to get to Hector faster.

"Please, come in," he said as he reached Hector. "It's too cold to be out here without a coat and—"

Isaias stopped short, pausing in front of Hector. While the snow cut into his exposed skin, the chill set deeper still when he saw the expression on Hector's face. With snowflakes clinging to Hector's eyelashes, his eyes looked too wide, too round as he stared in alarm at the rectory. Not the church, not the graveyard next to it, but the place Isaias lived. His blue-tinged lips were parted around shallow gasps, his breath steaming against cold air, disrupting the fall of snow.

This close, Isaias could feel Hector's fear radiating off of him intimately. This was no demon, was it? This frightened man, out in the cold.

Touching him would surely magnify the feeling tenfold—make Hector's pain his own—but Isaias reached for him, anyway, cupping numb fingers over the chapped skin of Hector's cheeks. Hector's fear hit him as a shock colder than the winter air, but he forced it down. For Hector.

Brushing snow out of Hector's hair and beard, he whispered, "Please come inside. You'll freeze to death out here."

It took a gentle pressure from Isaias's hands, but Hector finally tore his eyes away from the rectory and looked at—no, not *at* or even *through*, but *into* Isaias, like he was seeing the very core of his being. Isaias felt his emotional resonance respond in turn, baring his soul to Hector without intending to, letting Hector see into him. He felt vulnerable, suddenly—and like maybe it was possible for someone to understand the deepest parts of him, after all.

He wondered if Hector might understand, for even a moment, what it was like to be Isaias—to know too much, feel too much.

But then Hector's gaze broke away, and Isaias saw that his eyes were unfocused, distracted, still full of fear.

Isaias felt lonelier and emptier than ever. He remained a mirror, reflecting everything, seeing others but never himself.

"Please come inside," he repeated, allowing himself to near begging. Hector nodded mutedly, and Isaias took off his coat and draped it over Hector's shoulders—though it wasn't quite large enough for him—before guiding him toward the rectory. Isaias felt the chill intimately, the cold settling deep beneath his skin, but he was less hurried now that Hector was in less immediate danger. As they approached the rectory, though, Isaias found Hector slowing down in his grip, his steps dragging. By the time they reached the front step and Isaias opened the door, it was difficult to get Hector across the threshold. He froze there, just at the entrance, and Isaias shuddered, his body longing for the warm air that inched tauntingly through the open door.

"Come inside," Isaias pled again. He placed his hand on the small of Hector's back and nudged him gently. Another breath passed between them. Finally, slowly, achingly, Hector crossed the threshold. As he crossed, he looked to either side, then around the front hall of the rectory. He had visited Isaias there before, but he seemed to slowly take in each detail, as if he were seeing it for the first time.

Isaias closed the door behind them and felt painful relief as the heat of the building burnt life back into his bones. When Hector made no move to undress himself, Isaias took his jacket from his shoulders. Only then did Hector seem to realize what he should do and took off his boots. Isaias did the same, though every movement felt forced. He was about to go to the kitchen to offer tea when Hector interrupted him suddenly, as if he had arrived normally, as if he had not been in some kind of trance until that very moment, as if nothing had happened. "Thanks for inviting me over. What did you want to talk about?"

Turning back to Hector, Isaias tried to form a thought that might pass for coherent. Hector had his hands in his pockets, an overly casual stance despite the snow still clinging to him—maybe he had more of an idea of what had just happened than he was letting on. Hector stood at a slight distance from him, making no move to touch him—no ordinary hug in greeting. Isaias felt the absence of it, but made no move of his own.

Before he answered, Isaias took a moment to reach out to sense Hector's emotions again, now that they were in something resembling the safety of a home. Hector felt strangely calm, mostly, but there was something odd about the feeling, as if it was muffled behind something, something masking his true feelings from Isaias in a way that he was unfamiliar with. Against his better judgement, Isaias pried deeper, let his emotional sense creep further into Hector's consciousness. For the briefest of moments, he thought he felt something else. Something closer to fear. Something *real*.

And then it was gone, his emotions pushed back out by whatever was blocking him before he could figure out where that feeling had come from.

Isaias had to brace himself against the shock of it and stand strong to avoid betraying that he had tried anything at all. He didn't normally try to read someone so closely, he didn't dare expose himself so clearly, but he had never felt that kind of rejection before. It couldn't have been Hector, though, he thought. Hector wouldn't have even known that Isaias was trying to read him. Hector didn't understand, despite that brief thought that he might, one day, grasp what it was like to reflect everything around him. Hector wouldn't have known to reject him, let alone how.

Isaias felt a deep regret, starting in the pit of his stomach and slowly spreading outwards. He tried to ignore it and instead just brought himself back to the present—he hadn't answered Hector's question. For his own part, Hector was watching him, patient—ever a gentle man, even with something burning in his soul. He swallowed, his throat feeling tight, his heart hollow. "Tea?" he asked. His voice came out smaller than he wanted it to. "It was freezing out there, I think we could both use something hot to drink." Mrs. Marsh didn't stock coffee, seeing as Isaias never drank it, and anyway, it was probably too late for that much caffeine. No, tea was better—it would relax them both, he hoped.

"Sure," Hector said. "But you're stalling, aren't you, priest?"

The term of address felt bitter—that wasn't Hector. Not literally, Isaias hoped, but in that it was out of character. That was all. "No, I'm not," Isaias lied. He still felt thrown somehow; like that glimpse of fear could have come just as easily from himself as from Hector. "I'm just trying to be a good host."

"Right."

Hector on his heels, Isaias went into the kitchen. He flipped the light switch and there was a brief pause where he was worried the power was faltering again—for a moment, despite turning on the lights, nothing happened and there were left with only the light of the hallway behind them and the dim light of the moon filtering through the window. Then the lights turned on after a moment's delay, like everything was just slightly out of sync with Isaias's actions. He put the kettle on, listening as if he expected the roiling of water to also come too late, not at the right time, before looking back to Hector. Isaias leaned back against the counter, hands braced on either side of him. Hector had his arms tucked close to his body, watching Isaias carefully; guardedly. Both his hands were still wrapped in bandages from his cuts the night before.

Isaias glanced away a moment, looking back to the kettle as it heated up. He thought about lying again, seeing as Hector had been nearly erratic, bordering on hostility at times before in his mood swings. But that would get them nowhere. "I wanted to see how you were doing," he said, feeling that he shouldn't beat around the bush. His words, too, felt like they came out on a time delay. "You seem to be under stress, so I was hoping maybe I could relieve some of that for you. By being an ear to listen, at least, given..." He trailed off and turned back to try to smile to Hector. "If I'm good at anything, it's listening."

Hector was watching him. Isaias wanted to try to read his emotions again but was scared to feel something in Hector push him away again. Instead of going deeper, he instead tried to find the barest sense of Hector, like an anchor point. The smell of vanilla was a bit more distant, but the campfire smoke sensation was stronger. Neither meant anything, he was sure, but it was nice to feel out the room, feel out *Hector*. He felt familiar; safe, somehow, despite Violet's accusations. He was a comfort, despite the fear Isaias felt.

Isaias doubted, again: how could there be anything less than *good* about Hector, this man who felt like warmth against the cold of the winter night bearing down outside?

"I'm guessing Violet told you about me acting weird," Hector said slowly. Isaias dared hope for a moment—it was already more promising than anything else he had gotten out of Hector so far. "And after what you saw, too. I know I said that there were some pressures, so I'm sure it's got you worried. But I'm—it'll be fine. I'm fine, Isaias."

Isaias paused. Was Hector sincere? He sounded like he should be, but something rung hollow. "What has you acting this way and worrying us both, then?" he asked, hoping for a frank answer that could put Violet's mind at ease—and his own, God willing.

"I was looking up my niece on social media, after hearing from that side of the family."

Isaias frowned. Hector didn't keep secrets, but this was a surprise. Isaias had thought that Hector had no contact at all with his family. It was him and Violet against the world. "I didn't know that you had a niece."

"Well, neither did I," Hector ventured. His voice sounded tight. "I mean—I knew, but I didn't *know*. I've kept an eye out for her for a few years, now. Just checking in every now and again, right?" Isaias nodded but chose not to say anything. He didn't understand—he couldn't. Isaias had no family at all, and he had never dared trying to trace his roots, afraid of what he would find. Instead, he let Hector continue. "She used to be this rough and tumble kid. Played a lot of sports with the boys. Seemed like a normal kid. I dared to leave her a message once or twice, nothing much but enough to let her know she could reach out if she wanted to. I've never heard anything back."

Isaias gave Hector space in his pause to elaborate, but he didn't. Able to guess at what came next, Isaias asked, "Did something happen to her?"

"I don't know," Hector said, then abruptly added, "Never mind."

The smell of burning suddenly re-emerged, so sudden and strong that Isaias nearly gagged on it. Was it just his emotional senses acting up? Was it real—was any of it ever real? It was so hard to know when Isaias had never known anyone like him at all. Bishop Reid had promised him it was real, as real as God Himself, but what if Isaias was the one who was being led astray—not Hector?

But Violet had seen something. Violet doubted her father. Violet believed in *something*.

Unsure what else to do, Isaias asked, "Is that what that late-night call was about?"

"Violet told you about that, huh?"

"She did. She's very worried about her father, Hector. And so am I."

"Well, it was. It was the middle of the night. It was her father, my brother. Telling me to back off. He threatened me. It was the first time I'd heard from him in years, the only words he'd spoken to me in over a decade, and..."

Hector trailed off in silence and Isaias felt the need to fill it, to offer comfort. He had nothing else to give. "I'm sorry, Hector," he said softly. But the smell of burning lingered in the back of his throat. And Hector's feelings were unreadable to him somehow, even with a gentle push. Like he was still being blocked somehow.

Oh, Hector, Isaias thought.

"He wouldn't dare try anything," Hector said suddenly. There was a knife-edge to his tone. "But the fact that he threatened me, thought he could *do* something—" Hector's face fell. His lips twitched, holding something back. He lowered his eyes. There it was—the emotional whiplash. Even without making a push to read the emotions dancing across Hector's heart, Isaias could feel them vibrating under the surface. "Shit, it broke my heart, Isaias."

"I'm sorry, Hector." Isaias could barely manage more than a whisper. He was about to say more, but his attention was called away by the steaming kettle, so he pushed off of the counter and turned away to bide himself a moment's time. He removed the kettle from the heat to let it simmer down a moment while he got out the mugs and tea bags. Once the water was no longer too hot for the tea, he poured it over the bags, allowing the soothing scent of chamomile to waft through the kitchen. Turning around, he handed one mug to Hector, who accepted it with a tired smile and a weary thank-you. He seemed normal again—or at least calm.

"What are you going to do?" Isaias asked softly, tempering his words carefully. He walked out of the kitchen, not letting himself look at Hector's face, and led him to the study when he was sure that Hector was following. It would be more comfortable. They could sit. He could try to piece together the story in a more relaxed atmosphere.

Maybe Hector would be more honest with him, then.

"I don't know," Hector said, his answer brusque. "Seems too late to do much of anything, doesn't it? We've all damned ourselves."

Isaias shivered. He knew Hector didn't mean it literally—he never would, he was as irreligious as they came—but it made him uncomfortable, especially with Violet's accusations against her father's soul seeded in the back of Isaias's mind. Hector was not damned. He could not be damned.

Isaias couldn't allow it.

Measuring out his words as he pulled a chair closer to the desk for Hector, Isaias brought his desk chair around to sit in front of it, making room for them both to sit. Finding himself at a loss and knowing only what would comfort himself in these moments, he said, "I have no doubt that God will show you the way."

But Hector didn't seem to be listening anymore. He was staring off into the corner behind Isaias, his eyes unfocused, like they had been outside in the cold. The wet beads of melted snow in Hector's beard served as a chill reminder of the tension they had just been through.

The room's temperature seemed to plummet, as if someone had opened the office window, though neither Hector nor Isaias had moved. Distantly, Isaias heard the tinnitus hum of something in pain. The screams he had detected when he had pushed too hard into Hector's emotions.

"Hector?" he asked. Hector did not reply. He stared, glassy eyed at the wall. "Are you okay?"

"Oh, sorry," Hector said, peeling his eyes from the wall. Isaias looked to where he'd been staring, seeing a crucifix hung on the wall behind the desk, above the open window. When had Isaias opened the window? Given the sharp cold in the room seeping in through the gap in the glass, he was positive that he hadn't. The open window was undeniable, though. Isaias looked back to Hector when he spoke again. "You're right, Isaias."

Isaias shook his head. He didn't feel doubt from Hector, who was a sworn atheist. He hadn't been listening at all. While Hector sat—seemingly unbothered by the cold—Isaias went to close the window. He shivered against the chill breeze, shutting the frame tight. The crucifix on the wall shifted slightly, and Isaias took a moment to right it before he turned back to Hector. He sat in his desk chair, while Hector sat in the more comfortable guest seat, less than a foot of distance between them. "I'm always right," Isaias teased, though his heart wasn't in it. But he had another, more dangerous, path he needed to follow, and Hector hadn't been listening anyway. It was a path he needed to take, though he dreaded to follow it. "I'm sorry to ask Hector but—you haven't been relapsing, have you?"

Hector blinked at Isaias, confused, then laughed sharply, loud in the small room. "God, no. I haven't touched a drink in years, and I'm not going to let anyone take that from me. My family bullshit aside, I'm not touching anything to drink."

Isaias relaxed. Hector, for a moment, felt more like himself again. Honest and earnest. Isaias didn't doubt that this was actually Hector talking to him, right then. He smiled. "Good. Just checking. I'm sorry I had to ask."

"I know," Hector said, leaning forward somewhat, closer to Isaias. Their seats so close, it brought Hector into Isaias's space, near enough that Isaias could swear he felt Hector's every move. Isaias saw something shift in his eyes, from gentle to predatory. "I'm sorry to have worried you."

"It's okay," Isaias said, but he felt his voice catch in his throat. He looked at Hector a moment longer, feeling the intensity of his gaze. He shifted and tore his gaze away, not sure what to make of the heaviness of it, but that somehow only amplified his awareness of Hector there, so close to him. In an instant, he could sense Hector again, the sheer weight of his feelings. There was something strong there, yet unidentifiable. Something Isaias wasn't familiar with, despite the sheer power of it.

"Thank you, Isaias," Hector was saying. "For worrying. For being a good friend, for being there for me, even if I don't always know if I want you to be."

Isaias first felt pain at the words, but then was distracted as Hector's hand brushed against his knee, settling against Isaias's leg. He heard the scrape of Hector's bandaged palm against his pants. Isaias's heart raced, painfully aware of the weight of Hector touching him. "Hector?"

"Yeah?" Hector asked. He didn't move his hand. The emotional weight that Isaias had been feeling was gone. The smell of something charred was back. Then, in a dangerously low voice, like an animal watching its prey, Hector asked, "You think you can't be corrupted, man of God?"

The lights flickered but Isaias barely registered them, feeling suddenly numb. He didn't recognize Hector's voice—a voice that normally brought him comfort was unfamiliar to him. The tone of it was all wrong. He could think only of Violet's warnings.

A demon?

Or something changed in Hector?

Isaias shifted, wanting to stand up, but not fully daring to move. Hector didn't move his hand, either, and his grip was strong, making Isaias hesitate further. The grip didn't feel affectionate. It felt like something somehow better and worse at the same time. Isaias felt uneasy at his own conflicted feelings—this wasn't Hector. He had no right to think twice about that. Demon or not, this wasn't *his* Hector.

"Let's go to my office," Isaias said, scrambling for what to do next.

"In the church?" Hector asked. Isaias nodded, dazed. "Why?" Hector pressed. His voice was still low. His hand was still on Isaias's knee. Isaias could tell he was daring Isaias to justify himself. "We just got here."

"I know, but there's—I remembered there's something that I want to show you that I forgot there."

Liar, Isaias thought to himself, though the thought seemed foreign to him. He didn't know what felt worse: the uneasiness coiling in his stomach at the touch, the way he *welcomed* Hector touching him, or the fact that he lied to Hector's face to get himself out of the situation.

But was that justifiable, when Hector might just be under the influence of the Prince of Lies? A lie for a lie. Assuming Isaias believed that to be the case. He doubted himself, but he also doubted Hector. It felt wrong. Something was wrong.

He didn't want to lose Hector, or to lose Hector's touch, but he was afraid.

"I don't want to go into the church," Hector said gravely. His voice took on a rough edge, sharp and uneven. He still didn't sound quite like Hector. "I never go."

That's the point, Isaias thought. "Why not?" Isaias asked, trying to laugh a little, as if he could just joke through the strange sensation in his stomach. Hector's hand on his knee, almost aggressive, was too present—the frightening appeal of it. The wish that Hector had ever touched him before this, before he wasn't right. Was that the influence of a demon, too? "If you don't believe in God, what does it matter to you? I want to show you—"

"You believe," Hector pointed out. His grip loosened on Isaias's knee, but didn't lift, and Isaias was distantly aware of Hector's shifting emotions, at least what he could sense of them. The grip on his leg made Isaias more aware than he had been before, as if it whatever was blocking him couldn't hold the emotions back any longer, not with their closeness. Something like worry, something like regret, crept into Hector's emotions like a crawling vine. Still, though, the words sounded like a threat: *you believe.*

Isaias wet his lips. When he spoke, it came out in a rasping whisper. Reverence and awe mixed with his fear. Like a fear of God, he was enraptured by Hector in that moment. "I do."

Hector still didn't move. His grip tightened again, drawing Isaias's eyes to him. Steadily, calculatingly, he stared at Isaias. "So, then it matters."

Isaias swallowed, nervous at the intensity of Hector's voice. In a rush, he suddenly smelled vanilla so strongly it was cloyingly, dizzyingly sweet. He felt overheated; not a hot flash but like sweat sticking uncomfortably to the back of his neck despite the cold, as if the entire world had just shifted under his feet. "Hector—"

"What?"

Trying to gain his courage, he said, "Please don't touch me like that." It came out as another whisper, a desperate plea.

"Yeah?" Hector asked, and his grip loosened again, now no more than a ghost of a touch. Still there, still giving in to the temptation to feel, but barely there. *Taunting.*

"You know I—"

"What?"

"You know," Isaias repeated carefully. Then again, emphatically: "*You know.*" He finally relaxed as Hector removed his hand, feeling the cold rush back into him, especially in the space left behind by Hector. Nonsensically, he wanted to cry. Why must he doubt? "I'm sorry," Isaias said, again in a whisper. He tried to place the swirl of emotions he was feeling, categorizing them so that they wouldn't leech into Hector. Fear. Shame. Guilt in his gut that didn't fade away even when Hector moved farther away.

"No, it's my fault." The words sounded honest enough, but Isaias still doubted the apology that followed. Not with the way that Hector had felt. Not with the way that *Isaias* had felt. "Sorry, Isaias. I shouldn't have done that if you didn't want me to."

Isaias nodded but didn't agree or argue. He didn't want to commit to anything, to potentially lie to Hector again. He swallowed, looking away for a moment, then made to stand again, now that he felt he had full range of movement back—not that he couldn't have broken away from Hector at any time, but he had been frozen in place all the same. "Come with me?" he asked. "To my office?"

Hector didn't rise to meet him. "No."

"Please, Hector," he insisted, not entirely sure why it was as important as he was sure that it was. It had to be important. Maybe he'd feel less guilty if they were in God's house. Then again, maybe he'd feel worse.

But he did think that he'd feel *safer*.

"No," Hector insisted, voice laced with anger again. He looked up at Isaias from where he sat, baring his teeth at him like he might bite. It wasn't a human expression. "I'm not going."

"Hector—"

Distantly, Isaias heard a *click* from the direction of the door before the lights to the study died, plunging Isaias and Hector both into darkness. Isaias heard something slam open and a burst of cold air—fiercer than the wind outside—dropped the temperature into the room from chilled to frigid. Suddenly shivering against the freezing cold, Isaias could only see eyes in the dark. He shouldn't have been able to see Hector's eyes so clearly while his own were struggling to adjust to the sudden change in light.

He didn't think they were Hector's eyes.

The lights flickered back on once, twice, three times—then stayed on.

"I'm not going," Hector repeated, low and slow.

"Okay. That's okay." Isaias shuddered and walked on unsteady legs to the window again, closing it tight and locking it this time, as if he thought that would do any good. He looked over his shoulder at the door to the study—had he closed it behind him? had he locked it?—but didn't make for it. "We can just stay here."

"Okay," Hector—and was it really Hector?—said.

Isaias stood there at the window for a moment longer, his heart hammering in his chest once more. He still felt shame, he still felt guilt, even though he had done nothing at all. "I—have something for you, actually. I almost forgot."

Hector said nothing, only watching Isaias, who walked back to his desk. He dug through his desk drawer for some papers, only pausing when he could swear he detected roses and sandalwood. He wrapped his hand around the rosary, tucking it out of sight, then walked back over to Hector, still sitting in the chair and watching Isaias steadily; warily.

"Hold out your hand for me," Isaias said softly. His heart was in his throat.

Hector stared a moment at Isaias's hand, now outstretched, balled around the rosary, trying to hold it in such a way that Hector couldn't see enough to guess at what he held.

Isaias could feel the suspicion dripping off of Hector when he asked, "What is it?"

"Just take it," Isaias said, was tempted to plead, but tried to keep his voice gentle instead of desperate. "Please."

Hector paused one more time, then held his hand out and up from where he was still sitting. He trusted Isaias. Taking a breath, Isaias placed the rosary in the proffered hand, resting it on the bandages on his palm.

Hector flinched, hard, and the rosary clattered to the floor as Hector dropped it, retracting his hand to his chest to cradle it in his opposite hand.

There was a hissing noise, and it took Isaias a moment to realize that the sound was coming from Hector himself. He barely had time to register it before it morphed into a gurgling growl in the back of his throat, like a displeased and hurt animal warning Isaias away from him.

Isaias hesitated, but then knelt next to Hector, despite the apparent warning. "Are you alright?" he asked, though he was not sure what he wanted to hear. He didn't look at Hector immediately, instead picking up the rosary and holding it in both hands in his lap.

He looked up from where he knelt when Hector spoke. "You—what was that?" Only then did Isaias notice that Hector's eyes—those beautiful, kind eyes—looked so pained that it hurt. Whatever guilt that Isaias had felt before increased tenfold.

Isaias let go of the rosary with one hand and reached out to take Hector's hurt hand with his free one. Hector looked at him skeptically, so he asked, "May I see?"

Hector looked at Isaias for a moment, then stopped hugging himself. He offered the injured hand to Isaias, who took it gently in his own, turning it over to look at Hector's palm, running his thumb over Hector's heart line, partially obscured by the bandages from the night before, then down the lifeline, tracing around where the cross of the rosary had touched him. The bandages were blooming with a line of blood across the centre, as if the rosary had reopened his wound despite no damage to the bandages themselves.

The skin of Hector's hand was soft in places, calloused in others. Isaias took a moment to allow himself to familiarize himself with the patterns of it again. Gently, he pressed his thumb into the fleshy heel of Hector's hand, testing for pain but unwilling to go too near to the blood. Hector watched him, confused and hurt, not reacting to Isaias's hands on him.

What he was looking for, though, was mostly intangible. While the pain and uncertainty in Hector's eyes were a guide, he was searching for his feelings the entire time. Prolonged skin to skin contact helped more than any touch to his thigh would have, or even a hug. And what he felt broke his heart.

Hector felt heartache and pain, but they were distant. He was *afraid*, maybe even of Isaias, but clearer than anything else was the fact that Hector's emotions were far away from him; strained. What Isaias had thought was something blocking him from reading Hector was something far worse than he had allowed himself to imagine.

The fire inside of Hector was dying.

What did you do to me? Hector's emotions were asking, and Isaias wasn't sure who he was asking. A demon? God? Isaias?

"Hector, I—" Isaias paused, looking at the deep uncertainty in the other man's eyes, yes, but feeling it more in his heart. The fear. The regret and grief. Guilt. He was *suffering*. He was suffering so much that Isaias had to ask, knowing no other tools at his disposal, "May I pray for you?"

For a second, Isaias thought that, against all odds, Hector was going to accept. But instead, he said nothing as he drew his hand back out of Isaias's grip. Isaias felt a pang of his own heartache at the loss of Hector. He fought the urge to reach back out, take his hands again, ask him to never let go again. Anything to keep Hector there with him. Anything to prevent Hector from slipping away from him.

"Okay," Isaias said, slowly, taking Hector's silence as him not wanting to hear Isaias pray for him. Then, with all the conviction that he could muster: "God willing, Hector, I will not lose you."

"Whatever you say," Hector murmured, then stood slowly. He looked unsteady on his feet. His face was flushed. "I think I should go, Isaias."

Isaias nodded but stayed on his knees, looking up at Hector. He didn't speak because he knew the only words that he would be able to muster would be to beg Hector to *stay*. He watched Hector walk to the door, unlock it when it had never been locked in the first place, and finally close it behind him. He heard, a moment later, the main door of the rectory open and close, the sounds of the night outside trying, and failing, to reach him.

Distantly, Isaias was aware that Hector had left an untouched tea on the desk. The steam from the mug had long since died in the too-cold air of the rectory. Isaias gripped the rosary in both hands, bringing it to his lips, and waited for the scent of sandalwood and roses when all he wanted were the smell of vanilla and the warmth of a campfire that meant that Hector was there with him.

Isaias bowed his head and prayed for him anyway.

XI

Tuesday morning. Isaias had slept fitfully at best. Every time he closed his eyes, even as he struggled to stay alert in the shower that morning, he saw Hector's sad and wounded gaze looking back at him, clutching his hand to his chest as if Isaias had burned it. In the dark of the night, so late it was the early hours of morning, Isaias had dreamt that he saw a sense of betrayal there that he could no longer remember whether had been there or not on Monday night. He had lay in bed, staring at the clock reading three am, struggling to fall back to sleep. When he finally managed sleep again, words he couldn't remember Hector saying rang through his dreams instead.

What did you do to me?

When he woke up again at six, he gave up on anything resembling rest and got up to start his day.

Now, Isaias scrubbed his face as he stepped out of the shower, then pulled back his hand when he felt something sticky on the surface of his skin. Blood, he realized, that hadn't entirely washed off in the shower. He must have nicked himself shaving. He hadn't noticed the pain. Isaias applied a gentle pressure to the cut to stem the last of the bleeding as he thought of the sticky heat of Hector's own blood on

Sunday night, the wounds in the flesh of his palms, and of Hector's hand on his knee on Monday evening.

Hector, who Isaias could not allow to suffer.

But was it hubris to believe that Isaias had any hope of saving him? *I think my dad's possessed.*

Violet had more faith in Isaias than he had in himself. But maybe with God on his side, he could do something. He had to do *something*.

Isaias went downstairs mechanically. His legs felt leaden. "Good morning, Mrs. Marsh," he said when he entered the kitchen.

"Good morning, Father Flores," she greeted him back cheerfully. She was hovering over the stove, her grey hair tied back into a loose ponytail. Isaias smiled tiredly when he saw the mug of hot tea already steeping on the counter next to her. "Heard you coming out of the shower, dear," she said. She looked up at him and raised her eyebrows in polite surprise. "I thought you could use something warm to wake you up, and seems I was right."

Isaias grimaced. "Do I look that bad?"

"Terrible," Mrs. Marsh said before she grimaced. He felt a pang of her own guilt, for being so bluntly rude to him. "Forgive my frankness, Father. Are you alright?"

"Nothing to apologize for, I appreciate your honesty. I'll be alright, though—I just didn't sleep very well, that's all," Isaias said. First Hector, now he was lying to Mrs. Marsh as well. And hadn't he lied to the bishop and Violet, as well? How far was he falling in so few days? To seek comfort, he took a moment to reach out to Mrs. Marsh's emotions. The weight of them displaced the oppressiveness of his dark dreams. He didn't let himself linger in them long—he was slipping, too ready to test the water of the emotions of others. The bishop would be unhappy with him. "I'm fine. Thank you for the tea. I'm going to get my laptop from the church office, but I'll be back in a few minutes. I just want to do some research in the study. I'll be there for a little while if you need me."

"No breakfast?" Mrs. Marsh asked. "I was just starting something."

Isaias shook his head. "No, it's alright. I'm not really hungry, anyway."

"Nonsense," Mrs. Marsh said. "You need to eat, Father."

"I can't say I have an appetite." A half-truth, this time. He felt worn and thought food could help him feel energized—but his stomach roiled, and he wasn't sure he could keep anything down. Maybe abstaining would help him clear his head. "I just have some work to do."

"Do your research in the study," Mrs. Marsh said sternly, "but I'll bring you something to eat shortly, Father."

Isaias knew he wasn't going to win that fight. He smiled tiredly at her. "Alright, Mrs. Marsh. Thank you." He drank more of his tea before setting the mug aside—he could finish it when he came back—and going to the front hall to gather his coat and put on his boots. He pulled on his toque and gloves as well before heading out into the brisk morning. It was still early, and the dawn light was only barely filtering over the horizon but its reflection off the snow brightened the morning despite the cold. He adjusted his clerical collar—there was always Mass to tend to, after all—with one hand under his thick coat as he went, his gloved fingers not nimble enough to make the adjustment easy. The rectory was just behind the church, so it wasn't much of a walk, at least; a fact he was grateful for when the air was this bitingly cold.

With his free hand, Isaias checked his phone as he walked, snow crunching under his boots, and saw a voicemail from Hector, left at about three in the morning. Isaias remembered lying awake, having dreamt of betrayal in Hector's eyes and struggling to sleep again, watching the time on his clock creep further and further past that very time. He hadn't noticed anything on his phone at the time, but he supposed in the middle of the night, weighed down by exhaustion, he hadn't been thinking clearly or paying attention.

Isaias called up his voicemail box to listen to the message. When there was only silence at first, he thought it might have been accidental call. Then he heard the breathing—and static. Over the course of several seconds, both increased in volume and pitch until Isaias couldn't tell them apart. When the noise sharpened to a shriek, piercing his eardrum, Isaias abruptly dropped his phone. He bit back a curse—even then, he couldn't disappoint God or the bishop—and picked his phone up out of the snow, accepting the wet discomfort of slush soaking into the fingertips of his gloves.

Isaias was glad to see that the message had ended. He fumbled to take his gloves off for a more responsive touch to the screen so that he could delete the voicemail without further delay.

It was nothing. An accidental call in the middle of the night, nothing more. The noise was interference from nearby. Isaias's heart raced anyway.

Pausing as he approached the church, Isaias glanced up at the back window. One of the stained-glass windows—one that looked into his office, in fact, sandwiched awkwardly as an afterthought between two plain picture windows—was shattered in the centre, jagged edges of broken glass spearing into a hole in the stained-glass Sacred Heart that Mother Mary held in her hands. There was blood smeared across what remained of the glass heart like it was bleeding, and black feathers stuck in the clotting gore. The blood and feathers both had already begun to frost over, and snow lazily drifted through the jagged hole in Mary's heart into the church.

Something had exploded through the heart, tearing through Mary's chest, killing her—and probably whatever had broken her heart in the process.

Isaias picked up his pace the last few yards to the church, careful on the frost-bitten path but making his way to the back door two steps at a time. He turned the corner to his office, and there he saw it: the crow on the floor just below the window, in a shattered nest of glass. A gentle dusting of snow was already blanketing its body, a deceptively serene image of winter peace, if it weren't for the bright blood on the glass. The early morning sunlight filtering through the broken window reflected off the coloured glass to give the corpse a magical appearance.

"You poor thing," Isaias murmured as he walked closer to the body of the bird. Its wings were bent all out of shape, and it was still; lifeless. Isaias felt tears in his eyes—a sensitivity to the pain of all living things, feeling the lingering sensations of the bird's final moments of suffering—and knelt on the floor carefully, feeling the chill of the wooden floorboards in his knees, and avoiding the glass as much as possible, to look at the body of the crow.

The instant he reached out to touch it, the crow's head snapped up at him with a crack, crying out at him. He jerked his hand back before it could bite at him, but it was in that moment that he felt the life force of it, the pain of it, for just a moment before it died, and he *felt* its heart stop, its emotions just *end*.

Isaias's eyes welled with tears as he felt the crow's life disappear in an instant, and his heart constricted with the way that it went from alive, if afraid and in pain, to being... nothing.

Just nothing.

A life, gone just like that.

He hadn't even been able to soothe it in its dying moments. What was the good of his ability to feel and temper the emotions of others if he couldn't even offer a living thing comfort before its dying breath? All that the crow had felt was pain and fear. It was all Isaias had felt either, his own heart tricking him into believing the bird had already been dead because how could something still-living have been stripped down to only suffering?

Isaias's heart felt slow and heavy in his chest, and for a moment he worried that it would stop altogether. He felt the death of the crow lingering on his skin, seeping into his soul.

Bowing his head, Isaias crossed himself with his still ungloved hand. He allowed himself a moment of silence, in which he prayed for the lost soul of the bird.

He felt nauseous when he finally struggled to his feet, but his heart felt like it was returning slowly to normal, though his limbs felt heavy. He fought against it as he went to the small kitchenette near his office to find disposable gloves and a washcloth. Returning to the office with the gloves on, Isaias carefully picked up the body of the bird, wrapping it in the dishcloth so it would be protected. It was no burial shroud, but it felt more respectful than merely wrapping it in plastic. He would lay the bird to rest in the backyard of the church before he got his computer and did his research.

By the time he left the office, the room had become so chilled by the cold seeping through the broken window that he didn't overly miss any warmth from the church. Carefully cradling the wrapped bird to his chest, Isaias stopped by the shed that was set against the exterior wall of the church, a mismatched resin prefab that Hector had left them that didn't match the church's worn stone. After Hector had established the gardens of the Sacred Heart, he had been surprised to find that the church had no proper shed, even despite the small graveyard on the grounds, albeit that the cemetery was largely unused these days, bar the occasional visit and a periodic tending to the graves. But Hector had insisted on a place for proper storage of tools and had left behind supplies for the gardens as well so that they could be left in the church's care. Isaias hesitated only a moment thinking of Hector and his generosity, feeling his heart ache with Hector's absence, before he picked out a small trowel, thinking a shovel wasn't likely needed.

Once he had his tools, Isaias walked to the edge of the cemetery that was in the opposite corner of the grounds from the rectory. He found a pine tree just at the border, near the portion of the graveyard used for the burial of children and the innocents, where the branches had blocked the worst of the snow, leaving less for Isaias to have to dig through. With the bird tucked against his winter coat with one arm, Isaias used the trowel in his free hand to clear snow until the dirt amongst the tree roots was visible. He knelt, grimacing as wet snow soaked through his pants, and dug.

It was a struggle, the dirt half-frozen this deep into winter, but Isaias eventually broke through to softer dirt below the surface and was able to create a small grave for the bird. He rested the wrapped corpse in his lap and dug the shape of the hole out with his hands. The cold of the dirt penetrated his rubber gloves and left his fingers numb, but he ignored the pain of the cold in favour of making a proper grave for the bird. More than cold, Isaias felt emotionally drained. Not sure what else to do with the emotions of having felt something die, and still remembering how he had apparently hurt Hector, Isaias cried the whole time he dug the miniature grave. His tears burned cold streaks into his face. His chest ached from sobbing in only dry, cold air. He let himself sit there, in the snow, after he had buried the crow; let himself cry and whisper a prayer for the lost life.

By the time he had finished, grabbed his laptop, locked up, and headed back to the rectory, he felt like he had been awake for an eternity. His heart ached more than it should—the bird was not the first thing that he had felt die, but somehow, he felt at fault. Perhaps something in the office had caught its eye through the distorted light of the stained-glass window and called it to its death.

Isaias couldn't bear the thought that he might hurt anything else.

"That took you a while," Mrs. Marsh remarked when Isaias came back in, calling out to him from the kitchen as he closed the door behind him. "I just served breakfast."

"A bird broke into my office," Isaias murmured, still feeling rattled. He rubbed his eyes with the back of his hand, trying to wipe away the rawness. His cheeks still burned with the trails of frozen tears. "Would you mind clearing out the glass when you have a moment?"

Mrs. Marsh peeked her head out of the kitchen to look at Isaias. She frowned at him, and Isaias sensed her concern and felt some vague comfort from it. "Of course, Father. Whatever you need."

Isaias collected his plate of breakfast—and, despite his earlier protest and his lingering nausea, Isaias was eager to dig into the potatoes and pancakes with warmed maple syrup, hoping the food would be a comfort—and went to the study with his laptop safely tucked away in its bag. He set up at his desk, fortunately still tidy from his over-cleaning the night before. He normally wouldn't work and eat at the same time, taking the time to appreciate the good food that Mrs. Marsh had provided him, but Isaias wanted to get through things more quickly, and felt stretched too thin to properly take the time for much of anything. He took his first bites—finding that the syrup in his throat was a comfort even if it sat heavy in his stomach—while he pulled up a search engine to begin to do some research.

He would ask Violet if they could reconvene again after she finished school that day, so he wanted to get some research done before work to know what he wanted to present to Violet as his conclusion. He still didn't know what to make of anything that had transpired the night before. Hector's erratic behaviour, the door locking, the window opening of its own accord, and the lights failing. The way Hector had seemed burned by the very presence of the cross on the rosary. Everything pointed to something deeply, seriously wrong, but Isaias was afraid to let himself conclude anything.

But the crow, dead in his church that morning—had it been a sign? Had it died to send a message to Isaias? He did not ask if God could be so cruel to discard one of His own creatures to make a point—for were they all not God's creations to do with as He pleased? If so, Isaias wasn't sure what God might want him to discern from his message, except that this was real, this was *true*, and he should take this suffering seriously.

For a moment, the maple on Isaias's tongue tasted bitter—even burnt—and he set his fork down to open his desk drawer to find the rosary where he had returned it the night before after Hector had left. He picked it up and put it around his neck, tucking it into his collar and out of sight. It brought a strange warmth with it, only pleasant sensations despite the distance of the family it—and he—had come from.

Isaias ended up with two main search topics, and he was not happy with having to search either. In one window, alcoholism. In the other, demonic possession.

What was the world coming to, that either seemed like distinct enough possibility? And was it wrong that he wasn't sure which one he would prefer to be the root cause of Hector's problems? He wondered, though, if it was denial that he let there be any doubt in his mind. Neither was something he wanted for Hector, but could Isaias fight the very real trouble of Hector lapsing on his sobriety any more than he could exorcise a literal demon?

How could he ever choose which damned fate he would want to condemn his best friend to? Even the best-case scenario, in which Hector had been telling the truth—that Hector's brother had threatened him, had told him to stay away from his extended family on some level, that Hector's niece might be in trouble—how could Isaias wish that on Hector? Between all the apparent options, Isaias could ask for none of them to be the answer for why Hector was suffering.

There shouldn't have been anything wrong with Hector. He was a good, kind man. Why had God chosen him to suffer?

Hector didn't deserve what Isaias had felt the night before, the weakness of his spirit as it faded away.

Isaias put his remaining breakfast aside, the last dredges of his appetite gone.

In one window, Isaias had tabs upon tabs about how to help someone who was struggling with addiction, how to know when someone had relapsed, what to do to support them on their road to recovery.

In the other, signs and symptoms of demonic possession. Stories of psychiatrists working with priests to ascertain whether an affliction was mundane or supernatural. Health professionals writing on the difference, on how they came to face their skepticism.

Isaias did not think it was likely that he could convince Hector to see any kind of health professional—he had always been reluctant to see one for himself before, even if he would take Violet to as many doctors as needed to make sure that he had a medical opinion he felt confident in—but maybe there was someone else he could talk to for a more objective opinion. He thought briefly of the more academically inclined members of the parish, those who might know a health problem from a spiritual one—Violet's friend Poppy's mother was a professor of psychiatry, and she came to church just often enough to remind her daughter to be a good Catholic, that she was watched by God and should behave accordingly. Surely, she would have something to say.

But no, Isaias thought of someone else who might be able to help—someone he trusted enough to be honest with, though he wasn't sure how well their particular spiritual beliefs aligned.

Despite his doubt in everything else, Isaias felt sure that having a second opinion on the grief in Hector's soul would do him good. If nothing else, he felt confident that he couldn't do it alone, and so he pulled up the contact information for The Second Voyage.

XII

When Isaias entered The Second Voyage for the second time that week, he nearly ran right into Lena, who was hovering just inside the door waiting for him. Her eyes were darkened with a severity of concern that he didn't think he had seen in her before, though he had not been well-acquainted with her long enough to know if maybe this was a common side of her that he just hadn't met before.

"Let me take your coat," she said with some degree of urgency. Isaias reluctantly complied, though he was careful to not knock too much snow off onto the mat that provided meagre protection to the hardwood floors of Lena's shop. "Come in."

Isaias nodded and followed Lena in as she folded his damp coat on her arm. The fact that she had taken it at all told him that she intended to make him stay and talk—this would not be transactional. Something about that left him wary, as if he should be worried that Lena felt they would have a lot to talk about.

Like on Sunday, the shop brought a variety of powerful emotions with it from the side that housed used goods from citizens of Sainte-Thérèse. Despite it being a mere two days later, the exact depth and quality of those feelings had already shifted. Like the people in their town, The Second Voyage was changeable, *human* in its fickle emotions. It reflected all the nuances of pain and heartbreak and hope of the city back at Isaias. It was strangely comforting, just to know that this shop—and thus their city—was so *alive*.

Lena was ushering Isaias into a small storeroom behind the counter where her cash register sat, a room Isaias had been aware of before—it was hard not to be with a large sign above it that said 'enter if you dare', the threat undermined by a large and cheerfully yellow smiley face painted below the words—but had never once given a second thought to beyond acknowledging its existence. Once they passed through the sheer pink curtain that operated as a door to the backroom, Isaias became aware of the scents and sounds that curtain had been holding back. He heard a kettle bubbling away, fighting for prominence over the low beat of gentle electronic music, and smelled the pleasant burning of incense, something rose-like with a dash of cinnamon and citrus. It was a wonder that Isaias hadn't noticed any of these signs of life when he had been in the main room of the shop, with only the curtain to operate as a barrier, but he forgave himself. After all, he had been only in the shop for a few moments before Lena had brought him back there, and he was understandably distracted.

"Tea?" Lena asked, though she was already depositing loose leaves into reusable sachets and placing them in a pair of mugs, both shaped like cat heads. "You like herbal tea, right? Lavender and valerian root is good for stress."

"Please," Isaias said, honestly grateful for the offer, though he wouldn't have been able to decline anyway, not with Lena already pouring water over their tea bags. Awkwardly, Isaias sat at a small table in the back while he waited for her and looked around—the walls were dense and cluttered, filled to the brim with candles and incense, statues and iconography, religious symbols from a variety of faiths, as well as knickknacks of all variety of ages and styles and types. Curiously, as soon as Isaias turned his eyes back on Lena, he couldn't quite remember what he had seen on her shelves, other than a shrine that had prominently featured Mary watching over the room. He blamed it on his stress. The scent of the lavender and valerian tea was enticing.

Lena sat across from Isaias and placed the cat mug decorated like a calico in front of him. Its large eyes seemed to look into his soul without judgement. Lena kept a black cat mug for herself. Isaias cleared his throat and picked up the mug, sipping the steaming hot liquid from between the cat's ears. The tea wasn't steeped enough to have much of the floral or root taste to it yet, but the hot water was comforting, warming him from his throat and down into his chest as he swallowed.

"Thank you, Lena."

"Of course." She sipped her own tea before setting the mug down. She curled the fabric string of her tea bag around her fingers, distracting Isaias with the movement, and watched him for a long moment. Back here, in the dim light of the space, the steam from her tea seemed to somehow obscure her features. Long moments passed before she spoke again, long enough that Isaias couldn't quite keep track of how long he had been there. "So—you wanted to talk about a *spiritual* problem, right?"

Isaias blinked, coming back to himself. He nodded, then sipped his tea again—stronger already, the bitter valerian grounding him—to bide his time as he thought about what to say. Even after pulling up the phone number of The Second Voyage, he had hesitated to reach out to Lena. After all, what could he say that would be reasonable—both in terms of protecting Hector's privacy and Violet's trust, but also in terms of what Lena would even *believe*? It was no easier, sitting in front of Lena, to decide what to say. Ultimately, time was what made him speak. He had texted Violet to come by the church after school to talk to him, but that he would be out on errands before that in case she was out of school early—or so she said—again, and so he'd had limited time between finishing Mass and his most essential duties to make to The Second Voyage and talk to Lena before he would need to meet with Violet back at The Sacred Heart. Finally, he said, "Yes, that's correct."

Lena smiled fondly at him. "Forgive my saying so, Father, but I can't say that I'm used to being sought out for advice by someone so..."

"Catholic?"

Lena laughed, bright and cheerful. Something in her laughter eased him. "Yes, that's about right. Usually, people don't talk to me about spiritual matters if they're already embedded in a specific institution. I don't mean any offence by it."

"I didn't think you did," Isaias assured her. He smiled tiredly. "I've been struggling with defining a matter of... shall we say, spiritual pain, lately, and thought that I could use an outside perspective on it. Your belief system would provide a more unique view than asking those in my direct community."

Lena nodded. "I can see that. A lot of my own worship is rooted in similar beliefs to yours, even if what it looks like is a little different. I think it gives me a bit more flexibility about where to follow my heart."

Something in the words struck Isaias: the idea that Lena's beliefs were rooted in Isaias's familiar Catholicism but that she still followed her own heart. He felt, for a moment, the love emanating from her; not for anyone or anything in particular, but for all of God's creation. It made him distantly aware that the truths of Lena's soul were still somehow disguised to him, like he couldn't fully understand them, but it felt different from how he had been closed off from reading Hector. "Some might find the rules and guidance of the church helpful," Isaias said, noncommittally. He didn't know why he felt the need to defend the church. Lena was not anyone he needed to convince.

Lena shrugged. "And some find them restrictive. Have you thought about which of those people you are, Isaias?"

The question caught him off-guard, and he hesitated to answer, thinking it should be obvious. He was a priest, wasn't he? The structure was his life. But then, perhaps Lena didn't really care to know his answer—it was probably rhetorical, only challenging him to think. And had he ever *actually* thought about it? Had the decision to be ordained not been made when he was still a child, still learning about his belief in God?

Isaias cleared his throat. He wasn't there to talk about any of that. "I wanted to talk to you about what you know of possession."

Lena sipped her tea, then tapped his fingers rhythmically across the pointed ears of the cat-mug. "Demonic?"

"What other kind is there?"

"You'd be surprised." Lena shrugged, and the effortlessness of her answer threw Isaias once again. To speak of it so matter-of-factly—that possession was not only possible, and she was not surprised by the question, but that she would contemplate multiple causes. "Is this about Hector?"

Flashes of Hector appeared in Isaias's mind: exchanges of letters throughout their friendship, sometimes obvious, sometime surreptitious, the contents of them becoming more intimate over time; some six weeks ago, smiling in good humour as the two of them exchanged gifts, and Hector's eyes glowing when Isaias gifted Violet an art set that made her light up when she opened; the fleeting touch of Hector's hand on Isaias's shoulder as they made dinner together on one of Isaias's visits, but the visits gradually decreasing in frequency along with the letters. Blood on Hector's hands, his palms torn open by shattered ceramic. The feeling of his soul dying away. Tears stung Isaias's eyes and he lowered his gaze to the mug, making eye contact with the calico cat-mug instead, not ready to share the extent of his grief with Lena. "Yes, it's about Hector."

"I thought it might be." Lena nodded to herself, sombre. She was quiet a moment as she toyed with a pendant around her neck, tracing painted nails around the relief in the centrepiece. Isaias noticed after a second of the pause that it was a silver medal of Mary Magdalene. "The last time I saw him—when he brought the rosary—there was something wrong. You think it's a possession?"

"Violet thinks so," Isaias said. He felt something ache in his chest again, wondering if he was going to share too much. Violet had trusted him, not Lena—but Isaias didn't think that he could do this alone. And was Lena not a safer person to trust with Violet's fears than the bishop, who would think that Isaias should concern himself with the spiritual matters of the parish? "I don't know what I believe. I thought maybe it would be—" he cut himself off. He couldn't assume Lena knew of anything about Hector's personal troubles and traumas. He redirected his own words. "I thought maybe it might be a health problem, or some kind of stress, but I'm not certain anymore."

"You're worried that maybe the signs of mental or physical health are being misinterpreted as spiritual health," Lena said. Her voice was grave. She held fast to the medallion of Mary Magdalene around her neck.

"I am," Isaias confirmed. "I know clergy have done a lot of harm by making assumptions or assuming God is the only answer to someone's troubles. I don't want to pray for Hector if what he needs is—I don't want to be that person."

Lena softened. "The fact that you're asking questions is a good start, I think, Father. It means you have an interest in doing your due diligence before jumping to any conclusions. I think if you start by ruling out as many mundane causes as possible, that's a place to start, but if the only explanation you're left with in the end boils down to 'wild coincidence', then that doesn't feel much like it matches up with a Godly worldview, does it?"

Isaias nodded. He thought of some of the stranger occurrences that he had seen even in the past two days, the ones that were difficult—maybe even impossible—to explain by normal means. The pain he felt from Hector was explainable, but when coupled with doors opening and closing of their own accord, the strange voicemail, the video that Violet had shown him of Hector out in the street in front of their house the other night, the wounds on Hector's hands and the reaction he'd had to Isaias's rosary—it was becoming harder and harder to explain away. "No, it doesn't."

It was true, wasn't it? A God-fearing man like Isaias shouldn't hold so much doubt in his heart.

"So, if you are left with coincidence or God, it seems right to choose God, should you believe in Him—or any other divine power," Lena went on. She tapped her fingers against the relief of Mary Magdalene around her neck and dropped her hand back down to her mug of tea. "I know belief has been weaponized to hurt people in the past, but I think it's because a lot of God-fearing people saw what they thought were too many coincidences for them to ignore because they didn't fit into their worldviews. So, they thought, 'this must be something Godly'—or the opposite, as the case may be. We know more now, we know better, so the threshold is higher, but I still don't believe in coincidence. The world is both ordered and chaotic, but there are still *patterns*, I think."

Isaias tried to think of what God meant to him, in the end. Patterns, order in a world that otherwise felt inexplicable. Was that all God was? Or, he thought, perhaps that was enough: the comfort that faith brought him to believe that there was a *point* to it all. Even the darkest moments were a piece of something larger that happened, if not for a *reason* then at least as part of something intentional and purposeful, not *random*. Because Isaias could think of nothing more frightening than the idea that he was alone in the world, the things that happened to him only arbitrary. He couldn't say if God had some grand plan, that all pain happened for a reason, but more than anything, Isaias couldn't bear the idea of spiritual loneliness.

Isaias wished desperately that he could talk to Hector; confide in him; ask him to tell him that everything would be okay in the end. He hated that Hector was the only person he couldn't talk to about this. It felt like something special and good had been taken out from under him, leaving him incomplete, something less than whole.

But in the end, he was only left with one certainty. "I don't believe in coincidences, either."

Lena smiled at him. "Then you have an answer, don't you? Or at least part of one."

Isaias swallowed. Unsure he *did* have anything like an answer, he looked down at his cooling tea, meeting the eyes of the cat-mug. "And what do you think about Hector, specifically?"

In his peripheral, Isaias saw Lena running her fingers along the rim of her mug, back and forth between the black cat ears, as she took her time in answering. "There is something deeply wrong surrounding Hector," she said. "Or, if not wrong—*not Hector.* Do you understand what I mean?"

Thinking of how many moments, even over the past two and a half days, Isaias had felt like something was *not Hector,* he said, "I understand completely." And that statement, above all else, helped solidify in his mind that this was a very real possibility—that Hector was not himself, was *possessed,* and that Isaias needed to do something about it. He still felt doubt, but his mind felt clearer than it had since seeing Violet in his church on Sunday morning. He kept his eyes locked on the mug in front of him. "I just wish I knew what to do about it."

Isaias finally lifted his gaze from the mug when Lena laid a hand on Isaias's and squeezed it gently. At her cool but firm grip, he looked up at her. She was smiling—sadly, but smiling, nonetheless. "I think you'll figure it out," she said. "More than belief in God, you have belief in Hector. And I think that the love you hold in your heart will guide you to your answers. For what is faith about, if not love?"

Something about Lena's words sat strangely on Isaias's heart. Not wrong, exactly, but ill-fitting, like he would need to grow into them. He thought that later they might warm him, bring him confidence, but for the moment he wasn't sure if they laid his doubt to rest. He said none of that aloud. "Thank you, Lena."

Lena squeezed Isaias's hand again before she rose from the table. "I hope I was able to help."

Isaias stood as well, picking up his mug of tea and taking it to the small sink in the backroom. "You did," he said, despite the lingering uncertainty. "If nothing else, it gave me a great deal to think about. Thank you, Lena."

Lena nodded seriously. Her eyes were grave, but Isaias felt for a moment the weight of the care in her heart, the first real glimpse of her emotions after all this time. He thought that he understood her more than she likely knew: that she seemed simultaneously serious and inscrutable because she bore the heavy weight of her own heart.

Isaias hoped that one day he would be able to tell her that he, too, was weighed down by his own heart.

Instead, he thanked her again and stepped back into the body of the shop. While what he and Lena had talked about remained clear in his mind, Isaias found that as soon as he passed through the curtain into The Second Voyage, he was otherwise left with only vague memories of what he had seen there. He remained certain, however, that a figure of the Mother Mary had watched over him the entire time.

Dear Hector,

I just left The Second Voyage. I spoke with Lena. I tried not to tell her anything too personal, but I hope you will forgive me my trespasses if I said anything you would not want her to know. It's just that I'm scared—scared that I will never be enough to save you.

Do you even want me to save you?

Is it wrong of me to want to save you?

I wish I had answers, Hector. I wish I could ask you to give them to me. I prayed for you, despite your distaste for it. I prayed to God, but He gave me no answers about what I should do for you. I wondered, Hector, should I pray to You instead?

I hope God will forgive me these trespasses, too.

I don't know if I can give you this note. I hope that one day things will be right again, that I will be able to share my heart with you, and you can share yours with me again. If that's what you want.

I think what I am trying to say is: I miss you.

Yours,
Isaias

XIII

Isaias stopped by a café on his way back to the church to get another tea, the one at The Second Voyage that Lena had provided not having held him long enough to prevent the cold outside from leaving him numb. The barista who served him was an active member of the Sacred Heart's parish and took the time to chat with him, to try to make friendly conversation, and Isaias reciprocated but felt that his heart wasn't in it. It was an occupational hazard, meeting people in the community who wanted to stop and talk to him, to tell them all of their troubles, bare their soul to him even in the quietest moments of the day. Normally Isaias was happy for the chance to be a positive influence in someone's life, even outside the church. Today, he found the cheerful waves of energy coming off the young woman to be near painful, like the winter sun outside reflecting off the too-bright snow and hurting his eyes to look at; too much for him to absorb when there were so many tired emotions already clinging to him. The emotional whiplash of his pain against the eagerness of the barista was difficult to bear, and Isaias had to be careful not to let his bad mood leech into her better one. It wasn't right or fair to share his emotions with anyone, let alone a young woman who was just eager to share with someone she clearly thought of as a spiritual advisor.

He dismissed himself carefully, without saying much. He hoped the young woman didn't think it a failing that her priest was not the person she had wanted him to be in that moment.

Isaias was sitting at the desk of the church's office, staring at a copy of the Bible on his desk and sipping his tea, when the church secretary led Violet in. At some point the tea had steeped too much and become bitter. After thanking the secretary, Isaias set his cup aside in favour of turning his attention to Violet.

Violet took a seat without a word, looking at Isaias skeptically. Other than her purple crutches, which she continued to hold even as she sat this time, she was dressed in all black under her unzipped winter coat. Isaias hadn't known Violet even owned that much black, and it threw him off-guard to see her dressed like that. He thought to himself that Violet looked—and felt—like she was in mourning. Before Isaias could ask her anything, though, she seemed to notice the cardboard pasted up over the stained-glass window, the heart in the centre completely covered up by stiff paper. The result was the Virgin Mary holding up an unreadable brown box that hid away whatever was left of her heart.

"What happened there?"

"There was a crow—it must have gotten confused by the light in the church. It flew through the window." Isaias didn't want to add that it had died when he had arrived, that he had felt it die. "Did something happen with you last night, Violet?" He didn't want to tell her that he could *feel* that something was wrong, that something had shifted. He couldn't let her know that he didn't just think that she was in more pain than before, that he *knew* that she was.

Violet smiled tiredly. "It's a bad pain day," she said. Then she shrugged, as if dismissing her own ache—not just in her body, but in her heart. She tugged the zipper of her parka down away from her chin by a few inches and Isaias saw a glimpse of her father's rosary—the one Isaias had retrieved from The Second Voyage and then passed on to Violet—around her neck. He wondered how conscious of a gesture it was that she reached up and touched the crucifix where it rested over her sweater, tugging gently on the bottom, just below the wounded Christ. "Dad was acting super weird last night when he came home. He wouldn't really talk to me, at first. Then he got like—unreasonably mad at me for telling him to go see you. As if I had fucked up—sorry—for telling him to go see his friend. Eventually he changed course completely and, like, snapped at me. All, 'hey, I know you drank at the party last week, I know you fucking drank. Do you have booze now?'"

Isaias's heart sank, but he felt conflicted. He had started to believe Violet's theory. He had begun the process of preparing himself emotionally for whatever was to come, even if he didn't know what that was. Now it seemed he may have been right all along.

"And like, there's no way he could have known there was even alcohol at the party. I was curious, I kind of wanted to try Poppy's drink, but she talked me out of it. She was worried it was a bad idea, given my health and my parents' history. She'd said my dad would forgive me if I drank, but he wouldn't forgive Poppy if she gave me any and she needs to stay on his good side." Violet sniffled, smile sad but fond. "So no, I didn't have any, and dad couldn't have known there was any there anyway. It was just some stupid art kid thing. And even if he'd known—why did he want to know? He doesn't—he was acting like he wanted it, and I got all freaked out because what if I was wrong, and you were right? What if it's that he's drinking again and not the other thing?"

"Do you think it is?" Isaias asked, trying to keep his voice level. Not revealing what he thought, what he was scared of. "A relapse?"

"No," Violet said. Her grief became conviction. "I doubted for a moment, but I believe in my dad. And I know it's not that simple, that sometimes you're just so hurt that—it wouldn't be his fault, but I know my dad, and that's not what's going on. So I tried to throw it in his face. I asked him why he wanted to know, and he snapped at me, and I was like, 'What, you want to throw your life away *again*? Over what, what's your problem?' And—and here's the really freaky part, Father. He like... convulsed. And then collapsed. He was basically foaming at the mouth. And then I was trying to check his pulse and call fucking 9-1-1 when he started sobbing. He told me not to call, that he was okay, but he was sobbing the whole time, saying he was sorry, so sorry. But it wasn't me he was sorry to."

"Who was it?"

"I don't know. He said he was sorry to *Lily*."

Isaias frowned. He wondered how much of Hector's story had been true. "I'm sorry, Violet. Are you okay?"

"No." Violet laughed bitterly. "I mean, I'll be fine. I hurt today, but that's probably because I always kind of hurt. But I carry on. And it was really fucking—sorry, but it was scary as Hell, Father. After everything... I was scared I would lose my dad. I don't know what I would do without him." Her voice broke at the close of the sentence, cracking under all the weight she was carrying. Isaias felt her tears coming, the echo of so much pain in her soul, before he saw them begin to form in her eyes. It wasn't sorrow she felt—at least not alone. Her emotions were a shapeshifter, cycling through grief and anger and fear, then back again.

Isaias brought his hand to his neck, feeling the beads of the rosary under his collar. He tried to find comfort in the feelings that came with it—the distant memory of roses, of sandalwood. Violet couldn't imagine what she would do without her father, but Isaias couldn't quite imagine what he would do with a family. It was an unfair thought. The bishop had raised him. Isaias had a family. The church was his family. He shouldn't miss a different version of a family he'd never had, just as it was unfair to miss Hector when it was Hector who was in pain.

He traced the shape of the rosary down to the cross at its end, held fast against his chest under his vestments. "Last night, when I was with your father, strange things happened. Things I couldn't explain. He was behaving oddly again. And... when I gave him my family's rosary, he acted as if he was scalded by it."

"So, *is* it a demon?" Violet sniffed quietly as she wiped tears away from her eyes. "Am I right?"

"I don't know," Isaias said. He thought of Violet's story, about Hector demanding alcohol, and thought that even the timing of that outburst felt too much like coincidence, like it was staged. "But I spoke to Lena today about the nature of God and what we believe in. About the role of faith in our lives. About how it's in everything—that even randomness in the world does not happen in a vacuum." He took a breath. "I think that too many things have happened for it to be coincidence, these past few days. And this morning—well, I believe I saw what might be a sign this morning. I don't think God would mislead me on this one. I'm sorry for doubting you, Violet. But I'm scared that you might just be right."

Almost more heartbreaking than all of Violet's grief was the relief she felt in that moment, echoing out from her and into Isaias, making him wonder for a moment if the emotion was his own. How many times had she been doubted in her life that to be believed, even about fears so horrible, was such a *relief*? "I forgive you," Violet said softly. She sniffed, blinking away her tears. "What now?"

Isaias was quiet for a moment. "We have to be absolutely certain, Violet. We need to know that your father isn't himself. That something may be using him. And then..."

"And then," Violet filled in, voice grave, "we perform an exorcism."

Isaias knew that Violet was right, even if it scared him that she was the first person brave enough to use the word out loud. He knew she had to be right, because there was only one way to deal with a demon.

Exorcism.

The word sounded deceptively simple, despite the weight it carried. Isaias knew little about the rite. They were supposed to get proof. They were supposed to get approval. Would they be able to, even with their combined efforts? If they had so much difficulty convincing themselves, it would be even harder to convince someone else. Isaias's bishop hadn't even wanted Isaias to investigate his friend's troubles, had wanted him to leave well enough alone. It would certainly prove even more difficult to convince him that something needed to be done on this scale and magnitude.

"First, Violet, we will have to gather evidence. As much proof as we can. We need to be absolutely certain. And we need to take evidence to the bishop."

"But *you* believe me," Violet said carefully. He felt her hesitation, her doubt. Isaias felt guilty that he had doubted her so much that now she doubted *him*. "What more do we need?"

"I do believe you," Isaias promised her. He contemplated gathering feelings of confidence, of certainty, even if he still had his doubts, and sharing them with Violet. He could let those emotions reach out to her, suggest to her that there was nothing to doubt anymore, even if it was a lie. But it would be wrong to use his gifts that way. He was scared of how quickly they might become needed. "But it's not me that's the problem. It's the procedure, the way we have to do things."

"Dad isn't even Catholic," Violet said. Isaias could feel she believed in him, that he would guide them through this, but still she wanted to question the process. It was a testament to her own beliefs. "And don't we have enough proof? Can't your bishop just take our word?"

"I don't know," Isaias said earnestly. "I'm not sure how my bishop would react. He's a strong believer in doing things the right way. I'm not convinced that he would approve the exorcism without extensive documentation, which could take weeks or even months—"

The edge of Violet's emotions hardened into something blunt and deadly. "Dad doesn't have that long. There's no way."

Isaias thought of Hector's soul asking, *What did you do to me?* "That's what I'm afraid of Violet. But we can start by me seeing your father again tonight to decide if this really is the correct course of action. I can do my best to figure out what we need to do."

And if it wasn't—well, Isaias would have to find some other way to fight the forces of evil.

That evening, Isaias prayed for a very long time before he made his decision. He asked God for guidance, for answers, and to steady his hand however he might be forced to act. He prayed to the Lord to help not just him but Violet and, above all of them, Hector. To deliver Hector from evil; from the Devil himself if that was what Hector needed. To give Isaias the strength he would need to save Hector, whatever that might mean.

"Lord, You are my steadfast love and my fortress, my high tower and my deliverer, my shield and He in whom I trust and take refuge... please, Lord. Give me guidance in what I am to do to protect Your servants from the Devil. Show me the way to protect Hector from whatever avails him. Let not Hector, a good man, created in Your image, suffer."

Isaias waited a long time for an answer. To feel something in response, some sign of God's answer to his prayers. Anything to tell him that he was on the right path. That the choices he was making were right.

He wasn't sure that he felt anything at all.

Eventually, Isaias rose, feeling certain that nothing was coming and that he was alone in his decision, changed into plainclothes, and went downstairs to the main floor of the rectory. He was still wearing the rosary, tucked under the collar of his black button-up. The gentle aromas of roses and sandalwood enveloped him. Where God was absent in that moment, at least he had the memory of his ancestors to prove that he did not come from nothing.

Isaias allowed himself to stall for time for a few more minutes, setting the rectory to rights wherever Mrs. Marsh had not already done so, mostly in the study. A streak of mud sullied the floor, likely dragged in after he had buried the crow that morning, dark like blood where snowmelt had seeped into the hardwood. Isaias cleaned up the remaining mud, but the damp could not be lifted, permanently warping the wood in reminder of everything that had happened the past few days.

It was past nine at night. It was as dark as it ever would be outside, the sun having long since set. It was now or never—light was a long way away, and Isaias could delay no longer.

He texted Violet, *I'll be there in 15.*

The response was quick, and Isaias was certain that Violet must have been watching her phone for any word from him. *I'm in the park around the corner.*

Isaias pocketed the phone and gathered his things. The rosary was still around his neck, but he also collected a pocket copy of the Bible and tucked it into his winter coat pocket. He didn't know how much good it would do, but he felt somehow comforted by its weight as he pulled the coat on.

Despite putting on all the appropriate layers for a winter night, and not having even stepped out into the cold, Isaias felt chilled. He took a moment's pause at the mirror that hung from the front hall closet. He didn't much care for it being there, as it felt vain to check his appearance before leaving for anywhere. Maybe he would ask Mrs. Marsh to take it down, donate it somewhere, or maybe he could bring it to the next garage sale that the church participated in. After all, it didn't much matter to him, did it? Better it be used by someone who could appreciate its value. Besides, all he saw reflected back at him was a tired man without any answers.

Within the promised fifteen minutes, Isaias had arrived at the Montero home. He paused at the edge of the sidewalk, just before it turned into the path up to the squat bungalow that seemed to hold an air of more menace than was reasonable for a small family home. Surely it was just his own dread talking.

Before he could decide whether to be brave or to give in to his cowardice, the smell of flowers washed over him. Violet approached with her friend Poppy hovering just by her shoulder, hand halfway outstretched as if she was worried Violet would lose her footing on the frosty sidewalk. She finally touched Violet when they both paused steps away from Isaias, resting her hands gingerly on the sleeve of Violet's jacket, no longer in worry but in affection—Isaias recognized the deep fondness she held for Violet in the emotions he could sense from her.

"Hi Violet, hi Poppy," he greeted, trying to sound cordial despite the exhaustion he already felt. "How are you both faring?"

Violet grimaced and shrugged but said nothing. Isaias saw Poppy's grip tighten on Violet's sleeve as she looked to her. "Do you want me to go in with you, Vi?"

Shaking her head, Violet pivoted on her crutches to face Poppy to be heard better. "No, it's okay, Pop. I'll text you later. Try not to worry too much. I'll be okay, so will my dad. We've got God on our side, right?"

Poppy smiled nervously at Violet's words and the accompanying wink. After the forced humour evaporated, though, she leaned forward and rested her forehead gently against Violet's. Both girls closed their eyes and Isaias averted his gaze—not because he felt any judgement, but because it was clearly a private moment between dear friends. He recognized the love they felt for each other, more intimate for the fact that it was shared in this moment that was somehow personal despite Isaias bearing witness to it.

When Isaias heard Poppy stepping away, he looked back at the girls and recognized the pain of separation in their eyes. He thought to suggest Poppy stay after all, but he wanted to respect Violet's decision—and, more than that, he was painfully aware that he wasn't sure what would happen next, and he wanted to avoid putting Poppy in the way of any kind of pain or suffering. It was bad enough Violet was still involved, but it was her father, and so Isaias knew there was no other choice but to have her by his side at this time.

"Bye, Vi."

"Bye, Pop."

Isaias touched Violet's shoulder in an attempt at comfort as Poppy turned and walked a few paces down the sidewalk, though she didn't go far. Once she was at a slight distance, she paused and turned back, apparently determined to watch Violet enter her home and know that she was—for the moment—safe. Violet gave her friend a small wave before she tore her eyes away and looked to Isaias, seeming to wait for his direction.

"Shall we?" Isaias asked.

Violet nodded. Looked to the house, then back to Isaias. "I'll tell my dad I ran into you on my way home from Poppy's and invited you to come hang out for a bit. It's too late for dinner, but for tea or whatever. He won't mind that. And it's as good a reason for you to be here as any, right?"

"Alright," Isaias said dubiously, not sure how comfortable he was with how often he was lying these past few days. "You don't think he'll see through that?"

Violet frowned at him, giving him a side-eye. "Okay. Hey, Father, funny running into you, here. Want to come over, have tea with dad and me? There, now you don't have to feel bad if that's what you're worried about."

Isaias laughed without a single trace of humour. "Alright, then. Tea it is."

Violet smiled, equally humourlessly. She paused, then started up the path to her front step. As she approached, the porch light brightened as it detected her presence. Isaias walked a few paces behind her, his legs leaden as he took his time up the path.

He wanted to be wrong. And he wanted to help. He still didn't know if God had even heard his prayers earlier that evening. But when was the last time that he had felt confident that God had heard him at all? But God was still speaking to him, he thought—there were signs.

As he got to the door, Violet was already unlocking it and swinging the door open. She called into the house, "I'm home, dad! Sorry I was out kind of late. Hey, I ran into Isaias on my way home. I invited him to come by for a bit, is that okay?"

Like God, Hector gave no reply.

"Dad?"

Isaias picked up his pace and walked into the house with Violet. After only a few steps inside, Isaias froze in place when he felt an overpowering sensation.

No, not just felt, but heard, tasted, smelled, saw. Something burned across all of his senses, blurring his vision, scorching his nostrils and across his tongue, ringing in his ears, boiling his skin, overloading him. Like his whole mind was overcome, for one furiously dizzying moment, with the sensation of burning. What was—?

"Hector?" Isaias called. He could barely tell if the words had actually made it out of him with his head suddenly heavy and cotton-stuffed. He couldn't think. Distantly, there was the sound of shuffling from elsewhere in the house. Slowly, Isaias's senses cleared, except for a faint ringing that lingered in his ears like the screams he'd heard from Hector's soul days before, and he tried to figure out where Hector was. Where the *demon* must be, because nothing else could explain how his senses had been so overcome by something so foul.

Isaias held up a hand to signal Violet to wait, and carefully made his way to the far wall. While most of the sensory perceptions were leveling out to something that neared normal, Isaias felt hot. He walked slowly, step by step, trying to follow the sensations that were enveloping him, the faint noises, the feeling of *wrong*, though everything in his mind and heart and soul rejected this, made him want to turn and leave, go back to the church, give confession and pray for forgiveness. It got hotter as he walked, and his head swam, feeling heavy again. He came to the master bedroom, where the door was ajar, and slowly cracked it open.

Hector was on the floor in the centre of his bedroom. His chest heaved. His breathing was ragged, rasping out in pained gasps.

"Hector?" There was no answer, and Isaias started inching forward. He thought he should go closer, check if Hector was okay, but he was terrified to move too fast. He couldn't just leave Hector there in good conscience, though, in case this was a medical emergency. "Violet," he called out into the hall. "Stay outside."

He fished out his cellphone and pre-dialed emergency services but didn't hit the call button. His movements felt sluggish, not just from the heaviness in his head and in his limbs, but from the lack of proper mobility from still wearing winter clothes. Clumsier than he'd like, he crouched next to Hector and reached out to him.

Hector's head snapped up and he growled—truly *growled*—"Don't touch me!"

The sudden, jerking movement and the frightening quality of Hector's voice caused Isaias to snatch his hand back with such suddenness that he lost balance, falling backwards onto the floor from where he was crouched, dropping his phone. Instinctively, he scooted backwards, putting distance between him and Hector.

"Hector?" he repeated. His voice shook.

"Don't touch me, *priest*," the voice emphasized, and it was horrifyingly apparent to Isaias in that instant that the voice was *not* Hector's. "Stay away, lamb. Wool over the eyes, thinks he's so innocent when he's ready to become the wolf at any moment. A dutiful *sheep* but ready to *sin*—"

"Stop," Isaias said, but his voice cracked, lacking any conviction. He remained sitting there dumbly on the floor, staring in horror at the man he'd trusted and cared for, even as the shell of Hector slowly clawed its way up from his collapsed position on the floor. The movements were jerky; unnatural. "Whatever you are, you don't know what you're talking about—"

"Wanton, wanting, wantage, wantaway." Hector—whatever wore Hector like a suit—first sat up, then moved onto all fours; on his hands and feet, knees bent, ready to pounce.

"Stop," Isaias repeated, voice meek. His head spun, still heavy, still dizzy, now flooded with too many emotions to make sense of. Isaias heard footsteps and the tapping of crutches coming from just behind him. "Violet, stay away!"

"Isaias?" came Violet's voice from behind Isaias, just past the door. "Is dad okay? What's going on?"

"Violet," Isaias warned again, only for the door to swing the rest of the way open.

"Daddy—"

"Child of God," the voice snapped, but the words sounded choked, forced. Isaias felt tears in his own eyes, and it took him a moment to realize it wasn't just his own fear he was feeling, but Violet's pain, and Hector's, as a strange, convoluted flood of emotions that filled the room. The fear and pain were paramount, but there was also anger and guilt and so many more emotions that it was almost impossible to pin them down. His own anguish mingled with Violet's and with Hector's—or did the feelings belong to the demon? did demons know such pain, too?—and amplified it all to dizzying heights.

There was no time to try to make sense of any of the pain crowding out Isaias's heart, because Hector was rising from his crouching position on the floor in quick, jerking movements of his limbs. His limbs bent outwards. Up. Pushed him to his feet. His teeth gnashed. He stared Isaias and Violet down, eyes flicking back to them like a cornered animal—but was he predator or prey?

Hector's eyes were empty, Isaias noticed. Their characteristic kindness was hidden by something else; something unidentifiable and alien.

Distantly, Isaias heard the cat hissing from under the bed, saw the glint of her eyes as she watched Hector like a threat. He was glad to know that at least the cat was okay.

Isaias struggled to his feet slowly, scared that if he moved too quickly that Hector would pounce. He was filled with an unreasonable fear that Hector would *bite*, sink his teeth into Isaias. His movements were slow and awkward, his bones feeling hollow and too many layers weighing him down. He put himself between Violet and the twisted vision of her father. His heart was pounding in his chest, and he was scared that Hector could hear and smell his fear, but he knew that if Hector understood what was going on, he would want Isaias to protect Violet from whatever happened.

There was a growling noise coming from Hector, a deep rumbling in his throat that sent chills down Isaias's spine, as he swayed back and forth. The movements of his body were asynchronous with the movements of his eyes, making it hard to keep track of where he was looking; at Violet; at Isaias; at the door behind them, ready to make a break for it.

Hector's body took a step forward, the movement jerking and disjointed, his body not following the rhythm of a human. He clenched his hands open and closed, then snapped his head to look directly at Isaias.

Not knowing what else to do, Isaias said, projecting as much confidence as he could force into his voice, "Stay back, demon."

The demon—or whatever was inside of Hector—laughed, throwing his head back in a hearty cry before he swiveled his chin back down to look at Isaias.

"Oh, *priest*," he crooned, "so frightened, so afraid. So much delicious doubt in your mind and your soul. Where is your God? Are you afraid that He abandoned you, just like so many others have left you like dirt in the street? He has a habit of it, you know—leaving His creations to *rot*."

Isaias swallowed and resisted the urge to reply. This wasn't Hector, even though the voice was familiar, and the face was the same. Whatever the demon wanted to insinuate about the doubts in Isaias's mind, this wasn't his friend. Still, he felt tears in his eyes at the thought that Hector could say those words, pick at Isaias's doubts when he should have been trusted with them.

That's not Hector, he reminded himself. He knew that now. There was no room left for uncertainty.

"Oh, Father Isaias," the demon said, his voice thick with mocking and insult. "You think you can save anyone when you can't even save *yourself*? So many lies, so much doubt, so many lies, so much doubt, so many lies—"

"Enough," Isaias snapped, voice trembling. "Stop. Leave Hector now. Begone, demon."

"*Begone*." The word came as a hiss. There was a sudden jerk of his head, Hector's head, a swift movement back and forth like a dog shaking off water. "You—you don't know what you're doing. Silly, stupid man. No sense of his own heart."

Isaias felt Violet moving behind him and instinctively held out an arm to hold her back. She didn't move past him, but he heard her voice. "Dad, stop. This isn't you."

"No *fucking* kidding," Hector's face snapped. He sprang forward, an unnatural movement, swift but uncontrolled, lunging quickly at Isaias and Violet.

Violet screamed, and Isaias nearly did too, but instead stepped back, forcing Violet to take several swift paces back as well. The thing wearing Hector laughed again, then hissed as he rolled his head in a slow circle, like he was cracking his neck out. He looked next past Isaias. To Violet.

"Oh, little girl," he said, voice slick like oil. "You think your daddy is so good, so kind. You don't know he's a dirty liar. And the apple won't have fallen far from the tree. Sin begets sin. You're going to fuck up just like he did. Ruin lives just like he did. Are you ready for that, little girl?"

Isaias couldn't listen to his mockery of Violet. Remembering himself, he fumbled for his rosary, reaching into his shirt to fish out the beaded cross. He held it in front of him and watched Hector flinch away.

"Enough," Isaias said, but he could hear his voice lacked conviction, not able to imitate what he didn't feel. He tried again, tried to fake it, voice sterner: "Enough. Leave Hector alone. By the power of Christ—"

The demon flinched back but sneered. "You—"

Suddenly, the demon snapped his head from side to side. He growled, he hissed, he raised his hands to pull at Hector's hair. He closed his eyes tight, as if trying to block something out. A slow dribble of drool pooled out from the corner of his mouth. It dripped steadily to the floor in a long stream. Hector's body shook, even convulsed, rapid body movements that seemed unnatural, like someone was shaking him from side to side with invisible hands. The smell of burning intensified for a moment, was again near dizzying, before it suddenly, without warning, disappeared in a whoosh. Like the fire went out, leaving only ash.

Isaias took a gasping breath for air past the lingering, choking scent of smoke before the sensation in his lungs cleared.

Hector collapsed back onto the floor, a boneless crash as if whatever had been holding him up gave out without warning. Violet made it to Hector's side first, pushing Isaias aside with one of her crutches. Isaias followed mere seconds later. He crouched, reaching out to touch Hector's forehead, feeling the hot, feverishly clammy skin there. The rush of emotion he felt was indescribable, something pained and afraid but also so, so hungry. He brushed Hector's hair away from his forehead, then withdrew his hand from the unpleasant sting of emotions. He hung his head and whispered a prayer as he crossed himself.

"Lord, have mercy on Hector's soul. Guide him to Your path and deliver him from his pain and his sorrow..."

Distantly, he heard Violet joining in, repeating Isaias's words an instant after him, an echo in a young girl's frightened tenor.

They fell silent for a moment after the 'Amen'. The pause was heavy and full.

Violet broke the silence first, her wry voice trembling. "Do you believe me, now, Father?"

Isaias didn't look at her, instead staring at Hector on the ground. This was the man who had helped Isaias love the Sacred Heart. It was Hector who had come the closest to knowing all of Isaias's secrets and fears. Hector who had always been there for him, and who had been his dearest friend, his confidante, his anchor through all his fears and doubt.

"I'm afraid that I really do, Violet," he said softly. "And I'm not entirely sure what to do about that."

<h1 style="text-align:center">XIV</h1>

Isaias had come to no decisions by the time Hector woke up. He and Violet had gone back and forth on the evidence, now that the scales were tipping alarmingly in favour now for the case of demonic possession, to decide what to do next. Isaias wasn't happy with the conclusion, but what was he to do? Hector was not himself, and no mere lack of temperance would change him in the ways that he had been transformed. The voice he had spoken to Isaias and Violet in was not Hector's. Even how he had *moved* was unnatural. He had changed into something strange and inhuman and decidedly *not Hector*.

There was only one conclusion, with nothing mundane left to explain what was wrong with Hector: this had to be a case of possession.

Isaias was in the bungalow kitchen while Violet tended to her father. Isaias had been afraid to leave her alone with Hector, but she had told him to go 'chill out' for a few minutes. He retrieved a bottle of water from the fridge and sat at the dining table. The cat, Prue, was weaving around his ankles anxiously, having emerged from under the bed once Hector had collapsed, while Isaias screwed and unscrewed the cap of the water bottle until his fingers felt raw from the ridged plastic. He hadn't had a single sip of it, but after several minutes of obsessing over it, he paused and murmured a prayer over the bottle, blessing the water inside of it.

"Father?" came Violet's meek voice a moment after he had finished his prayer. He glanced up at her questioningly as he tightened the cap absently once more. "Dad's awake. He wants to talk to you."

Isaias felt alarmed that Hector had woken without Isaias knowing—had he left for so long that he could have put Violet in danger? But here Violet was. Safe. "Okay," he said. He leaned down and pet Prue between her ears to try to calm her—and himself—before he stood up and stepped over the cat. He followed Violet to the master bedroom, the cat trailing after them a few paces until it became clear where they were headed, at which point she turned back to the living area and hid under the couch.

Violet paused at the door and said, "He wanted to talk to you alone."

Surprised but unquestioning at this point, Isaias nodded. With his free hand, he pushed the door open, closing it behind him as he entered. He walked over to the bed where Hector lay and stood awkwardly for a moment, uncertain what he should do. It had taken some effort to get him into bed and under blankets, Hector a large man and with Violet unable to help, but he had managed. Now Hector mostly looked helpless, lying there. He had knocked the blankets back despite how cold it was in the room, and his face looked sickly; feverish.

"Hey, Isaias," Hector murmured, blinking up at Isaias. His voice sounded scratchy, like he had strained it. Isaias thought of the guttural, pained noises the demon had made with Hector's voice, the curses it had lashed out with, and thought that maybe he had.

"Hello, Hector," Isaias replied, his voice sounding weak. He knelt next to the bed and set the bottle of water next to him on the floor, then braced his elbows against the bed and folded his hands together.

"Are you going to pray for me?" Hector asked, and it sounded like he was trying to laugh, but the sound caught in his throat, trapped there, coming out as a raspy breath, a ghost of what it was supposed to be.

"I already did," Isaias confessed. He looked down at his clasped hands, fidgeting uncertainly. "Despite you asking me not to."

When he looked back up, Hector was frowning. "When have I ever asked you not to pray for me?"

Isaias paused. "Last night," he said. "At the rectory."

"I don't remember—I'm not sure if I remember being at the rectory at all." A breath passed between them before Hector said, voice uncertain, "Sorry."

"That's okay," Isaias said, even though it wasn't at all okay that Hector had gaps in his memory that large. "It's alright if you don't remember. You have nothing at all to apologize for."

Hector nodded, closing his eyes for a moment. Isaias took a moment to feel out his presence; the way his emotions spiralled through his heart. The vanilla smell was thick and sickly, like extract going bad, oil gone stale. The cherrywood was dull. And Hector's emotions were fleeting, moving quickly from one thing to another. Isaias could read them if he wanted, but no single emotion seemed lasting enough to try. It hurt Isaias's heart to feel Hector this way, his emotions thin and strained. And Hector's face—a face normally so warm, so kind, so *loving* looked instead weak, drained of life. If Isaias couldn't detect the emotions in Hector's soul, he would be frightened that Hector was lost to him already. As it was, he was scared he might lose his friend at any moment.

When Hector said nothing and only remained lying there, still, Isaias unclasped his hands and reached out to take one of Hector's hands in his own. Hector flinched slightly. "Sorry," Isaias murmured and drew away.

Hector squeezed Isaias's hand to hold him there. His grip was weaker and less sure than Isaias had ever felt it, and that, too, broke Isaias's heart. "It's okay," he said, even though Isaias knew that this wasn't okay, either. "It didn't actually hurt."

Isaias was certain that was a lie, but he nodded anyway, mostly as a gesture to buy himself a few fleeting seconds. As Hector's grip on his hands loosened, Isaias traced his fingers over the bandages across Hector's palm, around the edges of the wound he knew was still there. The bandage was sticky with dried blood—he would have to change it for him soon. Isaias asked, "What *do* you remember?"

"Not very much," Hector said softly. He squeezed Isaias's hand again, his eyes downcast. "A lot of things lately are a blur. I'm not sure where I am half of the time. What I'm saying or doing. It's gotten worse, lately. I lose more time than I actually remember and what I *do* remember is mostly just pain." Hector took a shuddering breath. "I remember you, though, Isaias," he whispered. "At least a few times. But not much of it is clear."

Isaias brought his other hand to Hector's, held it gently between his palms. He blinked back tears. "Do you know what's going on?"

Hector didn't answer right away. His eyes closed, and for a moment Isaias thought that maybe he'd fallen asleep. Eventually, he asked, "Is there something wrong with me, Isaias?"

"Not with you, my friend," Isaias whispered fervently, even though he knew he should caveat his words. "It's nothing wrong with you. But there is something wrong, and I'm going to help you. I promise you."

There was another breath of silence between them. Isaias wondered if Hector believed him, that he'd help. That he *could* help, never mind wanting to. He knew he could check, try to feel his doubt or his confidence, but he had to just trust Hector as he hoped Hector trusted him. As they had always trusted each other.

After a moment more, Hector looked at Isaias with sad, soulful eyes. "Tell me, Isaias. What's happening to me?"

Isaias paused, then let go of Hector's hand. He picked up the water bottle next to him. He held it up and asked, "Do you trust me?"

Hector nodded after only the barest pause. "Of course, I do. Always."

Isaias unscrewed the cap of the water bottle. He paused with it halfway open, doubting himself once more, then finished opening it, pouring a bit into a cup on the bedside. Before Hector could say anything, Isaias dipped his fingers into the water, wetting his fingertips, and reached over to Hector.

He murmured a blessing as he made the sign of the cross over Hector, tracing the path from Hector's forehead to his chest, crossing over his heart. Some of the water dripped from his fingertips, landing on Hector's cheeks and dribbling down his neck, leaving a wet trail across his skin. Hector hissed in pain as his skin steamed from contact with the blessed water.

Isaias withdrew his hand, preparing for the worst, but he detected only confusion and pain. Hurt, yes, but not fear or anger so much as unknowing.

Isaias wiped his hand on a damp towel that Violet had been using to mop up the sweat from her father's brow while Isaias had been out of the room. It would at least get most of the holy water off his fingers. "I'm sorry," he said gently to Hector. Hector had said that he trusted him, and this was what Isaias had done. "I had to try that."

"Was that—?"

"Holy water?" Isaias filled in. "Yes, I'm afraid so. Hector, I—Violet and I are convinced that you are possessed. That there is a demon inside of you. I'm so sorry."

Hector looked at him, eyes pained. "What?"

Isaias saw the incredulity in Hector's face and took a steadying breath. "I know you don't remember much. But that should be your first warning sign, my friend. "

Hector laughed, sharp and short; an almost mean sound compared to the soft rasp his voice otherwise was. It wasn't like he found it funny; Isaias could tell that there was more fear than humour in the sound. "What kind of religious bullshit are you feeding my daughter?" he asked. "No offence, Isaias. But that's…"

"Impossible? I hate to admit it, but I thought the same at first, Hector. It was Violet's idea, but she's convinced me. You're not yourself. And before we can let it get any worse, I have to—"

"What?" Hector asked, and the laughter was gone. He just lay there, searching Isaias's face with quick moving, frightened eyes. Isaias could practically hear the fear in Hector's emotions: *Don't do this to me.* "What?" Hector repeated. "Perform an exorcism?"

"I have to," Isaias said softly. "I don't know, Hector. But I can't leave you without help."

"Isaias, I..."

"You said you trusted me, Hector," Isaias reminded him, despite feeling like he was twisting the knife. He wanted to beg him, *Please, let me help you.* "Do you? It's alright if you don't. But I won't give up on you. If you say no, I'll find another way. I won't stop trying until I know you're okay."

There was another pause before Hector said, "I do trust you. More than myself. You and Violet... Violet is everything I live for. And you, Isaias—you help keep me steady, and make me believe I can be good enough. For my daughter. For myself. For..."

Hector trailed off, not completing his thoughts. Isaias mentally filled in the sentence *for God,* though he doubted that was what Hector would mean. He thought perhaps what he really meant was *for unconditional love* which was, after all, what God was supposed to mean. Love and order. Isaias reached out and took Hector's hand again, cradling the calloused and bandaged palm between his hands. He would change the bandages just as soon as he could bear to be away from Hector again for long enough to get clean gauze. Hector gripped Isaias's hands back, but it felt limp compared to the sure touch that Isaias was used to.

"I just want you to be back to yourself," Isaias whispered. He brought Hector's hands to his lips so that his words, his breath, ghosted across Hector's knuckles. "If that is what we must do..."

"I don't know if I believe what you're saying," Hector said. Isaias saw where it was going and wanted to weep. He wanted to say, *Please, believe me. Please, don't make me leave your side.* "That there's something in me. Demons aren't real. I don't believe in demons. I don't believe in God. But—"

"Hector—" Isaias started, but Hector cut him off.

"*But*," he repeated, "I believe in *you*, Isaias. And I believe that you believe. And if Violet is convinced—Hell, if Violet convinced *you*—then maybe it's worth a shot." Hector's voice cracked, and he took a shuddering breath. Isaias brushed his lips against Hector's fingers, not sure what he was doing but hoping it would bring his friend some comfort. Hector squeezed his hand. "Fuck, Isaias. I'm scared as Hell. I remember so little. This is the most lucid I've felt in weeks, and while I was awake you burned me with holy water." He laughed, darkly. "If it will make the pain go away, if it will make me able to be there for my daughter again—then do it."

Isaias felt a wash of relief, and he couldn't help but let it spread to Hector. It wasn't done—it was far from over—but Hector agreeing to let them *try* was a start. He was terrified of what came next, but it meant he could do *something*. He bowed his head, resting his forehead against Hector's knuckles, still holding his hand. "May I pray for you, Hector?"

To Isaias's surprise, there was no hesitation. "Yes, Isaias. You may."

Isaias gripped Hector's hand tighter in both of his, still gentle but firm, trying to emulate Hector's always steady but never hurtful grip, and he felt Hector's grasp tighten in turn. Isaias began: "O, Father who art in Heaven. Be my watchful guide to bring Your child Hector back into the light of Your love. Let him see peace again. Take him under Your wing and protect him from the powers of evil. Work through me to aid Hector in his troubles. Show me the answer through Your word. And help me help Hector to suffer no more..."

When he concluded with an 'Amen', he heard Hector echo the reply. He smiled faintly and raised his head to look at Hector. Said, "I thought you didn't believe."

"No, I don't," Hector confirmed. "But you do. If you care enough to pray for me, to ask your God to help me, I'm not going to disrespect that. It's—I don't know, touching, maybe. That you bring your beliefs to my side to help me when you're most concerned for me. It's part of your way of trying to help, right? No matter what I believe. No matter what's wrong, and if—if I can be saved from whatever it is. It's nice to know you believe. That you think that I *deserve* to be saved."

Isaias wanted to tell him that of course he deserved to be saved, but he wasn't sure if it would help. Instead, he nodded and traced his thumb over the back of Hector's hand. His heart pounded, feeling heavy in his chest.

He looked at Hector and he thought, *I will do anything to save this man.*

He looked at Hector and he thought, *I need him to know that I will do anything to save him.*

Isaias took a breath. He squeezed Hector's hand once more and carefully focused the energy of his emotions. He let Hector feel the care and concern he felt. He tried to show him exactly how he was feeling. That he would do anything for him, just so long as he knew that Hector was safe.

Hector looked at him with confusion. Gradually, some kind of understanding crossed his face, and Isaias could have wept for that brief glimpse of *knowing*, that someone understood what was in Isaias's heart. At the end of that moment, all Hector said was, "I know, Isaias. I trust you."

Isaias blinked back tears of relief, of joy, of fear—of all the complex emotions that he dared to feel just because Hector might, one day, understand Isaias's very soul. He smiled at Hector, already exhausted deep in his bones, feeling the desire to crawl into Hector's bed and hold his friend as if that alone could save him, but knowing there would be no time to rest. "Do you feel strong enough to come to the church with me?"

As he asked it, he became aware that he really did intend to conduct the exorcism himself. Violet was right—Hector didn't have long enough to convince the bishop, to find anyone else to help. And Hector had said he trusted *Isaias*—and so Isaias knew that he was the only one Hector would have faith in for this. And Hector's faith would be a necessary component of what was to come.

"I think so," Hector said. Isaias felt his fear and admired his bravery in saying it anyway. "Let's do this, then."

Isaias nodded. He took a breath, letting go of Hector's hand to allow the man the leverage to sit up properly. Isaias looked at the glass of holy water on the bedside table. He thought of the horrible things Hector had said in a voice not his own, words he could have told Hector to convince him something was inside him but couldn't bear to tell him. He thought of the crow, the doors locking, and all the other strange things that he and Violet had seen.

"Come with me," he said softly to Hector as he helped him to his feet. Hector, normally so strong, too weak to stand on his own. "And I will fight to save you."

XV

"Isaias? It's past midnight—what in God's name has you calling so late at night?"

Isaias took a breath and loosened his hand on his cellphone. As he exhaled, he watched his breath plume out in a thick, white mist in front of him. It was painfully cold, outside in the snow at that hour, but he had wanted some privacy for this phone conversation. What he was about to discuss was meant to be private—between him, the bishop, and God. He stood, listening to the breathing of his former bishop and mentor, allowing the bitter frost of midnight bite at his exposed skin. For a moment, he considered hanging up. Pretending it was an accidental dial. Saying nothing at all and letting the bishop wonder why he'd been woken in the middle of the night by a mysterious phone call. There were so many options besides committing to what he was about to do and what would come after. Instead, he said, "Your Excellency. I think that I need to make confession."

He could almost *feel* the puzzlement from across the distance. His empathy wasn't that powerful, he couldn't sense something like that, but he knew the bishop well enough to recognize that he wouldn't understand. That was why Isaias was doing it this way. He had realized this was his only option. "Isaias, my son. What's gotten into you that you need to confess at"—he paused, presumably to check his bedside clock, a dated night table alarm that Isaias could picture perfectly—"twenty minutes to one? It's well past midnight. What's going on?"

"It's a very long story, Your Excellency," Isaias said quietly. Something about being reminded of the hour seemed to demand softness. He resisted the urge to tell the bishop about what he and Violet had become sure was happening to Hector. About what Hector had agreed to allow them to do. If he told Bishop Reid what he was about to do, he would consider it completely out of the question. He would tell Isaias to stop. He would get out of bed despite the hour and come to Isaias's church in a heartbeat just to stop what was about to happen. Isaias debated if that meant that he should put a stop to it himself, even as he had become convinced it was true what was happening. Shouldn't he want to obey his bishop? Shouldn't he want to listen to the man who raised him? If Isaias was so convinced that Bishop Reid would tell him he was being foolish, he should take it to heart.

But he knew what Hector's heart felt like. He knew that what he had sensed wasn't Hector. And he couldn't bear the thought that maybe the bishop would deny that Isaias knew what was in his own heart, not for the first time.

The silence endured, the bishop perhaps waiting for Isaias to explain, to justify himself. Isaias knew that he couldn't. "Please, hear my confession."

There was another pause, and Isaias was concerned that the bishop would reject him. He felt relief when the bishop finally said, "Of course, my child. I'm just concerned about why you feel the need to confess tonight, at this hour. Is something wrong, Isaias? You can tell me if something is wrong."

Isaias was tempted to say, *Would I be calling to confess my sins past midnight if something weren't wrong?* But Bishop Reid deserved more respect than that. Maybe he even deserved the truth. Maybe Isaias should trust his counsel. Let the bishop take over, trust *him* to make the right choice where Isaias could not. "Please, Father," Isaias whispered.

There was another pause that went on far too long, even though Isaias knew it was only seconds ticking by. "A phone call confession is a bit unconventional, I'll admit," the bishop said. "But of course, my son. If you are in need at such an hour, it must be important. You may confess to me any time your soul is troubled. I am always available for your spiritual deliverance, Isaias. You know that."

Isaias took a breath. He needed to be honest here, or at least as honest as he could be. His heart and soul needed to be unburdened if he were to perform an exorcism. He needed to be pious and true. Pure. But were there not fears that he could not bring himself to confess?

Isaias began: "Bless me, Father, for I have sinned. It has been too long since my last Confession. My sins—my sins are many. I have lied. I have felt things die, felt them die in my heart, and never told anyone of the darkness that brings into my mind. I have used my gifts from God in ways that He surely did not intend, in ways that you have advised me not to. I have indulged in superstition. I have allowed myself to be tempted by wrongful thoughts, though I have not given into them. I have neglected, at times, the care of my spiritual self.

"I have doubted my birth family—resented that they gave me up, even though it was into the care of God and His house. I have doubted you. I have doubted, at times, even God and His signs. I have allowed myself to be misguided by signs of the Devil himself. And finally, I have despaired, instead of embracing God's love. I have doubted my place as God's child and as a carrier of His Word. I have thought myself unworthy of His forgiveness, the ultimate betrayal of God's loving nature."

Isaias's eyes pricked with tears, and he bowed his head as he awaited the bishop's response. Isaias had confessed many of these pains before, or variations of them. Many, but not all. And he felt guilt each time, as all of them still weighed on him even now. He needed to give them time to sink in for the bishop.

Was there more to confess? More to relieve from his soul? He wondered if he should confess to everything he had ever felt, everything he had ever wanted. He could barely categorize his own emotions, but he felt that so many of them must have been wrong—his emotions were to be wielded by God, not by any man, least of all Isaias. There were more doubts in Isaias's mind. And he could not bring himself to confess perhaps the more salient secret of them all: that he was about to contend with the forces of darkness without the authorization of his bishop. He would be putting himself, Hector, and likely even Violet in danger. Even more, he would be putting their *souls* in danger. He would go with God in his heart, but not with a blessing.

But how much choice did he have? Could they afford to wait? Could they afford to risk that Bishop Reid would simply tell him not to do it at all?

Isaias couldn't take that risk.

The pause dragged on, and Isaias wondered if the bishop expected more. If he suspected that Isaias was still lying by omission. Isaias was afraid, suddenly, that the bishop could see through him, read into his heart across the distance. That he was, against all odds, like Isaias and had simply never told him. Wrong as it was, he was afraid, and chilled by more than the frigid night air.

Suddenly, the bishop began: "God, the Father of mercies, through the death and the resurrection of His Son..."

Isaias followed suit: "My God, I am sorry for my sins with all my heart. In choosing to do wrong, and in failing to do good, I have sinned against You whom I should love above all things..."

"...and I absolve you from your sins in the name of the Father, and of the Son, and of the Holy Spirit."

"...our saviour Jesus Christ suffered and died for us. In His name, God have mercy."

There was a long, heavy pause on the phone line. Once again, the bishop seemed to want more. Isaias wished he could give him what he wanted, but he couldn't. He had to betray his trust. The fate of Hector's soul was more important.

"Thank you, Father," Isaias said. "I'll let you go now, so that you might sleep. I'm sorry for disturbing you so late, Your Excellency."

After another pause, Bishop Reid said, "Of course, my son. Thank you for your confession. It is always worthwhile to divest yourself in the name of God. And Isaias?"

Once more, Isaias was afraid that, somehow, the bishop knew. "Yes, Father?"

"I—Peace be with you, Isaias."

Isaias relaxed. "And with your spirit, Your Excellency."

The phone line ended in a definitive beep to indicate the bishop had disconnected. Isaias lowered his phone but stood there listening to the night air and watching his phone screen for a moment, halfway expecting the bishop to call him back, to tell him he knew Isaias was doing something he shouldn't be, that he was making a terrible mistake. Better yet, that the bishop would take it from here—he had a more direct line with God, after all, and could make the problem simply go away. He could save Hector's soul, not Isaias.

When nothing happened, and all he heard was the sound of distant traffic and the rustling of birds in the trees, he put the phone away, and turned to go back into the Montero home.

XVI

THERE WAS ONLY ONE logical place to hold the exorcism, though it was difficult to convince the still somewhat delirious Hector to get up and make the journey to the church. He had wondered if it might be worth it to simply hold the exorcism in Hector's own home, where he already was, but he would feel better—and frankly *safer*—if he were in his house of God. He would have everything he might need, he thought, and God would be close by; Isaias was sure he would feel His presence there, which was surely beneficial to casting out a demon. He had told Violet and Hector this, that it was better than doing it in their home, and they had somewhat reluctantly agreed to move.

It was a challenge for Isaias to help Hector, who was weak and still not fully aware of himself and his own body, even to his own car. Violet trailed behind, watching for any signs of trouble, before giving Isaias the car keys. They put Hector in the backseat—Isaias didn't want him within easy reach of the wheel—and Violet sat in the passenger seat while Isaias took the driver's seat. Violet had offered to drive so that Isaias could keep a watchful eye on Hector, but Isaias had said he would feel better if he took the wheel.

The drive to the church, albeit not far, felt tense—Isaias watched for anything suspicious, and felt nervous every time he drove over a patch of ice or a bit of snow.

The demon never seized Hector or made for the wheel, and they arrived safer than Isaias had expected. But after they parked and started to walk up the path to the church, through a gentle snowfall, Hector froze in place, causing Isaias and Violet to stop with him. Isaias, still holding Hector's arm to keep him balanced—and, perhaps more importantly, close by—turned to look at him. Hector was shaking his head slowly from side to side.

"I'm not going in there," he said, low and emphatic. There was a darkness in his voice that Isaias couldn't place and that brought ice to his blood. "I'm not."

His heart sinking, Isaias asked, "Hector?"

"I'm not going in there," Hector repeated. His voice was still his own, but it was filled with the abject terror that Isaias imagined might come from inside a man facing his damnation. Isaias contemplated reaching out to his emotions, verifying it was truly Hector, not a demonic imposter, but he was scared to feel Hector's fear. Isaias worried it would make him finally lose his nerve if he felt that pain for himself.

"Hector," Isaias said gently. He tried to put an emotional push behind him, something to tell Hector he was safe with Isaias, but it was difficult without opening up his heart to Hector's emotions, too. "You have to."

Violet approached cautiously from her near distance. Putting her weight more prominently on one crutch, she reached out with the other hand to touch her father's elbow. Isaias could see the pain in her eyes as she looked up to Isaias and her father. "Please, dad."

"No," Hector repeated. His voice trembled, and Isaias saw Violet look at where her hand touched her father's arm. He saw it, too, then: the shaking in Hector's extremities, shivering like an intense cold had come over him, freezing beyond the measure of frost around them.

Isaias was about to say something, to try to encourage Hector to *fight*, to fight whatever was telling him not to go into the Church, maybe even dare to open his soul up to what Hector was feeling just so that he could ease his fears, when he heard footsteps on the path behind him, boots crunching through freshly fallen snow.

Isaias turned in place and halted where he stood, panic overcoming him. "Mrs. Marsh?" he asked, disbelieving of the fact that he was seeing her there, in the darkest part of the night in the darkest month, wrapped up in a thick winter coat and a scarf over what appeared to be pajamas pants, as if she had hurried out of her home without dressing fully for the weather.

"The Bishop—Bishop Reid—he called me," she explained softly. She was looking directly at Isaias, for the most part, but her worried eyes flicked nervously to Hector and Violet. Maybe she could tell that something was wrong. "He didn't tell me anything, really, but he said that he was worried about you, Father. Since I live closer, I told him I would come see what was going on. Keep an eye on you, you see. We both thought that whatever was troubling you must have been serious if you felt that you should call him in the middle of the night."

Isaias cleared his throat. Looked back at Hector and Violet. He felt wisps of Hector's fear, and a waft of Violet's worry. He turned to face Mrs. Marsh again and said, "Mrs. Marsh, you should go home."

Mrs. Marsh looked curiously at him. Isaias could detect a speckling of what she felt too: confusion, concern. "What's going on, Father? Are you alright?"

Isaias hesitated. He did not want to lie to Mrs. Marsh, nor worry her more by dismissing her without an explanation, but—

"Stay away," Hector said, in a voice that was not entirely his own; something sickly sweet about it in its low baritone. Isaias's blood ran cold. He wanted to stop Hector—whatever was inside of Hector—from saying anything to Mrs. Marsh, but he couldn't think of anything to interject with fast enough. "Yes, stay away, Mrs. Marsh, unless you want to join your husband in the grave."

Mrs. Marsh eyes widened, and Isaias felt her shock. "Mr. Montero? I don't take kindly to threats."

"He's not himself, right now," Isaias cautioned, as if that was a real explanation. It wasn't untrue, but he knew that it would tell her nothing. He had to get her to leave, preferably by her own will. "But I'm going to help him. I think you shouldn't be here for this, Mrs. Marsh. Please go home." He didn't say, *I don't know if I can protect Violet, let alone the both of you.*

Mrs. Marsh took a few strides closer. Her eyes were bright. Isaias could feel her resolution, even marred as it was by her worry. Like Violet had been that first day she came to Isaias's church, she was confident even when she was afraid. "Father, if there's trouble, I'm going to be here for it. His Excellency may not be here to watch over you, but you're like a son to me, too, not just to Bishop Reid. I'm not going to let you get in over your head with anything."

Isaias exchanged a glance with Violet, who was stepping away from her trembling father. She looked at Isaias with helpless eyes. It seemed she didn't know what to do any more than Isaias did.

It had been bad enough to lie to the bishop, who was far away, but it felt like quite another to lie to Mrs. Marsh's face, with her right in front of him. She was kind and motherly to Isaias, who barely remembered his birth mother, and she had come out to his rectory at one in the morning simply because she was worried about him. If Isaias lied to her now, he would feel the need to confess all over again. There was something unforgivable about it.

Isaias looked at Mrs. Marsh and hesitated. He asked, "Do you believe in the Devil, Mrs. Marsh?"

Mrs. Marsh immediately crossed herself, from brow to breast, her eyes fluttering closed as she did so before she looked squarely at Isaias again. "I do, Father. I'm a devout Catholic, you know."

"I know, Mrs. Marsh," Isaias sighed. "But then you should know how dangerous this could become. You see, Hector is—he's—"

Mrs. Marsh's face was blank a moment, then filled with dull surprise, followed by horror. "Is this man possessed, Father?" she asked.

Isaias looked at Mrs. Marsh with his own confusion. Where he had taken days to convince, Mrs. Marsh was willing to accept it immediately. "You believe me?"

Mrs. Marsh's gaze held steady, something fierce in her eyes. "Of course I do, Father. Am I correct then? Is he possessed by a demon?"

Isaias nodded gravely. "I'm afraid so, Mrs. Marsh. And I intend to help him."

"Oh, Father. Bless this poor man's soul." Mrs. Marsh crossed herself again, murmuring a half-heard prayed under her breath, her words swallowed up by the gentle snow around them. Without further hesitation, she walked past Isaias, Hector, and Violet, and said, "Come on, then. Let me make you all some tea. You're going to have a long night ahead of you."

Isaias stared at Mrs. Marsh's back as she walked the last few paces to the church. He paused there, watching her without following.

Violet spoke, voicing the hesitation Isaias himself felt, the shock that Mrs. Marsh was so quick to support them. "You really do believe us?"

Mrs. Marsh didn't even turn around to face the three of them again. "Well, Violet," she said as she fished out her keys and opened the door, "I believe in Father Isaias. And I believe in possession, and I believe in the rite of exorcism. If you're certain that your father is possessed, then it's not my place to doubt how well you know your own father, or Isaias's spiritual expertise, or what it is that you need to do. It *is* an exorcism that you're planning, isn't it?"

Isaias glanced at Violet, who was looking at him with an expression that he dared not try to read the emotions behind, and then he looked back to Mrs. Marsh. "It is. But I don't want to put you in any danger, Mrs. Marsh. I don't know what it is that might happen in there."

"Well, I don't want you to be in danger either, Father, and I might be more help than you think. Demons can threaten me all they want," she added, casting a withering look at Hector, who remained quiet except for his breathing, staring blankly, "but I'm not going to let them put you in danger on my watch. If you are going to be facing Hell, Father, you shouldn't be turning away *anyone* willing to be your ally."

Isaias hesitated. He had so many questions, about *why* she was so quick to believe, why she felt so certain that she could help. He didn't want to doubt, though. Not someone like her, who was wise even beyond her years and who had unquestioningly been there for him—and was evidently there for him even when staring down the depths of Hell. "No, I suppose I shouldn't. Thank you, Mrs. Marsh."

Isaias placed a hand on the silent Hector's back and tried to urge him forward while Violet walked up to join the patient Mrs. Marsh.

Hector did not move.

"Hector, please," Isaias said gently. He moved around Hector's side to look his friend in the eye. Hector's breathing was ragged, and his eyes were somewhat glazed, unfocused. They were moving back and forth, almost twitching, like he was deep asleep but with his eyes held open. "Hector..."

"Don't touch me, *priest*," a voice said, falling from Hector's lips like spittle. The words seemed to freeze over in the night air, though Hector's breath did not frost as it was supposed to. Isaias was reminded of a performance he had seen once, a ventriloquist and his dummy, the thrown voice, the way it sounded disembodied when he knew where it was supposed to be coming from. "*Hector* is not going in there."

Isaias didn't allow himself to hesitate this time, seizing both of Hector's shoulders in his hands. Even through Hector's winter coat, even through Isaias's gloves, Hector's body felt ice cold. Isaias felt a wave of nausea as emotions hit him; Hector's fear was distant but unmistakable, wrapped up in something else that Isaias was beginning to recognize as the infernal emotions of the demon. Something pained and sick. He almost pulled away at the thought that he was sensing something of the demon's soul—if he even had a soul—but he held fast. He wouldn't let go of Hector. Not now. "Hector, I need you to fight this thing and whatever it's telling you. I know you're in there. You're almost there. You need to get to the church, and we can pray for you. We can save you—"

"I said," the voice coming from just outside of Hector growled, *"don't touch me, priest."*

Hector smelled of burning, and his shoulders went suddenly from unnaturally cold to hot to the touch, almost hot enough to burn even through the protective layers. While it hurt to hold onto him, Isaias refused to let go. It couldn't be real, and Hector needed Isaias to stay strong. For him. "Hector," he said, as calmly as he could possibly muster. He still heard his own voice tremble through his bravado. "Hector, fight this. Please."

"I—Isaias—I—"

"Hector, please," Isaias repeated. "You can do this."

"I—can't—"

"You *can*, Hector," Isaias insisted. The heat coming off of Hector was getting worse, but Isaias kept holding on, even as he felt sweat building in his palms. "Let me—let *us*—help you."

Hector trembled, tears filling his eyes. "Isaias, I'm sorry. Violet, I'm sorry. Lily, I'm sorry."

"Is that—?"

The question was cut off as Hector screamed out loud, a gurgling cry like an animal caught in a trap. With a sudden, jerking movement, he pushed Isaias off him, breaking the hold that Isaias had been desperately trying to keep on Hector, sending him sprawling to the ground. The water bottle in Isaias's coat pocket crumpled as he landed on it, bursting and soaking blessed water into the fabric of his coat, immediately chilling him. Isaias yelped in pain as he fell to the stone pathway, scraping open the palms of his gloves and tearing into his skin. He felt the sting of raw wounds, blood and snow mingling under his hands as he looked up at Hector with alarm.

Hector was hunched over, head bowed toward the ground, breathing heavily and raggedly again; laboured. His shoulders shook with the exertion of this hyperventilation. Isaias scrambled for the half-crushed bottle of water in his coat pocket, trying to prevent it from losing all of the holy water that suddenly felt desperately needed, but he couldn't take his eyes off of Hector.

"Dad!" he heard Violet cry from afar, followed by muffled murmuring from Mrs. Marsh. Isaias would have to trust Mrs. Marsh to take care of Violet. Isaias's limbs felt numb, but he knew that he had to protect them both from whatever might happen with Hector. And he needed to protect Hector from whatever was happening inside of him. He slowly rose, his body aching from where he had fallen on the pavement of the walkway, his palms stinging from where the asphalt had torn them up and where he had left bloody smears in the snowmelt. He lifted the partially emptied water bottle as he did so. He could feel the sopping wet copy of the Bible still in his pocket, could imagine the ink running from where holy water was surely ruining the good word.

Isaias swallowed hard and looked at Hector. He said, in his bravest voice, "Come with me."

The thing in Hector grinned, lips furling and baring Hector's teeth. For a moment, Isaias imagined blood in Hector's mouth. "Make me, *priest.*"

Isaias crossed himself and said, trying to compel his voice to become stronger, more sure, less afraid, "I order you, by the power invested in me by God, our Lord in Heaven, to *come with me.*"

Hector's head shot up, straightening from the hunched position he had been in, a rapid, disconnected movement that gave Isaias whiplash to look at. Hector hissed at him, a strange snake-like sound in the back of his throat that ended in a gurgle like too much saliva was gathering in his mouth.

And he lunged.

Isaias threw the holy water, plastic bottle and all, at the demon.

Hector's body stumbled back as the bottle hit him and, more importantly, holy water splashed onto him. He hissed louder, crying out in that unnatural, growling voice, clawing at his body where the water had splashed him, soaking into his clothes, chilling him. The bottle fell to the ground and Isaias took this instant of safety to unlatch the rosary from his neck with fumbling hands. He held it out toward the thing in Hector. The smell of roses and sandalwood intensified, nearly overpowering him. Isaias snapped, "By the power vested in me by God, I order you to stop!"

Isaias became aware as the demon's cries trailed off that there was a dim hissing, less like an animal now and more like steam from water hitting a hot stove. His heart raced, his pulse pounding in the wounds in his palms. He was afraid of hurting Hector, but he had to stop this *thing* from hurting Hector worse than Isaias ever could. He had to be strong.

But the demon had stopped making noise, and Hector swayed on his feet.

Cautiously, Isaias lowered the rosary and put it in his dryer pocket, the one that did not hold the ruined Bible. He walked a few steps closer to Hector, who simply stood in place. Isaias forced himself to take several deep breaths, picturing the way his lungs would expand and contract so he could calm his pounding heart. He stepped closer and reached one hand out, holding it the way he would reach out to an animal as scared of him as he was of it. "Hector?" he asked. There was a moment of silence. "Hector, are you—are you alright?"

Hector shook for a moment, shoulders quaking. "I—" he began, voice quivering.

"Hector, it's okay," Isaias said, though it was far from it and his cracking voice probably showed it. There was nothing okay with any of these displays of something terribly, terribly wrong. He reached out further, daring to touch Hector's shoulder, only for the other man to shy away before he could make contact. "Hector?"

There was a moment where Hector simply shook. But then the quiet shakes turned into something audible.

Hector was laughing.

A chill ran down Isaias's spine at first. But the strange thing was, he smelled more vanilla and melted marshmallows than he smelled burning or fire. Carefully, he repeated, "Hector." A statement, not a question.

Hector buckled over as the laughing became hysterical; manic and delirious. Isaias stood, frozen for a moment, before he simply closed the few steps left to stand directly in front of Hector. Unsure what else to do, Isaias wrapped his arms around Hector in a tight hug, allowing Hector to collapse into his arms and for the laughter to morph first into strangled breaths, then hoarse sobbing. The contact caused Isaias to feel an erratic flow of emotion, moving so fast it was hard to track a single feeling for long enough to identify what it was. He allowed himself to feel Hector's fear, sorrow, anger. Ignoring the ache in his own heart, Isaias held Hector close to his chest, tightening his grip despite the stinging in his wounded hands. He let himself take all of the negative emotions in. His heart was sure to shatter under the force of all of Hector's pain, but it would all be worth it if he could ease even the smallest amount of everything that hurt Hector. Anything, he thought, if it meant that Hector could breathe a little easier. He tried to will Hector to believe him that he would keep him safe. That he cared too much about him to let this pain go on for long. That he would bear it all himself if it meant that Hector got a moment more of peace.

"I'm sorry, Hector," Isaias whispered. "I am so, so sorry."

Locking the door of the church office with only Hector inside, Isaias turned back to face Violet, who was hovering anxiously, watching him. He had insisted that Violet stay out of the room as long as Hector was still calm enough that Isaias could handle him himself. There was no reason for Violet to witness her father in pain more than she already had.

"Is he going to be okay?" Violet asked. Isaias was too exhausted to dare to reach out with his emotions to verify how he knew that she was feeling, weighed down by the lingering effects of Hector's pain, but he didn't have to. He could easily recognize in her wide eyes, in her stance, how she was feeling: frightened and heartbroken.

Isaias hesitated. If lying to Mrs. Marsh would have been hard, lying to Violet would be even harder. He had the sense that he would do it if it meant protecting her, but he thought that he could avoid it for the time being. All they had was each other, and they were united in their singular mission to save her father. Isaias said, as neutrally as he could manage, though his exhausted voice probably betrayed him, "I will do everything in my power to help him, Violet. I promise that much."

Violet frowned but, before she could answer anything on her mind, Mrs. Marsh appeared from the church kitchenette. "Tea?" she asked the both of them, pausing just in the doorway of the kitchen. "I've put on a pot for us."

Violet looked exhausted, too, but smiled anyway. Isaias wondered how much pain she must have been in—not just her heart and soul but her body. But here she was, pushing through it all. "That sounds really nice, Mrs. Marsh. Thank you."

Isaias smiled, too, despite the tired ache in his bones that made even smiling seem like too much effort. If Violet was braving the pain, it was the least he could do. Still, he shook his head. "As wonderful as that sounds, Mrs. Marsh, I think I'm going to pass."

Mrs. Marsh frowned at Isaias, but didn't immediately say anything, instead heading back into the kitchen. Isaias and Violet stood in silence while they waited for her to return. Isaias was sure that Violet had more to say, but he stood close to the door of the office and listened for any signs of Hector while he picked idly at strands of acrylic and cotton from his ruined winter gloves that stuck to his bloody palms. Mrs. Marsh returned a minute later with a cup of tea for Violet.

"Thanks, Mrs. Marsh," Violet said, accepting it. She didn't drink any of the tea at first, simply holding the hot mug in one hand, leaning her weight on one crutch and blowing on the steam. Isaias wasn't sure if Violet even drank tea, but she seemed comforted by the gesture, so that was all that really mattered.

"Are you planning on eating or drinking anything at all, Father?" Mrs. Marsh asked.

He shook his head. "I think that I should fast, actually," he said. "It seems the best way to ensure that I am as pure of mind and body as I can be."

Violet, about to have a sip of her tea, paused. "Should I be fasting, too, Father?"

Isaias frowned at her. "I won't ask you to do that, Violet."

Violet echoed his frown back at him, then at her tea, then held her mug back to Mrs. Marsh with a sad smile. "I think that I should fast, too," she said.

While Mrs. Marsh hesitated to take the tea back, Isaias shook his head. "It's okay, Violet," he said. "It only matters for the priest hosting the exorcism. You're there as support, so it's more important for you to keep up your strength instead." He didn't know if it was true—he wasn't even sure he knew what either of their roles entailed, he felt too much like he was making it up as he went—but Violet nodded in understanding and kept her tea, so he counted it as a win.

"Okay," Violet said. She sipped her tea. Isaias, seeing the flicker of relief on her face as she drank the tea, as well as the proud look he received from Mrs. Marsh, knew that he had made the right decision. Violet needed any moment of peace she could get.

Mrs. Marsh glanced at Isaias's hands, where he was still picking at loose threads stuck to his wounds. She tsked at him and shook her head. "Let me get the first aid kit," she said. A part of Isaias didn't want her to treat the wounds—would the pain not bring clarity to his mind?—but he resisted the urge to argue. Instead, he nodded and waited for her to return with the small first aid kit from the church bathroom. He held out one hand at a time as she took antiseptic wipes—wincing as she did so—and cleaned his palms. "What now, Father?" she asked. "Do you know what you need?"

Truthfully, Isaias didn't know, and while he hesitated to answer so earnestly, he didn't think it would do any good to beat around the bush.

"Well, I haven't exactly received permission from my bishop to do this. So, I don't have access to the documents that I need to perform a proper exorcism, but—"

Violet cleared her throat, and Isaias looked to her. She was blushing, looking away bashfully. She said, "I have them."

"What?"

Violet looked up at Isaias, meeting his eye nervously, but with her chin held high in an attempt at self-assuredness. "I pirated them."

"You—" Isaias managed a startled laugh. But he saw the way that Violet looked like she was ready for a scolding, and so he broke away from Mrs. Marsh's attempts to bandage his hands and hugged Violet. She moved her mug of tea out of the way and didn't hug him back—her weight was balanced on one of her crutches—but she melted into the gesture. Isaias wondered how long it had been since her father, not himself, had hugged her. Violet stilled, relaxed, then leaned her forehead against his shoulder. Isaias felt her stop shrinking in on herself and instead bloom a little more in her confidence. "You're brilliant, Vi."

"You're not mad?" she asked as Isaias let go of her.

"I'm not acting on the authorization of a bishop. I didn't tell His Excellency what I was planning on doing. I think I would be a hypocrite if I complained about you retrieving the documents another way, wouldn't I?"

Violet smiled a little. "I *did* do my research, Father."

"I appreciate it," Isaias said softly. "These are extenuating circumstances, Violet. I think that God can forgive each of us our transgressions in this moment. So long as," he added with a wry smile, "we are contrite."

Violet looked at Isaias with a grave face, but her lips twitched tellingly. "I am very sorry that I illegally downloaded the supplications on exorcism," she said. "But I will do *anything* to save my dad from Hell."

Her conviction was heartwarming, even in the face of the fear that they all felt. Isaias smiled sadly. "So, will I, Violet. Anything."

Noticing that Mrs. Marsh was quiet, Isaias took a moment to look at her, to take her in. He wanted to think that she was too good for this, for whatever was that was going to come now. Too kind-hearted to face the demonic. But he could say much the same of Violet, could he not? Violet was too good for this. Too young, in fact, to become so jaded to the world. Isaias knew, though, that if he dared to consider asking Violet to reconsider her involvement, he would feel her anger, her pain, her betrayal. After all, she had been the one to come to Isaias for help. She had been the one who had to convince Isaias that there was something truly wrong with her father. And he knew that there was no way that Violet would leave her father's side. Not when he was suffering. And Mrs. Marsh would surely be angry that Isaias doubted her need to be there for *him*.

Hesitantly, Isaias let his guard down; opened himself up to their feelings. He could use their certainty.

Mrs. Marsh finished cleaning and bandaging Isaias's hands while Isaias felt out the emotions of her and Violet instead of contemplating his own. After a moment, he said, "I want you both to know that I will not let anything happen to you, no matter what happens in that room tonight."

Mrs. Marsh shook her head. "I'd say that of you," she replied. "I've made a promise to your Bishop—your *father*—that I would always look out for you, Father—Isaias. I won't leave your side, no matter the risk."

Violet, who had at first been looking to Isaias with wide eyes, relaxed her shoulders then lifted her head. "Me, too. You need us in there. We'll have your back as much as you'll have ours."

Before Isaias could try to argue—though he wasn't sure that he could—a crash came from inside the church office, followed by unintelligible yelling. Isaias moved closer to the door, pausing there. He heard a voice—*Hector's* voice, or a mockery of it—shouting in languages Isaias couldn't place, the words seeming to morph mid-syllable, sometimes overlapping. The words jumbled, then reformed in English.

"You'll all *rot*. Starting with him."

Isaias hesitated, then looked first to Violet, then to Mrs. Marsh. He thought that both of them looked frail in light of what they were going to face, together or not. Did they think the same of him, or did they have faith where he did not?

Both nodded to him, in turn. Isaias took a breath.

"Let us begin."

Hector,

I don't think I ever told you that I have dreamt of you. Like a beatific vision, you appeared to me, haloed by radiant light. I don't know what it meant, or if it had to mean anything at all. Maybe it was just my subconscious recognizing the divine in you.

I worried, at the time, that I was putting too much on you, so that's why I didn't tell you. And now, you have a dark presence in you, and I'm scared I'll never have an opportunity to tell you just how special you are. And here I am, wishing they had taken me instead.

It doesn't feel ironic, though, so much as prophetic: you are so *good* that of course the demonic had to come for you. Taking your goodness is a loss for the world, and a win for the forces of Hell, because what better way to crush hope than to take the best among us?

My loss would be nothing like yours, so of course it is you they wanted.

I'm sorry, Hector. For what I failed to tell you, and for

all the pain you bear, and for the fact that I can only do
so much to take that pain away from you. If we make
it out of this alive, I promise you I won't hold back.
I will tell you that you are divine. I will tell you that I
worship your goodness. I will tell you that you are a
bright light in this world. My world.
So please, Hector. Make it through to the other side.
I'll be waiting for you there.
Isaias

XVII

Isaias stood in the small Church bathroom, splashing water on his face to centre himself. He was tired, it was late, and he hadn't slept well in several days. Violet and Mrs. Marsh were in the kitchenette, waiting for Isaias to be ready. Distantly, he could feel their emotions wafting through the halls like smoke. He was familiar enough with them by now that he could trace their positions in the church, recognize the shape of their feelings. Even afraid, the sense of their souls was a comfort, drifting along the edge of his awareness.

Scrubbing wet hands across his face and through his hair to wake himself up, Isaias tried to avoid getting his uniform wet. Mrs. Marsh had retrieved his change of clothes from the rectory. He was now dressed in full regalia: cassock, surplice, a violet stole. The choice of colour seemed fitting. It was suitable, yes, to wear the colours of Jesus Christ's sorrow and suffering, but he was aware of the other significance of the vivid purple, with Violet just downstairs. Christ's suffering, the colour of healing, and the colour of the young woman who had brought her father to Isaias for help. He tugged on the sleeves of the surplice, feeling like it no longer fit him. That was ridiculous, of course. Nothing had changed about him in the past few days to make it no longer fit. He adjusted it a few more times, trying to make it rest on him more comfortably. It took a few tries before he gave up, accepting the fact that this was all going to feel wrong no matter what he did.

Everything about this was wrong, after all. What was one more thing?

Isaias sighed, then crossed himself. He clasped his hands together and prayed, ignoring the way his hands shook.

"Lord Jesus Christ, Word of God the Father, and God of all creation," he whispered to himself, "who gave authority to Your holy apostles to subject demons in your name and to tread underfoot all the power of the enemy...

"I humbly invoke Your holy name with fear and trembling, that, strengthened by Your power, I may attack with confidence the evil spirit who torments this your creature...

"Amen."

He didn't know if God was listening. He hoped He was.

He heard nothing in reply.

Slowly, Isaias unclasped his hands and examined his regalia once more. He didn't think he could make it perfect. He didn't think he could make himself perfect. Even with having confessed to his Bishop and father, he did not think he would ever be pure of heart enough to be truly ready for whatever came next.

That didn't mean it wasn't unavoidable.

Isaias opened the door of the bathroom and took a steadying breath before he exited. Mrs. Marsh stepped out of the kitchenette first, taking careful steps to avoid spilling the bowl of water she held, followed moments later by Violet.

Violet, grave faced and serious, looked to Isaias. Her voice was steady and she stood tall despite the fear Isaias could picture dripping from her spirit. "Ready?"

Isaias nodded but made no reply. He tried to extend his emotions to Violet, to bring her confidence, but he hesitated to know what to share with her.

In the end, he settled on love. He loved her as his own child, and maybe knowing how sincerely he cared for her would help her feel safe. Confusion flashed across Violet's emotions, then a shadow of understanding that bloomed into her own love. Her love for her father and, indeed, for Isaias, too. He didn't know what he had done to deserve that love—he hadn't saved Hector, after all—but it touched his soul to feel the echo of his own love reflected back at him.

Isaias blinked back tears and turned to face Mrs. Marsh, who raised the bowl of water like a devotional. Violet was studying Isaias, who bowed his head as he took the water from Mrs. Marsh with a quiet "Thank you." He held the hold in one hand while he made the sign of the cross over it with the other, and he prayed. "O water, I exorcise you in the name of God the Father Almighty, and in the name of Jesus Christ His Son, our Lord, and in the power of the Holy Spirit," he said, crossing himself thrice, at the moments where he needed to do so. "I exorcise you so that you may put to flight all power of the enemy, and be able to root out and supplant that enemy—"

There was a loud banging from inside the office, followed by a hollering. Isaias saw Violet flinch, but he closed his eyes to it. Instead, he continued: "—with his apostate angels, through the power of our Lord Jesus Christ, who will come to judge the living and the dead and the world by fire."

"Amen," Mrs. Marsh replied.

"Amen," Violet replied.

"Let us pray," Isaias started. He led them both in prayer, only to be interrupted, once more, by the banging. Isaias gritted his teeth, hoping to push through, hoping to force himself to get through the prayer so that they would be ready.

"Father," Violet interrupted this time, "maybe we should…"

Isaias closed his eyes and counted backwards from five. When he opened his eyes he said, "You're right." Lowering the bowl of blessed water and cradling it in both hands, he nodded to Mrs. Marsh, who fished out the key to the study and went to unlock it. "Wait," Isaias said, one last doubt attacking his mind. He had thought he could not ask Violet or Mrs. Marsh to not be here, but he knew in his heart that he needed to give them one last opportunity to back out. "Both of you—*neither* of you need to be here for this," he reminded them. "If either of you were in danger, I—"

"Don't be stupid, Father," Violet snapped, and Isaias felt the flare of anger that he had expected. It didn't supplant the love he felt in her heart, but instead the flames of each emotion fed the other. "It's my dad. I *have* to be here."

Mrs. Marsh just smiled sadly, saying nothing, and unlocked the door.

The heavy wooden door flung open in an instant, and Isaias stepped back in response, narrowly missing getting hit by it. The holy water sloshed in the bowl, some spilling onto Isaias's hands, soaking into his bandages.

Mrs. Marsh was less lucky, knocked to the floor by the force of the opening, crying out in pain as she hit the floorboards. "Oh, Lord above," she said, her voice strained with not the pain of it, but the fear.

"Mrs. Marsh—" Isaias started, but Violet was already by the older woman's side. She crouched, lowering herself on her crutches to check on the older woman for a moment, then nodded to Isaias.

"I'm okay, Father," Mrs. Marsh said softly as she pulled herself up, gently waving Violet off. "A demon would have to do much more than knock me on my bottom for me to not want to help you fulfill your mission."

Isaias braced to retort but paused and nodded. With a heavy, fearful heart, he looked up and into the office.

Hector sat in the centre of the room, tied to Isaias's desk chair by his wrists with rope. The stained-glass window of Mary above him cast dim moonlight in red and gold around the room. Mary's Sacred Heart was still broken and pasted with paper, leaving a patch of darkness that landed on Hector, leaving him a mere shadow. Even in darkness, Isaias could see that Hector was grinning at them like a vicious cartoon, the smile too big for his face. He looked *eager*. Isaias's hands, cradling the bowl of holy water, went numb, but still he stepped into the room, Violet and Mrs. Marsh a mere step behind him.

"Ready, *priest*?" the voice in Hector was asking, slow and slick, poison dripping from each word. "Are we ready to *rumble*, Father?"

Isaias stood steady. He would not let himself be goaded so easily. He took a deep breath and looked to the crucifix that hung on the back wall. He looked at the bookshelves with books designed to make faith easier for people, though it could never truly be easy. He looked to the portrait of Mary in his window, broken hearted though she was. He smelled roses and wondered if it was his own mother somehow watching over him, tied to him by the rosary he still wore around his neck, or if Mary herself watched over him now.

The door slammed behind Isaias, Mrs. Marsh, and Violet. While Isaias tensed, he did not jump, and nor did either of the women. Instead, he set the bowl of holy water down on his desk and retrieved his rosary and his waterlogged Bible. The Bible he set on the desk as well, but the rosary he held fast. He turned to face the demon in Hector, who watched him still with a wicked grin.

"In the name of the Father, and of the Son, and of the Holy Spirit," Isaias began through tight lips as the smell of rot and fire abruptly filled his nostrils. He had to push down the nausea as the sickly sweet and decayed scent filled the room. He could not, would not, be cowed by so simple a trick.

"Amen," Violet and Mrs. Marsh said behind Isaias.

The demon strained against the rope bonds at Hector's wrists, but with a leisurely slowness. The sight of Isaias, in his priest's garb, with his holy water and his rosary and his Bible, did not frighten it in the slightest. "What's this?" it asked in the mockery of Hector's voice.

"Ropes *and* witnesses? I never would have guessed *these* to be your kinks, *Father.*"

Isaias tried not to gag on the scent that washed over him with the taunts, increasingly stronger, all-encompassing. Someone had set fire to weeks' old garbage—spiritually speaking. Isaias continued, with a strained voice, "May God, the almighty Father, who desires that *everyone* be saved, be with you all."

"And with your spirit," Violet and Mrs. Marsh said behind him.

Hector's face was grinning ear to ear now, the smile somehow stretching even farther than it already had. Isaias momentarily thought that Hector's lips would split from the strain of it, his face cracking and defiling Hector's smile for good. Instead, he shook his head slowly, or the thing wearing him did. "And with your spirit," he repeated, mockingly, as if he were mere witness to the rites.

Isaias wet his hand in the bowl of holy water on his desk before he stood before Hector. His fingers wet, he sprinkled the holy water onto Hector. The demon-voice screamed wordlessly at him, the howl of an injured animal, something that had been hurt and didn't understand why. He caught a wave of his confusion and his anguish—it almost made him feel sorry for the demon, except that it was *Hector's* face that wore that pain.

"Behold water that has been blessed," Isaias said, keeping his voice steady. He made the sign of the cross over Hector's body. Hector's eyes, eyes that had always looked kind, looked *angry.* "May salvation and life be ours in the name of the Father, and of the Son, and of the Holy Spirit."

He heard Violet and Mrs. Marsh echo another, "Amen."

As the convulsions in the demon's body faded away into mild tremors, a light twitching against the ropes, his head rolled on his neck, chin touching his chest, before slowly lifting his gaze. The demon locked his eyes on Isaias's and licked his lips—Hector's tongue, Hector's lips—the appendage seeming too long, too thin, not human enough. Isaias tried to hold his gaze, fearing that if he backed away, the demon would see through him. That close, though, his fingers still damp with holy water as his hand hovered just above the crown of Hector's head and able to smell the sickening sweet scent of the demon, he couldn't keep the demon's eye long. Isaias looked away as he stepped back. He saw the demon smirking in his peripheral.

Isaias cleared his throat and tried to pivot. He turned back to Mrs. Marsh and Violet, who waited patiently for his direction. He took a breath but was aware of the way that he shook slightly; imperceptible, he hoped, to the two women. He had to lead them.

Closing his eyes, Isaias said, "Remember not, O Lord, our offences, nor those of our parents; neither take retribution for our sins."

"Isaias." His name sounded like a breath of air, barely audible—for a moment, he wasn't sure if he had really heard it. But the voice was one he knew well. Anytime, anyplace, he would not—could not—forget that voice. Opening his eyes, he turned to face Hector, still sat in the chair. There was something different in his eyes, maybe pleading, maybe hurt. But still not Hector. He would know Hector's eyes, after all.

Isaias stepped close again and made the sign of the cross over Hector. He mouthed the words of the Our Father to himself, this habitual, ritual prayer one that he knew better, that felt more comfortable and familiar. At its close, he raised his voice to a more audible volume. "Lead us not into temptation," he said, "but deliver us from evil."

"Amen," all in the room, save Hector, echoed. Hector stared at him still, his eyes growing dimmer, unfocused. Hector watched his movements, the cross made by his hand, tracing its movement, but somehow seemed to look through him.

Isaias tried another prayer, another plea. Another saviour. "Holy Mary," he said, "Mother of God, pray for us sinners, now and the hour of our death."

He saw a smirk manifest itself on Hector's lips. Isaias tried another. "I believe in God," he said, "the Father Almighty, Creator of Heaven and earth..."

Hector's eyes still tracked Isaias, but the demon remained silent. There was something vulnerable in his stare and Isaias, emboldened, stepped forward and began to make the sign of the cross over Hector once again, close enough to hear Hector breathing. "Oh Jesus," he said. "Forgive us our sins and lead all souls to Heaven, especially those in the most need of Thy mercy. O—Jesus!"

Isaias tore his hand out of his half-finished cross, taking an instinctive step back, feeling the *drag* of Hector's blunt teeth against his skin, ripping, tearing, drawing blood. Hector's bite lost purchase as Isaias fell backwards into his desk, but not before they tore a strip of bandage and flesh out of Isaias's hand. The bowl on the desk sloshed as Isaias collided with it, spilling holy water onto him. It poured down his back and pooled on the floorboards as Isaias cradled his bitten hand in its opposite.

"Father!" Violet called out, coming closer.

"Stay back, Violet," Isaias said through gritted teeth. He tipped his head momentarily toward the ceiling, closing his eyes against the feeling of blood throbbing to the surface where Hector's teeth had broken skin on the side of his hand, the wound pulsing just below his little finger. "Lord, forgive me for taking Thy name in vain—"

"Oh, *Isaias*," Hector crooned, his voice trembling with some mixture of emotions that Isaias didn't dare try to identify. "You think your God cares enough to be listening? He doesn't give a shit about this one. Not with sin in every crevice of his mind, his body, his soul."

Isaias took a shaky breath, steeling himself through the pain and looking up at the man seated in the chair in front of him, straining against rope hard enough that he could see blood swelling at his wrists, leaving bruises that were already forming, ugly and purpled. Isaias's blood was in the teeth of Hector's grin, along with cotton threads of his bandage. Isaias wasn't sure if he should have been able to bite that hard. "Hector is no sinner," Isaias said, his voice tight as he pushed through the pain, though he wondered how he could know that for certain. He only knew that he believed whole-heartedly that Hector deserved better than all of this. "And even if he is, it wouldn't matter. He is worthy of God's love and mercy, just like the rest of us. God loves even those who feel unworthy. That's the beauty of God's love."

"Oh, fuck you," the demon said, spitting blood into Isaias's face, causing him to wince as it splattered across his cheek, some of it landing on his parted lips. "Don't project. God hasn't been capable of love in two thousand years. He poured all that love out, out, into His creations, until He had none left to give. Now He doesn't give a single shit about you. You fucking people just refuse to accept that maybe you don't *deserve* love anymore, that you fucked it up and you're no longer worthy."

Isaias dropped his bleeding right hand and used his left sleeve to wipe his own spat-back blood out of his face, staining the surplice with a smear of blood and spit. The murky red stain stared up at him. His hands shook. He would not, could not, accept the demon's words. Love was all he had. Love was all any of them had.

Demons lied because *they* had no love left to give. Not God.

Using his uninjured hand to push himself up off the floor, Isaias turned to face Violet and Mrs. Marsh. He knew it was his own fear reflected back at him in their eyes. Violet's flower-scent smelled like mildew and root rot more than it did the usual florals. Mrs. Marsh reminded Isaias more of spoiled meat than a home-cooked meal. Even being in this room was poisoning them. Isaias, too, was being poisoned, he could tell—for when had he ever doubted God's love before?

Or was the demon simply speaking what he hadn't wanted to accept?

He had to be strong. If he wavered, so too would Violet and Mrs. Marsh. Hector needed them. Needed him.

"Beloved sisters," Isaias began, "let us humbly implore the mercy of almighty God, that, moved by the intercession of all the Saints, He, in His kindness, will hear the voice of His church for our brother Hector, who is afflicted by dire need."

Isaias turned back to Hector and knelt, then. He took to his knees and clasped bloody hands together, forcing his way through the pain. He heard Mrs. Marsh join him in supplication behind him, though he knew that Violet remained standing.

"Oh, on your knees, now?" the demon asked, leering at him, Hector's mouth stained with so much red. Blood and saliva dripped down his chin and was caught in his beard. How much of the blood was even Isaias's? He worried for Hector. Feared for whatever the demon was doing to his insides. "Come on, then," he said. "Suck your man Hector off. It'd be about damn time, wouldn't it? Maybe you'd be a little less *uptight*."

Isaias grimaced, trying his best to ignore the demon still, but finding himself troubled. He had to ignore the taunting, ignoring the implications of *sin*, the way the demon was trying to dig his nails into any doubts that Isaias had ever felt, but he couldn't ignore it completely. He broke from his script long enough to say, "Violet?"

"Yes, Father?"

"I think you should leave the room."

"What?" Violet asked, and Isaias could feel the dull surprise—but also the temptation to flee—in her emotions.

"I don't think you should be here for this."

"*What*?" Violet repeated, but then the dumbfounded tone turned to one half-laughing. Isaias didn't look back at her from his position on his knees, couldn't fathom trying to meet her eyes, but also wanted to remain firm. "Is—Father, is *that* the line? You don't want me to hear... crude sex jokes, but you could stand me seeing him projectile vomit like in the movies, if it came to that?"

Isaias blushed but, before he could say anything, Mrs. Marsh cut in. "Father," she said, "With all due respect, I think that Violet needs to see this through, at this point. To know this thing is not her father, but also to know that you are doing everything in your power to save him."

"I think—" Isaias began.

"Isn't that *sweet*?" the demon's voice cut in from Hector's mouth. Isaias stared him down to the best of his ability, trying not to let the laughter creeping into Hector's mouth to cause him to lose his nerve. "What's the subtext there, Mrs. Marsh? So that she won't blame Father Fuck Up when he fails? She'll know he *tried* to save her dad before he croaked? How precious. *Gold star* for trying, right?"

Isaias's heart hammered in his chest. He closed his eyes and clasped his hands tighter before himself. He tried to ignore the sickly, sticky feeling of blood on his fingers where it had dripped from the wound on the side of his hand. Some of it was absorbed by the tattered bandages, but the rest dribbled down the side of his hand to his wrist. At least it was only his own. He hoped it was only his own. He rose his voice and said, "Lord, have mercy."

Violet and Mrs. Marsh replied, "Lord, have mercy."

"Christ, have mercy."

"Christ, have mercy."

"Lord, have mercy," Isaias repeated.

"Lord, have mercy," Violet and Mrs. Marsh dutifully replied.

"Holy Mary, Mother of God," Isaias intoned. He took comfort in the scent of roses from the rosary around his neck. He tried to ignore everything else, except for the voices of the two women behind him. He tried to ignore the strange feeling that the demon's taunts had left on his skin. He tried to ignore just how much it hurt to see Hector tied to a chair, babbling now, laughing between the gurgles in his throat, not a thing like the man that Isaias cared so much for.

"Pray for him," Violet and Mrs. Marsh evoked.

"Saints Michael, Gabriel, and Raphael."

"Pray for him."

"All holy angels of God," Isaias added.

"Pray for—"

"Pray for me!" the demon yelled, cutting them off with his shrieking. Isaias opened his eyes and saw Hector's body writhing violently in the chair, straining against the ropes, rocking back and forth like something was overtaking him, and felt the faintest glimmer of hope. "Oh, Lord have Mercy!" he called. "It hurts, it hurts—"

Suddenly, the demon stopped moving. Hector's body stilled, and Isaias became more afraid than hopeful, afraid for Hector, reaching out to touch his soul, confirm he was still breathing—then the demon laughed, Hector's chin lolling against his chest. "Oh, just *fucking* kidding," he said, voice low. "Pathetic, all of you. But I almost got you, right? You almost thought this might be *easy*, didn't you?"

Isaias felt his hands shaking and grasped them together tighter to prevent the movement. He could not be seen to be weak. He must continue. "Holy Elijah," he said, hoping his voice wasn't shaking the way that his hands were.

"Pray for him," Mrs. Marsh said.

An instant later, a distant echo, Violet repeated, "Pray for him."

Isaias asked each saint for help, to *pray for Hector*, one by one: John the Baptist, Joseph, the patriarchs and prophets, Peter and Paul, Andrew, John and James, the Apostles, Mary Magdalene—*anyone* who might *listen* to his pleas, might do something to save Hector—and slowly the demon began to shake again, fighting against his bonds.

"Boring," he snapped, teeth bared and gnashing, struggling against the ropes. Blood welled from Hector's wrists.

Isaias went on: "Lord, be merciful."

"Lord," Violet and Mrs. Marsh said, overlapping slightly with Isaias in their eagerness to continue, "deliver him, we pray."

"From all evil," Isaias said.

"Lord, deliver him, we pray."

"From every sin."

"Lord, deliver him, we pray."

"From the snares of the Devil,"

"Oh, is *that* what you think I am?" the demon-thing asked. "Funny, I thought you didn't *really* believe, Father, that the Devil could be in any of us. Funny, given you're a fucking sinner by your own Book."

"From everlasting death," Isaias intoned through the sick feeling in his gut. He knew he had nothing to fear. He had confessed. He had told the Bishop the things that weighed on him. He was as pure of heart as he could be in preparation for this moment. He ignored the way his heart ached with something more, something he couldn't quite identify. He couldn't bear to look too closely.

"Lord," Mrs. Marsh and Violet were saying, "deliver him, we pray."

"I should be flattered," Hector's halfway-voice said, but it was weaker, suddenly. "What a party, all for me. You look good in purple, by the way, Father. I think Hector would find you pretty hot, praying for him on your knees. And the blood on your hands, on your face, on your clothes? Some people might be into that, too."

"...by Your Passion and Cross," Isaias said, not having paused for the demon this time. Trying his best to push through and ignore everything the demon was saying.

"Lord, deliver him, we pray."

"God," the demon called suddenly again. He rolled his head back. He screamed at the ceiling, voice raising, the crucifix on the wall near the window rattling, then hanging askew. "Do you *ever* shut up?"

"Christ, Son of the living God," Isaias said, pushing through.

"Have mercy on him," Violet and Mrs. Marsh said.

"You were tempted for our sake by the Devil."

"Boy, was He ever," the demon laughed. "You should have seen the sin and temptation on *Him*."

"Have mercy on him."

"You freed those troubled by unclean spirits," Isaias prayed.

"Have mercy on him," Violet and Mrs. Marsh prayed in return.

"You gave Your disciples power over demons."

"Oh, do you think you're one of His disciples?" the demon asked. He snarled at Isaias, still kneeling before the prostrated demon. "Oh, *honey*, no. You know you're not good enough for that. I told you: God doesn't love you, anymore. He's going to be *real* fucking picky with who He chooses to spread His word, now. Who ever told you that you were worthy to preach His word? I'm guessing it wasn't God Himself."

"Have mercy on him," Violet's voice came trembling, an instant early, overlapping with the demon's protests.

"Have mercy on him," Mrs. Marsh was saying, rushing to catch up to Violet.

"You are seated at the right hand of the Father, to intercede for us," Isaias said.

"Say," the demon interjected again, "Did they ever beat you, Father? Did they make up reasons to hurt you, just to keep you in line? Or did they have enough excuses to make you feel worthless, they didn't have to resort to such an old-fashioned one? What a loving home you grew up in. Almost as good as the mother who was ready to toss you out like yesterday's trash. Which was worse, can you tell me? The parents who thought you weren't worth the trouble, or the church that wanted you to stay in line?"

Isaias cleared his throat. His hands were shaking more visibly now, he could tell. He had to ignore the taunting. He had to, for Hector. His own pain meant nothing in the face of the pain that Hector would be feeling, trapped in his own body. Suddenly, though, the rosary around his neck seemed less comforting than before. It was a weight around his neck, now, but he did not move to take it off.

Isaias glanced back at Violet and Mrs. Marsh, who quickly added, "Have mercy on him."

"You will come to judge," Isaias said in voice, the trembling in his words matching the trembling in his hands, "the living and the dead."

"Have mercy on him."

"Be merciful to us sinners," Isaias prayed.

"Lord, we ask you," Mrs. Marsh said. Violet's voice was nearly inaudible to Isaias, but he could feel her conviction, still, though it was weaker. "Hear our prayer."

"Spare us," Isaias asked, trying to raise his voice to make up for Violet's.

"Spare *me*," the demon groaned, "from all this bullshit."

"Lord, we ask you, hear our prayer."

"Pardon us."

"Lord, we ask you, hear our prayer."

"Strengthen us," Isaias asked of his God, looking up to the askance crucifix on the wall and hoping to feel something there, "and keep us in Your holy service."

"This is getting old, you know," the demon droned, mocking. Isaias looked up at the demon again, tied to a chair before and above him, and found that their gazes met. The demon was scowling viciously. "How long are we going to keep going?"

"As long as we need to," Isaias snapped. "Until you return Hector to us."

The demon's scowl shapeshifted into a grin, and Isaias understood immediately that he had made a mistake. "Do you think you're going to miss Mass tomorrow, Father Fuck Up? Your parish might be disappointed if you use up all your energy on a non-believer."

Isaias took a breath. He ignored remembered words from his bishop. "Raise our minds," he said, as if he had never broken from script, "to heavenly desires."

There was no reply.

Unsure what else to do, not wanting to break script again and too scared to reach out to feel Violet or Mrs. Marsh's emotions, Isaias continued. "Grant that Your church may serve You in security and freedom." When there was no reply, he concluded on his own again. "Bring all peoples together in peace and true harmony. Graciously hear us. Christ, hear us. Christ, graciously hear us."

"Oh, did the flock waver?" the demon was asking. Outside, the wind was picking up. The light in the room had changed shape, too bright, as dawn crept toward the horizon. Isaias carefully stood. His hand throbbed in pain. "In this alone now, are we, Father Fuck Up?"

"O God," Isaias said once he was fully on his feet, "whose nature is always to forgive and show mercy, receive our prayer for this Your servant Hector—"

"Servant! Boy's a sinner, not a servant."

"—who is bound in chains by the power of the Devil. May Your faithful love and compassion mercifully grant him release through Christ our Lord."

Mrs. Marsh's trembling voice added, "Amen."

Isaias turned and reached out to help Mrs. Marsh to her feet, taking her shaking hands in his bloody ones. Violet, still standing a short distance back, was looking past Isaias.

"Violet?" he asked, gently. He wasn't angry, nor was he disappointed, but he was very concerned. She had stopped praying. Had this truly been too much to ask of her? He couldn't imagine the pain of seeing one's father act like a person you didn't recognize.

Before Violet could answer, the gusting wind outside rose to a crescendo. The paper pasted over the Sacred Heart of Mary in the window was torn from place and sucked out through broken glass. Pre-dawn light broke into the room, changing the colour of the room to cast Violet in a silvery light, and dropping the temperature in the room by several degrees. Faster than was reasonable, Isaias saw his breath coming out in frosted puffs. "Violet?" he repeated.

Violet said nothing, but instead used one crutch to gesture behind Isaias. "Look."

Isaias turned slowly and looked at Hector, who was painted in the same silver light as Violet, but otherwise still surrounded by stained red light from the window above. He sat with his head hanging, chin touching his ample chest, slumped forward with his wrists straining the ropes. Blood dripped to the floor from his hands, the gauze bandages again soaked through with blood. His breathing was heavy but regular, ghosting frozen air through the room on every exhale.

"Dad?" Violet tried quietly. She took a step forward, closer to the slouched figure in the chair, but Isaias stopped her with a firm hand on her shoulder.

"Wait a moment," he warned, holding her carefully back.

"What for?" Violet asked, voice coming out in a burst. "He's... he's okay, right? It worked, right?"

Isaias didn't say anything, instead taking strength in the warmth of the colour purple. She matched the violet stole he wore. The scent of flowers was present once more. Isaias felt her hope, but he couldn't let himself take it on. Letting go of Violet's shoulder, Isaias walked the few paces to Hector in the chair. He crouched by him. "Hector?" he asked. There was no reply. "Are you alright?"

"What do you think?" came the reply, low and gurgling, his mouth caked with spit and drying blood. Isaias's heart picked up in anxious fear, but he wasn't sure if he could place it as Hector's voice or the mockery of it, not so quiet as this.

"By God, if the Devil in Hector is speaking," Isaias said slowly, improvising, speaking through thick fear in his throat, "then I command it to silence. Let Hector speak for himself."

"Isaias..." started Hector's voice. He sounded weak. A wounded animal. His voice trembled, sounded wet, not just the spit and blood, but maybe tears, too. Isaias prayed he wasn't hurt.

The voice, though, didn't sound hostile. It was plaintive. Close to begging. Isaias's heart picked up in his chest, his heartbeat racing. Hector's voice had stirred something in his chest before, and now he desperately wished it really was Hector again. "Yes, Hector?"

"I..." Hector continued, in a voice so quiet that it was a whisper.

Isaias hesitated, coming close enough to hear better. He knelt by Hector, not for the first time. He moved his face closer. He feared being attacked again, but he wanted to believe that Hector wouldn't hurt him twice.

In his ear, Hector whispered, "Get fucked, buddy."

Isaias jerked back, but the demon neither said nor did anything more. Violet, behind Isaias, let out a choked sob.

"What now?" Mrs. Marsh asked as Isaias slowly rose and took a few steps back toward the two women.

"We begin again," Isaias said quietly.

"Oh, but we didn't even get to the *good* part," the demon said. "Why start over if you didn't even do the whole thing through? There's so much juicy stuff you could still use on me!"

Isaias resisted the urge to look back at Hector's body, because that was not the man he cared so deeply for—it was just his vessel. Nor did he cry, as much as the tears were a temptation. He could spare none. No, he had to be strong. For God. For Violet. *For Hector*.

Isaias repeated, "We begin again."

XVIII

It was five in the morning, once again in that breath of time between morning and night, maybe two hours from sunrise. Isaias was sitting on the floor of the kitchen, an ice pack held to his forehead. His head was aching, but he refused to take food, water, or medicine. He could probably bear to sleep a little, but he'd sent Violet to get some sleep back at the rectory. He'd tried to insist that Mrs. Marsh go home, or at least sleep on the extra linens that he had fruitlessly laid on the floor, but she'd been equally insistent that she stay awake with Isaias.

"You should eat something," she'd said, hovering over him at ten to five, once she'd cleaned and rebandaged Isaias's hand and taken the surplice and the stole from him to wash them and at least try to get rid of the worst of the blood. She'd returned from the rectory while they were in the laundry. The back of his cassock was stiff from dried holy water. "Or at least have some tea, dear."

"You know that I can't," Isaias had said sadly, though he would have loved a decent cup of tea. His throat was hurting from talking—*praying*—for hours on end. Tea with honey would have been perfect. For better or for worse, Mrs. Marsh had left it alone promptly enough.

Now, she sat quietly on the floor next to him. Isaias was about to speak after a lengthy silence, when Mrs. Marsh reached out and took his free hand—his left, the one that wasn't now wrapped in fresh bandages but was still wrapped from scraping it open on the asphalt—and asked, "May I pray for you, Father?"

Isaias stared uncertainly at her for a moment before he smiled tiredly and said, "That's my line, Mrs. Marsh."

"After holding a dozen exorcisms in a single night," Mrs. Marsh said slowly but firmly, "I think that you could use someone praying for *you*, Father."

Isaias thought to protest again but didn't end up doing so. Instead, he squeezed Mrs. Marsh's hand, giving up and allowing her to lead in prayer however she felt fit. His wounded right hand throbbed as if in sympathy, the blood just under the surface and threatening to break free again.

"Our Father, Who art in Heaven," Mrs. Marsh began, "give to us Your guidance and, especially, give to the good Father here Your word and Your love, as he is in need of it now more than ever. Father Flores is a good man, and he is trying his very best. Let Jesus speak through him and help him find peace at the end of this long, long night. Amen."

"Amen," Isaias repeated, smiling faintly.

Mrs. Marsh squeezed Isaias's hand. For a long moment, they sat together in silence, Mrs. Marsh holding Isaias's hand, before she asked, "Did the Bishop really hurt you when you were a boy?"

Isaias hesitated. He wondered what made Mrs. Marsh ready to believe it. The demon hadn't even said it definitively, only posed it as a hypothetical. Isaias liked to think that Bishop Reid was a good man. He had taken Isaias in when his parents hadn't wanted him, after all. "He didn't. No one at the church orphanage ever laid a hand on me, I promise. The things that happened were—" Isaias stopped himself. He took a breath. He couldn't properly explain exactly what had happened in the walls of his childhood church without Mrs. Marsh knowing what, exactly, was different about Isaias. "No one ever hurt me," he said instead.

Mrs. Marsh studied Isaias with a look he couldn't decipher. He dared not try to read her emotions—he was afraid of what would come next, if he knew that she doubted his insistence. "Well, I'm sorry, anyway," she said.

Isaias didn't deign to accept the apology, let alone to make justifications for anything. Instead, he sighed, and said, "I'm very sorry you were there for all of that, Mrs. Marsh. That was—troubling."

"I knew what I was getting into," she said, though her voice was soft.

Isaias wondered what she had thought she was getting into, if it had really been what she had expected. She had remained steady, as strong as always, through it all, but he didn't know how she could have ever expected any of that. He wished that he hadn't let her participate, in the end, no matter what she thought. It was bad enough that Violet had insisted on being there. Isaias squeezed Mrs. Marsh's hand, then let it go.

"Get some rest," he said to his housekeeper, then slowly stood. "Please, Mrs. Marsh."

She hesitated, then nodded. "Where are you going, Father?"

"To check on Hector."

He saw Mrs. Marsh pause. She said, "Be careful, Father."

"I will."

After putting the melting icepack back in the freezer and gathering the small first aid kit that Mrs. Marsh had left on the counter, Isaias filled a bowl with water and grabbed a hand towel, then headed to the study. The door was locked, and he had one of only two keys. He unlocked it and stepped inside. While the rest of the church was awash in pre-dawn twilight, the study seemed to exist in a plane of its own. Mrs. Marsh had apparently covered up Mary's broken heart again—how long had passed that Isaias hadn't been aware of?—forcing the room into partial darkness. The stained-glass window stained the light red and gold, but the gold stood out the most now, magnifying the pre-dawn twilight. The picture windows on either side of Mary had the blinds drawn, but dim rays of early sunlight filtered through. The room seemed almost to glow.

In the centre of the room, Hector sat in the chair, still tied to the arms of it with rope. His head was hung, and, for a frightening moment, Isaias doubted that he was breathing. He did see the slow rise and fall of Hector's chest and, perhaps more importantly, Isaias could feel that he was not alone in the room. Hector's presence, while dim, was clearly alive. Lack of sleep was surely driving paranoia.

Walking toward Hector, Isaias knelt before him and placed the bowl of warm water on the floor beside him. He looked up at Hector's face, trying to determine if the man was sleeping or not. He hardly looked at peace, but his eyes were closed. Isaias frowned faintly, then decided to chance it. He dipped the towel in the bowl, then reached up to gently dab the blood and spit out of Hector's beard. Most of it wouldn't give, much of the blood—*Isaias's* blood, he remembered—was dried in the wiry hairs, caked there with saliva. Still, he tried to remove the worst of it with a careful hand, as if cleaning Hector's face would do anything in the end. After, he switched to cleaning the blood from Hector's wrists, dabbing it away from the bruises and welts that the ropes had left against Hector's struggles. Hector flinched, but didn't stir, at first. It wasn't until Isaias was almost done cleaning the blood from his wrists—the water turning pink from the rinsing of the blood off of the towel—that Hector's eyes opened, and he spoke. "Isaias?" he asked softly, in a voice that was all his own.

Relief flooded Isaias, even though he was scared to let himself hope. He set the towel down partially in the bowl, soaking up the bloody water, and reached out to take one of Hector's hands. He could have cried at the way that Hector's emotions rushed into him. They *hurt*, they were fear, they were exhaustion, they were pain—but they were

Hector, through and through. "I'm here, Hector," Isaias promised him. His own voice was scarcely above a reverential whisper.

"I—is Violet okay?" Hector asked. His voice sounded hoarse. Weak. "Are you?"

"She's sleeping."

"And you?" Hector insisted.

Isaias smiled sadly. "Worried about you, my dear friend."

Hector slowly leaned back, lifting his head finally, though not far. He blinked past Isaias with tired eyes. With his head raised, Isaias saw that Hector looked ill; pallid, sweating, his face gaunt and haunted. "What are you worried about?" Hector asked in a weak, halfway laughing voice that broke Isaias's heart. "What could possibly be wrong?"

"Oh, Hector," Isaias said gently, not wanting to follow along with any attempts at joking. Not after everything that had already transpired in that room. With his free hand, he reached out to touch his friend's forehead. Hector flinched at the touch, and so Isaias dropped his hand and let it join his other on Hector's instead. He stroked his thumb over Hector's knuckles. They felt thinned, not like the robust man with strong and warm hands he knew so well. "I am so, so sorry."

Hector squeezed Isaias's hand, but his grip was weak, like all of his strength had simply vanished through the night. "I know you're trying for me. I know you aren't about to give up on me."

"Of course not," Isaias said. Without letting himself overthink it, he bent his head and kissed Hector's knuckles gently, still holding his hand in both his own. With his forehead resting against the back of Hector's hand, he felt some unidentified emotion flutter in Hector's heart, and Isaias's spirit stirred in reply. "I will do everything in my power, in God's power, Hector, to save you from this curse."

"I know," Hector said. Something comforting was in his heart and it gave Isaias the first real glimpse of hope that he had felt all night. It was cloaked in so much pain, but it was *Hector*. Hector, who now tried to squeeze Isaias's hand again, weak as it was, and said, "We match. Our hands—both injured, you know? We fit together."

Isaias didn't lift his head from where it rested on Hector's hand, held between his own, Hector's fingers a breath away. He traced his fingers across every part of Hector's hand, committing every part of him to memory not for the first time. He traced over the rough edges of his bandages, allowing the fabric of his own to brush against Hector's, their blood separated by such flimsy barriers, and wondered if Hector remembered where Isaias's injuries had come from. If Hector remembered the taste of Isaias's blood. "We do. I think we always have."

Hector didn't respond, and Isaias let them sit in silence for a time. He was aware of the room slowly lightening by the rising sun outside. Soon, he would have to leave Hector's side, deliver Mass, act like everything was normal. How could he pretend that anything was okay, when he would know Hector was suffering without him by his side to try to make it right, to ease his pain?

Tears pricking at his eyes and not knowing what else to do, Isaias slowly lifted his head and looked at his friend. Hector was filthy—the remaining blood on his face, his clothes, his lips, but also how he was soaked in sweat, urine, and the stench of human misery—and maybe it was a small thing, but perhaps Isaias could alleviate some of his discomfort. Reluctantly, but knowing he could not be selfish by holding fast to Hector, he pulled away and bent to remove Hector's boots, still wet from the winter night outside when he had been brought in so many hours ago. Hector looked at him in some kind of puzzlement, but made no protest, only watching Isaias.

He allowed himself to take his time—removing both boots carefully, setting them aside, then both socks and laying them flat across the tops of the boots so they could dry from the dampness of sweat. He would have to ask Mrs. Marsh to help retrieve clean clothes for Hector.

Isaias picked up the damp cloth, soaked in the bloody water, and wrang it out before he held one of Hector's feet in his lap and carefully wiped and cleaned it of the sweat and grime. What little relief he could give Hector, he should. Anything to show his utter devotion to him. *Anything.*

Isaias knelt there, cleaning Hector's foot gently, relishing in the soft but firm arch, relishing in this small comfort he could offer him, before he placed it back on the floor and then rested the other foot in his lap and did the same with it. It was an alien closeness, to hold Hector so, but he knelt there, tending to Hector in this way that felt small—too small—until his knees hurt and his eyes stung with tears.

He felt love and grief in Hector's chest, so entangled that Isaias could not separate them, could not tell where one ended and the other began. They were, in that moment, the very same emotion.

Blinking back tears that were somehow both his own and Hector's, Isaias finished washing Hector's feet and then gently replaced them on the floor. He rang the cloth out into the bloody water once more and took a moment to steel himself before he looked up at Hector, who had watched him only in silence. Isaias met his gaze but could say nothing.

Eventually, Hector broke the silence to ask, "Isaias?"

"Yes, Hector?"

"I want you to know that—that whatever happens..."

Isaias hesitated, his heart picking up. He shook his head but remained kneeling before his friend. "No, Hector," he said.

"Please, Isaias."

"No, Hector. I know, and I—"

Hector hung his head. Softly, he said, "I'm scared, Isaias."

"I know," Isaias whispered. He didn't need to try to read Hector's emotions to know that it was true. Everything in Hector now was a reflection of Isaias, and everything in Isaias was a reflection of Hector—his fear was their fear, his pain was their pain. His grief, his love—their grief, their love. "I am, too, Hector. Me, too. But do you know what God says of fear?"

"What does He say?"

"'Fear not'," Isaias repeated dutifully, "'for I am with you; be not dismayed, for I am your God; I will strengthen you, I will help you, I will uphold you with My righteous right hand'."

There was a moment's silence. Hector shifted to reach his hand out to Isaias. Bound to chair as it was, he could not reach far, and Isaias lifted his hand to take Hector's. The bloodied bandages on both their palms really did fit together, just like Hector said. "What if I don't believe in God, Isaias? You know I don't."

"Then know that *I* am with you," Isaias whispered fiercely. "I am with you, and I will strengthen you. I'll still pray for you. You still deserve to be saved—and I will do *everything* in my power to save you. So will Violet."

Another pause, their shared emotions intensifying through the contact, Hector's heart swelling in time with Isaias's as Isaias vowed to help him. Hector said, "I know, Isaias. Thank you."

Not knowing what else to say, Isaias reluctantly let go of Hector's hand. He picked up the bowl and towel and slowly stood. He stood before Hector for a second longer before leaning forward to brush his lips across Hector's forehead, tasting the salty sweetness and iron pang of his sweat and blood on his skin. When pulled away, he could not meet Hector's eyes and had to take his leave, before their bonded souls would reveal to Hector the deepest fear in Isaias's heart:

That 'everything' was simply not enough.

XIX

Isaias knew that Wednesday was going to be a difficult day when he nearly fell asleep in the shower. The night had dragged on long—the exorcism, caring for Hector, moving Hector to the rectory when it became clear that they were nowhere near done in their fight against evil. Soon, parishioners would be in the church, believing that it was a normal day. And Isaias would preach to them, as if it were a normal day. As much as Hector took priority, Isaias couldn't let him stay so near to innocent lives when he could be a danger. There would be no coming back from it if something were to happen—for anyone.

None of them had exactly gotten a good night's sleep.

Stepping out of the shower with a sigh, Isaias splashed water from the sink onto his face. He took a moment to examine the bite wound on the side of his right hand, trying to decide how obvious it was that it was blunt, human teeth that had made the gouge in his hand, then tried to shave. Somehow, he managed to not cut himself too terribly, but the pain of the blade skimming into his skin felt refreshing, if anything. No—that wasn't the right word.

Maybe it was just waking him back up to the reality of his situation.

Isaias washed his face again to get rid of the bloody nicks, then bandaged his hand to hide the wound from sight. Better not to risk anyone being able to identify what kind of teeth made it.

After all, he would have to face the parish that day.

Isaias sighed again, then rubbed both temples with his fingertips.

"God, give me strength..."

As Isaias made it to the bottom of the stairs of the rectory, dressed in only the cassock this time, Mrs. Marsh appeared from the kitchen.

"Are you certain you shouldn't eat, Father?" she asked. "I'm worried about your strength. Or perhaps the bishop could send in a replacement for you to say Mass today, so you might rest a while before we continue—"

"I'll be alright," Isaias promised Mrs. Marsh, holding up both his hands in a gesture of peace. She eyed the bandage on his right hand. Isaias dropped his hands and folded them behind his back. "I promise. How is Violet faring?"

"I convinced her to eat something, no thanks to your self-sacrifice, Father," Mrs. Marsh sighed. "The girl needs to take care of herself, if you won't."

After a hesitant moment, he said, "Maybe tea won't hurt. If you can use it as leverage to make sure that Violet is eating and drinking."

Mrs. Marsh slumped slightly, some kind of weight off her shoulders. She nodded eagerly, then went to the kitchen. Isaias stood, not sure what else to do with himself, and found himself staring at the door to the study. The study where Hector was now being kept.

Kept. Like an animal.

Isaias knew that it was a necessary evil, but his heart ached at the thought of Hector in there, suffering alone.

Before he could think too much of it, Mrs. Marsh returned with a cup of tea. Isaias thanked her as he took it, his throat suddenly feeling cracked from dryness. He took a long drink of the tea, feeling the sweetness of smooth honey sweep away some of the pain in his throat that he didn't know that he was holding onto. Hot tea, softened with honey, the heat almost too much to bear, but ultimately healing. He thought again of Hector.

Isaias let out a soft sigh. Breathed in the comforting scent of tea. He smiled to Mrs. Marsh again. "Thank you. For helping her—and me. Now, I have to—"

"You have to work. I know, Father. Take care of your parish, of course. Just don't hurt yourself in the process, will you?"

"I won't," Isaias said. He paused, and abandoned his tea on a side table before he hugged Mrs. Marsh tightly, then left the rectory and headed down the path to the church. He paused halfway down the path as he saw a crow swoop low overhead and fly off toward the edge of the graveyard. He could hear cawing coming from that direction. There was nothing inherently strange about it, but after the last several days, Isaias wasn't willing to take chances. Isaias checked the time briefly, decided he had time before he had to be at the church proper, and went in the direction of the crow.

Under the pine tree at the edge of the cemetery, there was a large murder of crows, at least a dozen of them, crowded around the spot where Isaias had buried the dead one the day before—and had it only been a day? They screamed their crow-calls at the sky, cutting through the frosty morning.

One of the crows looked at Isaias and suddenly the cacophony died, the cawing ceasing as each crow, in turn, turned to face Isaias. The silence was far worse than their outcries. Isaias felt their accusation in their stares. He considered reaching out, trying to sense what was going on in them, but his heart raced with the thought of making that unknown known.

Softly, he said, "I'm sorry to interrupt your mourning."

For what else had he walked into but the grief of crows?

Isaias crossed himself and whispered a prayer for their relief before he turned and walked briskly back to the church, his breath puffing out like frost and his boots crunching in the snow.

When he unlocked the back door to the church, nearest his office, he quickly encountered the church secretary. Stopping in his tracks, Isaias fought to prevent himself from looking at the office door. He had left it locked, but what if someone had realized something was wrong? He and Mrs. Marsh had tried to clean up the blood and other bodily fluids, and mask the scent of suffering and chemical cleaner with candles—but what if someone noticed?

"Good morning, Father—"

"Good morning, Josephine," Isaias cut her off. "I need to get ready for Mass, still. Is there something you needed urgently?"

Josephine frowned but shook her head. "No, Father, that's alright. I didn't realize you were still busy. It can wait."

"Thank you," Isaias said—and, truthfully, he *did* need to prepare for Mass. He hadn't given it much thought, not even what subject to preach on. He still didn't know how he was going to focus at all—but he had to keep up appearances.

Isaias went first to the study to make sure it wasn't disturbed and was relieved to find it in the state they had left it. The broken-hearted Mother Mary in the window watched him as he checked through the room and righted anything that he could to make it less obvious something had happened in there. He couldn't do much about the puckering hardwood where holy water had seeped into the floor, or the stains from snow and blood, but he opened the window next to Mary, even though the temperature in the church would at once plummet, and he pushed the chair Hector had been tied in closer to the desk to not look so conspicuous. He tucked the ropes into his desk drawer.

It was like he was cleaning up a crime scene in his own church. His rosary felt heavy against his chest, resting above his heart.

Isaias wanted to ask God again for aid, for some sign to ease his heartache, but he was afraid that He might not answer again. Instead, Isaias turned to the broken stained-glass window and lifted his gaze to Mary. She looked down at him not in judgement, but with compassion and sympathy. Isaias crossed himself, clasped his hands together, and closed his eyes.

He found himself praying not in words, but in feelings. He had always tried to put his intentions into sentences, into speech, into tangible concepts. But this time, praying to Mary, he found his prayer came more naturally as the shape of feelings.

His grief, his heartache, his hopes, his dreams. All of his desire to do the right thing, all of his fear that he would fail. All of his love for Hector and for Violet and even for Mrs. Marsh. These were the things that he prayed with: his heart was his prayer, and it felt sublime.

And when he felt something stirring his heartstrings in reply, he sobbed.

It was gone after only an instant—but was that Mary, who had heard him, who had whispered through him for a moment? Had she spoken God into his soul? Or perhaps he'd imagined it—but he didn't think he had.

For a moment, he had felt something touch his soul, and maybe everything would be okay. If he prayed with love, maybe it would all be okay.

In the nave of the church, shortly before Mass would begin, Isaias found Poppy. She was sitting in one of the pews, head bowed, and hands clasped, praying, as Isaias had prayed.

Isaias approached carefully and knelt by the edge of the pew. When Poppy did not acknowledge his presence, he waited for her to mouth an 'amen' and reached out and gently touched her shoulder. She startled and looked up at him before gesturing to him to wait. She pulled hearing aids out of a case resting next to her and put them in. Isaias waited for her to indicate she was ready.

"Sorry, I didn't hear you, Father," she said. "I don't like wearing my hearing aids sometimes, even though my mother likes to guilt trip me about it. She says it makes me ungrateful for the gifts I've been given."

Isaias shook his head. "You don't have to apologize—you can do whatever you like with them. They're yours."

Poppy nodded, though she didn't acknowledge his specific answer. Instead, she said, "The quiet makes me feel closer to God. It helps me cut out all this other stuff," she gestured around her, the otherwise empty church, "that gets in the way. Besides, I can hear okay without them, mostly. It's too loud with them sometimes."

"Then it sounds like you know what's best for you. But don't you have school today?" He knew that she did because Violet did, too. Violet had told him, before going to bed that morning, that she would call in sick on her own behalf. Her disability didn't guarantee that the school would accept her word as truth, but Hector didn't necessarily need to be the one to call in sick for her. And if the school chose not to believe her, she'd said, that was their problem. Isaias worried about potential truancy problems down the line if the school was already predisposed to believing the worst in Violet, but he had to concede that maybe school could be figured out once her father was better.

Poppy looked at Isaias for a moment before saying, "You look tired, Father."

Isaias smiled faintly. "Worried about Violet?"

"Absolutely. She texted me that she was okay and going to get some sleep, but after last night I'd really like to hear her voice and—" Poppy cut herself off and blushed. "Her voice is really the only thing I'm interested in hearing, most of the time. But since I wanted to let her rest, I thought you could tell me if she's okay."

Isaias hesitated about what to tell her, but he thought he understood. Sometimes, the world focused down into one single point, and that point was an individual. For Isaias, that person was Hector. "She really is okay."

"You're taking care of her and her dad?"

"I am," he promised Poppy. "I'm doing everything in my power for both of them." If he could give Violet's best friend anything, he could give her that. He had made the promise to more than just her, after all.

Poppy nodded, then slowly stood. Isaias did, too, and moved out of her way. "Thanks, Father," she said. "I hope you keep that promise—if I can't be there for Violet, I need to make sure someone is. I know she can take care of herself pretty well, but we—Violet and I always stick together, you know?" She blinked rapidly, and Isaias thought he saw tears in her eyes. "Sometimes it's like she's all I have, and I know people tell us that's stupid because we're just teenagers—but that doesn't matter, because right now it's true. Right now, she's the most important person in my world, and *that* will always matter."

Isaias felt the full force of Poppy's emotions—the way she truly *loved* Violet so fiercely. Isaias realized that he had not fully understood their friendship. It ran far deeper than he had let himself contemplate. "You're right," Isaias said. "You know your own heart, and you shouldn't let anyone else try to tell you how you feel."

"Thank you, Father." Poppy bowed her head before she stepped out from the pews. She smiled to Isaias before she left. "I guess I'll go to class, that way I can help figure out what Violet missed in the classes we share. But tell Violet I came to check on her, okay? So, she knows I'm thinking of her."

"I think she already knows."

Poppy's heart warmed—Isaias could feel it—and she said, "You take care of yourself, too, Father."

Before he knew it, Isaias was alone again in the church.

It had been a long time since Isaias had approached the pulpit feeling at a loss for words. Normally, preaching God's Word was natural. He believed, and so he simply had to pour his heart into his sermon.

But his heart was occupied. He had spent little time preparing for Mass, and he felt sure that his parishioners would see through him. Standing there, before an attentive crowd—Wednesday Mass drew a smaller group than Sundays, but a more attentive one—he felt himself wavering. His vision, from exhaustion; his spirit, from the same. He braced himself against the dais, afraid he might lose his footing, too.

Despite it all, he began to speak.

"When I am afraid," Isaias began slowly, not sure what else to start with, "I put my trust in God. As should we all. God does not leave us," he promised. "Nor does He forsake us. The words the Bible has for us about dealing with our fears, our anxieties, they should put us at ease. But, sometimes, it does not feel that our Lord delivers us from our fears. What then? You might ask. Then... then we must determine why it is God is testing our strength of character, and we must act."

Isaias took a breath. He tried to suppress the growls of his stomach, the throbbing pain of a migraine growing behind his temples.

"God loves us, I promise you that. But sometimes—sometimes we cannot rely wholly on God. We put our faith in Him, our trust, but we must act. Because He, too, has put His faith in us, in humanity—we are His creations, and He expects us to behave as though we were made in His image because we *were*. We cannot sit by and make excuses for why things do not go our way... we pray to Him, but we must also be ready and willing to put in the work to receive His answer. For you see—"

Isaias felt the rush of emotions hit him like a gale wind a split second before the back door, leading from the back rooms of the church, swung open, stopped short of hitting the wall. Isaias nearly lost his footing at the force of feeling, gripping tightly to the pulpit. There was a confused murmur from the pews as Mrs. Marsh hurried up to Isaias, saying, "I'm sorry, Father, I'm sorry," repeatedly as she crossed herself, pre-emptively asking for forgiveness for interrupting Mass.

"I'm sorry, everyone, just—give me one moment," Isaias said, stepping away to meet Mrs. Marsh. "What is it?" he asked her softly, heart pounding in his chest with fear. It reflected her own—but most of all, he feared for Hector.

"It's Hector," Mrs. Marsh said in a rushed breath, barely over a whisper and confirming Isaias's fears. "There's something wrong. You have to come, quickly."

Citing a family emergency—close enough—would have to do to dismiss the parishioners, but truthfully Isaias barely spared it a second thought, giving only a hurried word to those gathered there for Mass before he rushed off with Mrs. Marsh. His singular thought was: *I need to get to Hector.*

But when he was within a few meters of the rectory, he buckled over and vomited, sickness spreading across the snow and melting the top layer on contact. Steam rose from the foulness, and Isaias's throat and nostrils burned, but more than that he was distracted by the *smell*.

"Dear Lord," he said, looking at Mrs. Marsh, who had stopped to check on him. "What's that smell?" he asked.

Mrs. Marsh paused, looking up at the rectory, then back to Isaias. "I don't smell anything, Father."

Isaias covered his mouth and nose with his bandaged hand to block out the smell and prevent himself from gagging but said nothing. It smelled of rot and fire—a corpse burning on a pyre, a smell Isaias wasn't even familiar with but suddenly understood. He felt dampness on his bandages and could only guess how much was sweat, despite the cold, and how much was blood, feeling the bite wound splitting open again. He could say nothing to Mrs. Marsh, who would not understand. When she reached out to touch his shoulder, to guide him, he shied away. "Best if you don't touch me, right now," he said. "I'll be alright. Let's go."

Mrs. Marsh hesitated, but then nodded and approached the rectory.

As soon as she opened the front door, screaming cut through the mid-morning frost.

Worried that someone from the church would hear, Isaias hurried inside with Mrs. Marsh, and closed and latched the door behind them. The stench was worse inside. So, too, was the cold. Isaias shivered. "Are all the windows closed?" he asked.

"I believe so," Mrs. Marsh said.

"Good. Is that Hector?"

"It is, Father."

"Where's Violet?" Isaias asked.

"Right here, Father," Violet said as she came out of the kitchen with a bowl of water in one hand, balancing her weight on one crutch. Some of her stickers on the body of the crutch were frayed and peeled at the edges. There were tears in Violet's eyes and Isaias immediately felt himself tear up in sympathy. She passed the bowl of water to Isaias. "Please help him, Father."

Isaias nodded, taking the bowl, and turning to Mrs. Marsh. "The stole and the surplice. Are they ready for me to wear again?"

Mrs. Marsh hesitated. "Not all of the blood came out," she said.

"That's alright," Isaias said. "That will have to do. Bring them to me in the study."

Isaias walked to the study and unlocked the door. The stink was nearly unbearable as he opened the door, but the screaming just *stopped*.

"Hello, there, Father," purred the thing in Hector's body from where Hector was sat in the chair. Newly surfaced blood was at his wrists where the ropes had bit into them. He grinned wickedly at him. "Finally, you've come back to me. I was getting awfully lonely in this room, in this body, without you. Hector and I *missed* you."

Isaias frowned at the demon-thing, still feeling ill at the scent of scorched refuse, though it had begun to dissipate now that the demon had his attention. "You stirred up trouble because you were bored?" he dared to ask.

"Oh, no, Father. Were you in the middle of something? Wednesday Mass, maybe? *So* sorry to have interrupted."

There was nothing to say to that. Isaias knew he shouldn't have responded to his taunts at all—demons said only lies and would try to break him down. He set the bowl of water down on the desk as Mrs. Marsh appeared with the surplice and the stole. As she'd said, both still had blood stains on them. "Thank you, Mrs. Marsh."

"Aw, Father Fuck Up, you sound tired," the demon said. "You didn't get any sleep at all, did you? What a shame. I could have kept you up all night in a much more fun way. Maybe *you'd* be doing the screaming instead of me."

Gritting his teeth, Isaias donned his regalia and turned back to the demon. "I won't stop," he promised the demon. "I won't stop until you leave Hector alone."

"How *sweet*."

Isaias looked to Mrs. Marsh and Violet, both now standing dutifully in the closed study with him. Violet had retrieved her other crutch and stood steadfast.

"Beloved sisters," Isaias began, "let us humbly implore the mercy of almighty God, that, moved by the intercession of all the Saints, He, in His kindness, will hear the voice of his Church for our brother Hector, who is afflicted by dire need. Let us begin."

Behind him, the demon cooed, "Seventh time's the charm, eh, boys and girls?"

XX

HOLY MARY, MOTHER OF God,
  Pray for him.

Isaias hadn't realized he had fallen asleep until the words of the exorcism rocked through his subconscious, haunting his dreams. He jerked awake with the image of blood-stained teeth in his mind's eye and hit his head off the wall behind him where he was lying on the linoleum floor of the rectory's kitchen. He'd only intended to close his eyes for a moment, let the cool tile of the kitchen soothe the pounding of his headache. Now, the floor was shockingly cold, and his head still *ached*. When he looked up at Mrs. Marsh and Violet he noticed a faint aura of blurred pinks and greens silhouetting them; couldn't quite make out the details. Isaias closed his eyes against a wave of nausea, but his stirring forced him to notice someone—Mrs. Marsh, he assumed—had draped a blanket over him. Instinctively, he huddled into the blanket.

"Heat's out again," Mrs. Marsh said, confirming Isaias's suspicions.

Isaias sighed and slowly opened his eyes and found it a little easier that time, but still difficult. Fortunately, the lights of the kitchen were not on and the light from outside was dim—a glance at the clock determined it to be ten to six in the evening. Isaias had fallen asleep and missed the last of daylight. Pushing himself off the floor into a sitting position—and biting his tongue at the way his head swam, feeling heavy and full—Isaias looked to Mrs. Marsh and Violet. The edges of his vision were dark, and his ears were ringing, but once his senses cleared he saw that they were both bundled in blankets as well where they sat at the table of the kitchen together.

Violet's eyes were red, her cheeks were stained with tears, and her voice was full of the threat of more tears when she asked, "What now, Father?"

"I—" Isaias started before he coughed, the word getting caught in his dry throat.

Mrs. Marsh immediately rose, resting her blanket over the back of her chair. She went to the counter and poured a mug of tea from a pot wrapped in a cozy. She knelt by Isaias with the mug between both hands. "I don't care if you're fasting, Father," she said. "If you lose your voice, we lose our only hope of winning against this thing."

Isaias sighed softly and took the mug of hot tea. "Thank you, Mrs. Marsh," he whispered hoarsely. Mrs. Marsh returned to the table and the blanket she was using to fight off the cold while Isaias sipped the tea—it was lukewarm, the pot only retaining so much heat, but it was soothing, nonetheless. The three sat silently while Isaias attempted to heal his sore throat. After he'd finished his tea, Isaias let them sit in silence a moment more. And he said, "I think that we might need of reinforcements."

He saw and felt Violet's hesitation. "Reinforcements?"

But Mrs. Marsh understood. She said, "Bishop Reid. Father, I understand, but he *will* wonder why you went above him in the first place."

"I know, Mrs. Marsh. But I don't know who else to turn to. I'm afraid I'm not convinced I'm good enough on my own—and I know he wouldn't have approved, but now that the process is begun, maybe he'll agree to help us finish this."

"He's an hour away, do you think we can take Hector that far?" Isaias hesitated. "I think we have to try. We need *help*."

"I don't get it," Violet interjected. "Does it have to be your bishop? We could ask Lena for help. I bet she would know what to do."

For a moment, Isaias considered it—Lena, who seemed to know more than could be accounted for, whose soul was surely good, who prayed at perhaps not the same altars, but similar ones. She *was* an option, wasn't she? But the rites of exorcism Isaias was using were the *Catholic* rites—would it only interfere to bring in someone of a different faith? But without help, without guidance, Isaias was lost. "In theory, a priest should never do an exorcism at all without the authorization of his bishop. I've already contravened that—so while I would prefer to get reinforcements from my bishop, it wouldn't hurt to consult someone closer by who seems to know something, first," he conceded. "I've already broken the rules. We can talk to her. I don't have her number, but maybe if we call The Second Voyage, we can catch her."

"On it," Violet said, already pulling something up on her phone with quick and sure swipes of her fingers. Within moments, she was calling the shop—and a few moments later, she had clearly connected. "Hey, Lena, it's Violet Montero," she said, surprising Isaias with how quickly she could pretend to be so bright and energetic. The switch was instantaneous, and Isaias wondered how often she had fooled him. "Sorry to call you and make a sort of weird request—would you mind coming to Father Isaias's rectory? I'm trying to bully him into asking you for advice. Yeah, you will? Thank you! It's at—" she looked at Isaias, who said the address, and Violet repeated it. "Can you come over soon? Okay, see you then."

"Well?" Isaias asked as Violet put her phone back down.

Violet's mock cheer from the phone call immediately drained from her and she looked up at him. "She'll be here in like twenty."

Isaias's own energy sapped out of him, and he sagged. He was relieved to have someone else to talk to about it, but it also made him feel more powerless.

He just prayed Hector remained asleep for the twenty or so minutes it would take for Lena to arrive.

When Isaias sensed someone approaching the rectory, he barely held himself back from rushing to the door until it was obvious to everyone else that Lena had arrived. The night was absolute darkness behind her except for the cutting brightness of snow flurries in the air. "Thank you for coming," he said as he closed the door behind her.

Lena reached for her powder blue peacoat but paused and said, "Cold in here, eh?"

"Heat's out," Isaias confirmed.

Lena nodded and instead only unbuttoned the top few buttons. Isaias noticed the flash of her Mary Magdalene pendant as she bent to take off her boots, unlacing them and politely placing them to the side. When she stood, she looked behind Isaias, where Mrs. Marsh and Violet had appeared. Lena frowned in particular at Violet's tear-streaked cheeks. "You know, I had hoped Violet called me because you wanted advice about—but I see it's something much more solemn."

"It's about my dad," Violet said.

Something flashed across Lena's eyes as she pivoted to look at Isaias again. "Take me to Hector."

Isaias thought to ask how she knew that Hector was at the rectory but dismissed it as unimportant. Lena knew more than she let on, and Isaias would not question it anymore than he questioned his own intuition. While Lena's heart was normally closed off to him, he could sense now the urgency within her. She neither wanted nor needed an explanation. "This way."

Walking to the rectory with dread in his heart, Isaias led Lena to the study where Hector was trapped, Violet and Mrs. Marsh following along behind. When they reached the door, Isaias hesitated before he turned back to Lena. "Pray with me, first?" he asked. "Just for a moment."

Lena nodded and solemnly reached her hands out to Isaias, who took them gingerly in his own. Lena's palms rested on the stained bandages on Isaias's hands, and he saw something sad cross her eyes again before she closed them. Isaias closed his eyes, too, shutting out all of the external.

He did not pray in words, then, and nor did Lena, but he still felt something connect them through their cold hands. He understood more of Lena's heart in that moment—her love, her sorrow, her aged grief—and he shared in turn—his love, his sorrow, his grief both new and old—and regretted that he had never truly tried to be her friend before. He vowed that once he was on the other side of all of this, he would reach out to her again and understand what made her heart ache.

Once Isaias let go, he stepped away and turned back to the door. He took a breath to steel himself and opened the door.

"*Company?*" the demon's voice rasped before Isaias's eyes even fully adjusted to the light, as the study was in perfect darkness, swallowing up the light from the rest of the rectory. "You spoil me."

"Oh, Hector," Lena breathed from besides Isaias.

Isaias made to turn on the light, but the bulb only flickered before it burst, a shock of golden light and the plastic housing of the bulb cracking. He flinched, but Lena did not. In the brief illumination he had seen Hector grinning at them, but now with his retinas momentarily burnt he lost all vision of Hector. Something about it caused fear to sink its grip into his chest and his breath to quicken but he stepped forward anyway, willing his eyes to adjust faster but hoping that by being nearer to Hector he would know that he was there, that he was alive. For a moment, all he saw was the puff of his own breath, the study colder than even the rest of the rectory.

His fingers quickly became numb, but when Isaias felt himself close, he reached out and brushed unfeeling fingertips against Hector's forehead. Neither the demon nor Hector seemed to react. Instinctively, Isaias traced his index finger, no matter how numb, down Hector's forehead, then across it, drawing an invisible cross below his hairline. He felt and heard Hector's ragged breath as he tipped his head back to meet Isaias's touch. For a moment, Isaias believed that maybe it *was* Hector, seeking the tenderness of Isaias's touch, but then his fingers stung with the poisonous heat of the demon, and he slowly pulled his hand away.

He blinked as his eyes adjusted and asked over his shoulder, "Mrs. Marsh, could you please get some tea? It sounds like Hector could use it."

Mrs. Marsh didn't reply, but Isaias heard her exit. In her place, Lena and Violet stepped up on either side of him instead. Violet stayed a half-step behind, but Lena knelt before Hector and took his hand in hers.

"Hello there," the demon whispered in a cracked voice. Hector's eyes flashed in the darkness. "Fancy seeing you here."

"He really is possessed," Lena whispered with something close to reverence. It wasn't a question. After her conversation with Isaias at The Second Voyage—how long ago was it? Isaias was losing his sense of time—he knew she understood.

"He is," Isaias confirmed. With the same hand he had used to cross Hector, he now crossed himself. "You recognize it?" After everything, he wasn't surprised.

Lena nodded but didn't explain further. She instead bowed her head and whispered something to herself—a prayer, Isaias thought, though not entirely like his own. When she lifted her head, she said, "The demon is weak, but only because Hector is. A demon can only be so much stronger than its host—like a parasite, it risks killing the innocent soul it has latched onto."

Isaias couldn't say he was surprised, but it broke his heart all over again. Had he not himself felt that Hector's soul was truly suffering under the unbearable weight of the thing using him? "I've been performing an exorcism—exorcisms," Isaias corrected himself. "So far, nothing has worked. I need help."

Lena nodded to herself but kept her eyes on Hector for a moment more. She squeezed his hands before she stood and faced Isaias. "You're not whole enough," she said softly. "I can sense it. There's something damaged in you. That's what's stopping you."

"Can you help me?" This time, it was Isaias's voice which cracked.

His eyes adjusted to the darkness now, Isaias saw the soft, sad look on Lena's face. She took Isaias's face in her cold hands and leaned forward to kiss his forehead. It was strange—Isaias had assumed she was about his age, but suddenly he suspected she was much older than he had imagined. When she stepped away and smiled to him, and Isaias's heart broke all over again at what he knew was coming. "This isn't my story to tell. It's yours, it's Hector's, it's Violet's—I can offer you only my advice. But I can't help."

His heart in the pit of his stomach, Isaias asked, "And your advice?"

"Physician, heal thyself—you can't save someone's soul if you won't save your own, Isaias."

"I don't understand," Isaias said, even if he thought he might. He needed—or at least wanted—more. He needed *help*.

"What is your greatest strength, Father? What is it in you that Hector was drawn to in the first place?"

While he wasn't sure if he fully knew what she meant, Isaias bowed his head. He felt defeated more than anything.

"Is that it?" Violet said, breaking into what Isaias had forgotten for a moment was not a private rite. Her voice was softly fierce. "What now?"

Lena looked to Violet and smiled. "Find the source of all the pain," she said. "Trust me, Violet, okay? I wouldn't leave you here if I didn't think you could do it."

Isaias saw Violet tearing up. "Why can't you just help?"

"I'm not the right person for the job. I'm sorry, little flower—but trust me. Please."

Violet sniffled and lowered her head, saying nothing.

Lena turned back to Isaias. "You try to trust me, too, will you Father? This isn't where the story ends."

Isaias wanted to reply, to ask Lena to reconsider, to say anything at all, but he nodded.

Lena said, "Take care of yourself, Father, as you have always cared for others. And take care of Hector and take care of Violet. I'm sorry, but I can't do more. I've seen it too much—there's a set path you're on, and I can't take you away from that. How you walk it is up to you. Remember, Isaias—patterns in the chaos. Maybe not a reason, but an orderliness."

Isaias remembered, but he wasn't sure it brought him a great deal of comfort in that moment. What good was it for God to have set him on his way if He could not save Hector Himself?

But he knew that was it—Lena had deemed herself to not be on the same path as them, and he knew that he could not convince her. "Goodbye, Lena. I hope we see you again."

"You will," Lena promised with an air of prophecy.

As she exited, she passed Mrs. Marsh who looked mostly confused. She looked between Isaias, Violet, and the still raggedly breathing Hector, who was strangely silent. But Mrs. Marsh didn't question it and instead brought Isaias the mug of tea she had promised him.

Isaias took the mug and knelt by Hector and brought the tea to Hector's lips. Gently, he tipped Hector's head back—no longer afraid to be bitten—and gently massaged his throat to encourage him to drink. Hector did, slowly, and something like relief passed over his face.

Despite the closeness, Isaias felt Hector's spirit only dimly. He wanted to cry for him as much as he had prayed for him—but he could not let himself be ready to mourn. Not for Hector.

Not yet.

Hector,

I know you don't believe in God—but do you believe in me?

Lena tells me that I need to save myself before I can save you—but I'm not sure if I can. I don't know how to pray for myself, let alone heal myself. And maybe it's because I don't want to, really—for what have I ever done to earn true forgiveness, true redemption? It's not that I think I am irredeemable—but God has His purpose for me, and that is all that I am. Why should I ever presume that God would deem me worthy of a life other than what He has planned for me?

But Hector—a part of me thinks, perhaps Lena is right. Maybe if I first tend my own garden, then I will be able to tend yours. And then, when we come out on the other side together, we will both be stronger. Maybe I will finally be worthy of having you in my life. Our garden, together—

I don't know what I mean. I don't know what to think

anymore.

Is this proof that my soul is not pure enough?

I must want to save you only selflessly. So, I am afraid that I don't know what this means—this desire to build a life after this pain but with you as a part of it. Is that something for which *you* would deem me worthy?

One day, possibly, maybe—Yours,

Isaias

XXI

Isaias stood sentry outside the study, fidgeting with his mother's old rosary around his neck, until Violet emerged. After giving Hector the tea and helping restore him somewhat, he had become briefly lucid—Isaias had wanted to give that moment to Violet alone, though he longed for the chance to talk to Hector again. He satisfied himself by standing outside and being close physically, if not spiritually—and that allowed him to keep watch. Who knew when the demonic entity inside of him would re-emerge? Who knew if Isaias was putting her in danger by even letting her speak to Hector?

But Violet emerged after a short while, unharmed if tired. She smiled a little to Isaias and said, "He wants to talk to you, now, Father."

Isaias felt a selfish relief that Hector still wanted to talk to him at all. He replaced the rosary into the collar of his shirt, hidden away. Violet was watching him. Isaias asked her, "How are you feeling, Violet?"

"I don't think I've been in this much pain since Mom left," Violet said softly. Isaias saw her shift her grip on her crutches. "I'm stressed and not sleeping and so everything kind of hurts worse than usual. I'm always in at least a little bit of pain. But it gets worse when things are bad because then I know I'm not taking care of myself. There's always flare ups, but I know I'm not doing anything to manage them. So, I guess I'm fucking *tired*, Father."

"I know you are, Vi," Isaias whispered. He felt terrible that Violet was in so much pain and he hadn't realized just how bad it was. "Do you need to rest?"

Violet shrugged weakly. "We'll be leaving soon. I'll nap in the car."

Isaias was worried that wasn't enough, but what else could he do? "If there's anything I can do to help—"

"There's not," Violet said firmly. Then she softened. "Father—Isaias, you know I've always appreciated you've never—you've never prayed for me to 'get better'. Lots of people would have, in your position. Hell, even Poppy's mother said she would pray for me. I wanted to freak out on her, tell her if God made me disabled, then I'm disabled. That's just who I am. Praying isn't going to change that. And I don't want—I don't want her pity, or anyone's. But I know she does the same and worse for Poppy so I kind of swallow it down. What's one more thing that hurts when everything hurts?"

Isaias chose his words carefully. "I'm sorry to hear that."

"Don't be," Violet said, but less fiercely this time. She shook her head. "It sucks, but I'm used to it. This is my life. I don't want anyone praying for me or feeling sorry for me because they think my life isn't good enough. I don't like it when everything hurts, nobody *wants* to hurt so bad it's hard to get out of bed, but it's *my* life. Mine alone. And—Poppy gets it because she lives it. And Dad understands. And I'm glad you do, too, on some level. Because you never prayed for me. At least not like that."

Isaias smiled. "I've prayed for you for other reasons," he said. "Like when you were nervous about that art project. I don't know if God helps people get As, but I thought I would put it out there to Him."

Violet laughed. It sounded wet. "Thanks, Father. I think I got that A all on my own, though."

"I think you did, too."

Violet smiled tiredly. "Dad's waiting for you."

Isaias accepted the dismissal with as much grace as he could and went into the study. It wouldn't do to keep Hector waiting any longer.

"Hello, my friend," Isaias said gently as he closed the door behind him. He could barely meet Hector's eye—Hector, who looked like a shadow of his former self. Normally vibrant, eager, and cheerful, now he looked exhausted to his very bones—and felt it, too.

"You're going to give me a complex if you keep calling me that," Hector murmured tiredly. Isaias said nothing, and in the space of the silence Hector asked, "Are you okay?"

Isaias frowned. "I think that question would be better posed to you, Hector. Are you alright—all things considered?"

"You know I'm not. We probably both look like shit, but I at least have an excuse. Have you looked in a mirror lately?"

Isaias frowned, looking down at himself, as if that would help him see. He had to admit that Hector was probably right, he probably *did* look quite badly: he could imagine bags under his eyes; cuts on his face from mis-shaving, despite the re-emergence of stubble; his hands looked paler than normal, the skin sallow where it wasn't swallowed up by bandages.

"Yeah, see?" Hector asked. "You know I'm right."

"You might be," Isaias admitted. He walked closer to Hector and knelt by his side. He reached out and took Hector's hand, who did not grip back but curled his fingers weakly around Isaias's. "I'm sorry, Hector. For all you've been through in the past few days."

"It's not your fault, Isaias. You've been doing your damnedest to save me. I just wish you weren't wasting the effort. I still think you look handsome, though—the ragged look kind of works on you."

"Hector," Isaias said, and he saw Hector flinch at the nearly harsh tone in Isaias's voice. He lowered his voice. "Sorry. But I'm not wasting any effort on you. I'm giving you exactly what you deserve—someone to fight to their dying breath for you."

"Not everyone is so lucky," Hector said, laughing meekly.

"That doesn't mean you don't deserve it."

"Right," Hector said softly. "Well, thanks. I appreciate you trying so hard. But—can you promise me something?"

"Anything," Isaias said gravely.

"If I don't make it—"

"—anything except that," Isaias clarified quickly. "You're going to make it, Hector. I promise you." He paused, then said softly, "No matter what, Violet will have a safe home, and a safe family. I will see to that."

Hector nodded, understanding in his eyes. "Okay. Thank you, Isaias."

"Of course, Hector."

In the proceeding silence, Isaias, knees aching from the amount of kneeling and praying he'd been doing, shifted to sit cross-legged on the floor instead. He resisted the urge to rest his forehead on Hector. He would not give in to any weakness, no matter how much he wished he could lean on Hector for comfort for even a single instance.

Hector said, "Violet tells me we're going to go on a bit of a road trip."

Isaias nodded. "Yes. Violet and I will be driving you to Sainte-Jeanne, the town nearby, to meet my bishop. I think that he'll be able to help you."

"That's your father, right? Bishop Reid?"

"Not exactly—"

"He raised you, didn't he?"

"Well, yes," Isaias said slowly. "But it's more complicated than that."

"I don't see how," Hector murmured, frowning. He sounded like he wanted to fight, and Isaias felt the will to argue in him, but something wavered. Hector's head lolled for a moment before it jerked back up, like he was struggling to keep awake. He shook his head, then looked straight-on at Isaias. "Okay, so we're driving us to

Sainte-Jeanne. The good bishop helps us with the exorcism. That's it, then, right?"

"I hope so," Isaias whispered. He reached up to touch the rosary beads at his neck under his collar. He started counting them in his mind's eye.

"Alright. Well, I hope he's as good as you think he is."

"He is," Isaias said firmly. "His Excellency taught me everything that I know."

"And yet he's not your father."

"No. Not really, anyway."

"Okay."

Isaias shrugged slightly, helplessly, not sure what else to say. He watched Hector struggling to keep awake in the chair. "You should rest," he said to Hector. "I'll get Mrs. Marsh to bring you some food and water, but then you should rest until Violet and I are ready to go. Have you been sleeping?"

"I—don't know. I don't remember large swathes of time. I don't think it counts."

"Probably not. Try to rest for a while, if you can."

"I will," Hector promised. "I'll try. But... yeah, food and water sound good, first. I don't remember the last time I ate or drank anything. When you took me to the bathroom last, maybe? I don't know, it's kind of a blur."

"We've brought you food and water post-exorcism a few times, and when Lena was here" Isaias reminded him gently, but realizing it was probably futile to hope Hector remembered much of anything. The lack of recognition on Hector's face hurt, but Isaias wasn't sure if he wanted Hector to remember more, either.

"Well, thanks," Hector said. "I appreciate you trying so hard."

"I think you said that already," Isaias murmured. He slowly rose, letting his touch linger on Hector's hand as he did. He wanted to stay, to hold him, to pretend things were okay. He wanted Hector to hold him, too, for Hector to be able to promise him that things were going to *be* okay. "I'll get Mrs. Marsh to bring you some clean clothes, too, before we leave. Hopefully we have you long enough to get you dressed and cleaned up. But for now: rest."

"I'll try," Hector promised. "And Isaias?"

"Yes, Hector?"

"Thank you."

Isaias nodded but did not accept the thanksgiving. He didn't think that he deserved it.

He turned and left the study.

XXII

Isaias knew that it was a dream when he started bleeding profusely from his hands and feet, stigmata appearing where there had been none before. It was, after all, the only reasonable explanation, to be a dream—Isaias was not a man touched by God more than any other priest, certainly not beyond gifts that were not truly his except to use in God's name.

That did not make him closer to God, he thought. Not any more than he deserved to be, which was—

The pain was almost unbearable with its sudden clarity. He cried out in his dream-state, clawing at his own hands as the blood boiled to the surface.

Why? he asked, but his voice made no words. He wondered what would happen if he bled to death if only in a dream.

Priest of motive unworthy—will you betray Him with a kiss?

No, Isaias tried to say, but there was still no voice to be found in his throat. I will not betray him.

Isaias's hands, feet, side, all hurt so, so much. The blood was bubbling through his cassock on his side. *O God*, he pled silently, his mouth falling open in prayer. *Don't let me die before I can save him.*

No reply came this time.

Isaias woke up, shouting, to Mrs. Marsh shaking his shoulder.

"Father," she was saying urgently. "It was just a dream, Father. You're alright now."

Isaias looked down at his hands, which were shaking in his lap, clasped together. There was a hole torn into the palm of the bandage wrap on his right hand, the cloth pulled away to expose his palm, where he had seemingly dug a trench into his own skin where it had already been raw from being scraped open the other night. The wound bled into the bite-wound Hector had left on his hand. Traces of the fabric were under the thumbnail on his left hand, along with his own blood.

Seeing where Isaias was staring, Mrs. Marsh said, "Let me get you some ointment and a fresh bandage."

She started to stand back up from where she was sat on the edge of Isaias's makeshift nest of blankets and coats on the floor, and Isaias was overcome with an enormous sense of grief—he didn't know if it was hers or his own, and so he reached out with his hurting right hand and took her hand before she could get too far.

"Stay for just a moment, Mrs. Marsh," he asked of her.

She looked at him with a concerned softness in her eyes before she settled back down. She removed Isaias's hand from hers and instead hugged him to her chest.

"It's alright, Father," she said softly. "I've got you."

Isaias was only distantly aware that he was crying. He let Mrs. Marsh hold him, petting his hair and whispering soothing nonsense words, until he had exorcised the worst of his grief. Once he had cried himself out, he said, voice as raw as the stinging wound in his palm, "I hadn't realized I'd fallen asleep."

"Clearly you needed it," she said gently. "I put Violet to bed, too. I thought some rest would do her some good."

"Thank you, Mrs. Marsh."

"Of course, Father."

Isaias sat up slightly and Mrs. Marsh let go of him. "I suppose we'll be driving in the morning at this rate, then."

"I think so—I don't think any of us are in any condition to drive. I'll probably be the most ready, I think."

Isaias frowned. "Well, you wouldn't be coming—"

"What nonsense," Mrs. Marsh scoffed. "Why on earth would I not be going, too? I've been here thus far, haven't I?"

"Well, for two reasons, I think," Isaias said. "First, I need you to cover for me when people come to the rectory looking for me. If I cancel Mass—especially more than one day in a row—someone might come to check up on me. I'll need you to be here to answer the door and to tell anyone who comes knocking that I'm too preoccupied—maybe too sick to answer myself."

"Canceling Mass for a few days because the priest is sick or occupied with a personal emergency is hardly an unheard-of circumstance," Mrs. Marsh protested with a frown. "And the second reason?" she asked.

"Well, someone is going to have to feed the cat."

Mrs. Marsh laughed—startled but earnest. "You want me to go to the Montero home to feed their cat?"

"It would be a great favour to all of us," Isaias said gravely. "And, actually, I was thinking that Prue could come stay in the rectory while we were away. She'll be awfully lonely without company for a few days. I worry about her."

Mrs. Marsh smiled faintly but shook her head. "If you say so, Father. But you would owe me a raise, at that rate. Exorcisms *and* feeding the cat. Goodness—wouldn't it be better to let Lena watch over her, since she said she can't help with the exorcism?"

"Well, I suppose—"

"I'm sure she would feel grateful, in fact, that she is able to help in a smaller way. She seemed to regret that she couldn't do more."

"I mean—"

"We'll call her in the morning," Mrs. Marsh declared. "And drop off the cat before we start on our drive."

Isaias deflated. He wanted to remove Mrs. Marsh from danger as well—it would be impossible to convince Violet, so one of them out of trouble was better than none—but it was clear he wasn't going to win the argument. "Alright."

Mrs. Marsh patted Isaias's knee and said, "Do think about that raise, though."

Isaias laughed wetly. "If I had control of such things," he said, "you would be retiring before we got back home from Sainte-Jeanne, ready to live out the rest of your days in a sunny beach home somewhere. Maybe in Florida."

"Florida might be nice—much nicer weather than this." Mrs. Marsh gestured around the dark kitchen, the windows frosted over from the still-broken heat. "Well, at least put in a good word with Bishop Reid for me, will you?"

"Only the best word," Isaias said gravely. "The Word of God."

Mrs. Marsh swatted gently at him with one hand before she climbed to her feet. She returned to the counter where she had a mug of tea. She picked it up and grimaced in displeasure—presumably at the temperature—but looked back at Isaias. "Please tell me you weren't going to try to convince Violet to stay back too, were you?"

"I thought about it," Isaias admitted. "But I thought she would call me stupid for even suggesting it."

"She would—and she would be right."

"I appreciate your vote of confidence."

"You're very welcome." Mrs. Marsh smiled faintly. "So, when are we leaving?"

"Whenever Violet is awake and ready to go," Isaias said with a faint shrug. "We'll have to go to get her things before we leave, so she has any necessities in case we're away for a few days, but beyond that, well—just figuring out the cat."

"She's still sleeping, then?"

Isaias nodded, taking a moment to feel out Violet's presence in the rectory. He could faintly detect Violet's soul above them, in his room, asleep. He wouldn't disturb her rest unless necessary—she needed to take whatever time for herself she could get. It was a comfort, to feel her in some fleeting semblance of peace—not fully restful, he was sure, but it was something. He felt as if her presence was the feeling of flowers just waiting to bloom.

For a moment, it brought him hope.

Isaias managed a bit more sleep where he had created a small nest on the floor of the kitchen, but it was difficult to really *rest* when he kept such close track of all the presences in the rectory:

Mrs. Marsh, anxious and worried about everyone except for herself.

Violet, afraid but defiant, desperate to save her father but struggling to keep afloat.

Hector, a flickering ghost image of a man, being swallowed up by—

Something darker, something angry. Something lashing out, ready to bite.

Isaias wondered what his own soul would feel like if someone else could sense it; if they could see his spirit, what would they find? If any of his friends, his *family* here, knew the true nature of his heart—would they still deem him worthy?

When the dawn light was filtering through the kitchen window, and Isaias realized he was not going to be able to sleep any longer, especially with the morning arriving, he got up and took a very long, very cold shower. The cold water was punishing against his skin, and the rectory's heat still broken meant he received no relief when he stepped out of the water. His skin was pocked with goosebumps and his shivering didn't let up until he wrapped himself in his clothing—all black, a step shy of his uniform, and a thick sweater. The shower had not been for comfort, but to purify his soul again, to wash him clean of any lingering sin, and to force himself to alertness after fitful sleep. In his misery, he felt a renewed sense of vigor in the need to do the right thing for Hector.

Isaias went downstairs to where Mrs. Marsh had set out his cleaned cassock, his surplice, and his stole. Each still showed signs of wear, stained with blood and sweat. Mrs. Marsh's cleaning could only do so much to hide the signs of suffering. He packed them into a luggage, along with his water-logged copy of the Bible and his mother's rosary. To this, he added two bottles of water after whispering a blessing above them. Once Violet woke, he would go to his room to find another change of clothes in case he needed it, and anything else that might offer him comfort. So too would he retrieve some of his letters from the study after they roused Hector—or whatever lay within him.

Not wanting to wake Mrs. Marsh, Violet, or whatever was currently dormant in Hector, Isaias put on his coat and went outside to make his necessary phone calls.

Bundled tightly against the cold and feeling the bite of cold air against his still somewhat damp skin, Isaias sat on the cold stone of the front step of the rectory as he dialed one of the priests in the city that he knew best, though to call him a friend would be a stretch.

"Father Winnick speaking."

"Hello, Father Winnick. It's Father Flores calling."

"Isaias! We're up early to be calling before Mass—not that I can judge at all. How are things?"

Isaias fought down the nearly overwhelming urge to confess everything to a priest he scarcely knew. Instead, he said, "I'm afraid that I'm feeling quite sick today and I'm not sure it will be a quick recovery. I was hoping that you would be able to send someone to give Mass at the Sacred Heart over the next few days."

"I'm very sorry to hear that, Isaias," Father Winnick said. "But that's not a problem at all. I have an assistant who would be happy for the experience. I can't promise your parish will be particularly *happy* with the sermons, but I promise he'll be eager. Will you be back on your feet by Sunday, do you think?"

Isaias struggled for a moment to remember what day of the week it was. Everything since the last Sunday had blurred together, and he was losing his grip on the passing of reality. But it was only Thursday. Would it be possible for him to have saved Hector in three days' time? "I certainly hope so."

"Good. You see, I don't want the boy to miss Sunday Mass over here, if he doesn't need to... Have you let Bishop Reid know?"

"Not yet," Isaias said with no shortage of guilt. "But don't worry—he'll be hearing from me, soon."

"Alright. Well, I'll send Jonathan over with some soup when he comes to say Mass today. He'll give it straight to Mrs. Marsh, so as not to disturb your rest, on my orders."

Isaias smiled faintly. "That won't be necessary—Mrs. Marsh is already preparing a week's worth of soups for me."

"If you insist."

"I do. Thank you—and Jonathan—for your help, Father Winnick. Peace be with you."

"And with your spirit, Father Flores."

Isaias hung up and stared uncertainly at his phone.

He dialed Bishop Reid.

"Isaias, my boy," was the immediate greeting after only a few short rings. "I hadn't heard from you since your midnight confession, the other night. Mrs. Marsh insisted she would let me know if anything was serious, but—I was hoping to hear from you soon. Is everything alright?"

"Good morning to you, too, Your Excellency," Isaias said tiredly. "I'm—it's a very long story, and one I'd rather give in person. I was thinking I would come up to Sainte-Jeanne sooner than expected. Later today, in fact. I hope you're alright with a visitor on short notice."

Isaias felt the weight of the bishop's hesitation. "Of course, Isaias. I trust you've made appropriate arrangements?"

"Father Winnick at Saint Paul's has agreed to send Jonathan, his assistant, to say Mass today." He neglected to clarify that he had told Father Winnick that he was ill—the good bishop would surely understand soon enough the regretful reason for deceit.

"Well, I'm glad he was able to help you out. I won't ask too many questions now, though, son. Not until you get here. Are you driving?"

"Yes, I am," Isaias said. "It's only an hour away, so it seems best, rather trying to arrange something else."

And, more importantly, Isaias left out that it would be difficult, he thought, to get Hector to cooperate on even a short trip anywhere. At least Isaias had some agency and control over the circumstances if he were driving.

"Of course, my child. Just take care of yourself, won't you?"

"Of course, Your Excellency. I'll see you soon. Peace be with you."

"And with your spirit, Isaias. Take care."

Isaias hung up and headed back inside. He immediately felt, more than he heard, the stirring of the other occupants of the rectory. He went into the kitchen to put on a pot of tea for the others.

Mrs. Marsh appeared first, as Isaias finished setting the pot of tea to brew. "Have you eaten anything?" she immediately asked. "I don't want you to become faint when you're driving, Father."

"People can go longer than two days without food," Isaias pointed out mildly. "And I've started drinking water and tea again. I'll be alright."

"I don't care if you can go longer. You need your strength. Violet, and Hector besides, need your strength."

Isaias's stomach constricted—beyond hunger, he felt *hollow*—and reluctantly nodded his head. "Maybe something small won't hurt."

"It won't," Mrs. Marsh said and stepped past Isaias to rummage through the cabinets. "I promise you that. I don't think we can make much without the heat on, but I'll see what we can make do with.

We could always stop by somewhere for some breakfast on our way to Sainte-Jeanne, as well..."

"I defer to your best judgement," Isaias said with a tired laugh. He poured himself and Mrs. Marsh a mug of tea each and a third for Violet when she appeared a few moments later. He set Mrs. Marsh's mug on the counter and his and Violet's at the small table. Violet sat at the table and rested her crutches within arm's reach. She had carried a throw blanket down with her, wedged under her arm. Once she was seated, she wrapped herself up in the blanket to ward off the still-cold rectory. She seemed to disappear under it, leaving only her round face peeking out from the plush white fabric enveloping her.

"We'll be leaving soon, I guess?" Violet asked. She snuck one hand out of the blanket to pick up her mug of tea and drink from it. Isaias watched the relief of the warmth of it pass over her features.

"We will be," Isaias confirmed. "We need to make arrangements for Prue to be cared for—Mrs. Marsh suggested taking her to Lena—but we'll leave before long. It's another school day, though—do you think your school might raise concerns about you missing so many classes?"

Violet snorted, a thick puff of mist escaping in the cold air. She sipped her tea. "No. All my teachers have already given up on me—except my art teacher, I guess. I'm too much work for everyone, they'll be glad to get a break from me."

Isaias frowned. "What do you mean?"

"Exactly what I said. I'm—I don't know, distractible and loud. And I have a hard time focusing sometimes so the teachers need to help me more and I can tell they all think it's a chore but then they feel guilty and like they have to because I'm their charity case student."

"There isn't anyone at the school who can support you?"

"They tried to pull me out of regular classes and put me in 'special' classes." Violet shrugged. "But I told dad that I was pretty sure they were just trying to shove me in a corner somewhere so I wouldn't be anyone's problem anymore, and he believed me, so he said no. He told them it would be better for me to keep up with school if I was in classes with all my friends. But they do the same thing to Poppy. Any time we need a little extra help... the art teacher is different, though. That's why I like it so much and why it's my best class. She encourages me to be as angry or hurt as I want in my work. She doesn't—I don't know, censor me."

"You don't think she'll worry that you're missing classes?"

"She knows that sometimes it's hard for me to go to school. If I'm in too much pain, she'd rather I be at home. I can do art at home, too. She'll figure out catching me up when I'm back."

Isaias nodded, reluctantly. He was worried about the long-term impacts on her academic career—what if they expelled her for truancy? He had seen it happen to other young people in the community—but it was far from his place, especially now of all times, to tell her that her feelings of frustration were misplaced. He believed her that she felt dismissed as much as she felt pitied. He couldn't blame her for wanting neither.

Feeling guilty for not having seen the full extent of her struggles before a crisis happened, Isaias resolved to ask if he could do more to support her success if they all made it through this in one piece. He knew she loved her art classes more than anything, but he hadn't realized how small school made her feel, otherwise. He would have to talk to her—if there was any help she wanted or needed from him, he would try to give it to her.

And maybe he could commission some art from her—something to decorate the previously mostly bare walls of the rectory. He had art projects of hers that she'd nearly discarded, but maybe he could ask her for something of her own original making, whatever *she* wanted to make, for him to put up. The thought brought him some small comfort, that he could have a piece of his little family hung up on the walls after all this was over.

"Well, I hope soon you'll be back to creating your art," Isaias said. He hoped it brought her some small comfort, as well.

XXIII

THEY ATE A MEAGRE breakfast, packed a few more things, including some letters from Hector just for the comfort they brought Isaias, and confirmed with Lena that she was able to watch over Prue. With all their mundane duties in order, they prepared to drive to Sainte-Jeanne—which meant rousing Hector.

Even when Isaias had been collecting the letters, Hector had watched him carefully. Isaias had expected taunts and torments, but instead he had been silent, and something about that was chilling enough. The study was the warmest room in the rectory, though Isaias wasn't sure if anyone else could tell—so as he had gathered the last of his things, the demon in Hector watching him with calculating eyes, Isaias had slowly become dizzy with the strange heat of the room. The room wasn't hot enough to justify it, but he had felt like the warmth had wedged itself into his insides, his blood boiling, his brain frying.

He had left quickly until they were ready.

Now, Mrs. Marsh helped Isaias carefully untie Hector's wrists from the chair. Isaias watched cautiously, ready for even the barest movement from the demon that indicated it might do something. Mrs. Marsh treated the wounds on Hector's wrists with ointment while Isaias treated them with holy water. Hector hissed in pain, then in threat, and Isaias had to look away from the wet spot gathering on the front of Hector's pants. The man he cared so much for looked weak, and it hurt to see—the urine on his pants was only one small things, in the face of it all, but he was fainter, he seemed to be losing weight though he was still a solid man, he stank of sweat and animal fear.

Isaias's heart ached in a way that was familiar but that he had never truly understood. The pain of seeing someone he wanted to only have happiness who was instead suffering.

If they made it through this, he knew it would be hard to ever leave Hector's side again. All of his longing for family, and it had been right there in front of him. Now—now he was so close to losing it all.

He couldn't bear thinking in 'if's. He couldn't accept the possibility of a future without Hector and without Violet. He couldn't deny any longer the necessary role that they played his life. Imagining a future without them would break his heart and it had already taken so much damage.

When Isaias looked back up at Hector, their eyes met. Something disturbed him about what he saw in Hector's gaze—not understanding, but instead something conniving probing him.

Isaias tore his eyes away from Hector's gaze and focused on the wounds on his wrists. He worried that the split skin might become infected. There were raised red welts, but where the rope had broken skin, the skin was yellowing in places, purpling in others. Pus bubbled from the deepest wounds.

Isaias washed the injuries out with holy water again, dabbing it as clean as he could. Mrs. Marsh applied ointment and wrapped them with gauze. After, she changed the bandages on Hector's hands as well. The wounds from Sunday still looked fresher than they should, as if his body was refusing to heal from the gashes he'd had cut into his palms. Isaias's own injured hand throbbed in sympathetic pain.

Another *if*: what if, even after exorcism, parts of Hector never recovered? How changed might he be—physically, mentally, spiritually?

Once Hector's wounds were treated, Mrs. Marsh said, "We should change his clothes again."

Isaias nodded mutely. Mrs. Marsh retrieved a fresh change of clothes for Hector from the things she had taken from the Montero home. She had changed Hector before when he was sleeping but now, with him awake, Isaias saw her hesitation, afraid the demon would do something to hurt her. "I can do it," he said. He took the clothes from Mrs. Marsh and laid them gently to the side before kneeling in front of Hector. Mrs. Marsh dismissed herself, leaving Isaias and Hector alone.

It felt different from the other night. Then, when he had cleaned the blood from Hector's beard and washed his feet and done anything he could to bring him comfort, it had been *Hector*, the man who held so much of his heart. Now, he was sure the silence was the demon watching him, waiting for any moment he might slip. Biding his time to seize a foothold and break Isaias down.

Stripping Hector of his clothes with some difficulty, Isaias averted his gaze at the appropriate moments. He bit back the bile in his throat at the overpowering stench of human waste, vomit, sweat, and blood. He put Hector's soiled clothes aside and reached for the fresh clothing.

"Oh, *Father*..." Isaias froze at the breathy whisper from Hector. "How long have you wondered what Hector might look like? Won't you look now—while you have your chance?"

Isaias swallowed his desire to reply, to deny it, to say *anything*—he would not engage with the demon. He would not acknowledge anything it said to him, no matter what it made him feel. And he refused to accept what it said, besides—it was Hector's *heart* that called out to him, nothing more. There was nothing more he wanted than the closeness of their hearts.

I know you heard me. This time—the voice in his head, echoing into his chest like a vibration. Isaias detected a ringing left in its wake, a buzzing in ears that rejected sounds he was never meant to hear.

He hurriedly dressed Hector without a word, avoiding looking too closely at his soft skin or wondering what it felt like, then called Mrs. Marsh back in.

"We need to take Hector out to the car," he told her, not quite able to meet her eye either. He stood on one side of Hector and Mrs. Marsh on the other as they helped Hector to his feet. The demon did not fight them but instead grinned wickedly even when Hector's legs buckled under him, weak after too long with so little movement and too little sustenance. Isaias once again feared for the damage being done to Hector, convinced that this thing was rotting him from the inside.

They guided him out of the study, where Violet hovered nearby. As they approached the door, Isaias let go to fetch a winter coat and boots for Hector to protect him from the cold morning air. They had to hurry, though, if they were to make it out before anyone from the church arrived and spotted them leaving.

The demon, though, now stood still and watched Isaias with something menacing in his eyes. "Father, I just had a fun thought—what if on our little road trip, I take the wheel? Send us all careening into a tree? The road to Sainte-Jeanne is dead at this time of day, I bet no one would find the scene of the accident for a while. Can't you picture it—Hector's body, pinned under the wreckage, impaled by debris, bleeding out on the asphalt with no one there to save him?"

Isaias did his best *not* to picture it, in fact—he tried to force the mental image out of his mind, viciously vivid in a way he had to assume was the influence of the demon. "I don't think you would do that," Isaias whispered, softer than he intended. "Your host is valuable to you."

"Oh, you think so, Father? You think I care if a single man lives or dies?"

"I think you do," Isaias said, and tried to hide that he was bluffing. "Or else you wouldn't have stuck around for so long. If you didn't have use for him, why would you tolerate so many exorcisms?"

"Maybe," the demon purred, "your little exorcisms aren't all they're cracked up to be. Ever think of that? That I think it's *fun* to listen to your little desperate prayers, begging for mercy from a God who stopped listening a long time ago?"

"In the name of Christ our saviour, you will walk out of here and you will get in the car, and you will behave peacefully. God compels you."

"That's cute."

"Hey," Violet interjected. Isaias looked to her where she stood near the foyer mirror, her back to it. She stepped out of the way, bringing it fully into view of Isaias—and the demon. "Look this way."

The demon did—and froze as he locked eyes with his reflection in the mirror. Isaias saw it too: a distorted vision of Hector, revealing the rot inside. There was something there, something *other*, something with skin sloughing off in necrotic chunks, bile dripping from his lips, eyes hollow and expressionless.

Isaias tore his eyes from the vision of a corpse-like Hector, but the demon didn't look away. "You think I'm afraid of you?" he asked in a harsh, angry whisper, but Isaias wasn't sure who he was addressing.

Violet, in all her brilliant bravery, said in what seemed like her best impression of Isaias's exorcism voice, "The power of Christ compels you to tell us your name—and obey."

The demon snarled, pulling Hector's lips back in a too-wide scowl, baring his teeth. But he didn't peel his eyes from the mirror and his strangely soft voice didn't match his expression. "No."

"We're ordering you," Violet said, her voice trembling with the strain of her courage. "Give us your name, so that we might bind you."

The demon scowled but, haltingly, his voice forced out like air after being struck, he said, "Carreau."

Relieved, Isaias said, "Then, Carreau: we order you to leave with us."

Looking up from the mirror, the demon stared Isaias down. Isaias stared back, his heart hammering in his chest. But just when he thought he would break, the *demon* backed down.

"Okay," he spat, as if they hadn't just ordered him by his own hellish name. "But only because I think it'll be funny to watch you fail in front of your Bishop Reid. I'll be *delighted* to see you lose his faith."

Isaias tried not to wince. He looked away, carefully passing his gaze over the demon's reflection in the mirror. The demon, too, tore his eyes away from the truth of his reflection—and the mirror *cracked* in reply, a sharp shattering sound as the glass bent inwards against all logic.

"Seven years' bad luck," Violet murmured with a nervous laugh. Isaias wasn't sure if she was joking.

Isaias cleared his throat. "We shouldn't be superstitious when we have God on our side."

"Sure," Violet said. Isaias saw her fumbling with her phone as she put on her coat. Isaias's phone chimed and he glanced at the text from Violet.

Was that too easy?

Isaias frowned, knowing that she was probably right, but not wanting to look a gift horse in the mouth. Perhaps luck was simply finally on their side, superstitions aside? Perhaps—

God is looking out for us, he texted back.

He saw Violet shake her head slightly, but she pocketed her phone without replying.

As the car rolled up to the Montero house, Isaias was surprised to see someone sitting on the front step. The demon had been surprisingly quiet as they drove, and Isaias had been focused on the road, but as he approached the house it was unmistakable that there was someone there.

"Poppy?" Violet asked from the passenger seat—Mrs. Marsh sat in the back with Hector, whose wrists had been re-bound to prevent him from easily going after Mrs. Marsh or, worse, grabbing the wheel while Isaias drove like he had threatened to.

As soon as Isaias was parked in their driveway, Violet was clambering out of the car, hurrying along on her crutches despite the remnants of fresh snow on the asphalt. Poppy equally sprung to her feet when she saw Violet and walked briskly to her friend. Poppy hugged Violet tenderly, and Violet leaned heavily into the other girl.

Isaias stayed in the car to avoid interrupting the moment between the girls sooner than necessary, but even from that short distance he could sense the immense relief in both of them to see the other again. It warmed his heart, to feel the love they had for one another.

He really hadn't understood just how dear they were to each other.

Isaias turned off the car and climbed out, Mrs. Marsh following after. Isaias engaged the child locks and pocketed the keys—it felt like a ridiculous way to keep the demon staying put, as he was sure no engaged locks or taken keys could stop him from doing something if he really wanted to, but it was a moment for small comforts. "Keep an eye out for Carreau trying anything," Isaias said to Mrs. Marsh. "And if he does—yell as loud as you can."

"Might disturb the neighbours," Mrs. Marsh mused, but Isaias knew she took it seriously.

Isaias approached the two teenagers still hugging in the driveway and cleared his throat slightly to interrupt the moment as gently as possible. Poppy remained steady as she waited for Violet to pull away, giving Violet the opportunity to get as stable of footing as she could before Poppy moved away herself. Still, she looked embarrassed and averted her eyes from Isaias. He saw Violet nudge the base of her crutch against Poppy's snow-crusted boot. "I didn't expect to see you here," Violet said once Poppy had looked back up at her.

"My mother was being—herself," Poppy said. She didn't elaborate, but Isaias felt the understanding pass over Violet. She knew what that meant. "I knew you wouldn't be home, but I thought you wouldn't mind if I used the key your dad gave me to swing by whenever. So I came to check on Prue and kind of be... anywhere other than home for a bit."

"That's okay," Violet said softly. "Why were you out here in the cold?"

"You said you were leaving town, and I knew you'd come here first. I knew you'd be here soon, so I came out to watch for you."

There was a moment of silence before Violet said, soft enough to indicate her desire for privacy even though Isaias stood less than a meter away, but clear enough for Poppy to hear her, "I missed you."

"Me too, Vi."

Isaias was loathe to interrupt the moment, but the air was frigid, and time was scarce. "We should go inside and make arrangements."

Violet nodded and Poppy led the way back to the Montero house, opening the still-unlocked door. She flicked the light on and closed the door behind Isaias and Violet as if it were her home, not Violet's.

Isaias didn't think much of it for long, though, as he was instantly awash with relief at the fact that the Montero's house still had *working heat*. The sting of it was almost painful against his numb skin. The car had had heat as well, but the drive had been so short that Hector's old car's engine had barely had time to warm up, let alone had the heat kicked on enough for him to truly *feel* it.

This, though, was a home.

It was strange how something as simple as *central heat* reminded Isaias just how much he had lacked something like a home.

Isaias felt badly leaving Mrs. Marsh out in the cold, but that just meant they couldn't linger long.

"Is your dad okay?" Poppy asked of Violet.

"No," Violet said. "But we're figuring it out. Isaias is—well, we're working on it."

Poppy seemed to choose her words carefully. "I guess he wouldn't bounce back so easy, eh?"

"Yeah." Violet shook her head before looking uncertainly between Isaias and Poppy. Bashfully, she said, "I told Pop my theory before I ever told you, Father. She knows what's going on."

Isaias let out a breath of relief. He had thought Poppy being present would prevent them from speaking frankly, but he hadn't known what to think. Poppy had clearly known something was wrong, but Isaias hadn't known how much to say. It was Violet's family who was hurting, after all, and it wasn't for Isaias to disclose, no matter how dear to his heart Hector and his daughter were. "Good to know."

"So, it's true?" Poppy asked. "Your dad is—he's possessed by a demon?"

"Yeah, he is. He's—he's in the car outside. We're going to take him to Father Isaias's bishop for an—for an exorcism."

"I'm sorry, Vi." Poppy's voice was filled with barely restrained grief. Isaias could tell Hector meant a lot to her, as well. It suddenly struck him that he had never met Poppy's father. Only her mother brought her to church, and on what seemed to be an 'as needed' basis, at that. Whenever Poppy's mother had wanted to remind her daughter of who she obeyed, God was brought into the picture.

Now, seeing her here, in the safe space of the Montero home, Violet reaching for her hand to share their sorrow together, grieving Hector in her own way but trying to not show it too much, trying not to burden Violet with it, Isaias realized there was another piece of the lives of his loved ones he hadn't seen before.

And as much as he mourned for all of their pain, it made him love them more. Their hearts were full of so much depth, so much wonder, and Isaias loved them for it.

"Poppy," Isaias interrupted softly, "are you going to be safe here, if we leave for a few days? I don't want you to go home if you're not ready to."

Poppy frowned at him. "Can I come with you, Father?"

"What? Poppy, it's dangerous—"

"Isaias," Violet interjected firmly. "This is my family. And you don't make our choices for us. If Poppy wants to come, then I want her there."

"I—Violet, I don't think I can condone bringing someone else into harm's way."

"Poppy is family, too," Violet insisted. She didn't sound angry despite her stubbornness. "If she wants to be there, she can be. She has that right."

Something in Isaias's heart ached. But he supposed it was true—one had the right to be with their family, no matter who that family was. If Hector had been physically ill, not spiritually unwell, would Isaias not be desperate to be by his side anyway? If Violet's health took a turn for the worse, would Isaias not want to be there for her? God willing, neither would ever suffer again—but would it not be natural for Isaias to want to be with them while they did, to offer any love and comfort he could in the face of their pain?

"You're right," Isaias said. "But if things become too dangerous—for either of you, or for Mrs. Marsh—then I will do whatever I can to keep you out of harm's way." He had promised Hector he would keep Violet safe, after all. He was sure it would extend to Poppy as well.

"I'll take it." Violet grimaced slightly. "Pop, we'll catch you up more on the way, okay? We should get out of here quick."

"Good idea," Isaias said. "Do you need help grabbing anything for you or your father?"

"Poppy can help me with my things, maybe you can get anything you think would be helpful for dad? And then I'll probably need help getting Prue into her carrier."

Isaias nodded. "Sounds good. We'll get going quickly."

The three split apart—Violet heading to her bedroom with Poppy in tow, while Isaias went to Hector's room. As he walked down the hall, Prue emerged, the cat weaving around his ankles. Just outside the bedroom door, he paused to pet the cat to buy himself a second of thought.

He had been in Hector's room before, when Hector had wanted to show him a home improvement project or a book he was reading, but this felt different somehow—private and personal, entering without Hector there with him. As he stepped across the threshold, he took note of how the room remained the same—woodworking projects half-finished on a small desk tucked in the corner, a book he'd been reading for months still barely begun on his nightstand—and how the room looked different—there was a lack of love in it, a lack of Hector's spirit. It truly looked abandoned, though it had only been a few days since they had found Hector there, convulsing, possessed by something from Hell. Despite it being mere days, there was a thick layer of dust on everything and a foul stench wafted from the garbage can next to the bed.

Isaias didn't let himself investigate the scent anymore than he could let himself imagine what this room would look like with more light, more life, more love. What he would change to keep it clean and tidy, what piece of himself he would leave behind in a room like this. It was an absurd imagining—this was Hector's room, Hector's space. Isaias would be grateful for what part he had in Hector's life and never ask for more than he had been given.

He quickly gathered a few changes of clothes for Hector before rifling through his desk to see if there were some objects he might collect to bring Hector comfort in this trying time. Surely, a reminder of himself, who he used to be, would help him hold on, give him the will to keep fighting back. He picked up a woodcarving project Hector had been working on, a hand carved rose next to a little bird house he was probably planning on putting up when the snow had melted, and spring had arrived.

Then, he found the letters and postcards—bundles of them, buried deep in the drawer. There were many Isaias recognized, his own handwriting recalling memories back to him, correspondence he had sent Hector, bringing him comfort that Hector held onto them just as he held onto his letters from Hector. But there were also postcards, newspaper articles, letters from and about people Isaias did not know. And, perhaps strangest of all, a stack of letters he almost missed because they were crumpled and pushed aside like Hector had meant to discard them. When Isaias smoothed them out, he saw his own name as the addressee—letters, perhaps dozens of them, that Hector had never sent.

On impulse, Isaias placed the letters with the wooden rose, but he left them behind, taking only the clothing.

Violet and Poppy emerged from Violet's room a few moments later, Poppy carrying a backpack of Violet's things. Isaias saw the way she brushed her fingers across the back of Violet's hand gently instead of holding it. He saw Violet nervously touch the beads of a rosary around her neck—Hector's rosary, the one from The Second Voyage—before returning her hand to the grip of her crutch.

"Ready?" Violet asked as Poppy retrieved the cat carrier from the hall closet.

"Ready," Isaias confirmed.

It would all be over soon, he hoped.

XIV

Once they were back on the road, and Prue was left with Lena along with some cat supplies, Isaias drove with Violet still in the front seat, Poppy joining Mrs. Marsh in the backseat with the possessed Hector, the demon—Carreau, he had called himself, a creature of heartlessness, Isaias had found through a quick search when he had a second to breathe—strangely quiet as they drove through the city streets. It was only once they had passed through morning traffic into the quieter roads leading out of town that something changed.

Isaias didn't notice the radio at first—it started subtle, a quiet white noise at the back of his mind that he at first mistook for the tinnitus that had been intermittently bothering him lately. Soon voices cycled in and out, various channels breaking through to announce the morning news, the weather, traffic reports. That static of it was grating, to say the least, and he could tell the others were uncomfortable, too, especially Poppy, who was grimacing in the back. Violet leaned forward to turn the radio off, but nothing happened.

"You don't expect me to sit back here, bored the whole time, do you?" Carreau purred.

"You," Isaias said, feeling momentarily brave, "are beginning to sound like a petulant child."

Something ice cold, colder than the wind outside as snow began to fall again, wrapped around Isaias's throat and he nearly jerked against the feeling but held fast, avoiding sending the car skidding. A chill ran down Isaias's spine as fingers—Hector's fingers, he could tell, though Hector did not control them—massaged against his throat, fingering his Adam's apple with surprising tenderness. Isaias's mouth went dry, and he fought to not swallow, not show any sign of fear that the demon would feel under his hand.

"Would you rather the alternative, Father?" Carreau purred in his ear. Isaias tried to focus on driving but struggled to remain composed against the feeling of hot breath on the shell of his ear. "I can be all kinds of things for you, besides petulant."

The grip on his throat tightened, though not enough to hurt, and Isaias cringed away—then inadvertently jerked away with the wheel in hand as a wet tongue licked into the curve of his ear.

The car skidded across wet, snow-slick roads, and car in the opposite lane blared its horn as it slammed on its breaks and narrowly avoided skidding, too.

"Isaias!" Violet shouted in alarm.

There was nothing on Isaias's throat, nothing on his ear, and the demon was seated in the backseat as if he had never moved. His wrists were still bound, unable to touch Isaias.

Isaias righted the car with his heart pounding in his ears. He ignored the driver from the other car making angry and rude gestures from their own front seat as they drove past. As the pounding in Isaias's head faded, he realized the radio was no longer making that awful noise, but its place had been taken by ringing in his ears that was just loud enough to make its presence known without leading yet to a migraine.

He knew that Carreau was watching him using Hector's eyes.

Isaias felt immensely grateful that the rest of the drive to Sainte-Jeanne passed without further incident. By the time they were in the town, he felt familiar enough with the roads that he could navigate to the bishop's home without much difficulty.

He hadn't been back for a long time. While nearby Sainte-Félicité was where he had completed seminary, this was where he had grown up. His earliest years had been spent in the churches of Sainte-Jeanne and the saint cities nearby, but the ones here were *home*. He had lived as a boy in their rectories, walked through their pews, broken bread and said grace in the backroom kitchens. He had even been homeschooled in the Sunday School classrooms.

It was strange, comparing his life as a child and as a teenager to the glimpses he saw now of Violet's life—it was so different. Somehow, it had never fully struck Isaias that it might be strange to have rarely left the church except to travel to a different one.

You are God's orphan, they had told him. The memory struck him quite suddenly, and he wasn't sure he could place why someone would have said such a thing. He wasn't an orphan. His parents still lived but had *chosen* to give him to God. That wasn't the same thing at all. He was given up to best nurture his gifts from God.

It unsettled Isaias, but he pushed through the unbidden memories and followed instinct instead to lead him to wrought iron strength. He parked on the street across from the church and its rectory and took a deep breath as he glanced at the clergy house. He tried to steady his nerves—whatever happened next, and he did not know what would, might decide Hector's fate.

"You okay, Father?" Violet asked softly.

Glancing at her, Isaias could tell that Poppy and Mrs. Marsh—and, worse, Carreau-in-Hector—were watching him, too. "I'm alright."

Something echoed out of Mrs. Marsh that felt like understanding.

Isaias turned off the car and got out before he could overthink it any further. He went around to the back to open the passenger door where Hector sat. The demon watched him steadily as Isaias pulled him from the car and to his feet. He was too calm; too quiet. Isaias had expected at least taunting but instead there was *nothing.*

Against his better judgement, Isaias reached out to Hector's soul and whatever clung to it, trying to understand what it was, exactly, that he was dealing with here.

The arrhythmic pulse of Hector's soul mimicked a weakening heart, faint and unsteady. Fading. Meanwhile something coated it like grease, difficult to wash off. The demon didn't have his own soul, surely, so it instead clung to Hector's like a film of oil.

Something sticky and foul touched Isaias's heart, too, trying to pass from Hector to him.

Isaias jerked back instinctively from the demon despite not being touched. He felt something like *satisfaction* dripping off him. He was smug over whatever had just transpired.

Isaias ignored the looks from Mrs. Marsh and Poppy, the latter pausing as she stood just outside the door where Violet sat, readily available if Violet wanted someone to hold onto as she got out of the car. Instead, he carefully took hold of Hector's ample upper arm again and led him toward the rectory.

It was unnaturally bright out, the sunlight reflecting off the snow in front of the Bishop's home, making Isaias dizzy. His ears were ringing again, and he wondered for a moment how long it really took for a lack of proper sleep to catch up with someone. He almost didn't notice the front door of the rectory opening, not fully registering it until Bishop Reid appeared on the front step. He had tugged a toque haphazardly over his ears before exiting, but otherwise was dressed as if he had barely woken from slumber. His grey hair poked out from under the wool hat in tufts and he wore a housecoat hugged tightly around his body against the cold. For a moment Isaias *did* think of the man as his father, with him looking like an ordinarily old man. He looked older than Isaias had remembered him.

"I didn't realize you were bringing company, Father," Bishop Reid said.

"Apologies, Your Excellency," Isaias said, momentarily letting go of Hector as they got close enough to the bishop to greet him properly. Isaias bent before his bishop-father, taking his hand and kissing his ring. "It's good to see you."

"And you, Isaias. I see Mrs. Marsh, but who are your other friends?" he asked, as Isaias rose to his feet.

Isaias glanced back at Hector, who stood between Mrs. Marsh and Poppy, and Violet who stood slightly to the side, watching steadily. "This is my dear friend Hector Montero," Isaias said. "His daughter, Violet, and Violet's..."

In the moment of hesitation before Isaias defined Violet and Poppy's relationship, Poppy interjected suddenly, "I'm Violet's friend, Poppy."

Isaias saw the sad understanding pass through Violet's eyes and felt for her. But he nodded and said nothing—he would never draw attention to anything that might make either of them feel unsafe. And it wasn't his place to define their closeness, either—he wasn't even sure if he fully understood, but it wasn't *for* him to understand.

"Well—hello to Isaias's friends," the bishop said, voice bemused and expression skeptical—until his eyes landed on the ropes around Hector's wrists and his expression fell into something grave. He shivered then stepped back into the house, gesturing for them to follow him out of the cold. "Well, no need for any of us to freeze death."

Isaias held the door open for the others. Violet entered first, then Poppy helped Mrs. Marsh with Hector. Staying silent as he closed the door behind them, Isaias tried to find his words to tell the bishop what, exactly they were dealing with. He was bringing a possessed man, even if he was a friend, into the bishop's home without his knowledge. He felt sick with the thought—and by the way the bishop was studying Isaias as he took off his boots, he knew it.

"What's wrong, boy?"

"It's—" Isaias began, struggling to put words to his concerns now that he was faced with his mentor, the man who had raised him. "My friend Hector, here—"

"—my dad is possessed," Violet blurted out.

Isaias flinched and looked to the Bishop Reid. He didn't know how the bishop would react to such a statement. He steeled himself for a raised voice, an incredulous denial, the man telling them to *be serious.*

Instead, the Bishop said, eyes narrowed, "Excuse me, Miss?"

Violet didn't budge. "My dad is possessed."

Bishop Reid didn't reply to Violet, instead turning to Isaias. "Isaias, can you explain this? Because it seems to me you've brought a delusional young woman—"

"Hey—"

"Bishop Reid, please hear us out," Isaias said softly. "We have reason to believe he is genuinely possessed."

Bishop Reid kept his eyes narrowed on Isaias, but Mrs. Marsh stepped closer. "Your Excellency, please."

The bishop raised his hand to dismiss Mrs. Marsh, who faltered in the face of his silencing. Instead, he addressed Isaias, "The man looks ill, Isaias. What precautions have you taken before bringing him all this way?"

"I did my due diligence," Isaias promised, though he wasn't sure if it would be sufficient for his bishop's liking. "The only reasonable conclusion was that Hector is possessed. Your Excellency, I know him—I *know* this man. This is not him."

The bishop's incredulity only increased. "You *know* him? Isaias, it is unacceptable to let your *personal feelings* get in the way of your judgement. I know your talents lie in your empathy, but you are to let *God* be your guide, not your *heart.*"

Isaias frowned, feeling like a scolded boy, an effect the bishop often had on him. He thought he might cry from the pure frustration of it all. "Your Excellency..."

"Oh, shut *up*," Hector hissed. His lips were curled back, baring his teeth at the bishop. Evidently, the demon had grown tired of being talked about like he wasn't there. "Don't act like you aren't pissing your pants in fear. You know a demon when you fucking see one, *Your Excellency*."

The bishop stepped backwards. He groped for a cross that stood on a side table. His face was steely, impossible to read, but his aura, his presence—it was full of awe and fear. "Isaias," he said, "you really did bring a demon into my home. I will grant the authority to conduct an exorcism. But we will need to have a talk about your flagrant disregard of protocol."

"Oh, gee, *another* exorcism," the demon crooned. "As if Father Fuck Up here needs your *permission* to do it, Bishop. He's just not strong enough to do it alone. And poor boy, thinks his daddy can save him. Sounds familiar, doesn't it?"

Bishop Reid shot Isaias a quick look, and Isaias felt his cheeks heat up in shame, but the look at him lasted only an instant before the bishop turned his attention to Mrs. Marsh. "Prepare a room. We will restrain him. I'll gather the rites and our tools." He turned to Isaias as Mrs. Marsh launched into action, stone-faced and serious. "We will begin post-haste. The children will stay in the living room while you assist me. You'll have to fill me in on what has happened so far—hopefully you haven't compromised the man's soul already. This is the friend you spoke of before, correct? Not Catholic."

Isaias was reeling at how quickly the bishop fell into step, gave orders, and put Isaias in his place—all in a few fell swoops of his words. "He's not, no," Isaias said, feeling cowed in the face of his own father figure.

"He was, once," Violet interjected. She lifted one hand from her crutches to touch the rosary around her neck, tucked just below the collar of her shirt. "I think my grandmother was devout. Dad must have given up on it after he lost her." She lowered her eyes, as if in grief. "He talked recently—when all of this first started happening—about losing faith, so he must have had faith in the first place."

"Good." Bishop Reid nodded perfunctorily. "That will make it easier to bring him back to God."

"And Your Excellency?" Violet asked, voice and gaze firm. "Poppy and I will *not* be waiting outside. That's my dad. I'm going to be there."

"Excuse me?" the bishop asked. "You'll simply get in the way—"

"Violet can hold her own," Isaias stepped in before more damage could be done. "And as family, I think she deserves to at least observe. And if she would like her—friend there, then I think that she has that right."

"This is God's business, not hers." The bishop shook his head. "She'll be a liability. It's much too dangerous."

This time, it was the demon who broke in. "Really, sir? Do you think that if I really wanted to hurt the kids, that a few walls would stop me? You should know—your kind is all about hurting kids. You wouldn't let just anything stop you."

"*My kind?*" the bishop snarled.

"You know exactly what I mean."

Isaias ignored the discomfort of whatever the demon wanted to imply, cast it aside for the sake of Hector. Instead, he said, "Your Excellency, we don't have time."

The bishop tore his eyes off the demon. "You're right. Fine, the girls can be there, but they will *not* interfere. Do we know the demon's name?"

"Carreau," Violet supplied. Isaias felt a hint of her dark pride that she had solved that mystery.

"A demon of heartlessness," the bishop said softly and fiercely. He cast his eyes to Isaias suspiciously, and Isaias felt something like distrust—as if perhaps the bishop suspected Isaias would withhold something from him when telling him everything. He said nothing more of it, though, and instead turned to the demon. "By the power invested in me by Christ our Saviour—"

"Oh, I *know*," the demon said, spitting at the bishop's feet. He mutated Hector's once kind smile into a wicked snarl. "You don't have to tell me. Let's just get this over with, shall we?"

"Let us bind thee," Isaias cut in, improvising to support his mentor. He put on his bravest voice. "With us, you will face God—and repent."

The demon looked at Isaias with pure hatred in its eyes, and Isaias's heart sank into his stomach to see such a horrible, raw emotion on Hector's face, a face he would have only wanted love for. But Carreau bowed Hector's head as if in concession. "Let's do this then. The *real* fun is about to begin."

XXV

Standing in his childhood bedroom as he dug through his duffle bag, Isaias felt irrationally embarrassed for the fact there were traces of blood on his surplice and stole still, and that soon His Excellency Bishop Reid would see that. Not only would that show that he really had conducted exorcism without his authorization, a breach of protocol that risked the souls of both himself and of Hector, but it was categorical proof that he had *failed*.

He was changing into his uniform in the very room he had resided in as a boy. Not much of a child's room, he would be the first to admit—but it had been his. It didn't much matter if a rectory was not meant to be a home for children and that the room had always been bare walls and impersonal decorations. It had been the place that had given him a home after he was rejected.

No, not rejected. He would not allow himself to believe that. He was given to a higher purpose—not discarded but pushed to brighter things.

Dressed in his cassock and with the blood-spattered surplice and purple stole around his shoulders, Isaias stepped into the hallway and walked to the bishop's room. The clergy house felt smaller now, as an adult—distances that had once seemed vast now felt claustrophobic and tight.

He knocked lightly on the bishop's door, another thing that had once felt like a daunting task.

"Come in, Isaias," the bishop called. Isaias opened the door and stepped in, closing it behind him. "How do I look?" Bishop Reid asked with a weary smile.

"As Bishop-like as always," Isaias answered, looking over the man in uniform. He stepped forward to help his mentor tie off the purple fascia. He kept his head bowed solemnly, even as he stepped back.

"Thank you, my boy." The bishop took the time to examine Isaias's own uniform, then. "Blood?" he asked. "So, you really did try to perform an exorcism alone. Let me see you hand," he commanded, holding his own hand out to Isaias, who hesitated before he held out his bandaged hand. The bishop took it gentler than expected, but still firmly, turning it over in his palm as though to examine the wounds, though they were completely covered by the bandage. "Tell me everything that happened."

Isaias teared up immediately. He felt the bishop's tumultuous emotions mingle with his own, channeled through the contact where the bishop held him fast in place. Concern, but disappointment. Dread, but resignation. Isaias didn't fully understand what his bishop was feeling, but it confused his own heart. His grief, his longing for peace—for himself, for Hector—his childish desire to somehow turn back the clock. It had been a long time since he had wished that was possible. God made time march only steadily forward—Isaias would never have a say in that, no matter how desperately he wished to have time to *breathe*.

When Isaias didn't answer, the bishop sighed. "Oh, child," he said. "Your gifts are not serving you well, here, are they?"

"No, they aren't," Isaias said softly. The tears started in earnest. "Well, they are, and they aren't. They help me tell the difference, between Hector and the beast inside of him. They helped me see the difference. And sometimes I feel like I can *almost* reach Hector and help bring him to the surface—but it's painful. I feel the demon inside him, his anger and hatred. Magnified by Hector's pain, and Violet's—even Mrs. Marsh's—all of the pain and the scorn and the fear feels like too much."

The bishop was quiet for a moment, and Isaias felt the shape of his emotions shifting. He could tell the bishop was weighing something, judging something. Then—he let go of Isaias and the connection was broken. He felt his mentor close himself off, something most people didn't do because they didn't know Isaias could sense their hearts in the first place. The bishop didn't have Isaias's gifts—but he was a master of compartmentalizing his emotions and shutting Isaias out and always had been. Even when Isaias had been a child, the bishop could easily shut his emotions out. "I was afraid of that," was all he said. He explained no further. "Have faith, Isaias. It will all be over soon."

Isaias felt no confidence in the words. His own or the bishops. "Yes, Your Excellency."

"Now, to begin: you must confess anew. If we're going to do this, I need you to be completely clean of spirit," the bishop said firmly. He casts a steely look at Isaias. "And I suspect, now, that you kept some things from me when you confessed the other night."

Face awash with shame, Isaias bowed his head. He did not say that he felt discomfort confessing face-to-face, without even the confessional booth to offer a shadow of privacy. He did not say that he didn't even understand the full extent of his own sins. And he did not ask, *And what about you, Your Excellency? Do you not need to confess?* "Bless me, Father, for I have sinned. It has been—" he paused, trying to remember the course of events, how long it had been since this had begun and he had confessed to clear his soul "—a day and a half since my last Confession."

"Go on, my son," the bishop said when Isaias hesitated. His tone was flat, betraying nothing.

Isaias took a breath, wondering if he should start from the beginning of his life. From his earliest days, every sin that had shaped him. But he had confessed it all before, he thought—no more good would it do. God forgave. God forgave until Isaias sinned again. He would forgive and forgive again, as men—men like Isaias—would sin and sin again. That was what men did, and so that was what God did.

Assuming that God was in fact acting through the Bishop as His vessel. That there was more than just indifferent silence waiting for him.

"I have lied to you, my father, my mentor, my bishop. I acted in the name of God without your authorization to do so. And I did not tell you of the exorcism sooner. I put myself and my friends in danger without first seeking your guidance. I did not seek to be right by God and thus put our souls on the line."

A heartbeat of silence passed, and Isaias felt certain that the bishop was waiting for more. For Isaias to confess another sin. Isaias nearly did—he did not know which of the feelings of his heart might be deemed sinful, but he nearly poured his entire heart out just to fill the silence. When he didn't, the bishop began, "God, the Father of mercies, through the death and the resurrection of His Son..."

Isaias began, in turn, "My God, I am sorry for my sins with all my heart. In choosing to do wrong, and in failing to do good, I have sinned against You whom I should love above all things..."

"...and I absolve you from your sins in the name of the Father, and of the Son, and of the Holy Spirit."

"...our saviour Jesus Christ suffered and died for us. In His name, God have mercy."

The words of absolution said from both of them, Isaias kept his head bowed and said nothing more. He waited for the bishop to provide him his cue for what to do next.

"Are you ready, now, my son?" the bishop asked gently.

"As ready as I will ever be, Your Excellency."

And yet, Isaias doubted.

Standing in the centre of Bishop Reid's study, Isaias looked around to make note of what they had at their disposal. It wasn't so different from Isaias's own study, at his own rectory. He remembered this study from boyhood, and he saw much of it reflected in his own home. The pieces of Isaias's personality from his own were stripped out, leaving only the barest elements of the space. All the familiar religious iconography was there, of course; so, too, was there a simple desk and chair, to which Hector was now strapped with belts around his chest and middle. Better than rope, Isaias supposed. That was something. The bishop had quickly come up with something more effective than their haphazard attempts at binding Hector.

The bishop stood watching, waiting. Mrs. Marsh stood a few feet behind Hector. Violet and Poppy stood to one side, inseparable now that they were reunited.

Hector was lucid, for the moment. Isaias recognized him in his eyes, his heart. The demon, for the moment, was dormant—even though Hector's eyes looked fogged, his face flushed, and he was having trouble keeping his head up. He looked drunken, or drugged, the effects of the demonic possession wearing on his consciousness and eating away at his sensibilities.

Approaching, Isaias knelt by Hector in the chair, reaching out to take the other man's hand. "Are you ready for this?" he asked him softly. His voice low, he made an attempt at privacy. Selfishly, he wanted this moment with Hector to himself. He missed him.

Hector's gaze passed over Isaias's face at first, struggling to hold his gaze—and, perhaps, even to recognize him. Once recognition finally crossed his face, he answered, his voice weak. "As ready as I'll ever be." Then, more firmly though still struggling, he said, "Do it, Isaias. If anyone can..."

Isaias nodded, even though he didn't entirely agree. He squeezed Hector's hand in his, and Hector squeezed his back, before Isaias stood and turned back to the women and the bishop. Bishop Reid was watching Isaias steadily.

"Shall we, Your Excellency?" he asked the bishop. He didn't address the scrutiny in his gaze.

The bishop shook his head. "I think you should lead, Father," he said. "Not me."

"What? I trust your judgement, Your Excellency—but why?"

"This man is your friend, first of all," the bishop said, starting to list the reasons. "You know him; I don't. That does give you an advantage. And you could always use affirmation of your faith—grappling with the Devil is a sure way for you to remember your place in God's creation. Besides," he added, smiling wryly, "this is the kind of thing that takes a young man's strength."

"But Your Excellency—"

"Isaias, remember your place and your heart." The bishop's face had returned to deadly seriousness. He cast a pointed look at Isaias. "I think that God has chosen you for this, Isaias. And I think you are the right choice. Has God not given you His gifts—do you not think this is what He wants of you?"

It had crossed Isaias's mind before—despite the bishop noticing the way the exorcism was wearing on Isaias, that he was also well-positioned to see into the hearts of others using his gifts from God. Was it possible, that this was what God had always wanted for him? That *this* was his purpose—there was no divine loneliness, for he carried a piece of God's divinity in his own hands?

Isaias took a breath and turned back to face Hector once more. "Then let us begin."

Violet—ever his helper, his disciple—crossed closer to Isaias, Poppy following behind. "Save my dad," Violet whispered fiercely as Poppy handed Isaias a bowl of blessed water. "Please."

Though he could make no promises, he nodded to her as he took the water from Poppy.

Dipping his fingers into the holy water, Isaias reached out and brushed damp fingertips across Hector's face, tracing the sign of the cross first from forehead to chin. Isaias's heart raced and he held his breath as his fingertips passed over Hector's lips and felt the hard press of his teeth behind them. The bite wound on the side of his hand pulsed in remembered agony, but the demon, while he growled low in the back of Hector's throat, snarling in anger and in pain, did not bite again. Isaias lifted his fingers once they caught in the wiry hairs of his beard, and he lifted his hand to start in the opposite direction of the cross on Hector's cheeks. Something sizzled as his holy water dipped touch passed across Hector's increasingly gaunt face and Isaias fought not to recoil as boils bubbled up from his skin where Isaias's fingers had just passed—burns appearing on a few second time delay, marking the shape of a cross over the planes of Hector's face. Isaias swallowed his fear and his disgust at the stench of burning flesh and closed his eyes tight against the sight of it. He rose his voice in prayer to drown out a sound like water popping in oil. "Behold water that has been blessed. My salvation and life be ours in the name of the Father, and of the Son, and of the Holy Spirit."

Behind him, Violet let out a strangled cry and Mrs. Marsh whispered a prayer before exiting the room.

"Here we go again," Hector's voice gritted out, each syllable an exertion.

Isaias braced himself for impact—for the demon to *bite*, to fight back—but with no further reaction from the demon, he turned to his companions. He took a breath. "Beloved brother and sisters," he said, "let us humbly implore the mercy of almighty God, that, moved by the intercession of all the Saints, He, in His kindness, will hear the voice of His Church for our brother Hector, who is afflicted by dire need."

Isaias knelt before Hector and said, "Lord, have mercy."

"Lord, have mercy," replied the witnesses. Violet's voice rang loudest.

"Christ, have mercy," Isaias said.

"Christ, have mercy."

"Lord, have mercy."

"Lord, have mercy."

"Holy Mary, Mother of God," Isaias continued.

"Pray for him," the witnesses returned.

Isaias began the listing of the saints, naming each in turn, allowing for the watchers to ask them to pray for Hector. As the litany of the saints drew to a close, Isaias grew nervous.

Strange, for a demon so opposed to his own exorcism to be so silent.

Isaias rose for the next part of the exorcism. "O, God," he prayed, "whose nature is always to forgive and show mercy..."

Still, the demon said nothing. Isaias hesitated as he concluded the prayer, and before beginning the psalms. He took a moment to feel the presence of the demon.

He was momentarily blinded by his complete *indifference*.

Their routine of exorcism—of Isaias begging the saints to pray for Hector—had become so unimportant that the demon simply didn't care anymore. And if the demon was indifferent—what did that say of God? Was God not watching? Did He not care, not strike fear into the hearts of His opponents?

Was Isaias alone in this, after all?

"Father," the bishop's voice pressed from behind Isaias, low but with a harder edge under the surface of his voice. "Carry on. Fear not."

Concluding the psalms, Isaias walked back to Hector. He placed his hands on his friend's head, palms pressed against his temples and fingers caught in the curls of his hair. The heels of his hands rested just above the boils that had bubbled across Hector's skin. *A trick*, he told himself. *The imagination of the Devil. Not real.* He prayed for Mrs. Marsh to return with first aid supplies quickly. "Let Your mercy be upon us, Lord, as we have placed our hope in You."

Finally, the demon smiled. He looked at Isaias with earnest eyes and said, "The laying on of hands, eh? I bet this is the part you look forward to, each time we do this little dance. A convenient excuse to touch Hector, isn't it? *Oh*, how it must hurt to lie to yourself, Father Fuck Up. How it must torment you so to *sin*."

In the breath it took for Isaias to find his words, Mrs. Marsh returned to the study with a damp cloth and a first aid kit. "Allow me, Father."

Isaias nodded and let go—his hands lingering for a moment too long on Hector, dragging his fingertips down his hairline as if holding on would help *Hector* hold on—and gave Mrs. Marsh space. "Send forth Your Spirit," Isaias whispered as Mrs. Marsh dabbed the washcloth over the burst skin on Hector's face, pus and slime oozing from the burnt cross scarring Hector's cheekbones, "and they shall be created, and You will renew the face of the earth."

"*Feel* him, Father," Carreau whispered in a hiss with Hector's voice as Mrs. Marsh applied ointment to the burns. Hector's eyes looked past her and locked with Isaias's. "Not just physically, but emotionally. *Know* him. What's he smell like to you, feel like to you? *Taste* him, his soul. Feel the last ounce of him before I drain it all away. Last chance, Father Fuck Up, before I have him all to myself."

Isaias's stomach roiled with nausea, and he resisted the temptation to listen to what the demon said, to feel Hector's presence. To check on him, body and soul, and to prove the demon wrong. He was too afraid of the opposite—that it would simply prove the demon *right*.

Behind him, the bishop and Violet said, "Lord, have mercy."

"Save Your servant who trusts in You, my God," Isaias continued, carrying forth with the exorcism even as Mrs. Marsh tended Hector's wounds.

"Trust! No, Hector doesn't trust God. He trusts *you*, though, Isaias," the demon breathed. Despite the other four people in the room, it felt private. *Intimate*. Taunting.

Isaias closed his eyes to avoid looking at the snake head-on.

Behind him, Violet, Poppy, and the bishop said, "Lord, have mercy." Mrs. Marsh, by Hector's side, repeated the same, creating an echo chamber of prayer.

"Be for him, O Lord," Isaias said, keeping his eyes closed. He reached for the rosary around his neck and clenched his hand tight around it, the beads quickly becoming slick with sweat. "Be for him," he repeated, losing track of himself, "a tower of strength in the face of the enemy."

"Who's the real enemy here, *Father*? You know what you want. Is it wrong? Or is robbing children from their cradles the real crime, here?"

Isaias's mouth was dry. He wished he could drink the very holy water he was using for the exorcism. Behind him, the bishop and Violet said, "Lord, have mercy."

"Let the enemy have no advantage over him," Isaias said, but the words were a struggle, catching in his dry throat, "nor the son of iniquity persist in harming him."

"Iniquity: immoral or grossly unfair behaviour," the demon recited. "Who's *really* unfair, though, *Father*? The father of lies, or the fathers of men who hold no love for their children? Man was created in God's image—and it shows."

"Stop," Isaias whispered fiercely. He didn't know if the others could hear him, though he saw Mrs. Marsh shift her weight and lower her gaze even as she finished tending Hector's wounds, making him think that she must have heard. "Just stop."

As if Isaias had not broken the flow of the exorcism, Violet and Poppy said behind him, "Lord, have mercy."

An image of steel crystalized in the room. The bishop said, voice sharp and hard, "Isaias, continue."

Isaias swallowed hard. "Send him help, O Lord, from the sanctuary, and give him support from Your Holy Land."

"Lord, have mercy."

He doesn't want you to listen, something spoke in Isaias's soul. His heart swelled with an intrusion of emotions, and he felt a dizzying rush of feelings course through his body. His head spun and his heart raced. Stepping back, Isaias stared at the cold eyes in Hector's warm face. Not his eyes, not really even his face—a face of lies, worn on the wrong body.

"Isaias," the bishop warned.

Isaias looked over his shoulder at the bishop and swallowed hard. Then he nodded, turned back to the demon, closed his eyes, and continued. "I believe in God," Isaias said, not sure who needed convincing. He believed in God. That was one of the only things he knew to be true. He *believed*. "The Father almighty, Creator of Heaven and earth, and in Jesus Christ, His only Son, our Lord, who was conceived by the Holy Spirit, born of the Virgin Mary..."

"*Isaias*," a voice snapped.

Startled, Isaias opened his eyes. He saw, for half an instant, what had to be a reflection of the true face of the demon once more. The death-mask version of Hector distorted by the demonic force inside him, the cross marked in boils on his face oozing pus that dripped into his eyes, mingling there with tears as the demon wept, sobbing ugly tears. Hector's lips were peeled off, exposing rotten teeth. Bile dripped from the corners of his lips, meeting the pus and tears, his face a disgusting mess of fluids.

The vision disappeared in the space of a single breath, but Isaias knew he would remember it for the rest of his life.

There was only Hector—or the shadow of him, weak and ill and his eyes not shining like they used to—and no one and nothing else. Even Mrs. Marsh had stepped out of sight. All Isaias saw was Hector, halfway between who he was and who he was supposed to be.

"Yes, Bishop Reid?" Isaias asked, unable to disguise the trembling of his voice.

"I said nothing," the bishop replied. "Continue, Isaias."

Isaias continued through the Creed, then turned his back on the demon. It was the only way that he could continue, and he thanked the rites of exorcism for allowing him to address his supporters in that moment. He took in their emotions—Violet's courage, Poppy's sorrow, Mrs. Marsh's care, and the bishop's resolve—and drew strength from their true hearts. "Do you renounce Satan?" he asked of them.

"I do."

"And all his works?" he asked.

"I do."

"And all his empty show?"

"I do."

Isaias completed this segment and hesitated once again. He knew that he was supposed to face the demon again now, and he could not bring himself to do so for a moment. But he saw Violet looking imploringly at him. Poppy hovered by her side, squeezing her friend's arm gently.

"Please, Isaias," Violet said. "For my dad."

For Hector.

Isaias turned to face the demon in Hector once more. He felt dizzy, but he continued with his waning strength. Focusing in on this singular task.

Isaias clasped his hands together. "Together, with our brother, let us implore God to deliver us from evil, as our Lord Jesus Christ taught us to pray:

"Our Father, who art in Heaven, hallowed be Thy name; Thy kingdom come, Thy will be done, on Earth as it is in Heaven. Give us our daily bread, and forgive us our trespasses, as we forgive those who trespass against us; and lead us not into temptation but deliver us from evil. For the kingdom, the power and glory are Yours, now and for ever."

The bishop stepped forward and offered Isaias the cross he had taken from his foyer. Isaias shook his head and instead reached for the rosary around his neck. The crucifix that hung from it felt heavy as he removed it from his neck, the worn edges of the cross catching on his bandaged palm. He held the crucifix out—a symbol of a family that was mere memory—and gritted his teeth as he pushed through.

The demon snarled, baring Hector's teeth. There was blood seeping through the thin gaps between the enamel. The bite wound on Isaias's hand throbbed against the bar of the cross at the reminder, though the blood then could not possibly be Isaias's.

"Behold, the Cross of the Lord," Isaias said. "Be gone, all hostile powers! O God, Creator and Defender of the human race, look with favour upon Your servant Hector, whom You formed in Your own image and call to share in Your glory. The ancient enemy is racking him fiercely—"

"—so fierce!" the demon called.

"—crushing him with violent force—"

"—so violent!"

"—tormenting him with wild terror—"

"—oh, the *terror*!"

The cadence of the words was familiar enough that Isaias knew they were drawing near the end of this portion of the exorcism again. But the demon continued to taunt him, continued to fight, and Isaias wasn't sure how much of his own fight he had left in him—or how much *Hector* had left. Isaias closed his eyes against the pain of tears before he decided to take a leap of faith.

Dropping the rosary to the floor as he stepped forward, Isaias knelt before the bound Hector in the chair. The demon stared him down using Hector's eyes, but Isaias imagined confusion in those eyes. On his knees in front of this man, his friend, his heart, Isaias took his face in his hands once more before curling his fingers into the hair at the nape of Hector's neck with one hand, the other grazing the skin just below his burns. Gently, he guided Hector's forehead to his own. Isaias closed his eyes and took a deep breath to brace himself. He let himself feel the ghost of Hector's breath across his lips, steeled himself against the intimacy of the touch while reminding himself that this wasn't Hector.

But Hector *was* in there.

Eyes still closed, fingers in Hector's hair and feeling their breath mingle in the minute space between them, Isaias let his emotions wash *out*, wash *into* Hector, sharing his deepest feelings with someone else in the most direct way he had ever done. And who better than Hector, even corrupted by a demon, to feel the most intimate depth of Isaias's love, his hopes, his fears? Who in the world would take better care of Isaias's heart than Hector, who already possessed so much of it? While Isaias didn't want the demon to touch any part of it, he was willing to push past the darkness in Hector to reach *his* heart.

"Hector," Isaias whispered, hoping this moment could stay between them, willing the words past the demon's control and into Hector's soul, "I know you're still in there. I know you can hear me. *Please* hear me." Isaias's voice cracked and he fought to control his volume. Fought to let this moment be *theirs*. Fought for him and for Hector. For the garden he still dreamed they could grow together. "Come back to me. To me, to your daughter, to—just *please come back*."

"You know nothing," the demon whispered, voice slick and slow as oil. Isaias's heart broke and he fought back a sob as he felt the demon lean forward in Isaias's hands, straining against the belts holding him to the chair, hearing the stretch of leather pushed to its limits. Carreau was so close that Isaias could taste his breath. Rotten eggs with a trace of sweetness. And the demon said, in Hector's own voice, "You know nothing. I *dare* you, Father Fuck Up, to try to understand. To try to understand why I have been damned. Feel it, Isaias. Feel me. Feel my pain, and my sorrow, and my damnation. Then maybe you'll understand. And what hope do you have of exorcising a demon if you deny the truth?"

Isaias kept his eyes closed, holding Hector's face between his hands, fingers tangled in the curls of his hair, feeling the heat of his skin beneath his palms, even through the bandages. He fought through the fear and at long last, for the first time since he was a boy told that his emotions were a dangerous thing to be locked away inside a box, he opened himself up to let his heart truly *feel*.

Isaias's vision went first, tunneling black into nothing, his head swimming at the sheer power of a thousand emotions hitting his soul at once, but he only remained conscious for a moment before he felt himself losing his grip on Hector and falling, falling into complete darkness.

XXVI

Isaias slowly stirred back to the world of wakefulness with a degree of reluctance born of fear, understanding, and an exhaustion that had nestled itself into the marrow of his bones.

"Isaias," Violet's voice broke through before anything else really came into focus. She was hovering over him, her eyes round with worry. "Oh my God, you're awake," she said, voice speeding along at a pace that was hard to track. "I was so worried—"

"Vi, honey," Isaias interrupted, wincing through a headache and closing his eyes again. "A little quieter, please."

"Sorry, Father," Violet said, much more softly. "But you scared us."

"I'm sorry," Isaias said, blinking up at her and slowly sitting up, looking around him. He saw quickly who 'us' really consisted of. Violet was perched on the edge of the bed in his childhood bedroom, where he lay, and Poppy stood close behind her, always on guard, always ready. Mrs. Marsh was at the head of the bed, reaching already for a mug of tea on the nightstand, which she handed to Isaias. He didn't see the bishop at once, before he spotted him in the doorway, his expression stony. Isaias couldn't quite meet his mentor's eyes and turned his attention back to Violet. "What happened?"

"You passed out," Violet said, her voice tight. Isaias could tell she was putting in an effort to hold herself back to avoid agitating Isaias's headache with the force of her energy. She couldn't have known that her speed and volume weren't the only factors—Isaias's emotions were an exposed nerve, raw and ragged, and he felt the sharpness of every feeling in Violet's soul, the edges of every heart in the room. "I don't know, probably because you've barely eaten for like two days, but it was really sudden. You just kind of—collapsed. Are you okay?"

"I'll be okay," Isaias promised. "Is everyone else okay?"

Behind Violet, Poppy lifted her chin defiantly. "We got out of there fast. I helped Mrs. Marsh carry you out and up here."

Mrs. Marsh smiled. "No easy task," she teased. "Poppy did most of the lifting."

"You might have a bruised tailbone later." Poppy ducked her head, smiling bashfully. "I didn't lift you very well."

"You're forgiven," Isaias said with a laugh he didn't feel. "Thank you, all three of you. And is Hector—?"

"Yes, Ms. Montero, perhaps you and your friend could go check on your father," the bishop cut in tersely. "And Mrs. Marsh, if you wouldn't mind supervising the girls to ensure the demon doesn't do anything untoward."

Violet hesitated, looking between Isaias and the bishop. "Are you sure—?"

"Please, dear. I would like to talk to the Father alone."

Violet frowned, glancing back at Isaias, as if for permission. Isaias nodded, slowly, and so Violet gathered her crutches from where they leaned against Isaias's bed and hoisted herself to her feet. She and Poppy left together, Mrs. Marsh following along behind. Mrs. Marsh hesitated at the door, pausing beside the bishop. She looked between them before lowering her head respectfully. "We worry about you, Father," she said before the bishop stepped away from the door and Mrs. Marsh closed the door quietly behind the women as they exited.

Bishop Reid sighed the moment the three were out of the door. He dragged a chair from the corner of the room to Isaias's bed. It was the same chair he would always sit in to read Isaias stories from the Bible when Isaias had been a small child, new to the bishop's care.

"I—" Isaias started, ready to defend himself.

The bishop held up his hands and Isaias stopped mid-syllable. "Why did you do that, Isaias?"

Isaias bit back the petulant urge to ask, *Do what?* as if he could possibly hide from the bishop that he had used his gifts on a demon—or at least on the man possessed with that demon. Instead, he answered, "It had a point that I should strive to understand the truth if I want to—"

"The Prince of Lies," the bishop said slowly, lowering his hands into his lap, "'had a point?'"

Isaias looked down at the mug of tea he held between both hands in his lap. His cheeks burned with shame. "That's not Satan."

"Excuse me?"

"The demon. We know his name, and he isn't the Devil."

"Is now really the time to mince words, boy? It's a follower of the Devil itself. It is a sinner and a liar."

Isaias kept his eyes fixed on the mug, watching the steam. "I'm not trying to—I'm not trying to contradict you, Your Excellency. Only to make sure we speak with clarity."

"Certainly," the bishop said, his voice dry, "but my point still stands: you were being foolhardy at best. Downright sinful at worst."

Isaias winced. "I just thought—"

"I know what you *thought*, Isaias. And you jeopardized the entire exorcism. As expected, it failed without you there to lead it. Though, it seems doubtful it would have succeeded regardless."

Isaias frowned but could not bear to look at the bishop still. "We likely would have had to repeat the process," he said. "As we had before. But that doesn't mean it would have failed. I would have kept going. I won't give up on Hector."

"Look at me when you're speaking."

Isaias winced, closing his eyes for a moment to steel himself before he looked to the man who had raised him.

"I think that it would have failed," the bishop said slowly, "because you have not confessed all of your sins, my son. If you aren't free from guilt and sin, why would God ever listen to you?"

Isaias closed in on himself, shutting down his own fear and shame. He didn't want to believe that God could ever turn His back on him—but perhaps God loathed dishonesty more than anything else? Isaias fought back his own feelings; did not show the emotions he knew the bishop would take as an admission of guilt. He didn't dare to feel what the bishop was feeling, but his emotional resonance was still like an open wound, and he couldn't completely avoid the sting of emotional agitation. He still detected the edge of the bishop's iron will, an unpleasant taste like blood in his mouth. He could only imagine the judgement, shame, and disappointment that he would feel if he let himself probe any deeper. "I don't know what you're talking about," Isaias said softly. But he was very afraid that he did, in fact, know what the bishop was so ashamed of.

"Isaias, the way that creature was speaking to you. The things it said. The way it taunted you—"

Isaias closed his eyes a moment. Took a low, steadying breath. It did nothing to still his pounding heart. The wounds on his hands—the torn-up palms, the bite wound where Hector's teeth had torn flesh—throbbed in time with his heart. "I thought you called him the Prince of Lies, Your Excellency. How can you trust him?"

"Do not pick and choose what you listen to of that beast," the bishop warned. "We do not cherry-pick the Bible. We should not cherry-pick our faith beyond that. And being a liar by trade does not mean that you only lie. We take his words with a grain of salt. But more important, Isaias, I saw the way that you hesitated, the way that you reacted. The way you held that man. And then to allow yourself to open your heart and mind to him..."

Isaias blinked back fresh tears. "Your Excellency, I—"

The bishop shook his head and leaned back in the chair. He crossed his arms over his chest. "Isaias, I cannot blame you for the temptation to stray from your path. The Devil tempts all of us, from time to time. And you said, in your confession, that you have not strayed. I believe you in that much. But Isaias, if there are other sins you have committed—"

"There aren't," Isaias insisted, his voice cracking. "Your Excellency, why do you believe a demon and not me? Did you not raise me to be faithful?"

Sighing, the bishop relaxed his arms, then folded his hands in his lap again. "Isaias, my son, I want to believe you. But if you cannot face yourself, then we are going to need an expert on our side. Perhaps if we went and petitioned the Vatican—"

Isaias frowned, though he was more than a little relieved for the shift in topic from himself. "Rome?" he asked, incredulous. "To bring Hector all the way to Rome, that would be surely be at least a day of travel. And to expect the beast to cooperate that entire time..."

The bishop lowered his face into his hands, shaking his head slowly. "You're right, of course. Perhaps we could petition them to send someone..."

Isaias hesitated. He took a moment to wipe his tear-stricken face with his sleeve. He noted that the tears soaked into the blood stain on his surplice. "I don't know, Your Excellency. Hector is one man—and not even a Catholic, at that. They won't send someone lightly." He did not say, *You didn't even want to help him.* "And Hector doesn't have *time.* I can't trust anyone else to help him."

Slowly straightening, the bishop said, "Then, Isaias, I think you will need to confront yourself. If you truly want to save this man, you will need to come at it clear of conscience, void of questions."

Isaias paused, dropping his hand in his lap. "Just tell me what to do. I'll do anything."

The bishop was silent for a long, painful moment. When he finally spoke, it came with an extended hand and a grave voice full of promise. "Pray with me."

"You're going *where*?"

"Sainte-Félicité," Isaias repeated, voice careful. He could barely meet Violet's eye as they stood in the hall outside the study because he knew what she must think of him in that moment. He had asked to speak to her privately and left Poppy and Mrs. Marsh to watch over Hector. "To see my birth parents."

"Okay, great. I don't get it. Why? Why, when dad *needs* you?"

Isaias tried not to flinch. "It's *for* your father, Violet, I promise. You see—when I was a child, my parents were called upon to give me to the Catholic Church to raise. My adoptive family—Bishop Reid and the church—they re-baptized me to cleanse me of any sins of my family. But... I was a special case. So, I need to talk to my parents, and apparently they're in Sainte-Félicité."

Sainte-Félicité, where Isaias had gone to seminary. A city so near to where he had grown up and to where he lived now, in adulthood. The third in a holy trinity of saint cities. His birth parents practically next door to him—but he couldn't even remember their faces.

Had they always been there? Was that where Isaias had been born and, in another life, might have grown up like a normal child? Or did they move there to be closer to their own alternate history?

And what did it mean that the bishop knew precisely where they were, knew exactly how to find them, but Isaias hadn't even known that they were near?

"Does this have to do with what happened in the last exorcism?" Violet asked.

"Yes, but I'm afraid I don't know if I can tell you everything, yet, Violet. I'm sorry. Suffice it to say, I need to confront all sins in my past, even those not my own."

"That's stupid," Violet snapped.

Isaias was taken aback. "What?"

"You think you're not good enough to save my dad. But I know my dad, and I know he thinks the world of you." Violet's hands tightened on the grips of her crutches, her arms tense. "I don't really give a shit if you think you're good enough for God because you're good enough for my dad. You're just being a coward."

Isaias flinched. "It's God's will that I—"

"God's will? Or man's?" Before Isaias could respond, Violet pressed on. "This is dumb. You can't carry the weight of other people's mistakes, it's—" she stopped herself, looking down at her feet. She blinked rapidly and Isaias resisted the urge to reach out to her, at least physically, and hold her. "Your parents did what your parents did. And yeah, maybe you bear the weight of that, but it's not your *fault*. Don't make me doubt that," she whispered fiercely. "After all this time, that's what I've got."

"I know, Violet," Isaias said, keeping his voice as gentle as possible. "But the power of forgiveness—my own and theirs—will go a long way to making sure that I have the power of God on my side. The power to save your father, Violet."

Violet didn't look up, nor did she protest. "Fine. Tell Poppy to come find me. I'm going for a walk—pray for me that I don't get kidnapped or whatever, I guess."

Violet used her crutches to pivot and hastened to the door, and Isaias held himself back from following. Instead, he crossed himself and murmured a prayer to God to watch out for Violet—only to ensure that she and Poppy would be safe, and that whatever journey Isaias took with his birth parents would genuinely lead him to being able to help Hector.

If the sins of generations were passed down to him, somehow, he had to try. Maybe that was why God wasn't listening to him, these days.

Isaias knocked on the door of the study before he entered, as if anyone inside had any sense of dignity or privacy left. When Poppy looked past him, then back up to him questioningly, Isaias said, "Violet said she's going for a walk and to send you after her."

Poppy pulled her phone from her pocket and looked at the time—it was just past sunset and getting cold as the darkness set—before she just nodded and said, "Thanks for letting me know."

Mrs. Marsh approached Isaias once Poppy had left and said softly, "Did you want to talk to him?" Her eyes were gentle—but sad.

Not wanting to look too closely at the expression on Mrs. Marsh's face, Isaias looked past her to Hector. His head was hung low, neck craned and chin resting against his chest, but Isaias could still see the burn marks on his face. His clothes were deeply stained, and Isaias could *smell* him from there. He was breathing, but it took a moment for Isaias to be confident of that—the movements in his chest were subtle until suddenly they weren't, Hector straining to breath and coughing. Isaias tore his eyes off the man he wanted so desperately to take away from all this pain and looked to Mrs. Marsh's too-knowing eyes instead. "Is it him?" he whispered hoarsely.

"I don't know." Mrs. Marsh looked back at Hector and crossed herself before she turned her sad eyes on Isaias. "He's not particularly lucid, so maybe he's—I don't know."

Isaias nodded and said nothing, but he didn't have to. Mrs. Marsh gave him a swift hug before exiting the study. She closed the door with a soft click, but the sound seemed to echo, embedding itself into Isaias's ear drum and causing his head to throb. Or perhaps his head was already aching—he had spent so long mired in Hector's suffering that he felt like he no longer had a proper sense of his own body. It had begun to feel not like his own, which felt unfair to think for even a moment.

Isaias was left alone with Hector—or what he hoped was Hector. The lights seemed too dim in the room, leaving space for the fading sunset to creep through the window. The air in the room was raw. It smelled pungent, something between death and—Isaias didn't know what, except that it contained a powerful body odour that was overwhelming to him. Now that they were alone, Isaias thought that he heard Hector's ragged breathing.

Isaias braced himself before approaching Hector's prone form in the chair. He knelt in front of the chair again—it was becoming a familiar pose. He saw Hector's eyes flutter, but it reminded him more of someone failing to quite stir from sleep than anything alert. "Hector, can you hear me?" he whispered, though he was sure he could not. When Hector didn't respond, Isaias gathered the bowl of water nearby that Mrs. Marsh must have been using to wash Hector's wounds and to care for him. Wetting the cloth, Isaias dabbed it gently across the angry wounds on Hector's wrists. He was scared that they would become infected, that the cross-shaped burns on his face would scar, but what else could they do? "I'm going to Sainte-Félicité," Isaias said softly as he wiped blood and pus from the belt around Hector's forearm. He picked fibres from his shirt out of the raw skin. "But I'll be back soon, I promise. And I'll finally be ready to save you." Hector stirred, but still did not speak. Isaias realized he didn't sense anything at all from Hector—not campfire smores, not sulfur and pain, just nothing. He bit down the fear of just how little of Hector that must be left. "My birth parents may be able to help me find forgiveness. And God will finally let me be strong enough."

"That's stupid."

The whisper was so quiet Isaias was afraid he had imagined it—but it was Hector's voice. It was *Hector's* voice. Isaias's eyes welled with tears and his heart became swollen with love. "Your daughter agrees with you."

"Smart kid." Hector's voice was nothing more than a raspy whisper that Isaias had to strain to hear but God, it was worth every aching moment just to hear Hector's voice be truly his again. "What's the problem? You're the kindest man I've ever met. What's to"—Hector coughed, and Isaias used the damp cloth to pat blood and spittle out of Hector's beard—"What's to forgive?"

"Perhaps," Isaias said, glad Hector wasn't meeting his eye, focusing instead on dabbing the cloth over Hector's wiry beard, wondering if there had been this many greys before, before everything, "I love too easily. And maybe I stray too easily from the path of loving God and only God."

"What?" Hector's voice was groggy; confused. For a moment, Isaias thought he might fall back to sleep—or whatever state he had been in before, not himself, not of his own body. Isaias hoped he dreamed. When Hector spoke again, his voice was even softer than before, barely audible. Isaias felt their hearts break as one. "*Oh*, Isaias."

"It's alright, Hector," Isaias said. He rested his hands over Hector's wrists, careful of his wounds. He pictured the wounds on his hands tearing open, his lifeblood pouring into Hector, finding its way to their matching stigmatic wounds. He pictured himself giving his life for Hector, making him whole again. Tracing his hands over Hector's skin, relishing in it even where it felt clammy, sick, not like Hector, Isaias moved his hands to the arms of the chair and used them to brace himself to stand. "I'll be back soon, my friend. A changed man."

"That's what I'm afraid of, Isaias."

Not knowing how to reply, Isaias stood there silently over Hector. He rested one hand on Hector's chest and felt for his heartbeat reverberating and the rise and fall of his breathing until it slowed to something less like fear and more like slumber.

When Isaias was sure that Hector was asleep, he finally allowed himself to bring his other hand to his mouth to cover up his sob, no longer needing to bite back his tears once only God could hear them.

XXVII

The next bus to Sainte-Félicité hadn't taken long to arrive, so Isaias opted for public transit. The trinity of cities were all connected, tied together by threads of fate that were built over with controlled-access highways.

Isaias would have driven—the car would have been faster than wait-times with other lost souls at the bus terminal—but he was exhausted and every time he thought about driving, he thought about their near-miss accident. Even without Carreau backseat driving, it seemed dangerous.

And maybe, if Isaias prayed enough, he could manage a few fitful minutes of sleep on the bus.

His prayers, it seemed, were answered when he snapped awake in the bus bay of the Sainte-Félicité terminal, the bus driver's voice crackling over a distorted radio. Isaias hadn't dreamed, but it took a moment to remember where he was and why, feeling just a single step outside his body. As if something material had changed about the reality he lived in between falling asleep to the chorus of highway droning and traffic vibrations and waking to a bus driver telling him he'd been transported to another place while he slept.

Taking advantage of others disembarking first to gather his bearings, Isaias closed his eyes against the thrumming in his head that had not softened with sleep. He wasn't sure if sleep had done anything for him at all, but it might have been too soon to tell if the bone tiredness and aches in his body had dimmed at all.

Outside the window of the bus, Isaias saw a small group of people mingling, ready to greet friends and families and lovers as they climbed off the bus. Isaias wondered if his parents were any of them. He would never have been able to identify either of them by their faces, and there were several older couples in the crowd that could have plausibly been his parents. He wouldn't know. The idea of family waiting to greet him as he stepped off the bus was a foreign one.

And had they even come? The bishop had said he would call and tell them to greet him at the bus station. He had not been allowed to talk to them himself. So, what if they had no interest in seeing him face-to-face? What if they chose to ignore it, to let him walk alone into a city barely-familiar, with no answers to be found?

Isaias waited until the last few people were climbing off the bus to pick up his bag and head for the stairs as well. He watched the last few passengers greeting the last few attendants until there were only two people standing and waiting for anyone on the bus.

They had to be his parents. Standing at a slight distance from one another, Isaias hadn't considered them because they didn't look like a couple. The man was bundled in a thick coat, arms crossed over his chest and hands tucked into his armpits, his back arched as he huddled against the cold air that had crept its way into the bus bay. The woman had a toque pulled down over her ears and a scarf wrapped around her neck that swallowed her up, but her posture was more upright—proper or tense, Isaias could not tell. Her hands were folded in front of her, but the gloved fingers of her right hand were prodding at a bump in the fabric of her left hand's gloves on one of her fingers. The world outside the overhang of the terminal was dark, but the fluorescent lights for the parking highlighted all the harsh lines and wrinkles in both of their faces.

Isaias still wasn't convinced it was them, even though there was no one else they could be waiting for, until he detected the edges of their emotional auras. The smell of roses coming from the woman who had to be his mother was barely perceptible, but he still recognized it, even though it had faded to nearly nothing. There was something stale about it, something aged. And the man—the memory Isaias had of sandalwood, woodsy but sweet, had become musty, almost fungal from moisture and rot.

He had wondered often if they were happy without him. He didn't know what to think of the fact that they might not be.

"Isaias?" the woman asked softly.

Isaias took the last step off the bus's stairs onto the tarmac. The city felt like another world. Yellow bay parking lines boxed him in, separated him from a place he might have known. "Yes, that's me."

At first, neither of Isaias's parents—he had to call them that, but the word felt alien, for who had ever raised him by the bishop and God?—made to approach, watching Isaias, who thought maybe he should make the first move. He was the one who had sought them out, after all, hoping they would divine some secret meaning that had been hidden from him, like a commandment called down from the mountain. But what words could he possibly have for them? All of the questions he had wanted to ask them, all the things he had wanted to know, but he wasn't truly there for himself. He was there for Hector, and any information that could make his heart sacred again.

His mother broke the silence first. "Marie," she said, as if that explained everything in the world. She cleared her throat. "My name is Marie. If you don't want to call me your mother."

"Marc," his father added, sizing up Isaias before he removed one hand from where it had been tucked away close to his heart to offer to Isaias.

As they spoke, Isaias noticed a light French lilt in both of their voices. He had never imagined that they would sound French, that they wouldn't sound the same as him. Shaking his father's hand, Isaias said the words he had never thought he would say to his parents: "It's nice to meet you both."

He felt something like distrust in Marc's grip, even though Isaias hadn't been the one to choose to leave.

"Should we get coffee?" Marie asked, looking between her husband and Isaias as their hands separated again. She pinched the bump on her finger under the left glove again.

"So long as it's somewhere that has tea." Isaias smiled tiredly. "We have a lot to talk about, I'm sure."

In a diner on a corner in a city he had never known might hold his birth family, Isaias sat across from his parents at a peeling plastic tabletop surrounded by a silence thicker than the layers of snow outside. Inside, the diner had its heat on so high that Isaias was sweating. He'd taken off his wool coat, his gloves and hat, and felt too open now. He was sweating, his back sticky against the chapped vinyl seat. After the cold outside, the heat inside was suffocating, leaving Isaias wanting to go outside and crawl into the night and into a snowbank for relief.

"Heat's stuck, sorry," a waitress had said without sounding all that apologetic, sweating herself, before she promised she'd be back to them with their tea and coffees. They all three sat in silence for the minute it took for the waitress to return with the mugs and pot of coffee, as well as a metal tea pot with the string of a bag of tea clinging to the condensation on the side.

Once they were alone again, it was Marie who first spoke. "You really became a priest." Her eyes were fixed on Isaias's throat, though he had changed before leaving to avoid drawing more attention to himself than necessary, and so wore no clerical collar.

"I did." Marie nodded. When she didn't say more, Isaias fought to fill the silence. "I shepherd over a church called the Sacred Heart in Sainte-Thérèse. It's not far from here. And it's humble, it's small, but it's"—Isaias cut himself off, watching the expressions on his parents' faces, especially Marie's; feeling the crushing oppression of grief and remorse on her heart—"but you knew that, didn't you?"

"We did," Marie confessed. Like a reflex, she crossed herself from temple to sternum, across her guilt-ridden heart. As if she could say the words of contrition and Isaias would be the one to forgive them. "I'm sorry that we never reached out to you."

Isaias looked from her to his silent father and weighed his words. He said, "His Excellency Bishop Reid, he thinks that there are doubts in my mind. About my place in the world, about my origins. He thought that I should set my mind at ease by speaking to you. And it was somewhat pressing that I do so soon."

Marc spoke after a sip of coffee. As he spoke, Marie seemed to remember her own coffee and took a drink as well. "What kinds of doubts are you feeling that we could do anything about now?"

Isaias thought of all the questions he had wanted to ask them since he was a child. *Why did you let me go? Was I too much trouble?* and *Did you not love me enough?* But he realized that most of those questions no longer mattered. He had Hector, and he had Violet—maybe he even had Poppy, given how much Violet seemed to love her. He had love he needed to return to, where his home was.

"What do you know about my—capabilities?"

"We know," Marie said, voice fast, almost tripping over her words. She looked nervously at her husband. Isaias saw her toying with her wedding band again, now exposed. "You were a precocious child, always. And you knew and felt too much, for a boy your age."

"You could feel things. And influence things," Marc added. "It was a lot, for new parents. We didn't know how to handle it. Can you blame us?"

Isaias didn't answer. "And you thought these were abilities from—from God?"

Marc shook his head. "We didn't know what to believe. Your mother thought they were from God. I was worried it could be far worse than that."

Isaias's heart sunk. "Worse? What made you think that?"

"Have you ever parented a toddler, let alone one who has a supernaturally keen sense of everything you are feeling?" Marc asked, voice dry. But Marie twisted the ring on her finger again as she glared at him. He lowered his eyes. "Sorry, it was—Marie was religious, I was reformed. She believed wholeheartedly still in God, and I wasn't sure what to believe."

"I see."

Marie cleared her throat. She stopped fidgeting with her ring and wrapped her hands around her mug of coffee instead. Isaias took the moment to finally pour his tea, ignoring the heat radiating off the metal surface making the overheated diner even more unbearable. "I took you to church," she said. "For baptism. And I spoke to the church officials, and they said no, our baby must be blessed. And they took us to Bishop Reid, and he said yes, you were certainly blessed. That's when he suggested we give you up to them. To the church."

Isaias's hands jerked as he poured from the tea pot, and some of the scalding tea splashed back onto his hand. Most was caught by his bandages, but some splattered against his skin. He didn't wince. He picked up some napkins and wiped the tea off his hand. "So, it was Bishop Reid's idea."

Marc was staring at his coffee as he said, "He said it was God's design, that you were a child of God. He spoke of Christ, of the work of the Holy Spirit to beget a child. He said that Marie had been a vessel for a Peacemaker to be brought upon the world. And what the hell is a new parent supposed to say to any of *that*?"

Isaias wanted to ask, *Did you even try?* but had to concede the point. What would anyone ever be able to say to that, to such bold claims from a man of God, who commanded such authority? "I understand. And there was no history of such things in the family?" he asked, using all his will to be practical, to ask the questions he needed to ask. He didn't know if this was what the bishop wanted him to find—but it was what he had found.

Marc and Marie both shook their heads. "No," said Marie. "Not that we know of."

Isaias sighed. He took a sip of his tea, ignoring the bitter burn of scalded leaves on his throat. It was better than letting his throat stay dry. "The bishop's concern was that perhaps there might be a generational tie to my troubles," he said. "That maybe there was something in the family, years ago, that would explain my abilities or my... my proclivities."

"Proclivities?" Marie asked. Isaias flushed but, before he could answer, Maria added, "What you mean is, where your sin originates from?"

Isaias nodded carefully. "If there were perhaps a generational sin—"

"I don't think such a thing would exist," Marc cut in. "Isaias, do you think your bishop was wrong, then? That Marie wasn't touched by God, but by the Devil? That this was no immaculate conception?"

Isaias wondered if perhaps she had been touched by nothing at all. That Isaias had just been a boy. That he was just a man.

Marie said, "We were making the choice that was best for you, Isaias. We were guided by God."

Isaias felt their suspicions come and go but, more than anything, he felt Marie's guilt transform into something new: righteousness. Surety that she had made the decision she had always needed to make. Doubtful that Isaias believed her.

It was a fair concern. He didn't know that he did.

"I'm sorry to say, Isaias, that we don't really know why you are the way that you are," Marc said. "As far as we know, you're unique in our family. But to be fair, most of our family doesn't really talk to us anymore."

Isaias frowned. "They don't?"

Marie shook her head, then looked down at her left hand again. She returned to spinning her wedding ring around her finger. It fit so loosely; Isaias wondered why she had never gotten it resized. "I don't think anyone understood the choice we made. I don't think anyone forgave us. But Isaias—*you* forgive us, don't you?"

Despite it all, despite feeling their guilt and their desire to be relieved from it, Isaias had not *actually* expected the question. He hadn't expected them to seek forgiveness, nor that it would rest in his hands. He wondered if they needed to ask for it at all. He wondered if he wanted to give it.

He looked at his parents, at two people he did not recognize, at the grief etched into their faces through wrinkles and lines around the corners of their eyes that did not suggest smiles, but sadness. Reaching under the collar of his shirt, Isaias retrieved the rosary that had sat so close to his heart for so long. He smelled roses and sandalwood, untouched by age, as he clasped the wooden beads and the familiar relief of Christ against his hands.

"God, the Father of mercies, through the death and resurrection of His Son has reconciled the world to Himself and sent the Holy Spirit among us for the forgiveness of sins," Isaias recited, the words of absolution familiar and practiced, well-worn by time into habit. He pressed the pad of his thumb over the chest of the figure of Christ, asking for his own forgiveness as he adjusted the words to be closer to what he thought was deserved. "Through the ministry of the Church may God give you pardon and peace should you be so deserving, and may God absolve you from your sins in the name of the Father, and of the Son, and of the Holy Spirit."

Isaias felt the relief of Marie and Marc as he unclasped his hands and stood. After placing a bill on the table for the tea he had barely touched, Isaias turned to the people who might have been his parents, standing over them now. "I think you should have this," he said, offering the rosary. "I think it was yours."

Marie held out her left hand, the wedding band loose, and Isaias pooled the beads in her palm before laying Christ to rest on top of them. Though neither of his parents spoke as he turned to go, Isaias understood the full depth of all of their emotions: the comfort of a burden relieved, the grief for a life they could have lived, and the realization that they were letting their son go for the second and final time. He was sure it was a heavy moment for them, but for Isaias, he wasn't sure it meant nearly as much as he had thought it would.

For once, Isaias felt nothing at all.

Dear Hector,

I sense an ending.

It has never been within the parameters of my gift to know such things, so maybe it's just a feeling I have, a feeling in my gut or in my heart. The feeling that something, somewhere, is changing. Something will die and, like Lazarus, like Christ, will be reborn. I don't know what Christ saw in those three days gone, but I wonder if He came back the same person as He was before. And, if He changed, was it for better or for worse?

You have been gone from me for longer than three days. It pains me to doubt how many days it has been that you smiled at me, and you were not wholly yourself. When was it last really you I was able to speak to? How long have you been taken from me?

Now, each moment where you are *you* is a blessing. Each moment with you is a miracle.

But then, they always were.

It's past midnight, as I write this. Friday has snuck

up on us. Soon, it will be the day of rest again, and a full week since Violet had the courage to tell me you weren't yourself anymore.

But I will not rest, not until we have you back.

Hector, I beg of you, hold on. Hold on for your daughter. Hold on for me. Hold on for the future we could almost have. I don't want to face a version of the world where you are a regret. Where I have to wonder what another life might have looked like, with you still in it. Where I can only dream of planting flowers in our garden together.

I will pray to you for forgiveness for my selfishness later. And I will pray to you to understand my heart. But for now, I only want for you to hold on.

Hoping to be yours,

Isaias

XXVIII

Isaias's phone was vibrating against his hip, jarring him from sleep. He'd fallen asleep again on the bus ride back, his body taking any minor relief it could get from his constant exhaustion. The notepad he'd been writing letters to Hector on had fallen from his hand in his sleep—he picked it up off the adjacent seat as he turned on the screen of his phone to check what was causing the vibrations. It was almost two in the morning, but there was a missed call and a dozen texts from Violet, and even a few texts from Mrs. Marsh and Poppy.

Isaias didn't read the texts and instead immediately called Violet back.

"Father, thank God you called me back," Violet greeted before Isaias could get a single word in, her voice a flood of emotions Isaias could detect even from a distance. "My dad—he—Carreau, he got out. I don't know where he is. But he hurt Bishop Reid and he'll be okay, but he's *gone.*"

"Slow down, Violet," Isaias said softly, more to give himself time to process what she was saying than anything. "Hector is gone?"

"I don't know where he went. But Carreau got free somehow. The bishop tried to stop him, and the demon he just—blew past him. He's hurt but Mrs. Marsh is taking care of him. But Carreau, he's *gone*."

Isaias looked out the bus window at the bright lights beginning to appear, breaking through the darkness outside that had previously only been interrupted by intermittent headlights. "I'm almost back to the city. Can someone pick me up from the bus station? We'll find your father, Violet, I promise."

"Okay." Violet didn't sound comforted, but Isaias heard her take a deep breath before she spoke again. "I'm sorry I yelled at you before you left, Father. I was angry—and I still am—but maybe I have to respect your process. I just don't want you to do something stupid that means you can't help my dad because you're doubting." Violet's breath came out shuddering, and Isaias's heart arched for her. He hoped he would be back soon, able to help her and her father. "I don't think my dad cares about what God thinks of you. I know I don't. I just know we trust *you*, God or no God."

"It's okay, Vi," Isaias promised. "I'm just glad you're okay. Maybe go be with Poppy, and I'll be back soon. Take it easy, okay? I'll see you soon."

After hanging up, Isaias gathered his things and was ready to go long before the bus had pulled to a complete stop twenty minutes later, hurrying to disembark with an urgency that he hadn't felt in Sainte-Félicité. He was surprised to see that Poppy was the one waiting for him in the bus bay, fidgeting with the keys for Hector's car, staring at an iced-over crack in the asphalt—the ice surely under the surface, which would cause further damage if left untended—until she saw Isaias's shadow approaching. She looked up at him and smiled tiredly. The harshness of halfway burnt-out fluorescent overhead lighting cast the deep purple bags forming under her eyes into harsh shadows that hollowed out her cheeks. It made Isaias wonder how much worse he and Violet looked, how exhausted Mrs. Marsh must be, if Poppy had only been directly involved more recently. He'd been so focused on the signs of pain and exhaustion on Hector, that he had almost forgotten to stop and consider the extent to which the others must be hurting, too. He hoped they would have some relief soon.

"Am I driving?" Isaias asked, making a concerted effort to speak clearly against the fatigue that fought to drag his voice into a mumbled swamp of words. The exertion made his voice feel too loud for his throbbing head and, for second, sound was blotted out by the sharp white-noise ring of the increasingly persistent tinnitus.

Poppy shook her head. "I could use the distraction."

Isaias conceded the point with a flip of his hand to ask for her to lead the way instead of replying in words. She didn't speak again, either, cutting instead through the bus terminal—past the half-empty vending machines, the deserted lost and found counter, the people slumped in peeling vinyl chairs trying to get a moment's shut-eye—and into the pick-up and drop-off lot on the other side of the station. Isaias immediately spotted the car parked nearby and followed Poppy the short distance there. He was frankly grateful to her for driving, as he wasn't sure how much more able he would be to keep himself alert for the drive. He needed to reserve what little mental energy he had left for finding Hector—and resuming the exorcism.

Poppy started the car and switched to drive silently, pulling out of the parking lot and starting down the road to go back to the bishop's home without a word to Isaias. He saw, though, the tight grip on the steering wheel as she checked the rearview mirror and every blind spot more times than was strictly necessary.

"How are you doing?" Isaias asked her, watching her profile for her reaction.

Poppy didn't answer at first, and Isaias had half a mind to repeat his question in case she hadn't heard him. But before he could, she glanced at him momentarily before turning her eyes back to the road and shaking her head almost imperceptibly. Streetlights flashed by, casting sick-yellow light on her face. "Hector is like a dad to me," she said. "More so than my biological father ever has been. And Violet is—I love her, Father. I know I'm not supposed to, but I do."

"You're supposed to love," Isaias said gently but firmly. "I know why you think you're not supposed to love *Violet*, but I'm just happy she has you. God's doctrine is love. *All* love. I don't think He would judge who you love, despite what some may think."

"That's kind of you," Poppy said, her eyes glued to the road except for when she checked the rearview mirror again, as if expecting some kind of spectre to be hiding in the backseat, ready to pounce. "God knows my mother wouldn't say such kind things. But do you really believe that?"

"What makes you think that I don't?" Isaias asked, holding the hurt out of his voice.

"Well, do *you* love freely?" Poppy glanced at him sideways, but it lasted only the duration of a streetlight blurring past before her eyes were back on the road, back on the rearview mirror. "You don't seem to."

Isaias bit back his immediate defensiveness. He locked his eyes on the road, too, letting himself mull over her accusation. He tried to do what he was trained to do: listen, weigh, offer guidance. But he had never done it for himself before. "For a priest, it's different. I'm dedicated to God, and only God. There's no room for love for anyone else."

Poppy drummed her fingers on the steering wheel. "Do you think that's true? That loving one thing, one entity, means you can't love anyone or anything else? I think that I love God, despite everything, despite my mother weaponizing Him. But I *also* love Violet. And I love Hector like my dad. Why should it be different for you?"

"Because as a priest, I have to make sacrifices. A lot of love requires sacrifice, and for me to hold the authority that I do, I have to make them, too."

"I don't think Violet would ever ask me to sacrifice something that made me happy and wasn't hurting anyone else," Poppy said firmly.

"I don't think that would be fair. I'm just saying, Father—maybe practice what you preach about love."

Isaias thought, for a moment, about how he might respond, but found none of his words felt adequate. He, like Poppy, watched the painted yellow lines of the road flash by in the dark of the night.

As soon as the door to the rectory was opened, Violet barreled toward Isaias, shifting one arm out of her crutches to give him a one-armed hug. "I'm so glad you're back."

"Me too, Vi," Isaias murdered, hugging her back, too. He felt all of the earnest relief in her and his heart echoed the same. "I'm glad you're safe. Can you tell me what happened?"

Violet stepped back out of the hug and returned her grip to her crutch. With that distance between them, Isaias could see the tired lines on her face, the bags that had set in under her reddened eyes. "It's my dad," she said, her voice cracking under the force and speed of her words. "I mean, Carreau. We had bound him, with the belts, and with his name, but he got away anyway. He was making this huge commotion, so the bishop and Mrs. Marsh went to try to calm him down. And I used his name to try to order him to be quiet, I tried to speak like—like God was speaking through me, like you do, but God didn't come, and the demon didn't listen."

"Deep breaths, Violet," Isaias said gently, resting his hands on her shoulders and trying to send her a gentle emotional nudge to calm her nerves. He saw immediate effect, the way that Violet relaxed in his grip. She stayed steady, though, upset and defiant. "It's okay. I'm here now. We'll find him."

Violet nodded brusquely. "He broke free of the restraints and grabbed the bishop. And just fucking—flung him into the wall. Like a stupid cliché. And while Mrs. Marsh was checking on the bishop,

Carreau broke the window and climbed out that way. And now he's gone, the bishop is hurt, and I don't know what we're supposed to do."

Isaias nodded as he let go of Violet. She was alone again for the briefest of seconds before Poppy appeared by her side, resting her hand in the middle of Violet's back. Violet's shoulders drooped, tension leaving her—far more relaxed than Isaias's emotional nudge had left her, through a simple touch from Poppy.

"Where's the bishop now?" Isaias asked. "And Mrs. Marsh?"

Violet frowned, but said, "He's resting, upstairs. Mrs. Marsh is keeping an eye on him."

"That's all I needed to know," Isaias said. "Let's go find your father."

Sainte-Jeanne was a quiet city at night. It had been a long time since Isaias had truly experienced it during the day, but it was a lively enough city. Festivals, events, music in the air. At night, though, it was like whatever voices flowed through the city—charged it with energy, called it into action—finally let the people rest and get some sleep. For a city with a lot of life in the daylight, it was a place with relatively little nightlife. In the cold of a winter night, nearing the witching hour, it felt like there wasn't a single living soul that dared be seen on the streets.

Of course, Isaias knew that wasn't true. As much as people were avoiding the bitter cold and the biting snow, he could sense life all around him as he drove Violet and Poppy through the downtown streets. And as soon as he sensed life, he knew where to look for it—the shadowy figures in doorways, the fresh footprints leading to and from storefronts that otherwise looked closed, the flashes of light briefly visible in windows overlooking the street before sinking down, down, down, into the depths of the bellies of whatever lived under the streets.

Most of the city slept, yes, free from visions that drove them to action. But for some, not even sleep was an escape from the call to action, the drive to climb the mountain and come back with a message. There was truly no rest from those tapped into the deepest veins of life beating through the city.

And here they were, driving around the city with the windows down on a mid-February night like he, Violet, and Poppy were looking for a lost pet and not a demon on the loose.

Violet was in the front passenger seat, staring out the window into the night, soulful eyes searching for her father on the side streets. Isaias was scared that she was soon to be lost to him, as if she were the one who needed searching for, not Hector. Isaias reached out to her presence for a moment, and she felt so much smaller than she was, like a child, and not almost a grown woman. And Poppy, in the backseat, was equally unmoored, but on rocky seas.

Isaias stared out at the road, searching, driving aimlessly, and not knowing what to do.

Except to reach out to Hector, and hope Hector would shine like a lighthouse through the dark that clouded his soul. With nothing but his heart to guide him, Isaias drove near aimlessly down street after street until he felt a strange warmth spread through his belly, up into his chest, through his shoulders. Like Hector was calling him home.

Following his heart, Isaias drove them out of downtown through residential roads, then industrial, then out into the suburbs—and soon the sensation became dizzying, more hot flash than comfort. His palms clung to the steering wheel, sticky with sweat, and his vision swam. He rolled down the driver's side window, letting the late-night air chill him. He saw Violet looking at him out of the corner of his eye, but still he drove until they approached not a lighthouse but the Sainte-Jeanne water tower, a stalwart sentinel on the edge of the city. The reservoir was encased in brick that made it appear more like a church clocktower or watchtower than an elevated water tank, or else it should have, were it not for the crumbling façade exposing the pressurized steel beneath. Flood lights encircled the base of the tower, illuminating the tower from below, casting it in a halo in light that cast the hollow opening in deep shadows and reflected off partially obscured graffiti that read GOD IS. The final word was cut off, obscured by deteriorating brick. Isaias felt no desire to investigate, to uncover the rest of the message.

Getting out of the car, Violet and Poppy followed but didn't ask for an explanation, trusting Isaias's faith that Hector was there. Because he *did* have faith that his heart had led him to Hector. He scanned the ground around the tower for any sign of Hector, hoping the contrast of the flood lights wouldn't make him harder to see.

Instead, though, they illuminated him—movement above brought into sharp relief by the dazzling light, drawing their attention. Far above their heads, Hector's body was scaling the narrow, grated safety walkway around the opening of the water tower, not making any effort to sneak around but instead walking boldly to the broken opening, head held high and proud.

Divine inspiration struck. Before Isaias could doubt the impulse, he stood, feet braced, at the base of the water tower and, with all the force of every emotion he could muster after all these days of pain and suffering, he called out, "Hector!"

The thing above that looked like Hector didn't still so much as fully *stop*, a cessation of motion so sudden that it looked almost like its own movement. Invisible puppet strings were pulled taut, preventing even the slightest sway of the doll attached. Slowly, and with a great deal of effort, the demon in the shape of Hector turned to face the guardrail and look down at Isaias. The spotlights washed out Hector's features and cast a long, dark shadow behind him on the brick of the water tower. The painfully bright contrast highlighted the lines of suffering on Hector's face, too: the stains from sweat and blood, the inflamed burn marks that marked the cross on his face. The light almost seemed to reflect Hector's grin, too wide, blood between his teeth. "Well, isn't *that* interesting," the demon called down from his perch, voice bellowing. "That's a new one, isn't it, Father?"

Isaias kept his feet braced, looking up into the light, to Hector. He kept his back turned to Violet and Poppy, who he could sense were standing behind him now—he felt their bewilderment, their hope, their fear. He didn't hear them approach, however, as white noise roared in his ears, a static growl that sounded both like pain and like song. Only his own voice broke through the noise—his and the demon's. "I am speaking to *Hector*," Isaias shouted, voice straining with the force of volume and of pouring all the energy of his heart into his words. "Not to Carreau. Come down now. Return to the church and let us pray together. We are going to end this."

The demon gripped Hector's hands tight on the guardrail as he tipped forward, leaning hard against the rickety metal. Isaias tried not to believe that Hector might fall, tried not to break his stance. But the demon didn't look like he was threatening to jump—only fighting to keep himself upright. "Fuck you," the demon snapped. "I was *summoned*, and you don't get to be the one who sends me back, sanctimonious Father Fuck Up. You felt all that pain. You don't get to decide when it goes away."

In Isaias's shock, the pain of the demon came flashing back to him, making the tinnitus scream and his head throb. He felt again all the suffering that he'd felt when he'd opened himself up to him. Not just the demon's own pain, but Hector's—and someone else's despair, a sorrow so deep it had called up a demon. "Who summoned you?"

The demon stared down at Isaias with Hector's eyes before he jerked backwards, straightening his back out, then arching like a cat. Before Isaias could register Carreau's plan, he gripped the railing and hoisted himself over it, lunging over the rail.

"Hector!" Isaias shouted, dashing forward, as if he could catch the demon on what must have been a hundred-foot drop and save

Hector's body. Violet and Poppy's shouts pierced through the white noise that still flooded Isaias's head, accompanied by their terror.

But the demon, nimble as a cat, landed on Hector's feet. "You want to know the full story? I'll put you to that challenge, Priest. Listen, and see whose justice you believe in."

XXIX

The demon was surprisingly quiet on the way back to the bishop's rectory, so neither Isaias nor the girls disturbed the rough silence. Poppy drove them back, Violet in the passenger seat next to her, while Isaias sat in the back, close to the demon in Hector's body, watching him even while his head spun from pain and doubt. As they approached the rectory, Isaias's vision seemed to blur and, for a moment, he could believe it was only Hector that was sitting beside him. Hector, who might have been the only person in the world who mattered in that moment.

By the time they parked, the demon had slumped forward, neck craned, and head lolled. Barely conscious. Isaias waited until Violet and Poppy were out of the car before he also exited, walking around to the other side to open the door and lift Hector out of the car. It was a struggle to support him, since Hector had always been larger than him, but Hector had lost a great deal of weight over the past few days, so he managed to get by. Poppy stayed a half-step away to be able to offer support at a moment's notice. Her gaze remained fixed on Hector, serious and inscrutable. Isaias made no effort to read what she was feeling. Violet trailed behind, leaning more weight than usual on her crutches, her worry written in the frown lines around her eyes and the bags under them.

Supporting Hector with an arm around his shoulders, Isaias helped him into the rectory. He was about to take him back into the study before he changed his mind and helped him upstairs, down the hall, and into Isaias's old bedroom. For what was the point of tying up the demon to a chair in the study if he could have escaped any time that he wanted? He might as well let Hector rest easier than he had thus far. It was a meagre comfort, but he would give any small thing he could offer to Hector to make his suffering less.

Hector blinked up at Isaias, finally stirring out of his halfway slumber as Isaias lay him down in the bed. He held onto Isaias's arms as he helped him settle, as if he were trying to balance himself, to not drop too quickly. Isaias had a contradictory image in mind of the demon in Hector's body dropping from the water tower with no issue, compared now to the way Hector held onto him as if he were afraid that Isaias would let go of him, as if he would break in the short fall to the plush mattress below. Never before had Hector, his strong, steadfast Hector, seemed so delicate.

Isaias was so very careful not to let him fall, lying him gently back on the pillows and blanket. He let go of Hector only once he was fully lying down, then brushed some loose curls away from his forehead. Hector's eyes opened properly, finally, and locked onto Isaias's. "Don't go," he said, his voice hoarse.

It really was Hector again. Isaias could have wept, but instead said, "Let me at least get you some water."

"Please."

Isaias glanced back at Poppy, now a few more steps behind, who said, "I'll get water."

Nodding, Isaias smiled to her in relief. "Thank you, Poppy."

As Poppy exited, Violet hesitated in the doorway. Isaias nodded to her, too, and she approached with caution. "Hey, dad."

"Hey, Vi." Hector coughed. "Sorry to put you through Hell."

"No kidding," Violet muttered softly. She didn't come closer. Isaias could see his own pain magnified in both of them. But nothing broke his heart more than hearing Violet whisper, "I miss you."

Isaias looked back to Hector and watched all of the emotions he could feel in him play across his expression. How exhausted, heartbroken, and hurt Hector was. How much he must have wanted to reply, *I'm right here.* Instead, Hector said, "I love you, little flower."

When Violet spoke, her voice cracked with the weight of her entire heart. "I love you, too, dad."

Isaias, once again a trespasser in the family he loved, stepped away from the bed, hesitating to leave Violet alone with her father when he might not be himself for long, but not wanting to intrude on the moment any longer. But Hector said, "No, Isaias, please stay."

Violet, too, shook her head. "Please stay," she echoed. "You're part of this, too."

Before Isaias could protest, insist he didn't belong with them, Poppy reappeared in the doorway with a glass of water in one hand and a damp cloth in the other. "Mrs. Marsh said we should clean Hector's wounds," she said bashfully, looking between the three in the room already. "Sorry, am I interrupting?"

"No, you're good," Violet said quickly, beckoning for Poppy to join her. "Thanks for getting water."

Isaias took the glass of water from Poppy once she came closer before he sat on the edge of the bed, near Hector's head on the pillow. With his free hand, he helped prop Hector up so he could drink and held the glass of water to his lips. Some of the water drippled down his chin and into his matted beard, glistening on the silver hairs threaded throughout now. Isaias carefully took the glass back once Hector started to cough and gently rubbed his thumb across the back of Hector's sweat-sticky neck in a hopeless effort to soothe him until he relaxed again. Isaias glanced back at Violet and Poppy but looked away again when he saw the tears in Violet's eyes.

As Hector lay back down on the bed, he asked, "How was your trip?"

Isaias was quiet for a moment, loathing that Hector would want to know even if it made perfect sense. Isaias had thought that seeing his parents would bring him answers. But they had known nothing. And all Isaias was left with was wondering what the bishop had seen in a child taken from his home. If he had ever seen more than a tool. And it felt wrong to doubt. "Confusing," he answered honestly, looking from Hector to the girls. "I learned some things, but it wasn't what I had hoped."

"Not surprising," Violet cut in. "No offence, Isaias, but that was stupid. Why would people you don't even know have any answers about who you're supposed to be?"

"They're my parents," Isaias protested softly.

"Are they though?" Poppy asked, her voice meek before she spoke again, this time louder. Something in her voice was tight, wrapped taut around a hard edge. "I know it's complicated, but—they didn't raise you. They were never there for you. And even if they were, that doesn't mean they *know* you."

"I was born of their blood, and if their sins carried forward—"

"I don't buy it," Hector said from below. His voice was faint, difficult to hear. Poppy strained, and Hector, noticing, spoke clearer. "I get what you believe about that. But you were also a kid. How could you have possibly been blamed for what they did or didn't do? By God or anyone?"

"It's not about being blamed," Isaias protested.

"Isn't it, though?" Violet asked, her voice wry. "How could you be cursed or something without it being about you deserving it? How could you think you're a sinner because of them, without thinking that means you deserve to be judged, too?"

Hector shook his head, the barest movement against the pillow. He reached for Isaias, who gave him his hand. Hector held on tight, though his grip was a shadow of his healthy self. "Violet's right. Isaias, you're one of the best people I've ever met. The only person that I—that I care about more than you is Violet and Poppy. Don't you think that counts for something?"

"But the sins of the father—"

Violet stepped forward. "What even *are* your sins? Have you ever done anything wrong in your *life*?"

"Plenty," Isaias said softly. He cleared his throat and repeated, clearer, "Plenty. I can't explain it."

"Name one thing that's worth this self-flagellation act you've got going on," Hector said. Isaias hesitated, not wanting to say his gravest fears out loud. Hector seized on the moment, his voice strained with the force of it: "You can't, can you?"

Isaias swallowed hard and looked down at his hand in Hector's. He considered pulling away, but Hector was holding him like a lifeline, and he couldn't bear to take that away from his friend. And, selfishly, he didn't want to be apart from Hector for even a moment until he had to. And soon, they would lose him again. But while Isaias tried to decide how to respond, Poppy spoke up. "It's about what you did at the water tower, isn't it?" she asked. She glanced at Violet, then back to Isaias. "We both felt it. When you spoke, we *felt* it."

"We did," Violet confirmed. "Is that what this is about, Isaias?"

Isaias's heart ached, even as he felt his breath quicken. It was a gift from God—so why was he ashamed that they had realized there was something about him that was different? "From the time that I was a baby, I was different. I could sense things, feel things, that other people couldn't. My parents didn't know what to do with me." Isaias looked from the girls to Hector, who lay still on the bed. Hector's eyes looked tired, distant. Isaias wondered how much longer they had with him before the demon reemerged. "The priests told my parents it was a gift from God, and that He had plans for me. It's why Bishop Reid adopted me."

Hector's hand twitched in Isaias, drawing Isaias's attention again. Hector's eyes were heavy-lidded, fluttering like something was dragging them down, dragging *him* down, but then the twitch in his fingers changed from a tremor to a hold and he gripped Isaias's hand harder. Isaias squeezed back—gently—and let himself feel the bravery of Hector, a man who was losing everything—not least of all his bodily autonomy—but still found it in his heart to love.

Violet, though, was the one who spoke. "So, your heart is just—bleeding, all the time," she said. "And what, you're worried this isn't actually a gift? That your God actually cursed you?"

Wetting his lips and looking down at Hector, not at the girls, Isaias said, "Or maybe it wasn't even God."

Hector squeezed Isaias's hand again, and Isaias looked into his face as Hector struggled to open his eyes. "All I'm hearing is that your sin is that you're afraid."

Isaias felt tears threaten him immediately, and the force of his own emotions forced him to lower his guard. He felt the sudden power of Hector's sincerity and care. How he saw no flaws in Isaias, only beauty. But the tears didn't fall until Violet and Poppy approached, Poppy hugging Isaias and Violet wrapping one arm around him. He felt his heart warming with the strength of their love, even through their exhaustion.

Smiling tiredly through his tears, Isaias fought down the force and pain of many nights, days, years, of self-hatred and grief and instead focused on the love he felt in Hector, in Violet, in Poppy. In the family that was there for him. That accepted him. That was going through literal Hell with him.

Perhaps, together, they might still have a chance of defeating Hell itself.

XXX

Isaias woke up to the rhythmic tick-tocking of the clock informing him of the pre-dawn hour. He slowly stirred, confused that someone was holding him. It took a moment to remember himself, his surroundings, why his face was sticky from dried tears and Hector was holding him loosely in his sleep. He must have fallen asleep there, with Hector, after they had talked. A dangerous thing to have allowed, but the exhaustion must have possessed Isaias to make a risky decision.

What was more, Violet and Poppy were both asleep nearby—Violet on the foot of the bed, stretched out the best she could despite the small space and Poppy on the floor, resting against the edge of the bedframe, Violet's crutches next to her. Neither could be comfortable, and Isaias worried for the pain flareup Violet would surely face later. For Isaias's part, his neck ached from where he was propped up like a discarded doll against the headboard, halfway curled into himself and into Hector, who held him loosely.

Isaias stayed very still for a long time, breathing slowly and steadily in Hector's arms. He watched the steady rise and fall of Hector's chest, a buoy in the ocean that was all this suffering. With his breath came the most peace he had felt from Hector in a long time. He knew it couldn't last, but he relished the warmth of Hector's aura, the comforting smell of vanilla and chocolate.

Reluctantly, but wanting to give Hector the peace he needed while he could, Isaias sat up to get off the bed. Hector stirred as Isaias tried to extricate himself from his grip, and his arms only tightened around Isaias. Isaias smiled faintly, feeling the exhausted determination of Hector to stay near a source of comfort, and Isaias felt honoured to be the source of that comfort, if only for a moment and if only because he was warmer than Hector was. Isaias settled back down and tentatively reached up to brush some of Hector's hair out of his face. Hector's eyes blinked slowly open, and Isaias felt a pang of guilt for waking him. He had hoped only that Hector could hold onto rest while he could.

"Isaias?" Hector murmured softly.

"Sorry for waking you," Isaias said, equally soft. He kept his hand on Hector's face for an instant more before he drew back.

"Don't go."

Isaias smiled faintly. "I should let you sleep."

"You can sleep, too." Hector shifted, bringing one hand up to Isaias's face and touching the dried tears on Isaias's cheeks. "You probably need it."

"Maybe," Isaias said. "But I should—pray. I don't think that I did last night."

Hector scoffed. "You're an idiot."

Isaias flushed. "What?" Hector dipped his head down to tuck his face against Isaias. From there, all he could reach was Isaias's side, chin nestled against his hip. "Hector?" Isaias asked.

"You are," Hector pressed, his breath hot against Isaias's skin where his shirt had ridden up. Isaias felt the hairs on the back of his neck raise. He'd never felt Hector so close before. At least, not physically. "Just stay here."

"Okay," Isaias said, his voice reverential. He smiled to Hector, ignoring the strong scent of vanilla invading his senses, becoming overstimulating. It was frightening. It was Hector. Hector, Hector,

Hector. Isaias repeated his name in his mind's eye—there was his prayer, his salvation. He imagined what it might be like to feel Hector whisper *his* name, to feel 'Isaias' in Hector's hot breath against his stomach where Hector's head now rested.

Isaias lay there quietly for another long time. For a moment, he thought that Hector had fallen back to sleep, until Hector softly asked, "Isaias? Are you still awake?"

Isaias smiled faintly at Hector's sleep-laced voice. If either of them could ever go back to innocence, unharmed by the world, it would be found in Hector's dreamy cadence in the space just between wakefulness and sleep. "Yes, Hector?"

"I love you."

Everything stopped.

In that instant, he realized: *this* was the prayer he had been waiting for. *I love you* was the key to the gates of paradise that Isaias hadn't known he needed. To be known, to be loved, just as God commanded. Love—love was God, after all. Love was God, and love was Hector. Isaias had just needed that delectable fruit of knowledge to tell him what love could *be*. To let him see through the veil into the world of possibility of what they could grow in their garden together. Not just flowers, but the fruits of knowledge, and love, and new beginnings.

He also felt his fearful heartbeat asking as it skipped a beat, *What happens next?*

As time tentatively rolled back to a start, Isaias said, "Hector, I—"

"Save it."

Nausea flooded through Isaias, and he nearly gagged on the sickly-sweet stench of burnt sugar. "Carreau," he whispered.

"Got it in one, Father."

The slow, dreamy quality time had taken on for Isaias shattered as reality surged back to meet him, to bring him back to the harsh truth of the matter: Hector was possessed, there was a demon puppeteering his words and actions. Doubt came back first—how many times had Isaias thought he was talking to Hector in the past weeks that it might not have been him?—and was swiftly followed by heartache—for his friend, most of all, but also for himself.

How many lies had been told? How many of his fleeting moments of comfort with Hector had been delivered by false prophets?

Isaias jerked away and off the bed, initially falling to the floor, but ignored the hollow pain of the collision and instead surged to his feet and rushed to the foot of the bed to get the girls. He reached for Violet, first, who was already stirring from the commotion. Isaias helped her to her feet, and she immediately reached for her crutches, which Isaias passed to her as she leaned on him. Poppy stirred from the movement—and leapt into action faster than either Isaias or Violet had, immediately launching to her feet and darting to Violet's side to be ready for her. Isaias knew Poppy's heartbeat was racing through the prey-reaction, how immediately alert and on guard she was, ready to pick fight or flight in an instant. Violet transferred herself first onto her crutches and then into Poppy's space.

"How long has it been you?" Isaias asked, stepping between the two girls and Hector, who rose from the bed chest-first, like something had embedded a fishhook into the bone of his ribs, hauling him up limply and against his will, before the rest of him followed. His grin was painted on, and the glint in his eyes spoke of malice. Isaias fought his nausea down at the emotional resonance of pain he felt—the suffering that stank of smoke and charred meat, burnt sugar too mild now to describe the foul stench. "What do you want?" Isaias pressed, fighting his own emotions down. He could not think. He could not feel. Not now.

"Dad?" Violet asked uncertainly, her voice meeker than Isaias had ever heard it before. He felt her quashed hope as well, mingled into her disorientation.

"That's not your father," Isaias warned her. His heart still felt like it was lodged in his throat. From the corner of his eye, he saw Violet tense behind him, and Poppy move forward, ready for a fight if it meant keeping Violet safe. "What do you want?" Isaias asked the demon again, forcing his voice steady.

"I want *you*, Isaias," the demon said, grinning a mockery of Hector's smile as he rose to his feet. Somehow, Hector's already impressive height and girth seemed larger—and more threatening—with the demon once again in control. Unless, of course, he had always been in control—and now he was only showing them just how *much* control he really had. "No, really. I thought you said you'd listen to me. I think now's about the time you do. Maybe we can help each other out."

From the corner of his eye, Isaias saw Poppy steal a look at him, glancing between Isaias and the demon, but he dared not look to her or Violet. He wouldn't take his eyes off Carreau. "Make your case, Devil."

"I thought we determined I wasn't the Devil."

"Whatever you are."

"You're going to hurt my feelings, Father Fuck Up," the demon purred, voice falsely sweet. Isaias said nothing, so the demon continued, "Sit with me. Maybe we can have some tea. I can tell you what it is I want."

"You can tell us right here," Isaias said. "We're not friends."

"Fair enough, Father," Carreau said. He looked from Isaias to Violet. "What's wrong, girl? Aren't you used to this by now?"

"Shut up," Violet snapped, and Isaias heard her tears. "What do you want? Just tell us, and then leave us *alone*."

The demon smiled softly, an expression that looked too much like Hector's own smile for comfort. "Deal," he said. "If you do what I ask, then I'd be happy to leave your dear Hector alone. The lot of you can be a happy little family."

"What do you want?" Poppy asked, this time. Isaias shifted closer to her, reached for her, but she shrugged him off—not forcefully, but insistently. "Just spit it out, already."

"I've been summoned to make a difference to the people here," Carreau said, voice slick like snake oil. "And you're going to help me fulfill that mission, since you've been so gracious as to bring me all the way to Sainte-Jeanne, from whence I was summoned."

Isaias's heart pounded heavy in his chest. Why Sainte-Jeanne? Was this where Carreau had always wanted to be? Had Carreau strung them along, just as much his puppets as Hector was?

Isaias could find no words in him.

The demon looked between them when they didn't answer him, then clasped his hands together. For a moment, Isaias thought Carreau was going to mock him with false prayer to a false god. But instead, he slowly spread his hands like he was stretching putty, and a bubble of impossible liquid appeared between his hands. It was a deep, uncomfortable red, too dark even for blood, and it floated between the demon's palms like air, despite looking heavy and thick; viscous liquid that had no business existing where it did, laughing in the face of all of God's patterns in the chaos.

"I want you to feed this to the town," the demon said. "I don't care how. I thought I would put it in the water supply, let it bleed through the faucets and into the mouths and homes of all of the future martyrs of Sainte-Jeanne."

Isaias was disgusted, but Poppy asked the question he needed to know, her eyes locked on the vile orb between Carreau's hands. "What is it?"

"Poison, my dear flower," the demon said, smiling still. With a flourish, he caught the bubble in his hand, then held it out for Poppy to take. Carreau kept his eyes locked on the girl. "But not just any poison. This poison is specially designed, you see. Those free from guilt will be fine. Only true sinners will be affected."

"Sinners how?" Poppy asked, reaching out to take the bubble.

"Poppy, don't touch it," Isaias said in warning, but it was too late. Poppy took it in her hands, staring at it with frightened hesitation.

"Pops, be careful," Violet said gently next to her.

"Like I said," the demon clarified, "only true sinners, the ones who have been building their place in Hell with their own hands, will suffer at the hands of this poison. Like, let's just say as a hypothetical, those who have harmed children. Put this baby in the water supply," he said, tapping the bubble that Poppy cradled in her hands, sending it rippling, the red light shining off her deep brown eyes, "and all those abusers who consume it will die. Leaves the world a better place, don't you think?"

XXXI

"WE HAVE TO DESTROY it," Isaias said the instant that the door to the bedroom was closed behind the three of them. He stepped quickly away from the door, Violet and Poppy following. "We have to find a way immediately."

But Poppy surprised him by asking, "Why?"

Isaias gaped at her. He stared at the bubble in her hands, a threatening red. It reminded Isaias, now, in a new light, of disease and death more than blood. Whatever it was, it was clearly made from evil. "Poppy—"

Violet watched her friend steadily, without anger, without judgement.

"I mean," Poppy quickly said, her eyes locked on the orb in her hands, "I mean, I know why. That's not how—how justice works. We can't be executioners. And thou shalt not kill and thou shalt not make unto thee any graven image—this isn't another God, but it's something divine, or maybe the opposite of divine, that isn't of *our* God. That's what you're thinking, right? Because it's what my mother would say. That we can't enact God's judgement. We shall be humble. But why *not*?"

"For all the reasons you said," Isaias insisted, not sure how this conversation was playing out the way that it was. He had never realized just how much doubt could be held in Poppy's heart. "We are not God. We are not even god-like."

"How would we even destroy it? If we incinerate it or something, for all we know it ends up in the air instead."

"Then we lock it away where it can't hurt anyone."

"It already exists, Father," Violet cut in. She stepped closer to Poppy. She let go of one crutch, reached for Poppy, before she changed her mind and replaced her hand on the grip of her crutch and held tight. "I don't think Carreau—or whatever his name is—is going to let us off the hook just because we decide we don't want to do something with it. He'll do it himself. If we do it—if we expedite God's judgement—then we get my dad back."

Isaias stared at Violet in shock. "Vi, honey—"

"I don't like it, either, Isaias," Violet said, and suddenly her eyes were brimming with tears. "But what else are we supposed to do to get my dad back? We've conducted a dozen or more exorcisms. How many more times can we pray for him, if no one's out there listening? Nothing's working. And Carreau said he'd leave my dad alone if we helped him."

Placing his throbbing head—the tinnitus ringing true like God's word again—in his hands, Isaias took a breath. These poor girls. When he had gathered his courage again, he stepped close to Violet and to Poppy and said, "He's a liar. He twists love." Hector's words—if they had ever been Hector's words—burned like a scar in his mind, like the cross marring Hector's face, *I love you* a heartbeat before Carreau bared his teeth. "We can't trust that it will do what he says it will do, let alone that he will finally leave Hector if we do this for him. I'm sorry, but I don't know if we could take that risk—even if we felt sure it was the right thing to do."

Violet did not cry. Her tears didn't ever fall. But she hung her head and Isaias's heart broke with hers. It was wrong for a girl her age to force herself to be so hard—to fear judgement if she did anything other than hold her emotions and her reactions back. "I don't know what to do, Father," she said, voice sanded down into polished flatness. Isaias felt too much of himself then in this girl who could have been his daughter—in another world, in another life. "I just want my dad back."

"Oh, Vi," Isaias whispered. He held his arms out to offer a hug and Violet nodded weakly. Isaias hugged her carefully, letting her lean into him for as long as she needed. He let go once she pulled away and turned to look at Poppy. "Let's put the orb somewhere safe for now, alright? And we'll figure out what to do with it together."

Isaias watched dozens of considerations flash in Poppy's eyes before she finally, reluctantly, handed the orb to Isaias. He took it with trepidation, cradling it in his hands with an irrational fear that he might break it and unleash the pain it contained upon the world. Or, worse, that he might hold it too close, and it would leech into his heart, forever changing him. The orb filled him with a strange sense of nostalgia, but also the rancid smell of rot. It burned to the touch, and his ears filled with the sound of a heartbeat not his own; staccato and unpleasant and clashing painfully with the already present tinnitus and sounding like it was coming from someplace outside of him, from within the walls.

It filled Isaias with nausea, but he didn't want Poppy to be holding it any longer, especially not with the way that she had been looking at it. He carried it down the stairs, and the two girls followed him like a funerary procession to the bishop's study. He found a letter box in the desk, emptied it of correspondence, and placed the orb inside—it seemed to melt into the corners of the box, filling it the brim, taking on its shape, and Isaias closed the box and locked it.

He began a half-remembered prayer, not questioning where it came from in his heart. "I take refuge in You, our Lord, and ask You humbly as Your servant to cleanse this object, and cleanse those who have ever beheld it, of all sin, all histories, and all defilement. As You cast out the enemy, so too may You cast out all evil that attaches itself to the souls of Your humble servants. I shall ever sing Your praises. Amen."

Violet echoed his "amen" in a soft voice, her hand travelling to her chest, touching something beneath her shirt. He saw a dark, thoughtful look in her eyes. Poppy remained silent. Once the words had melted away, Isaias placed the locked box into a cabinet and locked that, too. It had felt heavy in its wrongness, but he felt immense relief to no longer be touching the thing and hoped only that this was one thing that God listened to his prayers for, that the Lord would stay their hands and finally bring Hector home without any more pain.

I consecrate myself into a vessel for Your power, O Lord. Give me even a fraction of Your might to hold this thing bravely.

He still heard a heart pounding at a distance, having travelled now into the floorboards.

"Both of you should rest," Isaias said gently. He looked between them imploringly. "I'll figure something out."

Violet sniffled. "Promise?" she asked as Poppy wrapped her arms around Violet's middle, tucking her face momentarily into the space between Violet's shoulders. Both girls looked remarkably small, and Violet had already always looked young for her age.

"I promise."

Violet sighed and momentarily curled into herself, leaning backwards against Poppy, letting herself be held. Once she had collected herself, she said, "I'll sleep in here. Since it—since he's upstairs."

"Okay, sweetheart," Isaias said softly. "I'll ask Mrs. Marsh to bring you some blankets and pillows so you can try to make yourself more comfortable."

"Thanks." Violet sniffled again, then inched forward, signalling to Poppy to let her go, who did so without further prompting. Poppy still said nothing.

Isaias exited the study to leave the two girls alone, and immediately heard them speaking softly behind the door once they had privacy.

Isaias couldn't blame either of them. His ears still rang and the heart in the floor still beat, making it difficult to hear them even if he wanted to. Instead, he took a moment to unwind the bandage around his right hand, flexing it and looking at the still-healing wounds. The bite mark was barely distinguishable as such, but Isaias thought he could still make out the shape of Hector's teeth. It was torn skin and blood just below the surface, turning it purple-red with bruising and burst blood vessels ready to escape. The side of his hand was blooming with the colours of fuchsias, and for a moment Isaias thought that he might see flowers breaking from his skin, splitting him open and making him anew. Between the ragged wound from the teeth of a man who might have loved him, and his torn open palm still stinging all these days later, Isaias wondered if he would ever heal, or if he, too, would be forever marked, if flowers growing out of him would make him a grave.

He couldn't remember the last time he had truly slept.

The sound of a heartbeat travelled up into the walls, into the ceiling, before it faded away to *almost* nothing, leaving only the buzzing of white noise that had become familiar in Isaias's ears.

Tucking the keys to the cabinet and the box into his pocket, Isaias walked up stairs and back to his childhood bedroom. He opened the door without ceremony or process and saw Hector's slumped there, on the bed again, jaw slack and staring up at the ceiling. For a painful second, Isaias thought that he wasn't breathing. But then the thing inside of him looked at Isaias and said, "Back so soon, Father?"

Isaias closed the door behind him and said, "I want to talk to Hector."

"Why?"

"Because he has every right to tell me his side of the story."

Hector's eyes lit up with the demon's mirth as he rose to a more rigid sitting position. It was a mockery of the laughter Isaias used to know in Hector's eyes, the crinkling of the laugh-lines around his eyes and the way his smile tugged to one side and caused his beard to twitch. The gestures that should have been Hector were bastardized, no longer the man Isaias knew. "His side of the story, eh? After all this time, you want to know what *really* happened?"

"I don't want it from you," Isaias warned.

"Oh, no, of *course* not—but you don't get to make that call, now do you?" the demon laughed, sharp and hostile. "Funny, to try to call the shots about the truth now when you're still just as much a self-deceiver as the rest of us lowly souls."

Isaias held himself back from arguing, but he felt the pain of his anxiety radiating through his teeth and into his temples. He took a moment to deliberately release the tension and unclench his jaw. "If you were to tell me Hector's story, how would I know you aren't lying to me?"

"What interest would I have in lying?" Carreau shot back. "What good would it do for me?"

"I don't know," Isaias admitted. He wet his lips and ducked his head. "But you've been manipulating us from the start, haven't you? You said it yourself—you wanted to come to Sainte-Jeanne."

"Moving you like pawns is very different from lying to you." The demon smiled again, then climbed to Hector's feet. "Though truly, haven't you made all your choices yourself? That was the Devil's precious gift to you: free will, and God let you keep it. Every choice you've made is your own, setting you further down your path, and it's up to you whether it leads to Heaven or Hell. We don't need to lie to you, Father. Getting you on the path we want barely takes a *nudge*."

Isaias felt cold—and he let himself feel it, too. The numbness tingled in his fingertips and down through the wound on the side of his hand. He was fighting too hard. He leaned into it instead. "Then tell me Hector's story," he whispered, feeling like he had betrayed Hector in so few words, Hector who surely loved too deeply to be betrayed by a friend. "Tell me what I need to know."

Carreau smiled and swiped Hector's hand through his hair, slicking it back with sweat. Isaias had the unshakeable feeling that the demon was about to sell him on something. "Let me tell you a story," he said, a playful lilt in Hector's voice that caused Isaias's stomach to cramp. "Imagine, if you will, a little yellow house on a hill. Inside, lives a family—mom, and dad, and two boys. The boys are good friends, but they have to be, because dear old dad has a *violent* temper. He'd scream and scream and *drag* the boys to church with their mother. Make them get on their knees and pray to be washed of their sins. But no, nothing was ever good enough to cleanse them but pain."

Isaias's guts roiled with a force of emotion that couldn't be explained—he felt so impossibly small, like he was cowering from something larger than he could ever be. Like he was asking God not to hurt him anymore, and knowing somewhere, deep down, that God turned away in indifference. Isaias whispered "I'm sorry" like a prayer and hoped that Hector could hear him.

"Oh, but one day, mom had enough. Dad's out with the younger boy, and she goes to her older son, and she says, 'pack your bags'. Only, the boy's had his bag packed the whole time. He's always *been* ready to leave."

Closing his eyes, Isaias didn't have to imagine what it was like to be a child always ready to leave—there was something too-familiar in the words that turned to rot in his stomach, in understanding this was Hector, and this was him. But Isaias had been scared of being too small for God, and too unsteady for the path he had been set on. Hector had been afraid of his own father. The two couldn't compare, but Isaias felt the numb acceptance of the child that Hector had been, a boy whose life was transmutable at the whims of the adults around him. His heart hurt to picture a kind man, once small, with a backpack ready by the door, ready for the moment he needed to run.

"And Mom said to little Hector, 'Don't worry, we'll come back for your little brother later'. But mom couldn't go back, and courts demanded to know why she had taken her son away from his father, and she fought, and she fought, but that second little boy slipped further and further away until he was lost for good."

"What happened to him?" Isaias asked in a whisper. It felt wrong for anyone else to get to tell Hector's story, but there they were. It was too late now.

"Ashes to ashes, dust to dust—not dead, no, but returned from whence he came. The fear of God can be passed down from generation to generation. I would think you'd know that, Father Fuck Up. Around and around it goes, spiralling us all deeper down into Hell. I know more about the sins of the father than you might think. Who *really* created Original Sin?" When Isaias didn't dignify Carreau with an answer, he grinned. His eyes sparkled, like this was all some cosmic joke in all the chaos. "When a little girl grows up to realize she's a little girl, do you think a father like that takes it well? So, she digs through court records, and registered businesses, and names and dates and files. And she finds a man named Hector who might just be her uncle, and his little landscaping business, and all those photos of beautiful gardens he has cultivated. And a man who grows such beautiful gardens must be a good man, mustn't he? So, she reaches out—and she signs her name with a flower."

Isaias could have sworn his heart stopped. He remembered a word—a name—whispered by Hector with grief in his heart. "Lily," he breathed.

"And there it is," Carreau purred, grinning as Isaias. "That's who Hector is so sorry to. *Lily*. The little girl he could have saved but didn't know how to. And she prayed, you know—if nothing else, she had learned to pray. And God wasn't listening, but *I* was. And better someone answer than no one, don't you think? And so, I asked our dear Hector: 'What would you do, to end this cycle of sin and torment?' And he told me, '*Anything*'."

Isaias's head spun. Hector had said 'yes'. He'd consented to the possession. Was that why the exorcisms continued to not work—Hector wasn't ready to be saved? All he could think to say was "I'm sorry." He didn't know how much of Hector was left to accept the apology. He didn't even know how much of what the demon said was true, telling a story that wasn't his. But Isaias still felt his guilt and his grief—the weight of years dragging his soul down toward Hell.

Downstairs, locked away in a little box, was poison worth decades of pain.

Isaias bowed his head and crossed his injured right hand over his chest, stigmatic wound throbbing as it recognized his heart, and prayed silently to himself.

He would save Hector. It was the only thing he could do.

XXXII

Resting his forehead against the old wooden doorjamb that would lead to the bishop's room, Isaias examined the peeling white paint of the frame for a long time as he worked up the courage to knock, picking at the flaking white latex and relishing in the way it gave way under his fingers, the momentary comfort of something within his control. It was getting late in the day, having let the girls find what modicum of rest they could, and the bishop had been hurt—but Isaias couldn't delay speaking to him any longer. It would be necessary to tell him of what he had learned in Sainte-Félicité and what he had learned—supposedly—of Hector. Because now he knew: they had to find Lily to find Hector's salvation.

Isaias knocked, then slowly stepped into the room. He looked at the bishop blinking tiredly up at him, Mrs. Marsh at his bedside, and suddenly Isaias was so very aware of just how old the bishop was. He'd been too old for children when he had taken Isaias in and now, nearly thirty years later, he looked *weary*. The bishop, propped in his bed with his only friend by his side, coughed and said, "I'm surprised you didn't come see me sooner, my son."

Isaias bowed his head and crossed his injured right hand over his chest. "I'm sorry, Your Excellency. This entire situation has been incredibly difficult. I was told you were stable—and we needed to find Hector and make sure everyone was safe. I'm sure you understand. Are you—are you alright?"

Mrs. Marsh gestured for Isaias to pull up a small chair from a letter desk in the corner of the room, and Isaias obliged as the bishop said gravely, "I'll live. Frankly, I've had worse—I don't think it had any strong desire to kill me."

"That's good," Isaias said, clasping his hands in his lap like he might offer prayers and last rites to the bed-ridden man beside him. The demon had felt the bishop unimportant. That was better than the alternative.

"Well, has there been any luck? With your pilgrimage to Sainte-Félicité as well?"

Isaias struggled for a moment. He said, "Of sorts, Your Excellency. I think I may have answers about how to help Hector."

"And from your parents?"

"My parents knew little. They sought only my forgiveness."

The bishop watched Isaias for a moment, and Isaias felt the calculating weight of his gaze. "And were you able to forgive them?"

Isaias thought of the encounter. Of the prayer that he had given them, for God to forgive them. He thought, too, of them telling him that the bishop had suggested that they give Isaias up to the church. That they had gone to Bishop Reid for help, and he had left with a broken family in his wake.

"Yes," Isaias lied. He didn't feel a great deal about lying, in the end. The details didn't matter, at this point, not for the bishop—whatever Isaias chose to forgive of the transgressions against him was between him and his God.

"Good. And your own sins, Isaias? Do you forgive yourself?"

Isaias thought of the answer he wanted to give, and the answer he knew he was supposed to give, and tried to reconcile how different they were. Perhaps in substance they weren't the same, but in result they were. "Yes," he said. Without lingering, he pivoted: "My birth parents told me you were the one who suggested they give me up to the church. That you told them I was a Peacemaker." He watched Mrs. Marsh still next to him, then turned his eyes back to the bishop. "They believed I was born from some immaculate conception, for a purpose. Is that true?"

The bishop was silent for a moment. Isaias saw how pale his skin was, washed out and lined with age. His face held no laugh lines, only deep, bruise-like bags under his eyes and grooves that tugged his lips downward into a perpetual frown. He did not feel like iron anymore, his aura smelling instead of old copper pennies. "There is much darkness in this world, Isaias. When a child is orphaned by God—gifted, but lost if not given purpose—then there is a chance they can make peace. I saw that in you, my boy. I saw that maybe you could save our souls. I hope you find it in yourself to understand that, and to forgive me for not telling you sooner."

Isaias let himself weigh that burden he had never asked for, the weight of everyone's fates. He let himself, the bishop, and Mrs. Marsh sit in the quiet as he considered. He did not acknowledge the bishop's distant wish that Isaias might forgive him for not telling him. And finally, he said, "The only soul I want to save is Hector's."

The bishop's lips tugged down into a frown, his jowls drooping and his eyebrows furrowing. "I see."

Isaias made to rise, and Mrs. Marsh stood with him. "I know more now," he said. "And I hope we find salvation soon. Rest, Your Excellency. I'll take it from here." The bishop's doubt reached him, but Isaias did not bend to it. Instead, he repeated, his voice laced with sureness, "Rest."

Something seemingly involuntary twitched in the bishop's face, tugging at the skin just below his eye, but he nodded. "Peace be with you, Isaias."

"And with your spirit, Your Excellency."

Isaias exited the room with sure steps, leaving the bishop's doubts behind. It felt anticlimactic—that in the end, his answers were true, but the bishop would offer no further clarity or comfort. There was nothing left for him in that room. He was about to close the door behind him when Mrs. Marsh stepped out of the room as well. At first, they stood together in silence. Isaias reached his heart out to hers and felt her love and her regret. She, too, was aged—but her presence lay over him more like the comfort of a worn blanket, maybe thread-bare, but still treasured and warm, nonetheless. "Did you know?"

"Did I know why His Excellency adopted you?" Mrs. Marsh asked. She didn't wait for Isaias to confirm. "In a sense. He never said as much, but ever since I was a girl—and ever since I was friends with Bishop Reid—I knew there was a great deal of evil in this world. Some people seek out any advantage they can find. I've known the church to do as much. At some point, children aren't children—when they are touched by God, they become something else."

"Orphans," Isaias said, though he didn't know that he understood. Still, Mrs. Marsh nodded, and Isaias decided that perhaps it didn't matter—that there were many more important things now in life. Like Hector, like young women who needed help, like cultivating a future for all of them. "I think I know what I need to do to help Hector."

Mrs. Marsh held her hand out for Isaias, who took it gently. Her grip was firm, despite how frail she looked. "Go with God, Isaias," she whispered fiercely, tears in her eyes. "And I will be here waiting for you when you are done."

Isaias breathed deeply and swallowed back tears before he bent his head and lifted Mrs. Marsh's hand to his lips, kissing her knuckles in reverence. She wore no ecclesiastical ring, no amethysts or jewels, but Isaias thought that she deserved his devotion and his love. He would come back to her, and when they went home, he hoped that she would finally retire in peace.

Outside the door to his childhood bedroom, Isaias briefly heard the heartbeat in the halls again. He stood there for a moment, raising his chin to the heavens, and he murmured a prayer to himself, less in words than in intentions. His words didn't feel as true anymore as his heart did.

When Isaias entered, the demon stood precisely as he had left him, though Isaias could no longer remember how long it had been. "Back so soon?"

"Come with me," Isaias said as calmly as possible.

"You're really enjoying giving me orders, aren't you?" the demon purred. "Do you think you'd be this bossy in bed?"

Isaias steeled himself and refused to react, to let him sway his emotions. And he said again, adding the weight of all the things he wanted to express but had held back for too long, "Come with me."

Carreau's stance broke for a moment with a half-step forward, a movement too abrupt to be totally natural. And then the demon grinned. "Well, isn't that *delicious*? I knew you were special, Father, but that's something new, isn't it? You're learning how to make emotions a weapon, now?"

Isaias swallowed hard. He stood as strong as he could in the face of the demon. And he said, "Just come with me."

"No force, this time? Where's the fun in that?" Still, he followed when Isaias turned and walked out of the room, slinking along behind him like a shadow with a curious glint in his eyes. Not daring to look back over his shoulder, Isaias descended the stairs. The sound of a heartbeat intensified in his ears as he veered toward the study before it slowly grew to something almost unbearable, mingling with the ringing in his ears that increasingly reminded him of screaming. He knocked on the study door before he went inside, giving Violet and Poppy a moment to wake and to gather themselves.

Violet blinked up in confusion from the nest of throw pillows and blankets she was resting on. As she propped herself up with a wince, Poppy helping her move to a sitting position, she asked, "Dad?"

"Not yet, Vi," Isaias said regretfully. "But we're going to get this figured out. I'm going to take us to find someone who can help."

Poppy frowned. "Isn't that why we came to Sainte-Jeanne? The bishop was our backup."

"I think we're in the right place, but with the wrong person. I think there's someone who can help us more."

Both girls looked at Isaias skeptically before Poppy locked eyes on Hector, staring the demon down. Violet reached for her crutches and used them to help push herself up off the floor, and Poppy turned her attention back to Violet to watch if she wanted any help. Once both girls were up, they approached Isaias with caution—and stayed several paces away from the demon in Hector. Isaias exited the rectory, his strange companions in tow—a demon behaving suspiciously well, biding his time, the daughter of the possessed man that Isaias wanted so desperately to protect, and her friend, who cast a furtive glance back at the cabinet where demonic poison was locked away. He led them across the street to his parked car. He directed Violet and Poppy to sit in the back—he would manage the demon himself in the front. When they were all seated, Isaias turned to face the demon in Hector. "Can you find her?"

"What makes you think that I can?"

Isaias ignored the puzzled looks on Violet and Poppy's faces. "She prayed, and you heard—you *answered*. I have a hard time believing you couldn't find her a second time, if you wanted to."

Carreau sneered, lips curling to bare Hector's teeth. The way his face puckered drew tension across the boils on Hector's face, the bars of the cross twisting with the scowl. One of the bubbling burn marks split and yellowing pus dribbled down Hector's cheek and into the corner of his mouth, where it caught on his lips. "And why would I do that for you, priest?"

Steeling himself, Isaias took a breath. He thought that he might put himself at risk if he pushed too hard, leaned on the emotional influence too much. "Because you want something from me—or her.

Not just Hector. If you really wanted us to come to Sainte-Jeanne, take us to her."

The demon studied him before, instead of answering, he waved his hand toward the windshield. The message was clear: drive, then.

Isaias turned on the engine and looked to the road ahead, not entirely sure what they would find when they reached Lily.

"Where are we going?" Violet asked as Isaias pulled out onto the road.

"To be forgiven," Isaias said, glancing sidelong at the demon.

He just prayed it would work.

XXXIII

As they approached the house, Isaias's stomach curled around a heavy core of dread, like the hardened stone pit of a rotten, bruised apricot. The sun was setting fast, leaving the week behind, and the last rays of the sun shone into Isaias's eyes as they looked up at the little bungalow down the path, making it difficult to keep his eyes on the house for long. The block was lined with older, small family homes, a mix of bungalows and townhomes. The house that Carreau had sworn was Lily's didn't stand out much in the light, except to see where the siding and fascia were peeling, damaged by wind or snow, and where the paint colour changed abruptly around the windows, as if some sort of shutter or decoration had been removed, no longer worth the bother of repair. It was snowing as they approached, and the lawn and path were slick with fresh precipitation that hid most of the details.

Isaias walked ahead to help clear a space to walk for Poppy and Violet, Carreau a step behind him like a lurking shadow, while Poppy hovered by Violet, watching to make sure her crutches had purchase. Isaias noticed the girls were getting slower, and he couldn't imagine how difficult this was for Violet, how much pain she must be in—emotionally, physically, spiritually.

After Isaias knocked on the door, he quickly heard sounds from inside the house that set his nerves even further on edge, despite the fact that he couldn't identify anything particularly *wrong* about them. It was the emotions, maybe—distant and unfamiliar, but easily understood as poisonous, noxious fumes of feelings leeching out from the under the door and into Isaias. He steeled himself against the reflex to take a step back and waited for someone to answer the door.

When the door was finally answered, Isaias was momentarily taken aback by the appearance of the girl who opened the door, albeit she was barely visible through the crack. Without letting the door be anything more than ajar, the teenager was a mirror of Violet—at least, Isaias saw the shades of the girls in each other. The girl at the door, though, was somewhat paler, making the dark bags under her eyes stand out like wounds against a thinner, sharper face. Her hair was shorter—almost a bob, but choppy and uneven, an unprofessional cut done in haste. She wore a baggy, dull and pilling red-and-black flannel shirt, and black sweatpants, hiding most of her body under layers of excess fabric. The closest to a true splash of colour on her was a white bandana that she wore around her neck, tucked into the collar of her shirt but with the knot visible where it rested against her throat.

"Lily?" Isaias asked, voice low.

Her lips turned quickly as she violently shushed Isaias and moved with remarkable speed in her next few movements. "It's just a friend," she called back into the house before stepping out, closing the door with urgency but so gently it barely made a sound. Standing barefoot in the thin layer of frost that had made it to her front step, she turned wide, suspicious, and bruise-dark eyes on Isaias, unbothered by the cold. "What's a priest want with me?"

Isaias glanced back at Hector—or Carreau—and at Violet and Poppy before he looked to Lily again, finding that he wasn't even sure what to say after everything. He had thought about it on the way to her home, and yet faced with the reason for all this grief, and faced with her own pain written in her eyes and on her heart, he was at a loss for words. "Lily," he repeated, "I've brought your uncle all this way to talk to you."

Lily blanched. "Uncle Hector?" she whispered, voice immediately hoarse. "What's he doing with a priest?"

Before Isaias could answer, Violet interjected, "Wait, *uncle*? I have a cousin?" Violet and Lily's eyes met as Violet stepped around Isaias, past even Carreau, Poppy perpetually by her side. All three girls looked past him, through him, into each other. Isaias felt something stir in their hearts, something like kinship. "Hi, Lily. I'm Violet. And this is my—this is my girlfriend, Poppy."

Lily's frightened-rabbit expression turned bashful. She looked younger than Violet, though they were about the same height and build, though it was hard to tell sometimes with Violet's weight distributed with the crutches. Poppy stood a step behind Violet, taller than both the other girls. "Huh," Lily breathed out, awe in her voice. "I guess the flower name wasn't so creative, after all."

"My dad picked mine out," Violet said, smiling. "He likes gardening."

Lily smiled shyly but awkwardly, softening. "I picked mine out for that reason, too."

"Mine's a coincidence, I guess," Poppy interjected awkwardly. She reached one hand out for Violet's, brushing her fingertips over Violet's where she gripped the handle of her crutch, but stopped short of holding her hand or even lingering. "It's nice to meet you, Lily."

"You, too."

"Well, isn't this *cute*?" Carreau cut in, voice sickly sweet but not disguising the wicked mockery. In a flatter voice, he said, "Hello again, Lily."

Lily stilled as she looked to Hector—to *Carreau*. She crossed one arm over her body and picked at a pill of broken fabric on the opposite sleeve. But her eyes glinted with understanding, and Isaias felt her relieved wonder. "You listened," she said softly, her voice nearly a prayer of her own. "Someone really listened when I prayed."

"Lily," Isaias said quickly insistently. "This is a *demon*. He's here to hurt people."

Casting a furtive glance to Isaias, then back to the demon possessing Hector, she said, "I only prayed for someone to take me away from here."

"And how do you think he was going to do that?" Isaias asked gently. He hadn't thought that it might not have occurred to her what a demon might do to set her free. But she was young—young and in pain. Isaias's heart broke for her: a girl so scared that she didn't care *who* listened when she prayed. As long as *someone* finally did.

Something in her darkened, though, and she tore her gaze from the demon to Isaias. "My uncle didn't do anything," she said. "Nobody ever did anything for me. So why should I care?"

Isaias hesitated to ask a teenaged girl to consider the ramifications of her actions. But he needed her to understand. "Your uncle was so heartbroken to find out you were hurting that he let a demon take him," he said gently. "Lily, he cares. I promise."

Lily looked again to Hector, studying his face. Isaias wondered if she was taking in the cross he bore in a burn across his face that would surely scar, the blood and pus pooling in the corners of his mouth and catching in his beard, the stench of sweat and urine soaked into clothes that had begun to hang too loose, the blood on his palms that had long since dried in trails down to the tips of his fingers—Isaias saw all those things and more when he looked at Hector, when all he wanted to see was *Hector*.

"Can you prove that pain's for me?" Lily asked, her voice hard but earnest.

"Lily," Violet begged, asking a girl she just met to *understand*. Poppy remained silent, and Isaias couldn't parse the cycle of feelings from all three girls.

And Isaias could never fully understand Lily's pain—her pain was *hers*—but he could try to make her see the shape of Hector's.

Isaias took Hector's hand, letting the ragged, bloody bandages of his still-wounded right hand line up with the wounds on Hector, their blood and their bodies connecting, feeling pressure against the still-raw bite wound that Hector's own teeth had left on Isaias's hand. He felt an electric jolt down his spine for the contact that was so close to what he wanted, something that might have been godly in another time, another life. Carreau—or was it a shadow of Hector?—surprised him by holding his hand back, fingers curling around Isaias's, capturing him in place. Their hands together like that seemed to create a perfect circuit, through which Isaias's emotions flowed into Hector and from which Isaias finally started to feel what Hector felt again—*Hector*, not Carreau, not a mockery or a shade. Hector's soul felt far away, but Isaias felt a shadow of his hopes, his dreams, his fears, his secrets. More than any time before, Isaias felt that, standing there and holding him, he might have understood Hector with the utmost potential, have truly known his heart and soul, if only they had more time.

With his left hand—also injured, albeit superficially—Isaias reached out to Lily. She stared at him uncertainly, just as he could feel Violet and Poppy filled with doubt, but it lasted only a moment before something shifted in Lily's eyes again, something like knowledge, something like maybe she had glimpsed her own piece of Heaven, once, and knew it when she recognized it in Isaias.

Isaias opened his mind and his heart. His head ached, each burst of white noise static sending a throb of pain from the top of his skull down through the base of his neck. He heard a heartbeat and didn't know if it was his. His vision blurred for a moment, red spots like shimmering blood appearing in the corners of his eyes but disappearing just as quickly. He bit through the nausea as he opened his heart wider, splitting his chest open, welcoming Hector and Lily into his chest, welcoming Violet and Poppy, too, distantly, a radius of love and fear taking root among his ribcage.

He let their hearts merge with his own, let them truly *feel* what he felt, what they felt, the full spectrum of all their heartache.

Through blurred vision, he saw tears in Lily's eyes. He felt Hector's grip regaining strength, closer to the man he once was, as he held Isaias's hand desperately.

His fingers went numb first, his nerves on fire until they became ice cold, the frost of that winter night setting into his bones. He thought that he might cleave in two, starting with his chest, but this was what he had to offer. This was always what he had to offer: a heart too heavy to bear alone.

Isaias's vision went dark a single moment before his knees buckled. He didn't feel, at first, the damage it must have done for his kneecaps to connect with the concrete step, his skin and muscles numb to the point that the recognition of pain made it to the rest of him late. Instead, he was more aware that he was dragging Hector down with him, because while Lily had let go when Isaias's hand went limp, Hector did not.

He lost consciousness after that, his hand still held in Hector's.

THE FIRST THING ISAIAS noticed that was wrong was the silence. He had become so accustomed to the droning of tinnitus in his ears over the past week that he had forgotten what it was like to exist in the *quiet*. Somehow, that was more noticeable than the pain throughout his body—his legs filled with sharp pins and needles, his fingers so numb they burned, the pain that was burrowing into his brainstem.

And he felt like he was floating.

It wasn't death. *God*, it couldn't be death—after everything that had happened, he could not accept that there was neither Heaven nor Hell, but only emptiness. He could not reckon for even a moment with the idea that *that* was God's perfect, untouched state of nature: darkness.

No. It had to be something else.

His own, unique suffering. He was dreaming, trapped in his own mind, on the verge of consciousness where he couldn't quite make it back out to his loved ones.

Isaias wanted to call out to Hector, to ask him if he could still hear him. No words escaped, and so instead, he prayed for him.

Can you hear me, Isaias?

He thought the voice might be Hector's, but when he wanted to ask, to confirm, he found that still he could not speak.

Are you listening?

Isaias wanted to say, You're the only one I've ever wanted to listen to, but still, he could not speak. He hoped it was Hector speaking to him, reaching through the darkness. He thought that if this was over soon, Hector's voice would be the one he wanted to think of, to hear, last among all the world.

Isaias, tell me: what would you do, to end this cycle of sin and torment?

This time, still drifting but slowly coming back into his body, Isaias was able to answer:

"Anything."

XXXIV

Waking to the sound of his name from a chorus of voices, Isaias felt he was at a great distance from his body. His name seemed to filter through a fog that persistently clung to his brain, blocking out the depth and nuance of what those voices were saying. He recognized they were calling to him, but it took a long time for the full meaning to register.

When he finally managed to open his eyes, through a great deal of effort, he felt snowflakes sprinkle across his cheeks, cast loose from his eyelashes. How long had he slept there, on the step of a stranger's home?

Above him, haloed by the shining fluorescent porchlight, was Hector. He looked perfect, even with his face silhouetted in darkness and the light shining off the oily surface of his burn wounds. Isaias tried to make out Hector's features, to identify the precise angle of his nose, or the way tiny wrinkles drew a map around the corners of his eyes, but he couldn't bring himself to focus. He knew the details were there, but he couldn't see them. Everything felt far away, like he was on another plane of existence, and he was viewing Hector through a filter.

Hector, he wanted to call out. *Is that really you?*

On either side of Isaias were Poppy and Lily, two funerary flowers by his graveside, more distinguishable in their closeness, though Isaias still couldn't quite bring his eyes to focus. Violet stood at a slight distance, near her father but just out of arm's reach. Her expression was more readable than Hector's, but she was cast half in light and hurt to look at for long.

Something shifted in Hector. He looked up at the night sky, snowflakes gracing his cheeks, and his features lit up under the electric hum of the porch light, the burn on his face illuminating like holy fire, the stains of tears and pus glistening. He cast a long shadow across the porch, and Isaias could barely make out the movements of Hector's mouth, his face turned to Heaven, as he whispered something that Isaias imagined might have been a prayer.

To Violet, Hector said, "He's gone." Isaias struggled to hear the words through the film around his mind that hummed like the fluorescent bulb above them. "Carreau. He's gone."

Head snapping to her father immediately, Violet's eyes were wide in the light. "He's gone?" she whispered. She did not step closer. She stayed precisely where she was. Her voice trembled with the same frequency as the electric vibrations all around them. "Dad? Is that really you?"

Isaias wondered if it was too good to be true. If Carreau wasn't in Hector, where was he? But it was true that he didn't not feel the signs of the demon, the essence of spiritual rot and brimstone burning that came with his presence.

In fact, he didn't feel much of anything at all.

"It's me, Vi," Hector said hoarsely. He turned to his daughter, who stood still, a sentinel in the night. It was only when Hector held his arms open for a hug that Violet broke, letting out a whimper, then a sob, before she stepped forward and let her father hug her. "It's me, little flower. I'm here."

Isaias's vision blurred with tears watching Hector finally hug his daughter, truly hug her again. His heart swelled with love in the instant before his stomach roiled with nausea as vertigo seized him, the entire world tipping, feeling like he was falling backwards, headfirst, despite not moving an inch. The ringing in his ears reached a crescendo, momentarily whiting everything else out.

Lily, refusing to look at Hector and Violet, broke the moment as Isaias's senses came back to him. "Sorry to interrupt, but I think there's something wrong with the priest."

It sunk in, then—that his head feeling like it was stuffed with weighted cotton was surely not normal, that his mouth shouldn't feel numb and coated with film like he had eaten something spoiled that stuck to his tongue. He tried to say, *Lily's right, something's wrong.*

What came out was: "I'm okay. I just hit my head."

Isaias's heart leapt forward in his chest immediately and he tried to cry out. Instead, he was silent. Despite his racing heart, his body sat up calmly. Lily flinched away immediately, Poppy just behind. Violet broke away from her father's arms and took a step backwards.

Hector stared Isaias down, his expression inscrutable. It hurt to see Hector look at him like a stranger, after all this time.

Carreau? Isaias tried to ask—out loud, to God, to Hector, to anyone who would listen.

Of course, it's me, a voice like sour, fermented honey whispered in his mind's eye, somehow amplified by the pain of white noise. *And nobody else is listening.*

"Hector, it's me," he heard himself say. Isaias felt his voice, his real voice, the words he wanted to say, pushing at his throat, crawling up into his mouth like bile, before he swallowed it back down, his desperate prayers to be heard laying acrid in his esophagus. "Don't you recognize me?"

"I do recognize you." Hector's voice was cold. "Now get the *fuck* out of Isaias."

Isaias would have wept, if he had a voice. Still, his eyes filled with tears for a fleeting moment before they were blinked back. He stood, against his will. He stepped toward Hector, who immediately put himself between Isaias and Violet. Without wanting to, he *smiled*. "After all we've been through together, is that the way to speak to me, lover?"

"What part of 'get the fuck out of him' don't you understand?" Hector said, though Isaias heard the lingering rot in Hector's voice in the way the words trembled almost imperceptibly, the way his heart was still sticky with charred sweetness, the way he was still touched by that thing. "What more do you want from us?"

"Over three days straight of exorcisms, and you think I'd step aside just because you asked me to?" Carreau asked in Isaias's voice. He dropped Isaias's voice to a low, mocking purr. Isaias heard it from a distance, so much like the mockery of Hector's voice he had heard a thousand times, that he would never forget. At least, he thought, he isn't bothering to pretend. Hector saw Carreau for what he was. Hector didn't believe he was Isaias for an instant. Hector couldn't hear Isaias in that moment, but he *saw* him. "I'm not giving this one up so easily. Father Fuck Up, he's got the voice of *God*. You know what that means?"

A toxic flurry of emotions seemed to curl in Hector's chest and Isaias could still feel them—his hurt, his anger. That was when Isaias realized the same emotions were echoed in his own heart—Carreau? A deep tiredness washed over Isaias, a fatigue so deep it would have been easy to give in, to sleep, to sleep and let someone else take the wheel. After a week of sleepless nights, of pain, of praying into the night, it would be *so easy* to let himself slip away and rest.

When Hector leapt at him, tackling him to the ground, it caught both Isaias and Carreau by surprise—and Violet, apparently, judging by the startled shriek she let out. Poppy was on her feet by Violet's side immediately, guiding her away from the scene. Lily cast wide eyes back to her house, to the shapes of changing shadows inside, before she spun back to Hector, who had grabbed Isaias and was hauling him to his feet. Distantly, Isaias was surprised how much of his strength Hector had retained. But then, he had always been strong. "We have to go," Lily hissed in a forced whisper. "Now."

Hector nodded curtly. "Poppy, can you help me?"

Poppy looked first to Violet, who nodded back to her girlfriend, before she hurried down the porch step and to Hector's side to help wrangle Isaias—Carreau—and drag him to the car. Lily hovered by Violet an instant longer before both girls started following.

"Poppy, you drive," Hector was saying as they reached the car. Isaias heard himself growling, felt raw poison stewing in his guts, felt Carreau starting to fight back. He prayed, *Don't hurt Hector or the girls. Please, God, just guide them through this night.* "Violet, Lily—I need one of you in the back with me."

"I'll do it," Violet said, voice firm.

Isaias's vision was blotting out in the peripheral, tunneling into darkness before it wavered back into the dim light of the cold night. Carreau fought him down, and he tried to fight back—but he was so tired.

Being dragged into the car was a blur, Isaias's head swimming in and out of consciousness. He didn't know how long he could hold on, but Carreau hadn't had long to sink his teeth into Isaias's soul, and so he prayed, he prayed to God and he prayed to Hector and he prayed to three young women who were braver than they should have to be and who he wanted to see grow up into the saints they would one day be. He felt boundless love for them, love he could not let Carreau quash.

"Where are we going?" someone, Poppy, maybe, asked.

"Just drive," said Hector. Isaias felt strong arms wrap around him, pulling him against a solid chest. Hector's lips brushed past his temple, and Isaias felt the touch of his beard, still sticky with pus and blood, against his cheek. He wanted so desperately to sleep there, to just be held, but he needed to heed Hector when Hector commanded, "Just hold on."

Drifting in and out in fits, Isaias watched streetlights flash through the car window, drowning the five of them in sickly yellow light in intermittent flashes before the shadows returned, deeper than ever before. Traffic roared past them like the rest of the world, breaking briefly through to Isaias before his entire reality became the cabin of the car again, became Hector's arms around him holding him fast, became Poppy driving them anywhere and everywhere, and Lily speaking just to fill the air and pointing places for Poppy to go, and Violet watching her father and Isaias with determination and fear in her eyes. As streetlights flashed past, Isaias saw the snow picking up in fitful flurries.

Isaias fought—fought as hard as he'd fought for anything in his life, as hard as he'd fought for Hector—to break past Carreau, whose hold was still weak enough to slip past for just a moment, to speak. "I'm sorry," he whispered like a devotional.

"For what?" Hector asked.

Isaias wasn't sure. He searched through his heart, for the memories and the feelings that were already so far away. He pushed past the words Carreau tried to make him say. God, had it been so hard, every time that Hector had tried to speak to them? Had it been so much pain to fight through, for just a moment of connection? Isaias couldn't waste the words. Not if he might never get another chance to say them. Every word a monumental effort, a painful tear on his heart and soul, Isaias said, "For not loving you enough."

Hector laughed, a heartbroken and wet but loving laugh, and it cut through all the other sounds in the world to make Isaias's heart sing. "I think you maybe loved me too much."

I don't think I could ever love you enough twisted in Isaias's mouth as Carreau seized back his control and came out, "Is your sentimentality really worth sending yourself straight to Hell?"

Hector did not reply, only holding Isaias tighter and cradling his back against his chest, his breath a whisper against Isaias's ear. "Fuck you, Carreau," he whispered. "I'd go right to Hell for Isaias. In a heartbeat."

Isaias struggled to speak, to cling onto his freedom, but could not find the words. He did manage to shake his head—the barest movement, the outline of his desire to tell Hector no, not again, not this time. Hector held him closer instead, his right arm curling around Isaias's chest and resting his palm over Isaias's heart. He was safe in Hector's arms, against his chest. His extremities were numb, on the other hand, loss of feeling creeping up his limbs.

"We're not going to do this like you probably want," Hector explained softly as he held Isaias tight. Fighting to keep his awareness, Isaias focused on Hector's breath and on the passing lights and the shadows of telephone poles and wondered how many voices crossed through the wires that spoke of God. He wondered if he could find God there, too, in Hector's arms. "I'm no preacher. I can't bless water and toss it around like it's going to save anyone's soul. I don't know the names of all the saints, and I don't think I could lead these girls in ritual. I don't know if I'll ever be ready to ask God for help again. But Isaias—I love you, and so does Violet, and Poppy, and I think that Lily will, too, once you give her the chance to know you. Imagine the life we could lead if you just make it through this."

I have, Isaias wanted to say. *I have imagined so much of what that life could look like.* "Love won't save anyone's soul, Deadnettle."

Hector didn't budge. There was no doubt in him. Isaias knew—Hector, after everything, was here to finish this. "I love you, Isaias. I hope you still hear me—but I won't just say it. I'm not stopping there." Out of sight, Hector's breath sounded damp. He leaned in and brushed his lips against Isaias's temple. The next words felt intimate, soft and defiant, though the girls could likely hear—and Carreau had stolen Isaias's ability for those words to ever be private. "Fight for me, Isaias. I'm going to fight for you."

Isaias wanted to promise him he would—he would fight for Hector, he would fight for those three holy girls who were by his side, he would *fight*. He couldn't promise, he couldn't even nod, but he let his soul speak out, let his heart sing despite his fear, despite his ears ringing, despite pain throughout his body. He hoped Hector felt the vow. By the way he wrapped one arm around Isaias's waist and squeezed him firmly, Isaias thought he might have.

"Wait, dad," Violet said, her face haloed by passing headlights, the snow picking up outside visible behind her, held back by a single pane of glass. "Before we begin, I have something for you." She reached under the collar of her shirt and removed the chipped rosary that Isaias had retrieved from The Second Voyage what felt like so long ago. Violet had kept it close to her heart. Now—she returned it to her father. "I think this was yours. Or grandma's, once. You should have it back."

Hector moved one hand away from Isaias by only the barest inch to take the rosary, cradling it in his hands and brushing his thumb over the worn relief of Christ. "Thank you, Violet." He closed his hand around the rosary, before he returned his grip to Isaias fully, holding him close, his hand a loose fist over Isaias's heart. "Isaias, if I pray for you, it's to anyone who will listen. Even you. And you've always listened to me, prayed for me, so if I pray for you, I want you to listen. Listen when I tell you that every word I've ever written to you is true. Every little gift I've given you has meant the world—those tiny little ceramic creatures I know you still keep even though they're worthless, I saw them, and I thought, 'They don't fit in, but Isaias would love them anyway, he would give them a home'. Who better to love a monstrous little creature than Isaias, the man who loves so much he'd go to Hell not just for me but for a girl he barely knows, for a stranger, or for anyone the world believed a sinner—you wouldn't give up on them."

"You don't know what the fuck you're talking about," Carreau spat, beginning to struggle against Hector's arms. Hector held fast despite the exhaustion Isaias could detect in his bones, the way he wanted nothing more than to rest. Something was cracking inside

Isaias, he was sure the others could hear it with the amount of pain he was in from something *splintering*. But Hector kept holding him. "I'm not giving up someone with these gifts from God. Father Fuck Up is mine—can't you imagine the beautiful shades of red we could paint the world?"

"I know what I'm talking about: Isaias gifts aren't from God, they're from his heart. You don't get to twist his heart. Not like you twisted mine." Hector's grip turned more into a hug than a chokehold. "Isaias, listen to me: you found the rose, didn't you? The little wooden rose I'd carved? I know you did. That was for you, I made that for you. A beautiful flower that means love. I thought about giving it to you. I wasn't brave enough. I wasn't brave enough for a lot of this. But you remember, don't you? So, *fight*, Isaias, and cast Carreau out."

Carreau didn't reply, only screamed, the gurgling cry echoing in the tiny box of the car cabin. He made Isaias's arms and legs twist in ways they weren't supposed to, contorting to box him into that small space, to make him harder to hold onto, to fight his way free. Isaias thought his legs might break; his arms might dislocate. Hector kept holding on.

"And don't you remember," Violet broke in, "how every time I hated a piece of art I'd made for class, you told me not to throw it out because you wanted it? When we were in the rectory, doing all those exorcisms, I saw them. You really took them home. You *framed* them. It wasn't just that you wanted to make me feel better and not throw away something I'd created. You saw them worthy enough to put them pride of place in your home. So, *fight*, Isaias, and cast Carreau out."

Isaias could feel a growl in his own throat that become a choked gurgle as acid climbed up his throat and bile dripped from his lips. Carreau spat a glob of mucous, but it only landed on Isaias, a wet and slimy sheen of pale green against his cassock. His chin fell to his chest then seemed like it might keep falling, his neck stretching painfully. His limbs continued to twist. Isaias's eyes blurred with tears of pain.

Poppy's eyes were locked on the road, focusing on driving through the growing blizzard, but she said, "Father, do you remember how my mother would come to the church and pray to make me feel guilty? She's a Catholic when it keeps me in line. She's a Catholic when it hurts. But you never made me feel small the way she did. You didn't care if I turned off my hearing aids during Mass. You wanted me to find God *my* way—in the quiet moments, where I was alone with Him, not with scripture that my mother wanted to turn into a weapon. She tried to make the Sacred Heart a prison, but you let me make it whatever *I* needed it to be. So, God, please, *fight*, Father."

Despite all the pain, and despite Isaias's head swimming, his mind fogging over, he *fought*—to hold onto the words of these people who loved him, his own love he gave in return, for the petty, stubborn desire after all this time that once he was on the other side of this, he would make his choices, too.

He'd had enough choices taken from him. Carreau could get in line. His body stilled.

"Fuck you," the demon choked out. Isaias dry heaved, phlegm thick in his throat, stomach acid pooling against his tonsils. He thought he might vomit from the sickness in his stomach, the pain in his body, and the way his head spun. "You called me, you fucks," Carreau snapped. "You don't get to go back on that choice. This is *my* show now. And I'm going to use this man to rain Hell down wherever I please. I'll kill the girl's father—or maybe I'll send him off to hurt someone else. It would hardly take a *push*. You wanted out, this is what you get."

This time, Lily was the one who spoke. Her voice was low but clear. Even with the wind beginning to whistle past the car as the snow flashed in the buzzing lights that passed by, her voice rang true. "I named myself Lily because I choose peace, but not for him. I want him to die. I do." Isaias managed to look to her, to see Lily looking first at the road, then over her shoulder, to Isaias, to the demon. Her voice grew louder, firmer. "But I want him to die the slowest, most humiliating death possible. I want him to die of old age and heartache and loneliness, knowing that he did this to himself. I want it so that every time someone asks him, 'Whatever happened to your son?' that he chokes on his own failure and knows he drove away the daughter he wouldn't acknowledge just like he drove away everyone else. I want him to die *lonely*, knowing he let himself be a cliché. Hurt people hurt people, but not me. I will break the hurt like he tried to break me. And I want him to die wondering, 'whatever happened to Lily?' And knowing that the answer is that his daughter is a better person than he could ever be. The only one left hurting will be him, and it'll be his own damn fault."

Isaias felt his heart constricting, but it wasn't him—it was Carreau, angry and spiteful. "And why the fuck shouldn't I kill him?"

"Because you don't get to choose!" Lily's raised voice was full of tears, and her heart laden with suffering. "If someone else wants to cut their abuser's throat, good for them. Hand me a knife, I'll help." Lily cast her eyes to Poppy, whose hands were tight on the steering wheel. She looked back to Isaias, to Hector, to Violet. "If somebody wants to forgive the person who hurt them and build a bridge, they can do that. Hand me a hammer. But nobody gets to make *my* choice. It's my business whether I hurt him back or forgive him or let him rot. Nobody gets to judge me for my choice. If I choose to let him live miserable and die worse, that's up to me. After everything, *I* get to decide. So, too fucking bad what you want, Carreau—I brought you here, and I'm choosing to send you back to Hell. Fight, Isaias—because he doesn't have a damn right to make our choices for us."

Carreau struggled to speak again, and Isaias took the moment of control to bite down on his own tongue, forcing it into silence. He tasted the iron of blood in his mouth, but he was able to keep himself from screaming in pain as the demon clawed at his insides, trying desperately to hold onto Isaias, who thought of free will, of the most precious gift and greatest burden they bore. He thought of God's plan, not so much a set path but patterns in the chaos. Of the fact that there was something out there, something bigger than them, that they weren't alone.

"Isaias," Hector was saying, "if you can speak your heart into someone, do it now."

"No," Carreau choked out, blood mingling with the bile on Isaias's lips, his tongue stinging. "I refuse."

Hector ignored Carreau. "Isaias, listen to me. We need you to be in this, too. You have to make this choice, too. I know you can. These are *your* gifts, and you can choose to use them for *you*."

"I—" Isaias tried to choke out. He tried to find his words, to fight, to lay claim to everything in his power. He gathered all the strength that he could to put force to what came next. But he didn't put only his wants. He took his grief, his fear, his anger. His exhaustion at not having slept properly for days. The aches in his joints and in his head. The defiance he felt at wanting to lead his own life. And he reached out to Hector's heart, too, and Violet's, and Poppy's, and Lily's. He took all of their pain and anger and hurt, too. He put all their love into the words that came next, too. "I cast you out, Carreau!"

Pain ripped through Isaias, turning his vision black. Something *ripped*, deep in his heart, something dark cut from him and cast out. The noise in his ears become impossible to bear, and his chest hurt so badly he thought that his heart might stop. He was scared that wherever Carreau was going, he would take a piece of Isaias with him.

And then there was only silence, and darkness, and a tiredness so endless that Isaias slipped backwards into Hector and into a deep and dreamless sleep.

XXXV

"LOVE IS LOVE."

Standing at the pulpit in front of the attentive parish that filled the church's main room, Isaias regarded the churchgoers with love and adoration—but less nervousness than he would have expected. He felt more confident in his place than ever before. Not physically, but in what he knew that he had to do. He was, after all, only a man.

The room was hushed; anticipatory. After he had missed the previous week's Mass, spending Valentine's Sunday morning bed-ridden with Hector, he was sure the parish wanted to know where he'd been after a week and a half of sermons delivered by a different face. He was exhausted even then, his ears ringing, his body aching. It was hard to focus, even reading was difficult those days, so he hadn't bothered preparing any notes. Hector had told him to not go at all, to stay with him, but Isaias knew what he had to do. A pair of crutches leaned against the pulpit. He was still getting used to them, but Violet had helped. He didn't know yet whether they were temporary or not, but he thought that with the way his head kept spinning and his body kept hurting, with so many invisible fissures running through his body now, he would be using them for a long time.

The week since they had returned home to Sainte-Thérèse had been hard. Isaias and Hector had barely gotten out of bed, Hector's burns weren't showing any signs of healing, Violet was missing more school, and Lily—they were figuring out how they could make sure Lily stayed with them, and that her father never tried to take her back. She had gotten frostbite the night of the exorcism, having stood underdressed in the cold for so long, but she was healing alright—physically, anyway. She would take longer to open up to them fully, they knew that. If she ever did.

When Isaias woke from the exorcism that Saturday, Poppy already driving them home, one of the first things he'd thought to ask was what had happened to that demon's poison, that he'd locked away. Violet had said she'd retrieved it and given it to the person who had the most right to it: Lily.

Now, standing in front of a church that no longer felt familiar, Isaias didn't know what the parish was feeling, and he had no desire to find out. The emotions of others felt more distant these days, coming to him only in involuntary flashes, and when he tried to reach his heart out, his world closed to a tiny point of nothing *but* feeling. The fear of losing himself to those feelings and losing control filled him with so much dread that he hadn't pushed it.

And anyway, it wasn't the feelings of the people who mattered then. It was his own. And there he was, earnest and honest, and finally ready to bare his true self for all to see.

He finally collected himself, his spinning thoughts, to continue. "You see," he said, "when we say that God is love, we aren't wrong—but it's not the whole story, is it? We choose, every day, to love. We make the decision to love ourselves, our friends, our families. Our lovers. And love... is love. It doesn't matter if the source of your love is an active choice, a word from God, or something you just can't explain. Love just *is*. And love is beautiful, isn't it? But it's also hard."

These parishioners, maybe they loved him—but as a symbol, as a voice. And Isaias had to learn to find love for his whole. He had to find the things and people that *he* loved with his whole.

He loved Hector. He loved Violet. He loved Poppy. He loved Mrs. Marsh. He already knew that he loved Lily, too, even in these early days of knowing her.

And God, he loved himself. That was a new one.

"But love—love, my friends, also rejoices from truth. Being true to yourself. That's from Corinthians. And the truth is—the truth is that I have to be honest with myself. I don't belong here. And not because—not because of who I love, though love—love in the romantic sense, the idea that I could love another man as deeply as I do, that's something I'm still learning. No, it's because I can't keep serving others at my own expense. I can't be a tool of the word of God, anymore. It's time for me to live—and love. I still love God, I promise that I do, but I have to live for more than Him alone. So, I'm leaving. And I leave for love, and not for another man—but for myself."

Heart racing and head spinning, Isaias wished that Hector and the girls were in the pews, though he knew Hector would be waiting for him outside. But Mrs. Marsh was there—and he saw Lena, too, who had never been to the Sacred Heart before. She locked eyes with him and gave him a subtle wave, a waggle of her fingers at chest level.

Isaias breathed deeply, trying to steady himself. He couldn't drag it out. "I have to go. I will have to find God in other places than this. Maybe I'll find Him as I find myself."

Carefully, he let go of the pulpit and gathered the crutches instead. They were plain in colour—black and silver—but Violet had decorated them with stickers from her collection: blue and green flowers, a rainbow over a sun, a cartoon bear holding a heart. He'd been embarrassed at first about his new crutches being decorated like that, but he quickly grew to love the idea that Violet had picked them out just for him.

Before he stepped down from the platform with the pulpit, Isaias used one hand to remove the clerical collar from his shirt. He placed it on the podium. There was no noise when he set it down, the sound absorbed into the dull ringing in his ears that was becoming a near-permanent fixture in his life.

He didn't say goodbye, he didn't linger. He had made his choice.

Stepping down, Isaias walked through the aisle of the nave, his movement unsteady on the crutches but his choice sure despite the way his head and heart both felt heavy, wrapped in a thick layer of fog. Nobody stopped him, though he hadn't been sure that anyone would try to. He paused only long enough to awkwardly tug on his winter coat, not used to manoeuvring with the crutches. When he stepped out into the late February morning, the air felt crisp in his lungs and he took a deep, refreshing breath. It was still cold, but the skies were clear and with the sun on his face, he felt sure that winter would end soon enough.

He saw Hector's car parked across the street from the church and walked down the front steps with some difficulty. Hector was standing beside it, leaned against the hood. Before Isaias could cross, the door behind him opened and Mrs. Marsh and Lena exited. Isaias turned to face them, looking up at them from the bottom of the stairs.

Mrs. Marsh stepped down first and, when she did, hugged Isaias. He struggled to hug her back with one arm, the crutches in the way, but he leaned in and let himself feel matronly warmth, the way that she smelled like laundry soap even now. She whispered fiercely, "I'm proud of you, Isaias."

Tears immediately welled up in his eyes, but he blinked them back. "Thank you, Lisette. Are you staying?"

"I am," she said as she broke away and Isaias reoriented himself. "I can't leave, just yet."

"I had hoped you'd retire, after everything."

Mrs. Lisette Marsh shook her head. "No demon is going to scare me off," she said with deadly seriousness. "And someone needs to make sure the new priest doesn't suffocate in the very large shadow you've left on this place. Maybe you can check in sometime—at least to make sure he's not letting those beautiful gardens Hector planted go to waste."

Isaias smiled. "I'm sure we could arrange that."

They stood for a heartbeat's worth of awkward silence before Mrs. Marsh spoke again. "Isaias, about Bishop Reid—"

"It's okay," Isaias said, not wholly a lie. It wasn't okay that the man who had raised him hadn't said a word to him as he struggled to recover from all that had happened, and Isaias hadn't exactly tried to reach out, either. But it would be okay. One day. "I already know what you're going to say."

"I won't make excuses for him. I won't try to say it's only because of the demon and not because—but I *will* say I'm sorry that a man can give up so easily on a child he raised."

"He's not exactly the first," Isaias said. It didn't bring him any comfort.

"At any rate, I'm still here. Even whenever I do retire. The girls will need a woman in their lives from time to time, I think, just to help out, though I'm sure you and Hector will continue to do a wonderful job. Poppy has her mother, I suppose—but Violet, Lily, maybe they could use a grandmother. My niece could do to spare me sometimes."

Isaias smiled. He said nothing about how quickly she had slotted him into a fatherly role, the moment he left his title behind. "I'd like that, and I think the girls would, too."

Mrs. Marsh gave him another hug and whispered, barely audible to him but ringing true, "I'll pray for you, still, Isaias. But only that you're happy, and healthy, and loved. But I think God's seen to that, already."

Before Isaias could find words through the cotton coating on his mind, she stepped away and returned to the church. Lena, who had waited a polite distance away to let them have their conversation in private, approached. "I don't have anything terribly profound to say that I haven't said already," she said with a wry smile. "But I told you, right? This was your story. You chose the ending."

Isaias's smile wavered for a moment, exhausted already from the continued conversation. He didn't think he would ever stop feeling tired again. He fought to keep the smile up. "I guess you did tell me that."

Lena nodded, then seemed to become distracted, looking past Isaias, toward the other side of the street. Isaias looked over his shoulder to follow her gaze, bile in his throat—was something wrong with Hector?—but he saw nothing except Hector giving them both a small wave as he perched against the hood of his car. He looked back at Lena when she said, "It's your heart he's drawn you, right? That was the answer."

Isaias shook his head, though not to disagree. "I'm still not sure I understand what you meant, before. At least not completely."

Lena looked back at him and shrugged before she reached into her sleeve to pull a pink scrunchie off her wrist and tied her hair up in a messy bun. "That's okay," she said as she dropped her arms back down and shook them out with a few hearty flicks of her hands. "You don't have to. Listen, though, if Lily needs anything—send her my way. I could run my own Big Sister program for her."

"I will," Isaias promised, and didn't ask what it might be that she could help Lily with above others. Some of it, he could see—the rest, he thought he would know when he saw it.

Lena gave a little wave before she stepped away, tugging leather gloves on as she walked away. She stopped, then turned back to him. "Oh, Isaias?"

"Yes, Lena?"

She grinned. "Let me know when you want your cat back."

Laughing, Isaias said, "We'll pick Prue up tonight."

"Thanks. I'll see you later, okay?"

Isaias briefly let go of one crutch to wave her off and waited for her to start down the sidewalk away from him before he looked back at Hector, still waiting across the street. He barely looked both ways before crossing, not willing to hesitate any longer to be with him. Hector stood as Isaias approached and opened his arms. Isaias walked straight into his embrace and let himself be held close. He breathed in the sharp, cool morning air and the smell of Hector through his jacket: vanilla, chocolate, and the warmth of campfire smoke.

When they stepped apart, barely enough space for a breath, Hector brought his fingers up to Isaias's chin to tip it up gently. He leaned down to kiss Isaias—tender, sweet, but firm, like Isaias had always known Hector to be. Isaias's heart soared as he kissed Hector back, relishing every detail that was still new and exciting: the wiry touch of Hector's beard, the faint brush of his still-raw burn wounds against his nose, the taste of his chapped lips. Hector had been his first kiss, his tenth kiss, and he hoped he would be his last kiss, too, together now until the end of time. He didn't think he would ever get used to being held, and kissed, by Hector.

The kiss broke, but Hector kept cradling Isaias's chin gently in his hand. Isaias savoured the rough callouses on Hector's fingers where he held him as he smiled to Isaias. The light, at last, reached those kind eyes.

"Let's go home."

Isaias,

I can feel spring in the air. It's in the way that the sunshine's started to melt the snow. Soon, the grass will be green, and the flowers will bloom.

And I can't wait to see the garden we'll grow together.

Love,

Hector

Acknowledgements

To my beloved Frances, always and forever. Can you believe this book is finally here? You have stood by me the entire time, from the initial idea coming to fruition, to the tumultuous time in which I wrote the first draft, to the pain we went through that stopped me writing and now—and now, to the ending. You have been with me through every moment, and I couldn't be more grateful for the steadfast rock you have been. My life would be emptier without you, without our garden, without our Lola, without the home we've built together. I look forward to the spring and every spring ever after, together.

To the self I used to be when I first began this story, so far away from the person I am now. This book has transformed as much as I have, and we are both better for it.

And to my beloved indie book community—the authors and readers who helped me rediscover my love of reading and writing, who inspired me to find the best version of this story I could, who gave me faith in myself. I am so grateful to the support and the joy we find in one another.

Lastly, thank you to the reader who has given this story, and me, a chance. I hope you enjoyed the journey. I promise it won't be the last you see of me.

About the Author

Tyler Battaglia is a queer and disabled author of horror, dark fantasy, and other speculative fiction, and is especially interested in subjects that interrogate the connections between faith, monsters, love, queerness, and disability. He lives in Canada with his partner and cat.

Tyler sometimes isn't sure what he believes—but he desperately wants to believe in love.

With publications across a variety of online venues and anthologies, you can find Tyler on most social media at @whosthistyler and online at https://www.tylerbattaglia.com, including a full list of publications to date.